THE FUNDAMENTALS OF
MURDER

THE FUNDAMENTALS OF
MURDER

A NOVEL BY

WILLIAM F. LOVE

DONALD I. FINE, INC.
NEW YORK

Library of Congress Cataloging-in-Publication Data
Love, William F.
The fundamentals of murder / William Love.
p.   cm.
ISBN 1-55611-233-5
I. Title.
PS3562.0848F8   1991
813'.54—dc20   90-56076
CIP

Manufactured in the United States of America

10 9 8 7 6 5 4 3 2 1

Designed by Irving Perkins Associates

To the late Dan Kavanaugh,
whose wit and sense of humor I try,
not always successfully, to emulate in my books

don't!" I said. "You can't do this to me! I've got a date with Sally Castle—that Halloween party with the Irregulars. I put it on your calendar over a month ago."

Regan shook his head without looking up. "I'm sorry, David, but this is an emergency. You will have to cancel your plans."

I looked around for something to hit him with. The heavy gold candlesticks on the altar looked tempting. Nope. That could do permanent damage. To the candlesticks.

I gritted my teeth. "Will you please look at me? We need to talk! If you think I'm going to cancel something I've been planning for months just because some—"

"David!" He whipped off his glasses and tilted his face at me, green eyes blazing. "We can discuss this at eleven o'clock! Go phone my acceptance. Please!" He returned to the book. I stood there glaring down at him, but he ignored me. I went down the stairs fuming.

I'd definitely blown it. I should have remembered the conversation we'd had a couple of months previously when the announcement about the conference first arrived. The Bishop had taken an inordinate amount of time dithering over whether or not to go.

The thing is, he's absolutely loony on the subject of fundamentalism. But he finally told me to send his regrets.

"Absent my constitutional preference to sleep in my own bed, I'd go," he told me. "My aversion to fundamentalism is profound, and I'd have enjoyed sharing horror stories with my fellow scholars."

"So what's your problem with fundamentalists?" I asked idly, licking the envelope. "I thought you were one. Isn't that somebody that believes in the New Testament?"

Regan gave me a long, careful look. "You're serious, aren't you?" I gave him back my wide-eyed innocent look.

He shook his head. "No, David, I am most emphatically *not* a fundamentalist.

"Fundamentalism, for your information, is a misguided and simplistic reaction to nineteenth-century theological liberalism. It seeks refuge from modern science in the Bible, in which it claims to find not merely the inspired word of God, but the final answer to every human dilemma." He paused for a breath, but before I could say "Sorry I asked," he was off again.

"Worse yet, it condemns legitimate biblical scholarship. The word of

God, it opines, must be patent to every reader, however naive. According, it forbids any scientific inquiry into the Scriptures. Outrageous and ludicrous.

"But worst of all are the infernal, ubiquitous door-to-door salesfolk, rushing about, forcing their shallow biblical interpretations upon the unwary of every faith.

"I once permitted one into my office, thinking he might be amenable to some civilized discourse on matters theological. This was years ago, but the memory lingers on."

Regan shuddered and glared at me, which was unfair: I'm no fundamentalist. The Bible in my room—Jewish, of course—has been gathering dust for years.

"I spent the most exasperating hour of my life debating, of all things, Darwinian evolutionary theory with a self-righteous dunderhead whose ignorance of science was rivaled only by his misunderstanding of the Bible. Particularly aggravating was my utter inability to pierce the armor of nescience in which he had cloaked himself."

Oh.

As you can see, those fundies really get to him. Regardless, he'd finally decided to pass up the Conference. Until this morning. And now I had a problem.

I could see four options: (a) try to talk Regan out of it; (b) lie to Barry, tell him Regan said no; (c) quit; or (d) just cave in, do as the Bishop instructed, and cancel my date with Sally, probably ending what had been a long and interesting, if sometimes stormy, relationship.

Not a good set of options. At first glance, (d) was unpalatable, (b) was overly risky and (a) looked impossible. That put (c) at the top of the list, which wouldn't have been as drastic as you might think. Both Regan and I know, though he'd never admit it, that any quitting I do (or firing he does) is temporary. Fact is, he *needs* someone with the weird combination of talents I happen to possess: typing and shorthand capability; the strength to deadlift 165 pounds (for when he totals his wheelchair in one of his famous racing turns); and a hide thick enough to overlook his more-than-occasional rages.

Sister Ernestine, our housekeeper and cook, is a fine lady, and we'd play hell trying to get along without her, but she doesn't do shorthand. Furthermore, at seventy-two, she's not much into heavy lifting.

So the Bishop and I go through a temporary parting of the ways about twice a year. These usually last about a day, and both of us feel better about each other afterwards. *Cathartic*, he once called it.

So that looked like the ticket—at first. But back in my office, cooling off, I realized it wasn't—not this time. The Bishop would see my quitting as a ploy to make him change his plans, which wasn't the message I wanted to get across.

With much grinding of teeth, I decided (d) was the best of a bad lot. I called Barry and gave him the good news. He couldn't have been happier.

"Fantastic, Mr. Goldman! I can't thank you enough! *Magnificent* job of persuasion! I *know* how hard it is to get the Bishop to change his mind once he's made it up."

He probably wondered why I snarled and hung up.

I dreaded the next call—to Sally—but there was no way out. I won't go into the gory details, beyond saying it ended with our relationship somewhere in the general vicinity of limbo. By the time we hung up, about the only thing we still agreed on was that Regan wasn't going to get either of our votes for this year's Most Admired American.

Just imagine my frame of mind when at five to eleven, hard on the heels of my possibly final conversation with Sally, the doorbell chimed.

The sight that greeted me through the glass of the front door didn't change my mood any: a string bean in his early twenties in overalls and a John Deere baseball cap.

Probably, I figured, a mope looking for a handout. We get several of those a week, guys who figure—wrongly—that a church establishment must be an easy touch. My first reaction was to tell him to get the hell off the stoop and back in the street where he belonged. And if he didn't like that idea, a little physical persuasion would have been nice, just to soothe my ruffled disposition.

But I didn't yield to temptation. Opening the door, I fed him my standard "May I help you?"

Like lightning, a Bible appeared from wherever he'd been concealing it. If he'd been some revenge-seeking perp I'd once put behind bars, and the Bible his weapon, I'd have been dead meat. His smile was almost as quick.

"Ah've gawt good news fer yew, Bishop," he said, tapping the book with his finger, "'N it's awl raht here 'n this yere Bobble! It's 'bout Jesus, 'n' what he c'n dew fer yew."

Relieved to see it was only a Bible, I pulled myself together. "Sorry. The Bishop sees visitors only by appoint—" I stopped. An idea began to take shape.

"Umm, you say you have a message for the Bishop?"

"Yessir. And it's rale important. Ah'd lahk to—"

"Excuse me. Maybe we can work you in. I just need to know one thing: are you a fundamentalist?"

The young man's gaze was steady. "Dern tootin'. Proud of it, too. Why?"

"No reason," I beamed. "Come right in."

THE BISHOP ALWAYS COMES DOWN from his prayers at eleven. I had just enough time to invite the newcomer into the office (the Bishop's, of course, not mine), and to get some vital statistics.

Name: Jerry Fanning. Recent background: arrived two weeks before, with wife and baby, via Greyhound. Point of origin: Ada, Oklahoma.

Before I could learn more, the elevator door in the kitchen clanked open and the Bishop's wheelchair pounded down the hall to the office. He likes to run that hall at about eight miles an hour.

Doesn't sound so fast?

Take it from a guy that lives there and risks getting creamed every time he goes through a door without looking both ways: it's excessive and a definite safety hazard.

Sister Ernestine nags him about it constantly, but Regan's never been much of a listener, especially to criticism of his behavior. Me, I've learned the hard way. The less you criticize him, the better your chances of getting him to behave. So I grit my teeth and try to ignore it. Which, I've got to admit, has gotten us no farther than has Ernie's nagging.

About a second and a half from the first sound of the wheelchair, Regan came spinning into the office, head hunched forward with exertion, hands pumping the wheels.

Sensing an alien presence, his head flew up. He brought the chair to a screeching halt just before it reached the Karastan rug. His eyes flickered to me, then to Fanning, studying him. Then they returned to the usual suspect.

Missing from his expression were any of the warmth, sympathy and human understanding you'd expect after five hours of praying. And his voice was just as cold.

"Mr. Goldman. I was not aware of any appointment. An explanation, please?"

Yeah, he was mad. Regan loves routine and hates surprises. The drapes on the south window were open wide, and he wanted to wheel over there as usual, adjust them a little and admire the view. No matter that it consisted primarily of Mrs. Mueller's garbage awaiting tomorrow morning's pickup.

He'd want to verify that the IBM personal computer over on the west wall, the huge Webster's *Unabridged* on its low stand to the left of it, and the table with the antique chess set on the right had all been nicely dusted by Ernestine. And, if in the mood, he might spend a moment or two contemplating one of the Renoir or Van Gogh prints on the east and west walls. Or the crucifix over the door.

And finally he would get to his correspondence piled on his desk where I always leave it after culling out the items he refuses to be bothered with.

Instead, he was confronted with a strange individual, sitting there, John Deere cap in hand, occupying space and time he'd made no provision for. His morning lay about him in shambles. So the boss was good and mad. Though not, I trusted, as mad as he'd be in about two seconds when he learned he was in for another wrangle with a fundie.

I stifled a grin. "Well, it came up suddenly, Bishop. This gentleman has a serious matter to discuss with you. So serious that I'm convinced nothing on your calendar can possibly be any more important."

I gave Fanning, now standing, a bright smile. "Bishop Regan," I said politely. "Jerry Fanning. Mr. Fanning, Bishop Regan."

Fanning looked back and forth from Regan to me. He was beginning to realize he'd just been drafted into World War III as a foot soldier. And if you're thinking I was being unfair to the guy, you're probably right. Tossing an earnest young Bible-pounder into the ring with an internationally renowned scripture scholar—yeah, that's unfair. Well, them's the breaks when you go a-Bible-pounding.

But fairness to Fanning was the last thing on my mind. Way, way ahead of that were thoughts of revenge.

"God bless you, brother!" said the Okie in his down-home accent, swallowing and extending his right hand to the Bishop. "I got some good news for you, and it's all right here in this Bible."

Regan stared at him for a moment, trying to decode what he'd just heard. Then, realizing *Bobble* meant *Bible*, and that he was in for a homily from this ill-spoken rube, his head slowly swiveled and he gave me a long look through slitted eyes. As he stared, his eyes changed. Outrage shifted subtly to something else, something mean and crafty. Something I didn't like.

He turned and took the fundie's proffered hand, baring his teeth in what he probably thought was a pleasant smile. "Welcome, Mr. Fanning. You have something to tell us about the Bible, have you? How very interesting. Please, sit down and be comfortable."

Regan's syrupy tone added further menace to the look I'd seen. What was he up to?

"Pull up a chair, please, David. I think we should *both* hear what Mr. Fanning has to say."

So *that* was it. I'd broken a house rule and had to pay the piper, even if the piper had to suffer along with me. That's the trouble with working for someone whose I.Q. is twice yours—they've got twice as many ways to turn the tables.

"In fact," Regan went on smugly, tightening the screws another notch, "if Mr. Fanning's message is of the urgency you suggest, we daren't entrust it to my feeble memory. You will need to take notes. *Verbatim*, David."

I settled grumpily into my chair, on the starboard side of Regan's desk. Without taking his eyes off Fanning, the Bishop handed me the steno pad he keeps for me for emergencies. He tried to keep a poker face, but the gleam of satisfaction in his eyes was unmistakable.

Fanning didn't waste any time proving he was a true fundamentalist. He held his Bible high and demanded, "I got to ask it, Bishop. Do you believe on every word in this here Bible?"

That started a forty-five-minute argument. They went after each other hammer and tongs and I got the whole thing into my notebook, a useless exercise. And the fundie never backed off. I was impressed by him. In fact, I had him ahead on points, when Regan abruptly ended it.

Along the way they somehow got into Adam and Eve and Moses, which I followed a little bit; then into St. Paul (the guy, not the city), where they lost me fast. I'll give Regan this: as mad as he was when they started, he used a lot less sarcasm than I'd have predicted and actually got less mad the longer they argued. In fact, he seemed to enjoy the whole thing, which is more than I can say for me.

I was thoroughly relieved when he finally sighed and said, "No more, Mr. Fanning. I'm afraid we'll have to agree to disagree. Just tell me this: why did you come? What is it you want with me?"

"The Lord sent me," Fanning blurted. I glanced up from my short-hand. He was blushing deeply, glaring at Regan, expecting a challenge. The Bishop raised an eyebrow.

"Oh? And just how did the Lord communicate this mission to you?"

"You probably won't—" Fanning looked at the floor and took a deep breath. He seemed to come to a decision and met Regan's gaze. "Okay, I'll just plain tell it. I had a vision." I glanced over to get Regan's reaction and was surprised to see him nodding encouragement.

"I've had two of 'em," the Okie said. "The first one came last winter. That time, Lord Jesus told me I had to bring my wife and baby and come to New York City. He wanted me to convert the city to Him and His holy word."

That got me. I looked up from my notebook and stared at the guy. Fanning stared right back at me. "Yep, that's right, Mister, the whole dern city. And that's what I'm trying to do." He turned back to the Bishop, who nodded more encouragement.

"Well sir," Fanning continued, "me and Ida Mae—that's my wife— we got here two weeks ago, and I been going from door to door ever since, trying to get people to accept Jesus as their personal Lord and Savior." The fundie's face relaxed as he smiled and shook his head.

"I been trying, but they ain't been buying. I don't know why the Lord picked me, or why He picked this city—but He sent me and that's that." He pounded the chair arm decisively.

"Admirable," Regan murmured. Fanning, who'd been skewered by a couple of the Bishop's sarcasms earlier, looked suspicious.

"No, no," Regan said. "I mean it, sir. Would that every Christian— Hah! Would that I—were as faithful to *my* vision. What form did this vision take?"

"Oh, I don't expect you'll believe me. I had a hard time believing it myself. I didn't know *what* was going on. But I just *knew* it was the Lord. No doubt about it."

Regan's eyes narrowed. "What do you mean, no doubt about it?"

"It's real hard to describe." Fanning said, so softly I had to strain to hear him. "Kind of like a dream, only it was real, that's the only way I can say it."

Not very convincing, I thought. But Regan was still nodding. "And you say you have had two?"

Fanning nodded back. "Second one was last night. Jesus told me to come see you. See, I passed by your house yesterday and saw the gold plate on your door that says Catholic Bishop.

"Well, Jesus come to me last night and told me to come tell you about Him. Even told me your name: Francis Xavier Regan. Said, 'I love the man, but he needs to get to know Me.'"

I grinned at Regan but he was intent on Fanning. "'I love the man, but he needs to get to know Me'?"

"Yep. I didn't want to come at first. Way I was brought up, you didn't go near no Catholic priests. Much less no Bishop! But He told me to, and I finally decided the worst you could do was kill me."

I grinned, but Regan nodded soberly. "I suppose. So you came here to bring me that message?"

Fanning nodded. "Yep. Trouble is, I don't know if that's *all* what I'm supposed to do. I *know* Jesus wanted me to come here. But I don't know what for."

"Of course you do." The Bishop was brisk. "And you've done it. Told me that Jesus loves me, and I need to get to know Him."

I was looking back and forth at the two erstwhile antagonists. The conversation was taking a strange turn. The Bishop glanced at me.

"It's highly unusual, Mr. Fanning, that you got in. Normally, Mr. Goldman is Horatio at the Sublician bridge, heroically keeping away all comers, occasionally even my oldest and dearest friends. But he let you in. An extraordinary day, Mr. Fanning—for all three of us, I suppose."

Regan looked at a spot on the ceiling. "Albeit fearful, you came— bearing a message of love. A message available to me every morning at prayer, but seldom heeded."

Regan lowered his eyes from the ceiling, gave me another brief glance, and returned to Fanning. I realized I'd stopped taking notes and quickly resumed.

"I am in your debt, Mr. Fanning. If you ever need my help, I hope you'll call." Regan held the gaze of the embarrassed Okie and nodded significantly. Then he glanced at me again and exploded.

"Oh, put away that pencil, David, and stop embarrassing both of us! You know perfectly well I was *joking* when I told you to take notes!" I looked at him and slowly shook my head. Who said bishops never lie?

Returning to his guest, Regan gestured at his useless legs. "I suffered a gunshot wound six years ago, Mr. Fanning, resulting in—this. My disability can leave me—cranky, at times. This morning, in a moment of pique, I gave an ill-considered order to Mr. Goldman. I was exasperated, I suppose.

"Your admission here, as you have perhaps sensed, is due solely to Mr. Goldman's desire—a quite understandable desire, I must admit— to punish me."

That's as close to an apology as I've ever gotten from the man. I gave him a nod to acknowledge it, which he gave no sign of noticing. Except for a slight blush.

The visit ended soon after, but not, of course, without the fundie inviting the Bishop to pray with him. Regan surprised me again.

"By all means. I'd welcome it, sir. You may stay or go as you prefer, David."

I stayed. Maybe I'd been so startled by the apology, I thought he needed watching. Of course I didn't join in, Jesus not being among the people I pray to. Within five minutes I saw I'd made a mistake. The prayer was endless.

I quit listening after a couple of hours. Well, all right, it only *seemed* that long. I tuned back in when I heard that merciful word, *finally*.

". . . and finally, Lord, we just ask you to help the families of those two poor women. Just be with them in their sorrow, Lord. And touch the heart of that hate-filled man. Help the police find him and stop him from hurting anyone else. Let him see the suffering he's causing, and make him repent and turn to you, sweet Jesus. Amen."

Fanning was obviously referring to the latest serial killer on the loose in New York, the one the press had branded Strangler John because he was knocking off prostitutes, apparently pretending to be a john.

By the day of Fanning's visit, Strangler John had struck twice. The papers were filled with the story, as they always are when murderers are on the prowl.

I don't use words like *mystical* or *supernatural*, but in hindsight, it's kind of interesting that Fanning chose to end his prayer with that bit about Strangler John.

—3—

I SAID STRANGLER JOHN HAD ALREADY KILLED two prostitutes the day the Bishop and I met Fanning. He whacked another one that Friday, and a fourth the next. The victims were no one I knew, so after reading about them in the papers I put them out of my mind, though that was getting harder to do. With another corpse turning up every Saturday, people were growing panicky. The papers were complaining daily about the police. And the police kept promising a solution "soon," except soon never seemed to arrive.

The cops were feeling the heat, especially Kessler and Blake. That's Inspector Kessler, head of Homicide, and Lieutenant Charlie Blake, the guy in charge of the Strangler John Task Force, as the papers (not Kessler) were calling it.

As far as Blake goes (not very far, in my opinion), he deserved all the heat he was getting. Kessler was a different matter. He's a good, hardworking cop just unlucky enough to be in one of those no-win situations where everything favors the perp.

All homicide cops detest the psychopathic murderer and not for the reason you might think. Oh sure, they object to innocent people getting wiped out. But worse for them is the frustration of knowing the S.O.B. always has the upper hand; with no rhyme or reason that any sane person can see, the psycho can pick his own time and place to strike.

And like a blind fighter, all a cop can do is wait for the other guy to punch and then try to react, all the time getting his brains beat in by the press, politicians and public who can't figure out why he doesn't just go grab the perp and put him away. Having been there myself, I felt a little sorry for the cops. But it was no concern of mine. Yet.

If you're wondering about that trip to Philly and whether Sally and I made the Halloween party, the answers are yes and no, respectively. Yes, I went to Philly and no, Sally and I never made the party. Right after Fanning left, the Bishop *asked* me—as opposed to the *telling* he'd done earlier—if I would be so kind as to take him to Philadelphia on Saturday, and I said, sure, no problem.

So the Fanning visit changed nothing about our agenda, but a lot about the overall atmosphere. Around the mansion, that is. The atmosphere between Sally and me was a different matter. For a week she refused to even talk to me. Then for another week she did talk to me but the tone of the conversation made me wonder why.

Finally, on the Friday of the second week, Sally and I did something that's become old hat for us over the years: made up. I talked her into going to a Knicks game.

That day—Friday, November tenth—wound up being a very big day for the city as well as for yours truly, though the day was nearly over before I ever found out about it.

I'd been down in Atlantic City on a case and barely got back in time to change clothes and go pick up Sally. And I'd been listening to the tape deck instead of the car radio. So I had no idea what was going on.

The Knicks-Bulls game that evening was a disaster—unless you're a Chicagoan. Ewing, benched with a pulled hamstring, got to watch Air Jordan put on one of his patented shows. Michael J. did everything to the Knicks but give them a fighting chance.

Naturally, our fair weather locals either left early or stayed purely out of meanness, hooting at the home team and cheering Michael on to bigger and better stuffs. They even booed Phil Jackson, the Bulls' coach, when he took pity on his old team and yanked the star with five minutes to go.

"What a bunch of sissies!" was Sally's succinct summary of the Knicks' pitiful effort. We were leaving the Garden with the six or eight other dyed-in-the-wool fans who'd stayed with us to the bitter end. What she actually said was a bit earthier than *sissies*.

"Aren't you being a little hard on them?" I rebutted. "Look who they were up against: probably the greatest basketball player in the history of the world."

"Bullfrogs! Jordan's the most overrated player in basketball. You want to know the *real* trouble with the Knicks?"

I didn't, and you don't, but try telling *her* that when she's on a roll. She carried on till we got to O'Reilly's for our traditional postgame brew. That's where she changed the subject and the course of my life.

When she did, she caught me napping. Women can change gears faster than Ewing can slamdunk and I was suddenly aware she'd asked me a question that had nothing to do with basketball. I got something about Strangler John, and that was it. I asked her to repeat the question. She made a face.

"I said, what do you think about this guy the cops have grabbed? Think he's really Strangler John? I mean, you're the detective."

I stared at her. I hadn't heard about the cops' big break that day. Last I'd heard, ladies of all sizes, ages and sexes were still being even more cautious than usual in this mugger's haven of a city.

"What are you saying—they've had a breakthrough in the Strangler thing?"

"Davey! Sweetheart! Don't you even read big page-one stories written by your own dear friend and fellow golf hustler, Chet Rozanski? The *Dispatch* was sitting right there on my coffee table when you came to get me this evening. Yes! They've broken the case. They're charging some guy from out of town. Sounds like he's confessed."

I pumped her about what the paper had said, but she'd already told me all she knew—couldn't even think of the guy's name—and we quickly moved on to other more personal matters. After I left her in the early hours, I picked up a *Dispatch* down in the lobby of her co-op.

Only when I was back at the mansion, in my pajamas up in my bedroom, did I open it up. It must have been roughly five seconds before my eyes widened and my jaw dropped.

Give me one second to scan the headline, (POLICE NAB STRAN-GLER JOHN! in twelve-point type), another for the initial glance at the photo below, in which I recognized my one-time place of employment, Homicide Headquarters on Twentieth, and a couple more to grin at Charlie Blake's determined-looking face. (You don't often see a lofty lieutenant cuffed to a criminal. Unless there's a chance to make the news.)

The fifth and final second was spent in taking a close gander at the arrestee. Looking scared, shifty-eyed and guilty as hell was our Bible-pounding Okie, Jerry Fanning.

—4—

THE CAPTION CONFIRMED IT: "STRANGLER JOHN SUS-PECT: Lieutenant Charles Blake conducts prisoner, Gerald Fanning, from his cell at Homicide Headquarters to the interrogation room."

I looked at the picture again, frowning. How could Jerry Fanning be the Strangler? It didn't track.

In a moment of temporary insanity I even considered waking up Regan. But it was already after three and he'd be up at five to do his upper-body exercises. I quickly regained my senses.

Sitting back in my easy chair, slippered feet on the hassock, I read the story. Rozanski has that irritating *Dispatch* style, but he's a whiz on facts.

Nov. 10. Police today announced the arrest of the man they believe to be "Strangler John," Gerald C. Fanning, 23, of 212 Gramercy Park. Fanning arrived in the city, according to police, two days prior to the murder of prostitute Theresa "Little Teri" Langelaar, the first "Strangler John" victim.

At a hastily summoned press conference today at Homicide Headquarters, Inspector I. M. Kessler said the case against Fanning is "all but airtight." When asked to elaborate, Mr. Kessler refused, saying more information would be available "very soon."

Joining Kessler for the briefing was Lieutenant Charles Blake, head of the Special Task Force assigned to the Strangler John case. Reporters were not permitted to question Fanning, though Blake stated "... full opportunity for questioning the prisoner will be granted after he has spoken with his attorney." When questioned, Blake declined to say who Fanning's attorney is or whether he even has one.

According to police, Fanning has been living in rented rooms at the Gramercy Park address, with his wife and one child, since their recent arrival.

Independently, the *Dispatch* has learned that Fanning is unemployed. The Fanning family arrived October 11. The police consider it of considerable significance that the first Strangler John murder occurred two days later—on Friday, October 13.

At the press conference, Kessler stated that Fanning came to New York from Ada, Oklahoma, his home. To the question, "Why did he come here?" the Inspector responded, "I guess you'll have to ask him that. And you'll have that opportunity within forty-eight to seventy-two hours, I promise you."

I tried to recall what I already knew about the murders. There'd been four, all prostitutes but one. They'd happened on four successive Friday nights, the fourth the previous Friday, November third. From what I'd read in the papers the last day or two, the police didn't seem to be getting any closer to a solution than ever. But my memory needed refreshing.

I got up and went to the ancient wooden cabinet in the corner where I keep the most recent six weeks of the *Times*, *Dispatch* and *Post*. It was 3:14 by my Timex, but I was a thousand miles from sleepy. I fumbled through the papers in the cabinet, found the ones with something on the murders, hauled the armload back to my chair and educated myself on Strangler John and his murderous activities.

The first victim, Theresa "Little Teri" Langelaar, had been murdered during the night of Friday, the thirteenth of October, in a room in the Terrace View Motel, a fleabag at Forty-eighth and Ninth. That crime didn't get a lot of coverage—the violent death of a prostitute not being front-page stuff, even for the Manhattan *Dispatch*—until someone claiming to be the Strangler called the *Dispatch* the following Wednesday, October eighteenth. The caller spoke in a whisper, presumably to avoid identification. He said he'd murdered Langelaar "for sweet Jesus' sake" and threatened the life of every prostitute in the city. Not surprisingly, the *Dispatch* had played it up big. But the other papers barely mentioned it, and the Langelaar murder stayed in the minor leagues. *That* week.

When Joy Foxworth bought the farm the following Friday night,

strangled in identical fashion, the press—and not just the *Dispatch*—
was in full cry. Not only was the victim garroted the same way—the
police were guessing the killer had used piano wire—but it happened
on another Friday night. And the way the body was left begged for
headlines.

Little Teri's body, the cops finally admitted, had been left the same
way, but there'd been no photos of it—at least not in the papers. This
time the body was in public view—in the unfenced passageway below
the front stoop of a brownstone just west of Ninth Avenue, on Forty-
ninth. And a *Post* photographer got a closeup of it.

Wedged in the victim's bared teeth, a white card with big black letters
read REPENT! The photo also showed that the killer had ripped the
victim's earrings off, tearing the ear lobes. The late Joy's bloody left ear
showed up very plainly in the photo. The caption added that the body
was nude.

The murders were now solidly on page one. Where they stayed.

Of course the journalists soon had a nickname to go with it. That
came out of the press conference Blake put on, late Saturday afternoon.
Blake had Sergeant Joe Parker, a seven-year veteran of the Homicide
Bureau, join him for it. A reporter had lobbed a question about the
modus operandi, and Parker had fired back offhandedly, "Yeah, looks
like the strangler was her john."

Rozanski, who was there, picked up on it, and within twenty-four
hours the crimes had become the "Strangler John Murders," earning
Parker, I later learned, a good reaming-out by Kessler. Kessler's no
slouch when it comes to reaming, as a few ancient battle scars of my
own will attest.

The kettle got another stir the following Tuesday when the whisperer
called the *Dispatch* again. Same message as the week before, with the
more specific warning that he was going to strike again that Friday.

Sure enough, despite the public hysteria, hookers staying home (the
Dispatch estimated that the streetwalker population on New York sidewalks was down eighty percent that night, though they didn't say where
they came up with that estimate), extra police patrols and neighborhood
watch groups roaming the city, it happened. The third victim was
discovered shortly after dawn Saturday morning.

She was first identified as another prostitute, which was understandable. Not only was her nude body found in the spread-eagle posture,
REPENT! card in mouth, but it was in the identical spot under the

same stoop where Joy Foxworth's had been found the previous Saturday. The only difference was, no bloody ears, though they were bare of jewelry.

When the news broke that this victim was no prostitute but a well-known and successful high fashion model named Laura Penniston, the story went national. *Time* and *Newsweek* reporters were all over the place. All the evening news programs and "A Current Affair" did stories on Laura Penniston, who, two or three years back, had been on more magazine covers than Madonna.

Her face hadn't been as exposed recently, but that wasn't due to lack of interest. On the contrary, she'd parlayed her face into her fortune—in the form of her own modeling agency, Penniston Associates, Inc. According to the papers, it had become one of the more successful in the city.

This Penniston woman had made the transition from studio to executive suite without missing a beat. Never married, she'd dated the rich and the famous right up to the night of her death.

One hot item was Penniston's earrings. The cops apparently established from several witnesses that she'd been wearing earrings that evening. And they were missing. Why hadn't the killer ripped them off her the way he had the first two women? Theories abounded—none of them worth a damn, as far as I was concerned. Not that I could think of a better one.

But the police were spending more time on the killer's calling card in the victims' teeth than they were on the earrings. They seemed to be getting desperate. The following Wednesday they requested—and got—every paper in town to run a blow-up of the card.

Basically your ordinary business card in appearance and size, it had the single word, *REPENT!*, professionally printed, standard font type, taking up most of the space. At the bottom, in small print, were the words, "For as many as have sinned without law shall also perish without law." The words *sinned* and *perish* had been underlined in ink, presumably by the killer. The New York *Times*, naturally, had the exact reference for the quote: Rom. 2:12, whatever that is.

The *Times* also ran a short sidebar: an interview with an expert on the New Testament. His theory was that the killer was serving notice on the city's prostitutes that he was substituting his vengeance for the law's, since the law refused to act. The expert also said the killer's usage of the quote violated the "intention of the original author." It sounded like that violation bothered him more than what the killer had done to the women. I made a mental note to give my in-house New Testament expert a jab about that.

Anyway, Kessler was telling the papers that the cops were going public with this "vital piece of evidence" in hopes that someone with information about the cards would come forward. Such as the printer who made them, or anyone who might have seen them anywhere else. What Kessler didn't say, but had to be obvious to any cop or ex-cop, was that this was sheer desperation on his part.

A vagrant thought struck me, and I went back and reread a couple of the articles. In examining the three bodies, the police had found no signs of a struggle by any of the victims. No blood anywhere (except for those torn ear lobes—and forensics had shown that damage to have been inflicted after death), no skin under the fingernails, no bruised knuckles. Throat damage from the cord used and—except for Penniston—torn ear lobes were the only marks on any of the victims. Whoever he was, the killer was quick. And deadly.

By now I'd gone through about half the pile of newspapers. I dumped the ones I'd read, and picked up a new stack.

By the next Friday, November third, it seemed every woman in the city (certainly every prostitute) was staying locked up inside. There were hints that special police patrols were out, and that every female cop under sixty was stationed, all tarted up, somewhere in or around Times Square. It figured not to happen again, at least not that night.

And it looked at first as if it hadn't, as the city got through Saturday morning with no corpses turning up. But early Saturday afternoon, the weekend manager of the Hot Corner Motel at Forty-sixth and Tenth Avenue, came across in one of the rooms the spread-eagled body of one Billie Morgan, card in mouth. Another prostitute, same M.O., and again, no signs of resistance by the victim.

More press conferences, more screaming by politicians and pundits, more promises by Inspector Kessler, a lot more anxiety for the city.

So tonight, Friday, November tenth, had been shaping up to be the very peak of hysteria, the end of Strangler John Week 4, the night of the prospective fifth strangling. But the cops finally caught a break and nailed the guy—*if* you wanted to believe that Jerry Fanning was it. I had my doubts.

And I wasn't alone. I was back to where I'd started—today's *Dispatch*, Chet's story on the arrest. Make that yesterday's *Dispatch*: it was now 4:08 by my Timex. In the A.M.

Editorials of any kind, I try to avoid. But a box beneath Chet's story said, "For an editorial on today's events, see page 27." To my surprise, I found that whoever wrote it (and it might have been Rozanski himself) shared my doubts about Fanning's guilt, if not for the same reasons. It ended with this:

> . . . So let us by all means hope that Inspector Kessler is right and Mr. Fanning is indeed Strangler John, though we will take a good deal more comfort in the Inspector's assurances when he gets around to telling us the basis for the arrest. But for all Mr. Kessler's assurances, we cannot in good conscience advise the women of our fair city, particularly not the women of the street, to go out alone tonight. And our guess—certainly our hope—is that the police themselves are not resting easy. Only if the Strangler does not strike again tonight will it be time to breathe a tentative sigh of relief, and look forward to the trial of Mr. Fanning. If he is indeed the monster who has been committing these atrocities, no punishment is too severe. In fact, the citizens of this State should begin to take seriously our position on the usefulness and fairness of the death penalty, and insist that our legislature reinstate it, and our Governor, for once in his life, do the right thing and sign it into law.

As I dropped the paper on top of the pile on the floor beside me, I reminded myself to see that Regan didn't miss that editorial. His position on capital punishment is about as far from the *Dispatch*'s (and mine) as Ada is from New York.

My smile at Regan's probable reaction faded.

A mental picture of Fanning praying for the murderer's victims popped into my head. That I'd ever let him into the mansion had been, as Regan had said at the time, highly unusual. I couldn't help wondering, as I turned out the light and got into bed, whether destiny had played a role.

5

ERNIE HAD HER OWN OPINIONS on Fanning's guilt or innocence, as I learned next morning at breakfast.

(She's Sister Ernestine to everyone else in the world, but I get away with the "Ernie" because she's never figured out a way to make me stop. When I first started calling her that, she used to blush. Now she doesn't even notice. I've seen the Bishop grimace at it, but he knows better than to say anything.)

I was in the kitchen, wolfing down a superb Denver omelette she'd made me—our usual morning routine. If you forgive her occasional attempts at playing Jewish mama—nagging me about my marital status or the supposed advantages of hooking some nice Jewish girl—Ernie's okay.

"Well, David, have they caught the Strangler Jack?"

"Strangler *John*," I corrected. "You see, the word for the customer of a certain kind of, um, lady is *john*. Since the police suspected this guy of approaching these, uh, particular ladies as a customer, they're calling him—"

"Please, David. You don't have to treat me like some schoolgirl. I know about johns. *And* prostitutes. Even a nun hears a few things by—my age." (Ernie doesn't know I know her age. She'd die if she did.) She leaned over my shoulder and examined the big page-one photo. "But do you really think he *could* be the murderer? From the picture, he seems such a nice boy!"

I grinned. "Yeah, that's probably what those prostitutes thought. I'll tell you something, Ernie. Lots of nicer-looking boys than him have done just as bad." I sipped some coffee and reread Rozanski's story as she cleared away my mess.

21

"I still don't think he did it," she opined as I left the kitchen. I didn't answer. What can you say to an illogical female?

But the Bishop is neither female nor illogical (usually) and his reaction wasn't much different. I'd left the paper on top of the mail on his desk so the first thing he'd see when he came down at eleven would be Fanning's befuddled face. I checked my watch when his wheelchair passed my office. The buzzer on my desk sounded exactly twenty-eight seconds later.

Regan was jabbing at the paper with his reading glasses as I entered.

"David. What in heaven's name *is* this?"

"My God! Am I honored! A man of *your* intelligence, and you want me to read you the morning paper? Okay. It says, 'Police Nab Suspect in Strangler—"

He wasn't in the mood. "David! If you please. Your sense of humor this morning is more exiguous than usual. Thrusting that man upon me in the first place was beneath you. Tricking up a *Dispatch* this way is a singularly tasteless way to prolong it. If you think—"

"Hold it," I interrupted. "That's no fake. You're looking at two of your favorite people in the world: Jerry Fanning and Charlie Blake." I wanted to be sure he recognized Blake. After Blake's one and only visit to the mansion—in the Lombardi affair—Regan gave orders that the welcome mat for the Lieutenant be permanently retired.

"Can you believe the way that Fanning guy pulled the wool over our eyes? Hell, no wonder he prayed for the murderer: it was him!"

"Nonsense," Regan answered. "He's no murderer, David, certainly not a multiple murderer, and you know it as well as I. He's an earnest, somewhat misguided young man who, with fortune and God's grace, may eventually become the devout Christian he desires to be. But a multiple murderer? Arrant nonsense, David."

I shrugged. "Hey, the cops don't arrest people on a whim. He must have done *something* to give them the idea."

He closed his eyes tight for a minute, then gave me a wary look. "Do you really think it possible, David? You were with him the entire time he was in our house. Do you seriously believe he could have strangled four women?"

I got serious. "Yes, I do. When you've been around crime as much as I have, you learn that people do some surprising things. Even Bible-pounders."

He scowled at me for a moment, then abruptly pushed his wheelchair away from the desk and began to "pace."

I've learned to read his state of mind by his movements. When he crosses the office in a set path—say, from west wall to east wall and back—he's pursuing a definite and logical train of thought. When it's aimless, he's just processing a lot of stuff, with no particular plan. At the moment he was just processing.

I plopped myself down in my chair and waited. After three minutes and thirty-seven seconds (Sure, I timed him. What else was there to do?) he spun his chair to face me.

"I am on the horns of a dilemma," he said, frowning. "I made a commitment to Mr. Fanning, do you recall?" I tried to remember, failed, and shook my head.

"I told him," the boss explained, "I was in his debt for bringing me that message of God's love. I told him to call on me if he ever needed help. Well, his current predicament is itself a cry for help. And I am a man of my word." He put his hands on the wheels and I thought he was off again. But he settled for drumming his fingers.

"Clearly, I have no stomach for assisting the man who did . . . that . . . to those four women. But. If Inspector Kessler is barking up the wrong tree, I have an obligation to render aid. Utilizing your expertise, of course." He turned his head and studied one of the Van Gogh prints. I glanced at it, but it didn't seem to have any answers. He turned back to me.

"Kindly hand me the New York *Times*, David." I got up and brought it to him and he studied all the news that the *Times* saw fit to print about Fanning. I felt like telling him he'd do better reading Rozanski in the *Dispatch*, but let it alone.

"There's nothing here," he finally grumped, tossing the paper back on his desk.

I looked at him.

"I mean, nothing useful. Pointing toward either guilt or innocence. How can we find out what Mr. Kessler has?"

I shrugged. "Oh, there are ways. If you seriously want to—" I heard a buzz coming from my office: the sound of my private line. If I don't pick up by the third buzz, Cheryl Grossman will pick up in her office over on Broadway and take the message. So I raised my eyebrows to see if Regan wanted me to stay or take the call. He shrugged and gave a small wave of dismissal. I headed for my office to pick up before the third buzz. Barely made it.

It was Cheryl herself, so my hurrying had been wasted. "Dave wants to talk with you, Davey. Just a moment."

Cheryl's boss, the "Dave" who wanted to talk with me, was Davis L. Baker, fellow Delancey Street Irregular, my attorney when I need one (more often than I'd prefer) and my landlord/employer—at times. I.e.: he lets me keep my name on his office door and occasionally hires me to do some investigating. Cheryl, his secretary, handles any other work I need done, as and when I need it.

As you may have gathered, I hold down two jobs. I'm the Bishop's special assistant, a job I've had almost since I left the police force six years ago at approximately the same time Regan took a slug in the spine from a mugger, thus requiring the services of a special assistant. The job pays me a small but regular salary.

But Regan permits me (often to the disgust of his peers) to work as a private investigator on "my own time": all but the thirty hours a week he pays me for.

I insisted on the arrangement from the get-go. Being a glorified private secretary for a Catholic bishop is not my idea of an exciting way to spend my life. Regan didn't much care for my moonlighting at the time, but had few other options. Word about his temper had gotten around the archdiocese, and he couldn't find a priest to do it.

As it's turned out, the boss has grown to enjoy the arrangement. He gets to hear about my cases, and sometimes lends a hand. And, with his intelligence, that's turned out to be to my considerable advantage a couple of times.

But I digress. I was talking about Davis L. Baker. Dave is a whiz of a criminal lawyer, one of the best in town. He was in his usual hurry.

"Davey! Have you met a Jerry Fanning? I'm talking about the guy the police just arrested for the Strangler John murders." I tried not to let my surprise come through and did my lawyer impersonation that always irritates Dave.

"Can you lay a foundation for your need to know, counselor?"

"Come on, Davey, I don't have time for games. I've just been appointed to represent the guy. I met him briefly just now, and he says he knows you. Fill me in, will you? How well *do* you know him?"

I smiled and shook my head. No sooner does the Bishop ask me how to learn what the cops have on Fanning than we get a call from the guy most likely to know: Fanning's lawyer.

A holy life must really get you somewhere.

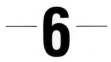

"WELL, WELL, WELL," I said. "Nice to see the poor guy get a break, getting you appointed his attorney." I meant it, even if I sounded sarcastic. Baker ignored the compliment.

"I'm calling to find out what you can tell me about him, Davey. He's in big trouble, and getting him off isn't going to be easy." So I gave him a brief description of that morning visit of two weeks before. He heard me out and blurted a word I'll omit. "That's it? What good is that? I thought you'd *have* something! So he came and tried to convert a bishop and a Jew to Christianity? And naturally struck out. Look, I need something to help get him off!"

"Tell you what, Dave," I said. "Tell me everything you know and maybe I'll lend a hand with my considerable P.I. skills. Right now, all I've got is Chet's article in the *Dispatch*. Which ain't much, as you can read for yourself. Well, plus this morning's New York *Times*, which is even less. That's it. Speak to me, my man. I'm a trained investigator. Let me solve it for you."

"Hah! You'll solve it? I'll let you in on a little secret, friend. Looks to me like the police already have."

"You mean Jerry's confessed?"

"Hell no, he says he's innocent. But get this, Davey. You know those cards saying REPENT? The ones in the dead women's mouths? They're *his* cards. He brought them here with him from Oklahoma. No doubt about it. Two of his prints are on one of them."

I went silent. When I spoke again it was in an entirely different tone. "What?"

"You heard me. Those REPENT cards are his."

"*His* cards? Are you kidding me?" This was going to be a real kick in the head for Regan. "Has he admitted they're his?"

"Sure. Not that it matters much. They got a search warrant on Wednesday and went to his apartment. Found hundreds of them. He says he brought them from Oklahoma to hand out to people on street corners.

"And he handed them out, all right—in Times Square. People saw him doing it. In fact, that's how the police found him—they got descriptions from people who saw him there that evening. Trouble is, he was handing them out on the fatal Friday the thirteenth. The night of the first murder." Baker chuckled unpleasantly.

"Think about that one, Davey. Fanning's seen handing the cards out in Times Square, roughly two hours before Langelaar gets iced. And guess where Langelaar was last seen alive?"

I nodded to myself, sure of what was coming.

"Yeah, you guessed it. The last whore who saw Little Teri alive says she saw her on Times Square—just a block away from where Fanning was handing out cards. And at about the same time. Doesn't look good for your buddy." Baker's voice now took on a new, insinuating tone. "I got all this, by the way, from, uh, Fran Wilson. Looks like Harrington's handing her the case. Lucky gal."

I understood the change in his voice. As he well knew, Fran and I had something going, once upon a time. She'd joined the D.A.'s office right out of law school during my last year on the force, and we hit it off right away. Good-looker with a great bod. I threw a pass, she intercepted, and the two of us scored some very pleasant touchdowns. Then Sally came along and—well, life changes.

But I never stopped liking Fran. I'd kept track of her over the years and been happy to see her—deservedly—move up the ranks. She was now an assistant D.A., one of Harrington's top three.

Of course, Baker's "lucky gal" comment had been sarcasm. For someone in Harrington's office, getting assigned a high-profile case like Strangler John was a no-win deal. Do everything right, develop an airtight case, and Harrington comes in and takes all the glory. Screw up and you die alone. Fran had drawn the short straw.

"Fran, hmm? What *else* has she got? I suppose they found all four sets of earrings in Brother Fanning's apartment?"

"Nope, no earrings anywhere. That'll probably come later, not that Fran necessarily needs them. She may already have enough."

"Such as?"

"Plenty, my friend. For openers, like I said, the REPENT cards with Fanning's prints on them. For another, before I got to him, they gave him a polygraph. He flunked. Inadmissible technically, but don't worry, Fran'll figure a way to get it before the jury. I'll scream about it, but with my luck, we'll get Perkins or someone like him, and he'll shoot me down. And juries go for that kind of crap.

"And then there's the little matter of Fanning's bizarre behavior on Wednesday when he was first approached by the police. Fran's really going to go to town with that. For witnesses, she's got two credible cops and two even more credible bystanders. Well, so she says. And I believe her."

I hated to ask but I had to. "So what did he do, Dave?"

"Well, it wasn't real bright—whether he's Strangler John or not. See, keep in mind, they weren't even thinking of him as the murderer; they just wanted to verify that the cards were his. And find out if he knew anyone who might have taken some. So the patrolman moseys up. And what does Fanning do? Cuts and runs!" He barked another unamused laugh, then continued.

"He's got to be the unluckiest guy in captivity. Because this patrolman—Bryant's his name—just happens to be a former high school track star who's still in tiptop shape. Guess how far Fanning got? He's got Fanning on the ground in two seconds, along with a probable promotion to detective. All he's done is find the number-one item on Kessler's Christmas wish list: a probable Strangler John."

I started to ask a question, but Baker wasn't through. "I got to tell you, Davey. Kessler's convinced that Fanning's it. And how can you blame him? Look at it. Here's a guy, comes to New York October eleventh, two days before the first murder. Since then there's been a woman strangled every Friday night—until guess when? Last night. Last night we didn't get one. And guess where Fanning was last night?"

"Yeah, yeah, in jail. But that's all circumstantial, man. Have they got anything hard?"

"Oh, rest assured, I'm pushing that angle with Fran. The answer is no, they don't. But give them time. They only picked the guy up on Wednesday. They're comparing his prints to every print they've been able to take anywhere in the vicinity of all four murders.

"Also they've got mug shots of Fanning in police stations all over town, they're showing them all over Times Square, the two hotels, Ninth Avenue in the Forties—anywhere the murderer is known to have been those four nights. If he did it, and he probably did, they'll find the evidence. Count on it."

"Probably did? Hey, whose side you on, anyway?"

Baker's tone was bored. "I've told you a dozen times, Davey, I'm paid to defend 'em, not believe in 'em. You better start facing facts, buddy. Take it from me, the guy's got a very guilty look about him."

I gave it some thought. I did respect Dave's instincts. That was part of the secret of his success. But, Jerry Fanning? The Bible-pounder?

I frowned. My earlier breeziness with Ernie and the boss was evaporating in the face of the probability that this nice fundamentalist was it. "Gee, I don't know, Dave."

"Hey, the guy's a fruitcake, Davey. He tell you about his visions?"

"Oh, he told you about that, too? Okay, yeah, that's on the weird side, I'll give you that. Still, there's something about him—I just don't think he's guilty."

"Well, I'm glad you feel that way, son, because he could use an investigator and he damn sure can't afford it. You want to help? Just for sweet charity's sake?"

I thought a moment, wondering whether to bring up the Bishop's interest in the case. I decided to wait.

"Okay, sure, Dave," I answered. "When do you want to get together?"

"How about this afternoon? I've got an appointment to see the boy at the jail after lunch. Want to tag along?"

—7—

By the time I slid back into my chair in Regan's office, I'd come to three conclusions. Number one, Fanning was in a whole lot of trouble. Number two, he wasn't guilty. (Maybe. And that one was strictly from my gut.) And three, I was glad Regan was on his side.

For once, the boss didn't try to ignore me. Generally, when I come into his office, he's either hard at work on a personnel file or trying to pretend he is. (He's personnel director for the archdiocese, a job the Cardinal gave him after the injury six years ago.) But this time, as soon as I entered he shoved away the pile of papers he was working on, tossed his reading glasses on top, and gave me his undivided attention.

"Hate to disturb a man at his work," I said, "but I just had a very enlightening conversation with Mr. Davis Baker about our friend with the visions. Would you believe Baker's been assigned to represent him?"

Regan's eyebrows went up. "Oh?"

"Yep. Good news for Fanning. But when you hear what Baker told me, you just might want to change your opinion about the boy's innocence."

"Indeed." The Bishop frowned down at his desk, rubbing his hand over his chin. "I suppose you'd better tell me, then. What does Mr. Baker think?"

"Thinks he's guilty as sin. Let me tell you what he told me. Then tell me what *you* think."

I talked and he listened. When I came to the part about the cards in the women's mouths being Fanning's, that got him just like it got me. His eyes got big and he cut in.

"Those cards were his?"

"You got it. What the police want to know is why he didn't come

29

forward, *if* he was innocent, when they put that thing in the papers, asking anyone who had any knowledge of such cards to come forward. I'm telling you, Bishop, when you put it all together, it looks pretty bad."

Regan looked shaken. He nodded slowly, staring into space. He squinted at his hands for a minute. Suddenly he swung his wheelchair away from his desk and pumped over to the south wall. He sat there looking out the window, nodded jerkily and muttered something. I don't think he intended me to hear what he said, but I did. Just.

"I have to know. I owe the man. I have to know."

He swung back to me and raised his voice. "So. You are going with Mr. Baker to the jail. I'd like you to form a firmer opinion as to his guilt or innocence while you're there. Perhaps you'll be able to give me some guidance as to where my duty lies."

I nodded and got up to go. He stopped me with an upraised hand. "One other thing. While you are with Mr. Fanning, I should prepare myself, in case we decide to help. A certain detail about those murders has aroused my curiosity, and I'd like to explore it a little. You keep the newspapers for several weeks, don't you?"

"Sure. The last six weeks' worth are up in my room."

"I thought as much. Would it be an imposition to ask you to cull through them, find the ones dealing with the murders and bring them to me?"

"Yeah, a big one," I said, hiding a grin. "It'd be a lot of work. I'd have to go all through them. But what the hell, anything for a friend." I turned to go.

"No." He was miffed. "I don't want to impose, David. If it's too much trouble—"

I waved it away. "No trouble. Just give me an hour or so and I should be able to find most of them."

He tried to call me back but I was gone. I raced to my room, grabbed the pile of newspapers off the floor where I'd left them the night before, and hustled back downstairs. Regan was at his desk opening a personnel file. He looked up in surprise.

"Did you forget something, David? What—?"

I walked over and deposited the pile of newspapers on his desk. "Wasn't quite as much trouble as I expected," I said, letting him see the grin. He stared at the stack.

"Sorry for the humor. I couldn't resist. You were being so polite—

so out of character—I decided to give you a hard time. I had them out last night. Naturally, I hadn't put them away."

He shook his head. "I must remember in the future to be less accommodating. The rule still holds, does it? No good deed goes unpunished?"

"Something like that." I turned to go. "Well, I'll put your buddy Fanning through the wringer and let you know how he does. And I hope those papers have a clue in them somewhere. Because I got to tell you, it doesn't look real good for the home team right now."

—8—

THE JAIL IS NOT THE MOST depressing institution the City of New York owns and operates. That honor goes to the morgue, hands down. But the jail's a clear-cut runner-up.

Baker and I would just as soon have been somewhere—anywhere—else that Saturday afternoon. But at least it was bearable, knowing we could get the hell out when the visit was over. That wasn't true for me on three other occasions I could tell you about, but I don't care to relive any of them, so I won't. But I probably will eventually. My mouth will see to that.

I took the Bishop's Seville and picked Dave up at his office on Broadway. We didn't have much to say. The weather—cold, steady drizzle combined with just enough snow to keep things gray—seemed to sap our energy. And maybe knowing what an uphill battle we had before us had something to do with it.

Things didn't brighten up any inside the jail. Even the fat desk sergeant looked dreary.

"Putcher John Q. right here, gents," he said tonelessly, pushing the register at us. He sat back in his swivel chair and watched us sign the book through eyes that disappeared into the surrounding flesh. He pulled the book onto his lap without taking his eyes off us. Finally looking down and studying our signatures, he spoke again in the same toneless voice.

"Which wunna ya's Baker?"

Dave flicked a finger.

"You're the guy's lawyer?" Without waiting for an answer, he switched his shrewd gaze to me. "'N who're you? Name's Goodman?"

"Goldman," I corrected.

He gave no indication he'd heard me. "'N what's *your* b'ness with the prisoner?"

"He's a licensed investigator working for me," Baker put in, irritated. "Show him your license, Davey."

I pointed at the desk where I'd already deposited my P.I. license. The officer looked at the license, at me, back at the license. Finally deciding it wasn't covered with deadly microbes, he picked it up and studied it. Suddenly he let out a bellow, in a voice I wouldn't have believed he had in him.

"Fernandez!"

My heart rate was working its way back to normal when an equally bored-looking but much younger and swarthier man appeared. "Take these two back to Visitors B, Josie," the sergeant told him. "'N get Fanning for 'em."

"Yessir," was the sullen response, followed by "It's *José*, dammit!" under his breath. He may not have intended the last three words to reach the sergeant's ears, but the smug look on the latter's face showed that it had. Sulkily, José took us through a door marked Visitors into a depressing room I've been in more often than I like to remember.

It's long, narrow and gray, divided by a windowed partition into two sections, Inmates and Visitors, and about the only good thing you can say about it is that it's functional. Six carrels for prisoners and their visitors, bulletproof glass separating the two. Each carrel with its own phone set-up to permit conversation through the thick glass.

The room was empty when we arrived. The carrel Fernandez directed us to had a double phone hookup on the visitors' side, permitting three-way conversation.

As Fernandez left to get Fanning, Baker put his briefcase on the shelf and glumly tried to get comfortable in one of the high-backed straight chairs. Deciding that shifting weight didn't help any, he gave up, closed his eyes and waited. My own shifting around helped just as little. The chairs were as lousy as they'd always been.

Baker opened his eyes, gave me a sidelong glance and a suggestion of a smile. "The last time I was here, you were over there," he murmured, nodding at the glass partition.

"Don't remind me," I mumbled, shifting again. I'd not only been on the other side of the partition, I'd just come from an interrogation by the one and only Charlie Blake, whose grave I'll never spit on only because I refuse to waste my precious bodily fluids.

To give Fernandez credit, he didn't keep us waiting long. We'd barely had time to settle ourselves when the steel door on the inmates' side of the room opened and the guard reappeared, Fanning behind him. Fernandez pointed at us, folded his arms across his chest and leaned against the wall so he could keep an eye on the situation. Jerry strode over and sat down opposite Dave and me.

His head was up. He didn't exactly look cocky, but he sure wasn't bowing and scraping either. The orange jail coveralls he wore were ugly, although stylewise about on a par with the clothes he'd worn two weeks earlier. And unlike most prisoners, he wasn't ashamed to make eye contact. The only indicators that he wasn't where he really wanted to be were his weary, bloodshot eyes.

Jerry nodded at Baker, took a second or two to recognize me, then gave me a grin.

Dave and I picked up our phones, and Jerry followed suit. Baker got his eye. "Remember Mr. Goldman, Jerry?"

The jailbird turned his eyes on me and, still grinning, gave me an incongruous wink. When he spoke, his voice came through thin and distorted and far away. The equipment in that place is a disgrace.

"Shore. How are you, Mr. Goldman?"

I grinned back at him, wondering how he could be so cheerful. "Hey, make it Davey. And I'm feeling lucky not to be where you are. What the hell's going on, Jerry?"

He grinned and shook his head ruefully. His tone was assured. "You got the right word for it, Mr. Gold—uh, Davey. This place is pure Hades, no ifs, ands, or buts about it!" He shrugged. "No Christian belongs in a place like this."

From the corner of an eye I saw Dave shoot me a glance. Without letting Jerry see, I flicked Dave a wink. He's heard me hold forth on certain late-night occasions, about the way we Jews feel when people use *Christian* to describe all that's good and proper in America. But I could hardly take offense at Jerry's remark.

"We've got some questions, Jerry," Dave said. "But first, why don't you go ahead and tell us everything you know about the whole thing?"

Fanning looked at him. "But like I told you before, Mr. Baker, I don't know *nothing*. That's what's so doggone frustrating about this whole dern—!" Jerry looked at both of us and took a breath.

"Well, *a'course* I knew about the Strangler John murders. Who didn't?" He looked at me. "You heard me *pray* on it when I was in your house, uh, Davey." Eyes back to Baker. "But, I swear, Mr. Baker, I didn't see no ad, or whatever it was, in no paper about them there REPENT cards I was handing out.

"That one policeman, that, uh, Lieutenant Blake, I think his name is? Yeah? He said he found that hard to believe. But it's true! You got to believe me!"

I nodded. "I do. How'd they arrest you, Jerry?"

He looked at me. "It was on, uh, Wednesday . . ." I could barely hear him and gestured at him to hold the instrument closer to his mouth. He did. "It happened Wednesday morning. I guess it was, oh, around ten o'clock. I'd just been to see some old folks—Mr. and Mrs. Kelly.

"I'd accidental left some of my literature at home and was goin' back to get it when this patrol car passed me on the street. I didn't see it at first, but they sure saw me. Then one of 'em got out and come at me. I guess I panicked."

He closed his eyes. When he opened them again he looked at the floor, frowning as he spoke. "See, Davey, I been in trouble with the law before—back in Ada. I was a wild kid. Got arrested a few times before Ida Mae led me to the Lord. Fact, that's where I was when I met the Lord. In the jail in Ada."

I studied Fanning's face while he talked. He seemed sincere.

"That's when my life changed, Davey, and all for the better. But Wednesday, when I saw that police officer, I just—well, I just panicked." He was suddenly finding it hard to meet our eyes. "I didn't know what he might want, I didn't even stop to think. Just cut and ran."

I gave him a level stare. "Not too smart, Jerry."

He finally met my eye and shrugged. "Nope. Stupidest thing I ever did, I reckon. Well, they run me down and jammed my face into a fence." He shook his head ruefully. "Them old boys up here are about as mean as the ones in Oklahoma. Almost made me feel at home."

"Then they brought you in?"

"Yep. They wanted to know all about them there cards."

"Was that what they mainly concentrated on, Jerry? The cards?"

Fanning became more glum. He started mumbling. "Well, I wouldn't say that. But they sure spent plenty of time on them. Where'd I get them printed? How'd I bring them here? Where'd they been all this time? Who might've got aholt of some of 'em? All stuff like that there. But that wasn't all. I guess day before yesterday it was—what's today, anyway? I'm having a hard time keeping the days straight."

"Saturday."

A look of pain crossed his face. "Saturday?" He shook his head. "Today's Saturday? I was a-going to surprise Ida Mae tonight. She loves Amy Grant—the Christian rock singer, y'know . . . ? And I was going to talk to Miz Billings about sitting for Joe Bob, and take Ida to the concert. Noticed an ad about it in one of the papers last week." A tear suddenly glistened in his eye. "I've let Ida Mae down so bad."

Fanning put the phone down and turned away. He took a deep breath, straightened his shoulders. He turned to us, looked at both of us and put the phone back to his mouth.

"Where was I?"

"The cards, Jerry," Baker said.

Fanning nodded. "Oh, yeah, okay, today is Saturday, huh? So it was, uh, Thursday. They had me in that there interrogation room just about the whole day on Thursday. They got real mad, too." Jerry grinned. "They were trying to feed me the answers they wanted." He looked triumphant.

"I got me one advantage on 'em. I been in jail before. Their tricks are the same here, too. So they didn't fool me none. I just tolt 'em what I knew."

Baker then asked the key question. "How about alibi, Jerry? The police are convinced that the same guy murdered all four women. Surely you've got an alibi for at least one of those Friday nights."

Jerry shifted uneasily in the chair and studied his shoes. "Yeah, they asked me what I was doing on those Friday nights. I told them I was home." The last three words were muffled. He tried looking at me and found he couldn't meet my eyes.

"They asked me, uh, they asked me if I, uh, if I went out at all those nights. I, uh, told them that Ida and me just go to bed early on a weekend night, same as any weeknight. See, I have to get up in the morning before little Joe Bob—"

Fanning's eyes filled and his voice caught. He stopped, looked at the ceiling for a few seconds, pulled out a dirty handkerchief, blew his nose and resumed, meeting my eye this time.

"'Scuse me. It's just that thinking about the baby—" His eyes dropped again and he mumbled, "Anyway, I was home ever' night."

Fanning took a deep breath waiting for the next question. I glanced sidelong at Baker, but couldn't read him any better than I can at poker. His face stayed with Jerry as he asked the next question.

"Did they tape the whole interview, Jerry?"

Fanning looked at him and nodded. "Yep. They played it for me later and asked me if I wanted to change anything." He grimaced. "It was too late by then."

José, still leaning against the door, caught our eye and tapped his wristwatch significantly. "We've got to go, Jerry," Dave said, sticking his notepad back into his briefcase. "Try to stay cheerful, man. Though you seem to be doing fairly well." He gave the prisoner a curious look. "How do you manage that? This is a pretty depressing place."

"The Lord put me here," Jerry answered, his mood brightening. "I think He wants me in here to spread His word among these poor fellows. I never tried telling no prisoners about Jesus before. There's a lot of old boys in here just yearning to know the Lord, you know. I've been trying to—"

Baker raised his hand and interrupted the flow, his eyes boring into the fundie's. "Look, Jerry. Right now you've got to concentrate on getting out. That's all that matters. Spreading the word is fine but you've got other things to worry about. I'd advise you to keep your head down and pay attention to business."

Jerry nodded glumly, eying the wall behind us.

As we walked down the corridor to the front door, Dave was gloomy. "No way I can put this guy on the stand, Davey. Can you imagine what Fran'd do to him on cross? The courtroom would be knee-deep in Jerry's blood."

I winced. "Yeah. I'm beginning to see Kessler's point. Jerry's obviously lying about staying home nights. And I don't like that criminal record, either. On the other hand, how could a liar that lousy fool Regan and me so completely?"

Baker grinned sardonically.

"Don't answer that," I added hastily. Pulling on my topcoat, I said, "Want to go see Kessler?"

"*You* go see Kessler," Baker answered. "I've got to get home. I'll grab a cab." He slipped on his own overcoat as we headed for the door. "The bond hearing's Monday at eleven A.M. McKinnick's courtroom. I'll file a discovery motion at that time. Come if you want."

I shook my head. "You don't need me, Dave. Just let me know what happens. And if I can find out anything from Kessler today, I'll call you. I'm sure he'll be delighted to find out you and I are working the case."

Baker raised an eyebrow. "Oh yeah, for sure. The only thing that'd make him happier'd be to learn he's been demoted to patrolman."

KESSLER'S REACTION OVER THE PHONE when I told him I was involved in the case confirmed Baker's assessment.

The inspector and I go way back. He's the guy that fired me the time—well, *one* of the times—I let my temper get away from me. Since I opted to go into P.I. work here in New York, events have thrown us together a few times, not always amicably. Fact is, he likes me getting involved in one of his cases as much as Jesse Helms likes hippies.

Hearing his fussy, precise voice on the phone made me feel kind of nostalgic. It had been several months since we'd talked. The conversation was friendly—till he found out why I was calling. The friendliness quotient nosedived when I asked to stop by. When I told him I was working on the Fanning case the expletives started.

"You know, Inspector," I said in a hurt tone, "you never seem to consider *my* feelings when you say things like that. I'd think you'd—"

"Stuff it, Davey. And stuff you, by the way. It's been nearly a year

WILLIAM F. LOVE

now since you've poked your nose into one of my cases—"

"Poked my nose? That's gratitude for you! If the Bishop and I hadn't solved that Barbara McClain thing, you'd *still* be looking for her murderer! You ought to be damn happy every time you hear we're getting involved."

Several seconds of silence. "Hell, come on over, Davey." Kessler sounded tired. "The day's already ruined."

The Saturday crew at Homicide Headquarters down on Twentieth Street is not your typical all-star line-up. It'll normally be a mixture of rookies, misfits, has-beens and never-wases. So I wasn't surprised to see Bill O'Grady manning the front desk.

O'Grady's a sad case. When I came into Homicide twelve years ago, he was a rising star. He'd cracked the Panzini case and was well liked by Kessler. In fact, he was actually being touted as the next inspector, once Kessler got kicked upstairs.

His fall from favor came about a year before my own, though for a different reason. In Bill's case, it was women. He'd been sleeping around and hadn't been careful about it. He was caught having lunch with the wife of one of the lieutenants in the department. What made it even worse was the rumor that he'd been running around with a mistress of some outfit bigwig at the same time.

So his career went straight into the toilet and stayed there. From a snappy, dapper up-and-coming young star he'd become a fat and sloppy has-been who spent all of his off-hours, and too many of his on- , inside a bottle.

Bill's formerly handsome face, now jowly and booze-reddened, lighted up when he saw me approach the desk. We'd always hit it off, and I'd made a friend for life when I took him out and got both of us drunk the night he learned about his demotion.

"How you doin', friend?" he said, pushing aside his girlie magazine. "What are you looking for this time? Gonna get another of your fair-haired clients off a murder rap?"

"Aw, come on, man, be fair. I only get 'em off when they're innocent. You guys just love to build up your big fat reputations by nailing us little guys."

Bill responded in kind and it soon became apparent he'd be only too happy to kill the rest of the day trading insults. I had to break it off. "Love to jaw with you, Bill, but the big guy wants to see me. He back there?"

O'Grady's jaw dropped. "You seein' Kessler? More'n I can say, man. Guess I'd'a been better off if he'd a' fired *me*, too. Then I'd get to see him once in a while, way you do."

"Whatta you mean?" I answered with half my brain, while the other half read, upside-down, the personnel sign-in sheet he'd left carelessly on the counter. "I wasn't fired, I quit of my own free will." He hooted, but I insisted, "Believe what you want, man, I'm sticking to it that I quit. I'd finally had it with all your damn insults."

O'Grady offered to buzz Kessler, but I told him I knew the way. We parted with the usual promises to get together soon, both of us knowing it'd never happen.

My plans had made a midcourse correction the moment I saw a certain name on the sign-in sheet. So, leaving O'Grady and entering the main hallway, I headed left for the squad room instead of right, to Kessler's office. I'd seen *Joe Parker* on the sign-in sheet. I had good reason to talk to him. Two reasons, in fact: aside from professional considerations, he's a friend.

Sergeant Joe Parker and I have a longstanding, informal arrangement which involves us slipping each other hot tips. And I knew he'd been on the Strangler John task force.

Brow furrowed, tongue sticking out of the corner of his mouth, Joe was typing so laboriously that he didn't hear me approach. So I pounded his desk and shouted, "Wake up, Joe! The criminals are in the building!"

He jerked up, startled, hair flying, eyes wide. "Shit, what the—" Seeing it was only me, he pushed his chair back, put his hand on his chest and took a deep breath.

"Jesus, Davey, what the hell you doin' to me? God awmighty, ya ever hear a' jus' walkin' up an' sayin' 'It's me, Joe'?" He wagged a finger at me. "You gimme a heart attack 'n' you'll have my old lady to deal wit'."

I grinned at him. "Hell, keep spending your Saturdays writing reports, your old lady's going to have more than a heart attack to complain about, Joe. And if you think Kessler's going to be impressed, think again. I tried it, and where did it get me?"

Parker sat back, hands behind his head, pulse rate apparently back to normal. He grinned. "See, Davey, that's the difference 'tween you and me. You did it to impress Kessler, whereas I'm doin' it 'cause I'm dedicated and wanna better myself. I could care less if Kessler knows I'm doin' it. I don't even know if the man's in the building."

Of course I had a choice comment on that bit of horsefeathers. That done, I got my butt on a chair and my elbow on his desk.

"I gotta talk to you, man. I'm working for Baker on the Fanning thing. You're on the task force. What have you got on the guy?"

"You gotta be kiddin', Davey! You're so far behind in gotchas, you'll *never* catch up! I told you when I saved your butt on that McClain deal, you were gonna have to come up with a *dozen* tidbits to pay that one back. And what have I got from you since then?"

He was right. But I didn't let that stop me. "Then give me something on the come, man," I pleaded. "What've you got to lose? I'll make it up to you, so help me."

Parker frowned, looked down at his desktop without seeing it, and seemed to come to a decision. "Okay. Gonna give you a hand, Davey, and not just for old time's sake. Kessler's so damn hot to nail someone, I don't think this Fanning guy's gettin' a fair shake. I don't think he's really it, and I'm not the only one. Doesn't smell right.

"Blake's all excited 'cause of a lotta circumstantial shit. Physically, the guy's big enough. See, from the angles of the cuts on their necks, the lab boys figure the killer must have been at least as tall as the tallest victim. Well, Penniston an' Morgan, they were both five-ten. Since Fanning's six-even, he coulda done it. Big effin' deal—so could half a' the men—an' some a' the women—in this city."

Parker had a few more choice comments about Blake, after which he began to get helpful. Joe's main job on the task force had been interviewing the last people known to have seen each victim alive. I pulled out my notebook and took plenty of notes as he proceeded to run down what he'd learned.

For "Little Teri" Langelaar, the first victim, the last person known to have seen her alive had been Angie Demopoulis, fellow prostitute. She'd seen Langelaar working the scene on the west side of Broadway between Forty-sixth and Forty-seventh shortly before midnight on Friday the thirteenth, an hour before the estimated time of death. Angie'd contributed nothing in the way of I.D.ing the murderer.

Joy Foxworth, the second victim, though also a Times Square regular, hadn't been seen at all that evening. At least not by anyone who'd come forward. Her mother had last seen the girl (Joy was nineteen) when Joy left their apartment in Harlem, presumably to catch the subway downtown, at seven o'clock that evening. Mrs. Foxworth had denied knowing that her daughter was a prostitute. Joe'd been sure she was lying about that, but couldn't see that it mattered. Nor could I.

Parker's job description had got changed when victim number three—
Laura Penniston—showed up. Blake had reassigned him to more routine
duties. Since Penniston was the only high-visibility victim, I was ready
to believe Joe when he sneeringly told me, "Blake was all over that one.
Not bein' one of your common whores, she had lotsa high-class friends."

Parker gave me a twisted grin. "People *you* like to pal around with,
Davey, you and the Bish. I think Blake was afraid I might do somethin'
crude. Like spit on their marble floors or somethin'.

"So me, I get assigned the lovely duty of goin' through Penniston's
little black book—she was a nut for phone numbers. We'd picked it up
out of her office by search warrant. Two hunnert and seventeen numbers
in that little black book by my actual count. Took me forever to run
'em down. The ones with names beside 'em weren't so bad but thirty-
three of 'em were just scribbled in without any name to go with 'em or
nothin'. But I ran 'em all down and, a' course, none of 'em led to nothin'.
But I guess it made Blake feel good to know I was keepin' busy."

But when the strangler got back to icing common whores again, with
the discovery of the body of Billie Morgan in Room 303 of the Hot
Corner Motel the following Saturday, Parker was back in the witness-
interviewing business. He'd gone to see the three other black prostitutes
Morgan had lived with.

They'd told him she was the only one of the four who'd had the guts
to go out looking for customers that Friday, November third. She apparently hadn't been afraid of Strangler John or anything else. She'd
left their apartment around ten, heading (the other girls assumed) for
Times Square, her usual stand.

And Parker had found a witness who'd seen her after that. This was
the only witness he'd been able to find who'd seen any of the four at
or near any of the places where they were actually killed.

"His name's Phil Martinez," Joe said. "Manager of the motel. He
happened to be workin' that night, an' he also happened to know Billie.
Said they were 'friendly,' for what that's worth. Denies they ever made
it in the sack, but—friendly." Envisioning the conversation between
Parker and Martinez and the kind of questions Joe must have asked to
get that denial, I decided Blake had had a point, keeping Parker away
from Penniston's friends and relatives. My friend Parker's not the
smoothest guy in the world.

"Anyhow," Parker went on, "when Morgan came into the motel,
about twelve-thirty, she flipped Martinez a hunnert-dollar bill—to pay

for the room. Martinez says he gave it a hard look, C-notes not bein'
his stock in trade much. Looked okay to him, so he changed it for her.
I got the receipt—thirty-four something, so she'd of picked up sixty-
five and change. That dough never turned up, of course.

"We also got the C-note from Martinez and dusted it. It had a partial
of Martinez's right thumb and a better partial of his right index finger.
Also a probable smudge of one of Morgan's fingers, which backs up his
story. That's it. No other prints.

"Well, the whore and the motel guy joked a little, he says, while he
was makin' change. Martinez says when he teased her about the C-
note, her comment was, 'Yeah, not bad for a old broad, huh?'"

I mulled that one over. "I thought I remembered Morgan only being
in her thirties."

"Yeah, well, thirty-eight. But most of the gals cruising Times Square
lately are teeny-boppers. Morgan's one of the older ones on the street
these days. She also had plenty of tattoos on her."

"Tattoos? What's that got to do with anything?"

"Well, it's a funny thing," Parker said, rocking back in his chair
again, hands behind head. "All three of the whores that got it had
tattoos. And the Penniston dame had some writing on her palm. A code
or somethin'. Burke chased that writin' all over the place, but he got
nowhere with it."

I frowned at him. "What do you mean, writing on her palm?"

"Just what I said. I saw the corpse, and I got pictures of it. There
was something written in ink on the left palm." I opened my mouth to
ask the obvious question, but Parker anticipated me.

"No, we don't know who wrote it. But some of us think that mighta
been the killer's way of makin' up for her lack of tattoos. Like maybe
the psycho's got a tattoo fetish."

I was interested. "Anything come of it?"

Parker shook his head glumly. "Not yet. Oh, Kessler went wild over
it—for a while. He and Blake had us goin' round and round on it. What
did it mean, did it have any connection with the tattoos on the other
three? The tattoo thing got a play around here for a couple days but
didn't seem to get anybody nowhere."

I returned to my first reaction. "And you don't even have a clue
whether the writing on the palm was done by Penniston, her killer or
someone else?"

He grinned. "All the above, Davey." He dropped the grin and shook his head soberly. "We don't know. We know that Penniston was right-handed, so the way it's written, on her left hand, it coulda been written by her. But Blake don't think so. His theory is the killer wrote it, but wrote it to try to make us think *she* did. To throw us off, I guess. I never figured that one out.

"Blake showed it to a writin' expert, along with some samples of her writin' on paper. Expert couldn't say. Mighta been, mighta not. Hard to tell, writin' on skin. And it's just a word was all it was." His face suddenly lit up. Glancing quickly in both directions, he reached into a drawer and pulled out a sheet of paper.

"Shit, here it is. Wanna see a picture a' the lady's hand? And re-member—you never saw it."

He flicked the sheet across the desk. It was a grainy 8½-by-11-inch photostat. Left hand, palm up—from just above the wrist to the fin-gertips. The entire palm was visible in the center of the picture. The detail was good: veins and hair follicles were faintly visible in the wrist. And, handwritten on the palm, aimed diagonally at the base of the little finger was some writing, smudged and faint. I held it up to the light and studied it. It looked like four letters: G O S T.

That's what it looked like. It wasn't easy to read, with the ink smudged and the imperfections of the photostat. I looked at Parker. "Shoot me a copy of it?"

He snorted. "You kiddin'?" He extended his hand. "Give it back. I could get my ass in a wringer."

Joe didn't change expression as he put the paper carefully back in the shallow desk drawer. He got to his feet. "'Scuse me a minute, Davey. Gotta take a leak." He turned and headed for the men's room just outside the squad room door.

I scoped the room to double-check I was alone and wasted no time getting the photocopy from Parker's drawer and heading to the Xerox machine on the west wall. Fortunately, it was turned on, so I didn't have to wait for it to warm up. Inside thirty seconds, Parker's copy was back in his desk drawer and mine was in my breast pocket, nicely folded.

Parker came back avoiding my eye. But dammed if he didn't open the drawer to make sure his copy was right where he'd left it.

"Anything else you can tell me?" I asked.

"Maybe. Besides the tattoos, the other thing we've been running around on is the earrings. All four of the victims had pierced ears. All four lost their earrings. But Penniston is the only one without ripped ear lobes. Also the only one not a whore. So what does it mean?"

"I'll bite," I said. "Tell me. Maybe Penniston wasn't wearing earrings that night?"

"Maybe," Parker allowed. "But she had them on earlier in the evening. We know that. But what I think is, uh, the worst thing the Mets could do is trade HoJo. He's the only real slugger they've got left with any consistency."

I stared at him. "HoJo? What the hell are you talking about? What does HoJo—?" I shut up. Something in Joe's expression—make that lack of expression—told me the squad room now contained more bodies than just Joe's and mine. And I had a funny feeling the third one was inhabited by Inspector Kessler.

A hint of perspiration began to form just below my hairline. If my feeling was right, Kessler had missed nailing me red-handed at the copy machine by just forty-five seconds. The results of that would have been disastrous for Parker and not too hot for me.

Riding over me in louder, argumentative tones, Parker continued. "But if we can trade Viola for a proven slugger like Clark, it's fat city, baby."

Joe looked up, over my shoulder. "Ain't that right, Inspector?" I turned casually.

It was Kessler and he was curt. "If you gentlemen are discussing the Mets again, count me out. I have no interest in that team. Or in anything else related to baseball. Hello, Davey."

Kessler's dark brown eyes showed both curiosity and suspicion. His pointed beard was as well trimmed as always, but had a little more salt and a little less pepper to it than the last time I'd seen it. In a year or two it would be completely white. But his head retained its luxuriant crop of dark hair, only a trace of gray around the temples. As usual for a Saturday, he was casually dressed in sweater and tie.

I got up and shook his small, well-manicured hand. "Hey!" I told him. "You've got to quit pushing my man Joe so hard. Saturdays, yet! I thought I trained him better than that."

Kessler looked up at me with a mock scowl. "Yes, you trained him all right, Davey. He's got every bad habit you ever had. I've given him a few good ones to try to overcome what you taught him." The inspector held my eye. "I trust you haven't been trying to inveigle some departmental information out of Sergeant Parker, Davey. That would violate regulations. As you know."

Parker involuntarily looked down to be sure his desk drawer was closed. Kessler's eyes seemed to pick it up. He's a hard man to fool. I tried to cover.

"Hell, Inspector, if I'd known writing reports was the way to get ahead here, I'd have done *that* instead of apprehending perpetrators. Maybe that would've kept me from getting my ass fired."

Kessler reddened and stroked his beard. I'd never used the dreaded *F*-word in his presence before. He opened his mouth, probably with a sharp reply, then closed it. A careful man. When he did speak, it was calmly.

"Well. You didn't come over here to talk about old times, Davey. And we're all three busy people. Let's get out of Joe's hair." Gesturing for me to follow, he spun on his heel and headed for his office.

I trailed after him, but not before mouthing a *later* to Joe. He winked at me, then scowled at his typewriter. He hates writing reports.

—10—

"Okay, Davey, close the door, sit down and get to the point," the inspector said as we entered his office.

I didn't obey. I was too busy scowling at something—the something being Lieutenant Charlie Blake slouched in a chair and sneering up at me. I turned to Kessler and opened my mouth to complain. But he beat me to the punch, as he settled in behind his big desk.

"I said sit down, Davey. I've, um, asked Charlie to join us, since he's handling the Fanning matter." The inspector looked nervously from Blake to me while he shuffled a few papers. Trouble was, he didn't keep enough loose papers on his desk to make it believeable.

Blake was loving it. "Got yourself another criminal to protect, Davey?" He looked at Kessler. "Maybe you and I should get ourselves fired,

Inspector. Then *we* could see how it feels to make lots of money, finagling perps out of jail."

His sneer broadened. "What's the matter, Davey? You don't get enough religious nuts over there on Thirty-seventh Street? You have to go out and dig 'em up as clients?"

I grinned and took a step toward him. I was studying the point on his jaw where a short right cross might make the biggest impression. Kessler must have guessed what I had in mind.

"I didn't invite you two birds in here to start a fight. Davey's got a legitimate interest in this case, Charlie, so never mind the extraneous comments. Davey! Sit!"

I took a breath and pulled a chair up next to Blake's. I hate to admit it, but he's not really that bad-looking. About my height and weight, and a couple years older, he keeps himself in shape; always has, going back to when we were rookies together. His sandy hair looked as full as ever, though I'm not particularly fond of the lacquered spray-on look. Charlie wore it that way back when it was fashionable and still does, now that it's not. My theory is, a guy that spends that much time on his hair is telling the world he hasn't got much else to offer. In Blake's case, that's definitely true.

At the moment he had the same triumphant glint in his eye that he gets when he's about to arrest his favorite felon, namely me. That's happened twice. Both were trumped up and later exploded in his face, leading to reprimands—once from the commissioner himself—but he'd enjoyed himself for a while. Currently he had nothing on me that I knew of, making me wonder what could have him feeling so good.

I sat down and tried a pleasant tone of voice. "How are you, Charlie? From the look on your face, you've got a surprise for me. Anything you can tell me about?"

Blake gave me his own version of a grin, as unpleasant as I could have wanted it.

"Yeah. The inspector and I have a friendly message for you, Davey: quit wasting your time on Fanning. Guy's loony, a religious fanatic, certifiable psycho. He did all four of 'em and we can *prove* it. Stick with him, boy, and you'll wind up wishing you hadn't. Right, Inspector?"

Kessler was nodding as he tamped tobacco into his pipe. He didn't speak till he had the pipe going to his satisfaction.

"Charlie's right, Davey," he finally said, sending some white smoke in the general direction of the ceiling. "We've had a breakthrough just this morning. We've now got plenty to go to the grand jury with, probably enough for a conviction." He glanced at Blake and added, "Though we're certainly continuing our search for more evidence. Right, Lieutenant?"

Blake nodded sourly, probably resenting the edge in Kessler's voice. Sounded like they'd had a go-round over whether to keep looking for more evidence. Charlie's been known to quit looking for hard evidence once he's got enough to convince himself.

I wondered what they had. Kessler was obviously impressed by it and he doesn't impress easily. I suddenly remembered the photostat in my breast pocket and wondered if a word on a dead woman's hand had anything to do with Kessler's breakthrough.

"Fran Wilson's on her way over here," Kessler went on. "We're going to fill her in. You'll probably hear about it when you talk with Baker. Fran wouldn't want us to tell the defendant or his counsel about it till she has a chance to review it. I'm sure she'll give Baker a call this evening and tell him all about it.

"But take our advice, Davey. Don't get involved with this one. You don't want to be associated with a guy like Fanning. Probably strikes you as a nice guy—just an innocent hick from Oklahoma. Well, he's not. He's an extremely dangerous psychopath. He's murdered four women and he'll do it again if we don't put him away."

I studied Kessler's face for a moment, then Blake's. They damn sure had *something*. That was clear from their expressions, Kessler's soberly satisfied, Blake's gloating. I couldn't recall when I'd ever seen Kessler so sure of himself. His idea that he now had enough evidence to get a conviction was disquieting. He doesn't say things like that lightly.

What worried me even more was Blake's presence—in the case, and in this room right now—and what that meant. It was Kessler's way of telling me I'd get no cooperation on this one. In the McClain case, he'd gone so far as to let me go through their files at one point, much to Blake's disgust. Blake sitting in today told me there was no way that was going to happen this time.

All in all, the Fanning case looked to be closed before it ever got opened. Well, you can't win 'em all—but I wasn't ready to give up yet. I tried a little stubbornness.

"Look, Inspector. You just said Fran'll tell Baker right away, and you know I'm working with him. What've you got to lose by telling me what you've got? It's obviously big or you wouldn't be—"

I stopped for two reasons. One, Kessler's expression told me I was getting nowhere. Two, there was a tap on the door, and Fran Wilson entered. I got to my feet, and Blake reluctantly followed suit. Kessler stayed seated, though he smiled and nodded at Fran.

She looked terrific, even better than the last time I'd seen her, maybe two years before. Fran's real little. The top of her head fits right under my chin when we dance, which is why we never went dancing much. And she's extremely—well, *stacked* is the only word that comes to mind. She was wearing a nicely fitted burnt orange suit that went well with her dark brown hair. Her eyes opened wide with surprise when she saw me.

"Well, Mr. *Goldman!*" she said, with a grin that produced a dimple I'd almost forgotten she had. "I didn't expect to see *you* here." She gave me her hand in a warm and extended handshake, and didn't seem to mind my caressing it for a moment with my other hand. Blake made a noise of disgust. We ignored him.

She finally nodded at him matter-of-factly, while I pulled up another chair. She sat down and, as she did so, Kessler rose. All the ups and downs were making Kessler's office feel like a Punch-and-Judy show. But Kessler wasn't clowning. He gave me a significant look.

"You'll have to excuse us, Davey. We have things to discuss. In private."

So I was bounced. "Watch these guys, Fran," I told her. "They *think* they've got something airtight on Fanning. So airtight, they're afraid to tell me what it is, afraid I'll tear it apart. Don't trust them, friend."

"And I suppose I can trust *you*, Davey?" Her eyes pinned me.

"Hey, have I ever given you reason not to? I mean, have you—? All right, all right, don't answer that. But the least you could do is give me one more chance." She didn't smile. Kessler cleared his throat.

"Okay, Inspector," I said hastily. "I'm on my way."

I closed the door behind me and slipped into my topcoat, thinking hard. Not about Fanning. On Fanning I had nothing to think about till I knew what Kessler had. No, about Fran: how was I going to get her back on my short list? She looked scrumptious.

—11—

KESSLER AND BLAKE HADN'T BEEN blowing smoke. What they had on Fanning was every bit as scary as they'd hinted, I learned as soon as I got Baker on the phone.

"Yeah, Davey. Glad you called. Just got off the phone with Fran— said she saw you, by the way. She sounded—well, I don't know. Interested. In you. Anything going on there?"

"I honestly don't know," I said. "I'd like to find out. She looks great, I'll tell you that."

"No argument there," Baker chuckled. He cleared his throat and got serious. "Well, get your mind off her bod now, friend, because she's after Fanning and loaded for bear. Thanks to Kessler. Well, actually, thanks to Blake. I got to tell you, Blake really pulled one off. Helluva job, I've got to admit. You know, I now see why you've always considered Blake such a genius."

I got short with him. A little of Baker's sarcasm goes a long way. "Yeah, yeah, the guy's a rocket scientist, we all know that. Get to it, Davis. I haven't got all night."

"A little touchy, are we?" Baker chuckled nastily. "All right, here goes. And I hope you're sitting down." He took a breath.

"See, all along Blake's had the idea that the wife knew something she wasn't telling. I mean Fanning's wife. Certain questions seemed to frighten her. Specifically the ones about where her hubby was on the Friday nights that the murders were committed.

"She'd been sticking to it that Fanning was telling the truth when he told them he was home in bed with her. But she was giving Blake clear signals she was lying, or at least not telling everything she knew. Blake also noticed that that's where Jerry really blew the lie detector

49

test. I've seen it, by the way, and Blake's right. The polygraph guy asks Jerry, 'Did you at any time on the nights of blah, blah leave your residence for any reason?' When Jerry says no, every squiggle on the sheet heads straight for the moon. Damn chart looks like a punk rocker's hairdo.

"So this morning Kessler and Blake stage a little impromptu drama for an audience of one: Mrs. Ida Mae Fanning. As an ex-cop, you're going to love this one, Davey. Blake's interrogating her on some minor item and Kessler comes storming in." Baker went into his Kessler voice, which he does superbly. "Says, 'Okay, that's it. Mrs. Fanning, your husband just told us the truth.'

"Well, little Ida Mae looks stunned. So Kessler keeps the pressure on. 'That's right, Mrs. Fanning. Now we *know* where your husband went on those Friday nights. Would you care to change your story before we start perjury proceedings?'"

Baker sighed mournfully. "I guess you can't blame the poor little broad too much. She's young, uneducated, scared. Stranger in town, husband's in jail. And here's this nice sympathetic policeman—no, two nice sympathetic policemen, both just trying to help. So she starts bawling and telling them how relieved she feels not to have to lie about it any more.

"Fran's got the tape of what Ida Mae told them then, and I'm going over to her office tomorrow and listen to it. I'll know more after I hear it but from what Fran says, it's a real ballbuster. According to Fran, Ida Mae told them that Jerry'd gone out—get this—every Friday night since they've been in New York. Went out a little before midnight and never got home before two." He paused, then added, enunciating every syllable like a lawyer, "*Every Friday*, Davey. That's four Fridays, four murders.

"What's even scarier to *me* is that the guy lied to his wife. Kessler asked her if she ever confronted Jerry about these walkabouts. And she said she did. But he denied everything. Told her she must have been dreaming."

Baker paused, possibly waiting for applause. Got none. Sighed. "And this is a guy who, I'm convinced, is genuinely devoted to his wife. So why'd he lie to her, Davey? Why? I know I've got an evil mind, but me, I can think of one very good reason."

I was trying to get my brain around this newest piece of news, but Baker wasn't offering any time out for meditation.

"I got to tell you, man, this guy's losing me fast. Oh, I'll represent him. In fact, as far as representing him goes, I'd say I've got a decent chance of getting him off. With a little luck. I mean, everything they've got is circumstantial. So I could probably throw enough dust to get a hung jury; maybe even a not guilty. I suggested as much to Fran, and asked about copping a plea. She sneered in my face, said I knew better than that. And, of course, I do. Fran'd never get away with plea bargaining this one. Can you imagine what the papers'd do to Harrington if he dared to offer a deal to Strangler John? Hah!

"Anyway, I can put on a case. Assuming the cops don't come up with a fingerprint or an eyewitness or some such. I just wish the S.O.B. would level with me. I mean Jerry."

I thought of something. "Hey, wait a minute, Dave. Fran can't use this, can she? In court? I mean, a wife can't testify against her husband, can she?"

He laughed at my naivete. "Don't kid yourself, Davey. That's what people think, but it's not true. At least, not in this case. In New York, as in most states, there *is* a spousal privilege that can be invoked by a defendant in a criminal matter.

"But that's only regarding hearsay evidence. It's the law's way of protecting what spouses tell each other in private.

"But that doesn't help Fanning. See, he didn't *tell* Ida a thing. All she'll be asked to testify to is what she saw him *do*. Which will be plenty to nail Jerry's hide to the wall. And there's not a damn thing I can do to stop it."

"News to me," I muttered. I thought some more. "But what if she refuses to take the stand?"

"Contempt of court, baby. She'll be under subpoena. Of course, the cops are redoubling their search for hard evidence, now that they're sure Jerry's it. And they'll probably find some. When they do, they won't need her any more. And Jerry'll be shit outta luck."

We agreed to stay in touch. Dave planned to have another longer and franker conversation with his client. My own immediate project was to fill the boss in. I doubted that he was going to be very happy with this new piece of information.

—12—

"WHAT? She said *what?*" Regan was mad at *me*.

"You heard me," I answered calmly. I had gone straight into his office with a quick tap on the door, interrupting his study of three impressive-looking books. (All I can tell you about them is that they were in three different languages, none of them English. And don't ask me where he digs them up. I haven't got a clue.)

At first the Bishop was annoyed at being interrupted. Annoyance quickly changed to shock as he heard of Jerry's Friday night prowl-abouts.

I couldn't blame him for being upset. A hell of a thing to learn you've probably been made a fool of by none other than Strangler John himself. That's how I was now reading it; I assumed he'd agree with me on that, after he'd had time to assimilate the news.

His eyes narrowed. "So he left their apartment every Friday night? And was gone for several hours? Without explanation?"

"You got it." I was trying to supply objectivity for both of us. Regan seemed to have lost his. He glared at me as he drew the obvious conclusion.

"What you're telling me is that Mr. Fanning is probably a multiple murderer." He shook his head. "How could I have misjudged the man's character so completely?"

He pounded his palms on the arms of his wheelchair, spun and began wheeling aimlessly around the office. Bad sign. He stopped abruptly and pounded the arms of the chair again.

"No! I *still* can't accept it. David, I must talk with Mrs. Fanning. Something's not right." He looked at the floor for a minute, then back at me. His eyes seemed to plead with me.

52

"Try to get her, David. I *must* see her as soon as possible. You can use my phone if you like." Regan swung around and headed for his beloved south windows.

"Hold it," I called after him. "You mean get her on the phone? Or go get her and bring her over here?"

A quarter-inch shrug of the shoulders was all my boss could manage. He *was* down. Well, if he wanted to act strange, so could I. So I did something I'd never done before: pulled my chair around and sat at his desk to call. I even considered putting my feet on the desk, but that was just a moment of temporary insanity.

I dialed the number from memory. I have a habit of memorizing numbers. Comes in handy once in a great while. Like this time.

The woman who answered had the right-sounding twang, but the timbre was middle-aged. "Ee-yellow!" was the way the word came out. Somewhere between three and four syllables, with a rising tone on the second syllable, falling on the last. I guessed this was Miz Billings, the acquaintance from Oklahoma with whom Jerry had told me they were staying. Whoever it was, she definitely hadn't grown up in the Bronx.

"May I speak with Mrs. Fanning, please?"

The voice turned vaguely hostile. "Who's callin'?"

"It's David Goldman, ma'am, a friend of her husband. May I speak to her, please?"

Silence for a moment. Then, "Idy Mae! 'S for you, hon."

More silence, broken intermittently by the sound of a baby gurgling, then a new voice, same number of syllables per word, but thirty years younger-sounding: "Ee-yellow."

"Mrs. Fanning? My name is David Goldman. Possibly your husband has mentioned me?"

Brief pause; then a torrent of words.

"Yes he did and I want to thank you for the hep you're being to him, Mr. Goldman, 'cause we just don't know anyone in this here city, and I just hate it, and Joe Bob's unhappy, and Miz Billings wants us to leave, and I just don't know what to do."

Her voice was starting to crack with the last few words, possibly from lack of oxygen. She took a breath and I jumped in.

"Mrs. Billings has asked you to leave? I'm surprised. Your husband told me she was a nice lady."

"Well, she is, Mr. Goldman. She even said she'd keep Joe Bob for us till we found a place—she really likes the baby—but she says she's tired of all the policemen hanging around. And now there's reporters too. So you cain't rightly blame her none.

"I just don't know where to turn to. That one policeman—that Lieutenant Blake—he was nice for a while and said he'd help, but now he's changed and won't talk to us and a body gets so unhappy you just don't know where to turn, you know? I mean, I just don't have anyone in this—"

I had to cut her off or she soon wouldn't have air enough to talk at all. "Excuse me for interrupting, Mrs. Fanning, but how about coming over here? Uh, for a while. We're only a few blocks away, and I'd be happy to—"

"No," she said firmly. "I'm about to put Joe Bob to bed and I got to stay here with him. I cain't go anywhere. I ain't been anywhere since we got here."

Ida Mae was starting to sound weepy. I looked at the Timex: 5:17. I had a sudden thought. Make that three.

One was that Jerry had mentioned he'd wanted to take Ida Mae to an Amy Grant concert tonight. I'd noted in the *Times* that the concert was at the Shubert and that tickets were still available through Hot Tix.

Second, Ernie had once worked in an orphanage, she'd told me on some occasion—part of her long and checkered career as a nun. It occurred to me that she'd probably changed a diaper or two along the way.

Three was that Sally was tied up this evening and I'd made no plans. A bachelor with nothing to do on a Saturday night is what Regan calls a *contradictio in terminis*.

"I understand what you're saying, Mrs. Fanning, but you know about us from Jerry. You know he trusts us, don't you?"

"I expect," she said reluctantly.

"Well, you're having a hard time over there from all the police and reporters. Let me come over and pick you and the baby up. No, no, please let me finish. I'll bring you here—we're only a few blocks away— and there's a lady here that knows babies backwards, forwards and sideways. You can trust her with, uh, Joe Bob.

"The Bishop wants to chat with you for just a few minutes, then I thought you and I could go somewhere, have a quiet, relaxing dinner. After dinner, if you're interested, we could go to a concert. Maybe you've heard of the singer, Amy Grant. She's at the Shubert tonight. And I just happen to have a couple of tickets."

There was a moment of silence. Then, in a small voice, "Yes, I've heard of Amy Grant. I *love* Amy Grant." Pause. "Are you a Christian, Mr. Goldman?"

I groaned inwardly. If I'd ever heard a question that answered itself, that was it. But I kept my voice serious, and hedged. "I hesitate to call myself that, Mrs. Fanning. But I *am* a big fan of Amy Grant."

Her next question signaled surrender. "Who's the lady that'd take care of Joe Bob?" I gave her some pertinent facts and figures about Sister Ernestine, and that did it.

"I could be ready in twenty minutes, Mr. Goldman. If that's not too—"

"Not at all. I'll be at your front door in twenty minutes." We hung up.

Regan wheeled in my direction. "Who's Amy Grant?"

"And you call yourself a Christian!" I scolded, vacating his desk. "She's only the finest Christian rock singer in the world is all!"

Well, that's what the *Times* had said someone said.

Regan rolled to his desk, shaking his head. "Christian rock singer." He shook his head again, then looked at me.

"But far be it from me to criticize your methods. Just please don't tell Sarah I'm responsible for your attending Christian rock concerts."

(The Bishop and my mother, who are pretty good friends, have an unspoken pact that he won't proselytize.)

He was still bothered by his apparent mistake in character-reading. He got my eye. "Answer this question, David. If you think Mr. Fanning committed these heinous acts, why is he carrying that Bible?" Regan shook his head. "He's surely not insane."

I shrugged. "Look, I'm no psychologist." The boss's expression didn't change. I was going to have to do better.

"Okay," I sighed. "Look at it this way. Here we have a guy with a criminal record: a *violent* criminal record.

"Think about it. He's a born-again Christian, comes to New York and these women are flaunting every standard he—"

"*Flouting*," Regan muttered.

"Yeah, that too. Anyway, not following the standards he finds in that Bible of his.

"Hey, he's a born-again Okie. He freaked out! Hell, I was born and raised here and it freaks *me* out sometimes! So—he starts offing sinners." I shrugged. "It happens."

The Bishop swung away from me. "Quite apart from your abominable phraseology, I can't agree with your assessment of the man's personality." He pivoted back to his desk. "Nonetheless, Mrs. Fanning's purported story is worrisome. How am I to account for those Friday-night absences? And his lies? And his guilty demeanor?"

He pulled a couple of personnel files toward him across the desk and put his reading glasses on his nose. "Well, thanks to your good offices, we'll soon be talking with Mrs. Fanning. Let's see what she has to say."

—13—

BELIEVE IT OR NOT, I actually found a parking place on Thirty-seventh when I returned with Mrs. and Baby Fanning. Twice in one day—undoubtedly a record.

I'd called Hot Tix and arranged for two Amy Grant tickets to be waiting for us at the Shubert box office. Then I went to pick up Ida Mae.

The place on Gramercy was a rundown townhouse. Mrs. Billings—stout, middle-aged, untidy hair ninety percent gray—answered the door and was friendly enough, but we didn't have time to get acquainted. Ida Mae came on with a rush, baby on her shoulder.

"Don't wait up, Miz Billings. I have my key. I'll come in as quiet as I can."

Ida tried to pull her inadequate cloth coat around both her and the baby. I hoped she had something warmer to get through the New York winter—if she was going to stay through the winter. I found myself wondering where she'd go if Jerry took a trip up the river for a stretch of life-times-four.

Joe Bob didn't wake till the end of the car ride, his head resting comfortably on his mother's shoulder. He did shift positions when she settled onto the seat, and stuck his thumb in his mouth. But his breathing stayed smooth and regular, his eyes closed.

But in the hundred-foot walk from the car to our front door he awoke with a vengeance. With nothing to shield him from the wintry wind but the lapel of Ida Mae's meager coat, he got very unhappy and wanted the whole world to know it.

The Bishop, alerted by the screaming, was waiting at the office door. He took Ida Mae's hand, saying around the wails, "I'm terribly sorry, Mrs. Fanning, about your predicament. Won't you please sit down?"

She didn't obey but did follow him into the office, continuing to pat the thrashing baby. I could barely hear her answer: "Thank you for having me over, uh, Bishop. I really appreciate you-all taking an interest in Jerry and all. I just—"

The Bishop interrupted her by wheeling to his desk and ringing the little silver bell to summon Ernie. I wondered how he expected Ernie to hear it over the racket, but he gave it a healthy jingle.

"Excuse me, Mrs. Fanning," Regan said, timing his words to coincide with Joe Bob's oxygen intakes. "We will do better, speaking of such serious matters, uninterrupted. Ah, Sister Ernestine."

I shook my head: Ernie had heard the bell. Had to be ESP. I'd been right there and *I* couldn't hear it. "This is Mrs. Fanning. Would you be so kind as to take young Joseph with you to the kitchen? We have matters to discuss."

"Oh, no," Ida Mae said. "Joe Bob won't go with—"

But the baby had other ideas. Ernie's long robes had caught his eye as soon as she came in the room. Curiosity soon became fascination. Holding out both hands, he smiled at the nun, making friendly coos and gurgles.

"Well, who do you think you're looking at, little one?" Ernie asked him, delighted at his delight. "You come right here, you hear?" She moved in and swooped the baby up with a by-your-leave smile at the surprised mother.

The nun executed a quick spin, drawing a happy squeal from her tiny burden, and turned back to the dumbfounded Ida.

"We'll just be right next door, dear. Don't you worry your head, we'll be fine. I've handled many a baby in my day." Before the startled mother could answer, Ernie was gone with a final flourish of her long dress and another happy yelp from Joe Bob.

Regan smiled. "Not to worry, Mrs. Fanning. Sister is extremely competent and, in any case, will be well within shouting distance. Please be so kind as to take that seat."

Now in control, the Bishop got down to business. Ida Mae let me have her coat and sank into the chair in front of the Bishop's desk, pulling her skirt over her knees. With the baby no longer blocking the view, I had a chance to look her over.

Not that there was a lot to look over. If she'd been a car, she'd have been a subcompact. Jerry'd said she was twenty-one; she could have passed for sixteen. Little feet, small, shapely legs under the worn cotton dress, petite body, small round face. The only thing big about her were her black, curious eyes. Also there was something odd about her, hard to say what. It had to do with youth and innocence, but I couldn't put a finger on it.

The Bishop tilted his head forward and studied her over his reading glasses. "Thanks for coming, Mrs. Fanning. It was kind of you to oblige me on short notice."

She tried to smile. "You're being awful nice to *us*, Bishop. By the way, is it right to call you Bishop? That's what Jerry said he called you." Regan nodded.

"Anyhow," she went on, "I guess the least I can do is try to help *you*, when you're trying to help Jerry. You *are* helping, aren't you?"

"Trying," Regan corrected grimly. He took a breath, continuing to study her. "Mrs. Fanning. As you know, your husband is in a great deal of jeopardy. Mr. Goldman and I were prepared to offer our services to help him, but—to be brutally honest—any assistance we could give would be based on an assumption of innocence. Speaking for myself, I was ready to make that assumption, based on the assessment I made of his character and personality during his visit here two weeks ago.

"But now it has come to my attention that the police have some highly incriminating information about him—information which I hope you can help me understand and perhaps dispel."

Ida Mae's big, dark eyes got bigger. I suddenly realized what was odd about her: she wasn't wearing a speck of makeup. Attractive enough as she was, she'd have been a sure knockout with some mascara, lipstick and whatever else women do to their faces.

"Why, I'll sure try," she said doubtfully. "I'll tell you what I can." I wondered if she was having a hard time keeping up with all those three-dollar words Regan threw around so freely.

"Good. First of all, let me ask you a question about your husband's past. The police are saying that he has a history of violent crime. Any comment?"

She reddened a little, but stayed calm. "Didn't Jerry tell you about that? I thought—"

She broke off. "All right," she resumed, nodding vigorously. "Back before Jerry and I were married; way before, back before he was even a Christian, he had him a wild streak.

"See, Jerry never had him a regular family, way I did. He grew up in foster homes from little on. Mr. and Mrs. Miller kept him the most, and they used to bring him to church with them—that was Christ Baptist, the same church I went to with my family.

"Well, when he was only thirteen, Jerry got in with a bad bunch, and got in trouble with the police, you know? And things just kept getting worse after that.

"And when he was, oh, about seventeen, he got arrested for robbing a liquor store—they called it armed robbery and I guess that's what it was, all right. He got convicted."

Talking about the man she loved seemed to brighten Ida Mae's whole personality. Her shoulders straightened, she sat up straight and her dark eyes glowed.

"Anyhow, they were going to send him to McAlester. That's a terrible place, and I was just heartbroken. See, I was only fourteen-and-a-half at the time, but I was already a Christian—I was baptized when I was eleven—and I was crazy for Jerry. Still am." Regan winced, but she didn't notice.

"Well, I went to my Aunt Ida, she's the one I was named after, you know? And Aunt Ida just couldn't have been sweeter.

"She marched me straight over to Mr. Paul Brown's office, he's just about the best lawyer in Pontotoc County, maybe the whole state, and she hired him on the spot. He filed appeals and I don't know what all, and he somehow got that case plumb thrown out on grounds of—Well, I don't rightly recollect what it was, it was some kind of lawyer talk, you know? But he sure got him off."

It was obvious the girl was coming to the good part, the way her eyes were shining. "Well, the other thing that happened when I was going so much to see Jerry in jail was that he become a Christian and got baptized. He just loved the Lord, and the way he's lived as a Christian ever since proves it!

"Course, my mom and dad said that was just to get me to marry him. But we didn't get married for three years after that, and that's *not* why he become a Christian! It's *not*!"

Regan changed the subject. "All right. Let's ignore the criminal record. But we have a more important, a much more worrisome development to cover. The matter of your husband's Friday-night peregrinations. Tell me about them."

Ida Mae looked away and blushed. "Do I have to?" Her voice had changed to a childish treble.

Regan's eyes were giving her no quarter. "Indeed you do, Mrs. Fanning. At least, if you want our help." She looked at him and took a deep breath.

"All right. But Jerry's real mad at me right now about it. Wouldn't look at me for the longest time today. Said, 'Why'd you have to go tell them that, Ida Mae?'"

She looked appealingly at Regan. He didn't change expressions.

She nodded. "All right, Bishop. I'll tell you what I told that inspector. But he *tricked* me! He wasn't being fair at all! He told me Jerry'd told them all about it!"

"Do you know where they got the idea of it in the first place, Ida Mae?" I asked.

She swung to me, blushing. "It's probably my fault. The first time they talked to me, they asked whether Jerry was always home on Friday nights, and I, I kind of hesitated." She looked angry. "I'm just not a good liar, I can't help it!"

"Nothing to be ashamed of, surely," Regan murmured.

"Maybe not, Bishop, but I sure wished I was better at it this time. For Jerry's sake. Anyhow, they kept after me and kept after me, and I just got so confused! Then, when they finally come in this morning and told me Jerry'd told the truth finally, I was so relieved! It was like the dam had busted, and I could finally tell them the real truth.

"And almost right away I knew they'd tricked me. I could see by the looks on their faces how happy they were that I'd said that. I felt like such a fool!"

The tears finally came. Ida Mae didn't try to hide them or turn away. She just sat there and bawled like a little kid. Kind of endearing.

Except tears always make me uncomfortable. I want to say something, do something. But there's never anything to say or do. Regan, on the other hand, didn't seem to mind in the least. He just waited patiently, staring at her, until she stopped. Then he turned to me, sarcasm in his voice.

"Some Kleenex, David. *If* it's not too much trouble." I jumped up guiltily and got it from his desk drawer. I guess there *is* something you can do.

Ida blew her nose and looked expectantly at the Bishop. As did I. How was he going to get Jerry out of this one?

Well, for openers, by asking ten million questions. He spent the next two hours going over the Fannings' nighttime routine. What time did they go to bed? Just when, on those Friday nights, had Jerry gotten up and gone? When did he return? Had he left on any other nights? I took a ton of notes, trying to ignore my stomach growling as the dinner hour came and went. Here's what it all came to:

The first Friday they'd been in town, October 13, Jerry had gotten home later than usual: a little after ten. He said he'd been handing out REPENT cards in Times Square. He'd told Ida how discouraged he was by the indifference of everyone—theater patrons, tourists, pimps and prostitutes—that hung out there.

"He was real down that night," Ida said. "I tried to kind of comfort him, but he was just real blue." He'd even shortened their evening prayers from half an hour to ten minutes.

"It was a couple of hours later," Ida Mae went on in a hushed voice. "Something woke me up. It was dark, but I reached over to feel, and Jerry was gone. I figured he must have gone to the bathroom—it's down the hall—but I waited and waited, and he didn't come back.

"I finally went and looked in the bathroom and in Joe Bob's room, but he wasn't there. Went downstairs, but Mrs. Billings's door was closed like always at night. He was plumb gone.

"I went back to bed and waited but I must've fallen asleep. Next thing I knew, it was morning, and Jerry was getting me up."

"Did he seem . . . different?" Regan asked.

Ida Mae looked at him and nodded slowly. "In a way he did. He couldn't look at me. Well—not until we prayed. Praying seemed to make him feel better. During it, he asked forgiveness of the Lord. Didn't say what for. Even cried when he did it. I wanted to ask him—I wanted to ask him about where he'd gone, but I didn't have the . . . the nerve, I guess." Her voice caught. "Now I wish I would of."

Regan frowned. "But I understood you *did* ask him." Ida nodded. "And when was that?"

"The next time. The same thing happened, only this time he woke me, coming in. It was after three, and I turned on the light. He said he was sorry, he'd just been to the bathroom. He had his pajamas on. I didn't say anything. I hadn't been awake, so how could I know?

"So I waited fifteen minutes till he fell asleep. Then I got up and went in the bathroom. And there were his clothes rolled up, lying on the floor. I felt them and they were still warm. Next morning, of course, he'd gotten up before me, and the clothes'd all been put away. When I saw that, I *had* to ask him. He told me I'd been dreamin'. I could just tell, lookin' at him tellin' me that, he'd worked it all out ahead of time, just in case I did ask. He tried to smile, only it wasn't much of a smile, Bishop." She started weeping again.

I shook my head and looked at Regan. Never had I heard a wife incriminate her husband so devastatingly. Was the Bishop reading it the way I was? His face gave no clue.

So I asked my one question. "In all confidence, Ida Mae, what do you think? Did Jerry kill those four women? Tell us what you think in your heart."

Ida lifted her chin and faced me through the tears.

"He most certainly did not!"

I was convinced she really believed what she was saying and wished I could agree. I'd now reached *my* conclusion. Jerry Fanning *had* to be Strangler John. I could almost see Fran Wilson licking her chops.

—14—

I WAS STIRRING SOME CREAM AND SUGAR into my coffee at 8:30 Sunday morning, watching Ernie bustle around the kitchen. Ernie's one of those people—usually women of a certain age—who are never happy unless they're doing something. When they run out of things to do, they'll undo everything they just did so they can get busy redoing it.

"You look better than usual for a morning-after, David," she commented.

"Morning-after? Are you kidding? Ernie, I was out with a *Baptist*! No smoking, no drinking, no dancing, no fun. If there's any difference between a Baptist and a nun, I can't tell it!" She glared at me, and I grinned back.

"Actually, we had a pretty good time. Amy Grant probably won't be my pick next time I go to a concert, but she's okay, and it was nice to see how much Ida Mae appreciated her. She had a great time.

"Then, since the boss's long-windedness made us miss dinner here, we stopped at Sarto's for a quick bite on the way back. That wasn't such a good idea. She was too anxious to enjoy the tortellini, not knowing what kind of torture you and the Bishop were putting Joe Bob through. So we got back early—as you noticed."

She sniffed. "Early by *your* standards, maybe. If I have to stay up till midnight again, I'm going to be old before my time."

"Aw, come on, Ernie. You'll never get old. And you didn't *have* to stay up! I told you, put the kid to bed and relax. Ida Mae says he never wakes up. Hey, he didn't even stir getting in or out of the car when I took them home."

"Oh, you *say* that, David, but whose fault would it have been if he'd

63

rolled off the couch and cut his precious little head open? I—"

"Don't feed me that line of bull, Ernie! You stayed up for one reason only—you wanted to look at the little guy. I bet you and the boss fought over him all evening!"

She smiled. "He *is* a nice boy." Then she glared at me again. "But it's a good thing the Bishop has no children. Another hour with him and little Joseph would have been spoiled rotten."

She put a substantial omelette in front of me and departed. Her Sunday routine is no different than any other day. She goes up to the chapel a little before nine to pray and "assist the Bishop at mass," whatever that means.

While I ate I checked out the latest on Fanning, "the alleged Strangler," in the Sunday *Times*. Under the headline, "Alleged Strangler Had Violent History," the story related some of what Ida Mae had told us the day before—i.e., Jerry's Friday-night outings and his criminal record back in Oklahoma—but with a very different slant.

The article cited "a highly placed police official who requested anonymity" and I had no doubt about it being Kessler. Kessler's a good cop, as cops go, but he's not above using the media to influence public opinion when he thinks it might help him win a case.

I called Baker from my office, catching him as he was heading for church. Learning that I had talked directly with Ida Mae, he promised to call me back as soon as he got home. Which he did, a little after ten, and I filled him in. Then he took a minute to think.

"Okay, Davey," he finally said. "It's a tough one. But I'm still going to bust my tail. I'll hear that tape of Ida this afternoon. And talk to Jerry first thing in the morning about copping a plea.

"Fran's not going to like it, and Harrington'll probably tell me to shove it where the moon don't shine. But he's a little scared of me. I've beat him more often than not. And there's lots of little technical things on this one that'll let me tie him up in knots for months.

"Maybe if I give him a pound of flesh—say at least seven years in the slammer, no chance of parole—he might go along. That's tough on Jerry. But you and I are now agreed he's guilty as hell, so screw what he wants or doesn't want. Anyway, thanks for the fill-in. Talk to you tomorrow." He rang off, leaving me wondering where this left the Bishop and me. That question was answered almost immediately. Ernie was in the doorway saying, "Bishop Regan wants to see you up in the chapel right away, David."

I stared at her. "Has he gone nuts? He *never* invites me up there. Do you think maybe God's finally told him the truth and he's ready to convert—to Judaism?" Ernie didn't even smile. Catholics can never take a joke.

He was in the usual spot, right in front of the altar. I wondered if Ernie had misunderstood his instructions. His eyes were closed and he didn't hear my approach. I finally gave a little cough and his eyes popped open.

"Ah, David. Thank you for coming up. I want to go visit Mr. Fanning at his place of incarceration. Arrange it, please."

I didn't bother to argue this time. For one thing, I was all argued out. For another, he'd closed his eyes and gone back into his private world. I had plenty of questions but he wasn't in the mood. I was on my own. I spun around and headed back downstairs to see what I could arrange.

—15—

I GUESS WHAT TICKED ME OFF MOST was Regan's total refusal to let me go with him into the visitors' room.

"But someone ought to take notes," I complained.

"Out of the question. Just wait for me here in the waiting room, David. A little patient waiting never hurt anyone; least of all one with the inordinate proclivity for precipitate action you constantly demonstrate."

"But—" He spun around, ignoring me. All my buts weren't going to get my butt into that visitors' room; his mind was made up. Off he went, following the guard, restraining his inordinate proclivity for precipitate speed in that wheelchair of his.

Getting him visitors' privileges hadn't been all that easy. I'd finally had to resort to calling Fran Wilson at her apartment. I'd had the foresight to hang onto her private, unlisted number after our short but steamy relationship came to an abrupt end three years ago.

Fran didn't exactly bubble over with joy when I told her why I was calling. But some adroit persuasion convinced her that for purposes of spiritual comfort, a bishop ought to be able to visit even Strangler John. She called the jail and gave the okay.

(My telling her that if she didn't feel she should do it I'd have to have Regan call Harrington and make arrangements directly may have given her the false impression that the Bishop and her boss are buddies. They're not. In fact, Regan can barely stand Harrington, a feeling I suspect Harrington reciprocates. But is it my fault if Fran draws the wrong conclusion from an offhanded comment of mine?)

Once Fran agreed to make the call, getting the Bishop to the jail was no big deal. Just took a little planning and forethought. I had the Caddy brought around to our front door by a guy at the garage where we keep it—Fred's, around the corner on Eleventh Avenue.

I bumped the Bishop down the eight steps of the stoop, and he got himself into the car with the help of a couple of steel bars he's had installed on it.

At the jail I got him up the ramp and inside with no difficulty. As far I knew, it was his first visit there, but it didn't seem to depress him as much as it does me. Maybe that's because he knows he's never going to have to spend the night there. That's an assurance sad experience has taught me I have no right to share.

After doing all the work of getting him there, being told I had to cool my heels in the waiting room didn't exactly fill me with joy. But during the forty-five-minute wait, sitting in a chair a lot more comfortable than the one I'd occupied in the visitors' room the day before, I began to see Regan's point.

He was undoubtedly talking to Jerry as a spiritual adviser. So it had to be alone. I guessed I could live with that.

When the boss came wheeling back into the waiting room, I tried to read the expression on his face. Wasted effort. And his mouth was as uncommunicative as his face. He didn't say a word till we were in the car and moving.

When he finally spoke, his tone was triumphant. "Mr. Fanning is innocent, Davey!"

My head swiveled so violently the car actually swerved. I wasn't so shocked by his announcement about Jerry, though that was startling enough. Nor by the unexpected certainty in his voice. It was his calling me Davey. He *never* calls me Davey.

"You're kidding! How can you be so sure?"

He calmed down. "Well, I shouldn't be so absolute. I've become a bit less sanguine over the past twenty-four hours regarding my ability to discern when people are telling me the truth. About anything whatsoever.

"However, Mr. Fanning has just made the most embarrassing of confessions. I am convinced—well, almost convinced—he was telling the truth. If he was, he is innocent."

"He made a confession? Of what?"

Regan waited. He wanted to have my eye. I slowed for a yellow light, and pulled up to the intersection as the light turned red. A couple of pedestrians gaped at such un-New York-like driving, but I ignored them.

"David," Regan said solemnly, holding my eyes with his, "it must be understood that my revealing Mr. Fanning's secret to you—" He raised a finger of warning. "—assuming he was truthful—is the moral equivalent of the seal of the confessional. What you're about to hear is as confidential as anything you'll ever hear from me. Mr. Fanning only agreed to permit me to tell you when I informed him I could not act without your knowing. As I'll explain in a moment.

"He absolutely refuses to permit me to reveal it to anyone else, not even to Mrs. Fanning—indeed, *especially* not to her. And not to the police, even though, if he's telling the truth, it would mean his immediate release."

I turned back to the street as the light turned green. "So," I frowned, accelerating, "You want an oath or something? Okay, you got it. Now, what's his secret?"

Regan struck me as a bit overwrought. And why was Jerry being so stubborn about it? If the Bishop was right—if Jerry could get out of jail by giving up his secret—why hold back?

The Bishop was silent till we came to the next red light and I looked at him again. His face was impassive as he divulged Jerry Fanning's secret. "Mr. Fanning is fascinated by pornography, David. He's been sneaking out of bed each Friday night to see X-rated films."

I stared at the Bishop. "That's it?" He nodded. A horn blared behind me, kindly alerting me to the fact the light had changed. I drove in silence for a couple of blocks, absorbing the revelation. It didn't make sense. Porno movies? Sounded like a lame excuse. But the Bishop was apparently buying it, so . . . maybe.

But . . . that Christian fellow? Inveighing against the crimes of the city while himself diving into its sleaziest sleaze?

Jimmy Swaggart came to mind, along with something someone had said about him: "The guy *had* to get relief. He was so busy keeping everyone else on the straight and narrow, he thought he was perfect. And that's a terrible thing to have to live with."

I started to chuckle, then immediately turned the chuckle into a cough. The clergyman on my right wasn't in any mood for chuckling.

But it *was* kind of humorous: the fundie sneaking into the theater with the other porno junkies—who'd split their sides laughing if they knew who he was and what he represented. And he'd die of shame if they ever found out.

Did it have anything to do with his marriage? I thought of young Ida Mae, too modest to use makeup. Did the sights of Times Square make Jerry crave something a little more . . . exciting?

The Bishop waited for me to process the information. He didn't speak till I finally shook my head and said, "I'll be dammed."

"So will Mr. Fanning," Regan said "or, at least, so he imagines. He is so distraught over his self-perceived failure to live up to his duties that he's not thinking clearly. I can't tell you how difficult it was for him to bring himself to confess that to me. Or how relieved he was afterwards." I glanced over and thought I saw a look of satisfaction. Regan doesn't hear many confessions. I guess he enjoys getting the opportunity.

"New York," he went on, "is the first place he had ever seen theaters blatantly advertising pornography. Nothing like that, I suppose, in Ada. And he found himself fascinated in a way that was both ugly and compelling."

I wondered how much of this was from Fanning and how much Regan's projection. I had plenty of time to wonder, since we'd now arrived at the mansion. I went around to the trunk and got out the wheelchair while Regan opened his door. When I had the wheelchair set he levered himself off the car seat and onto the wheelchair, using those steel bars. I pulled him back up the steps and returned the car to Fred's. Regan was waiting in his office when I returned.

"Each Friday night," he continued, as I sat, "a theater near Mrs. Billings's home—the Rialto—offers a new racy film. He happened to pass it on his way home from his first Friday night in the city trying to convert the unaccepting multitudes on Times Square—and found himself attracted. He says he fought the temptation all evening. Ultimately he found a useful rationalization: his inability to sleep.

"He slipped out of bed and went to the theater. Paid the exorbitant five dollars and fifty cents and went in. The film was horrifyingly compelling. I gather X-rated filmmakers these days don't leave a great deal to the imagination."

"Yeah, so I've heard." The boss was discreet enough not to raise an eyebrow.

"Yes. Well, in any case, Mr. Fanning had terrible guilt pangs the next morning. He wanted to tell his wife but couldn't bring himself to do it. Too ashamed. Once he'd confessed the sin to God, however, he felt able to face the world with a cleansed heart, convinced he'd never fall again.

"Only to find himself, the next Friday afternoon, drawn right back to the Rialto, curious to see what the new movie would be. And, of course, that night when he went to bed, he found his mental state the same as the previous week. And so on. All four Friday nights."

I raised an eyebrow. "And you believe him?"

Regan smiled. "I do. But as I said, I am not as sanguine about my ability to read human nature as I was yesterday. So we need to verify his story. As I told you, the only reason I made you privy is that you can do so.

"I suggested strongly that he tell the police and let them do the checking. He could then be released from durance vile. But durance, it seems, is less vile than telling even one more soul of his failure."

I thought a moment. "So you want me to check it out."

"I do. He tells me Mrs. Fanning should have several photographs of him. Obtain one or more from her, then go to that theater and question the employees. Given your skills, I should think you can establish the veracity of his story—or expose its falsity."

I shrugged. "Yeah, maybe. But where does that get us?" Regan looked surprised. At least I had his attention.

"Here's what I mean." I sat back and crossed my legs. "Suppose I do verify that Jerry's telling the truth. That'll be nice. We'll both know the guy's innocent, and your faith in your understanding of human nature will be restored. Great, right? But. What good's it going to do us? It won't—"

Regan cut me off. "You mean, of course, that lacking Mr. Fanning's permission to take our knowledge to the police, our knowledge will not be helpful."

"You got it. What good does it do us to know the guy's innocent when we've got nothing to take to the police?"

"We'll simply have to find the true murderer."

"With a psycho?" I laughed bitterly. "Lots of luck! What are you? An expert at finding a needle in a haystack? Look, Bishop. The only way we're going to be able to get Jerry off is to take this to the police."

"And violate the seal of the confessional?" Regan was outraged.

"Violate—?" I was sputtering. "What violate? The guy's got an iron-clad alibi and you're worrying about violating some corny seal? What is this?"

Regan took a deep breath. "What this is, David, is a solemn obligation I have undertaken. As have you, in agreeing to be bound by it. It isn't for you or for me to decide what's best for Mr. Fanning under the circumstances. We have undertaken an obligation. It's not up for discussion."

"Well, I don't see why the guy's so het up over a little fling. It's embarrassing, sure, but what's the big deal?"

The Bishop nodded. "The big deal is not Mr. Fanning's opinion of the gravity of his conduct. The big deal is the solemn obligation I—and you—have undertaken." He sighed. "Since I agreed to hear his confession—even extrasacramentally—I cannot do other than to honor his insistence. And, as I carefully explained to you, when I extended the obligation to you, neither can you. Going to the police, however wise that may be in abstracto, is not an option."

Regan held my eye till I nodded acceptance. "Just obtain that verification," he concluded. "Once we have that—if we get that—I have an idea or two to share. Our cause may not be as hopeless as you think."

—16—

No sweat getting the photo of Jerry. Ida Mae showed me a bunch and I picked the best one. *Best*, of course, is a matter of personal opinion. In this case, it meant the clearest and most recent exposure of Jerry's face. I took one Ida said she'd taken herself just three months previously. A full body shot, Jerry grinning, standing by a lake, displaying a freshly caught fish. He was barechested and even skinnier without his shirt on. (That's Jerry, not the fish.) I'd have preferred a blow-up of just the face, but this was okay. Ida Mae thanked me again for the concert and wanted to know if we were getting anywhere. I told her we were working hard.

I hadn't come up with an approach to the people at the Rialto. Nor did one occur to me on the drive over. Sometimes you just have to play these things by ear.

The theater wasn't doing much business at five o'clock on a Sunday afternoon, but it was open, marquee announcing *Daddy's Favorite Baby-Sitter* and *Papa Primed to Pump*. Apparently it was Father's Day in Pornoland.

The ticket window was lit but unmanned. I let myself into the dark, dingy lobby, also empty. I could hear faintly the sounds of the movie. Behind the tiny concession stand was a door marked Manager. I tapped a quarter against the glass counter of the concession. A few seconds later, the door opened and a short, stout middle-aged man emerged.

"Five-fifty," he said in a bored tone, giving me a glance and heading for the cash register. Something stopped him before he got to it. He took a long look at me.

"Vice?" he snapped. That gave me the opening I'd been hoping for.

71

I just stared at him. Impassive. Coplike. The man's eyes shifted. The snap turned into a whine.

"Hey, pal, I *told* Langford we'd comply. You guys keep hassling me, I'm going to the mayor, I swear to God! I've got friends, you know. I—"

I stopped him with upraised hand.

What you never want to do, unless you are one, is *tell* someone you're a cop. That can get you into trouble. Prison-type trouble. Impersonating an officer is a felony. On the other hand, you're not duty-bound to correct any and all misunderstandings that might arise.

As it happened, I knew Phil Langford. He'd been on the force forever. Went into Vice back when I was in Homicide. He's one miserable S.O.B. But if the porno man thought Langford and I were buddies, well . . .

"You the manager?" I asked, tight-lipped.

"Yessir. What do you—?"

I cut him off. "I'll ask the questions, sir. If you don't mind. Name?"

"Walter MacIntosh."

"Okay, Mr. MacIntosh," I said, pulling Fanning's photo from my coat pocket. "I'm not really interested in code violations. I'm not with Vice. Just want to know if you've ever seen this individual."

Relief showed in the manager's piggy little eyes. He took the picture and squinted at it. His eyes flicked back and forth from it to my face.

"Yeah, maybe," he said. "What's in it for me?"

Time to get tough. I jerked the picture out of his hand. "You don't want to play, hmm? Fine. I'll be back. With Langford."

"Hey!" he whined, reaching for the picture. "I only asked who he was. Is that a crime?" I let him take the photo back. He studied it some more.

"Uh, yeah, I've seen him, lemme think a minute."

"Take your time, sir."

The man squinted at Fanning's face for another few seconds, tilting the photo from side to side. Suddenly his eyes lighted up.

"The Eskimo Pie guy!" he exclaimed.

I waited, trying to be impassive.

The words tumbled out. "JoAnne was the first one to notice him. That's him! He's been coming in here the last few Fridays. We noticed him because he asked for an Eskimo Pie. A hick, right? From Tennessee or somewhere. Can you beat it? An Eskimo Pie! Shit, I don't have refrigeration—I'm lucky just to have a few candy bars.

"So JoAnne gets kind of smart-ass with him. Says, 'Sorry, we're fresh out. But we're getting a fresh supply tomorrow. Be sure to come back.' Then she tells me about it after.

"Says, 'Hey, Walter, we're getting a higher class of customer. They got to have Eskimo Pies!' We get a good laugh out of it, know what I mean? I told her to let me know if he comes back.

"And, sure enough, next week, the guy's back, wanting his Eskimo Pie! JoAnne gets me, playing along, you know. I tell him we just happen to be fresh out, and the guy's face falls. Same thing's been happening for weeks—it's got so JoAnne and I are looking for him on Friday nights to see him ask for his Eskimo Pie!"

This was good. Maybe *too* good. "How do you remember it's Friday nights?" I asked suspiciously.

He shrugged. "JoAnne only works here one night a week. Mostly I'm here by myself, but weekends I need some help. My son usually helps, only he's got class on Friday nights this quarter, so JoAnne comes in. Nope, it's Fridays, all right."

I had a few more questions for my new friend, such as time of arrival ("Probably around midnight. Maybe a little after"), time of departure ("Can't tell you, buddy—uh, *sir*. Never noticed him leaving"), and were there any side exits in the theater ("Nope. Not without setting off a fire alarm"). Jerry Fanning was off the hook.

"You *will* tell Langford, won't you, Officer?" MacIntosh called after me. "I always cooperate with you guys."

"Next time I see him," I promised, without turning or stopping.

—17—

AN HOUR LATER I WAS BACK HOME in the dining room with Regan, finishing a spicy bouillabaisse Ernie had been simmering all day. Two big bowlfuls each. A satisfying end to a satisfying weekend.

Regan had held up dinner till I got back from the Rialto, not that I got all choked up over that bit of kindness. I knew he knew that if he ate before I returned, I might just take off. Sally Castle is usually up for some evening fun and games. Then the boss'd have to wait till morning to learn whether his fundie buddy was or wasn't lying about those Friday nights.

At first the Bishop wondered whether our porno friend had been truthful with me. I set him straight.

"Was MacIntosh telling it like it was? You better believe it. If you'd seen the man's face when Langford's name came up, you'd know. Langford's the closest thing to the Narc from Hell you ever want to see."

I grinned. "And MacIntosh got the idea that Langford and I are buddies. Possibly from something I said. Believe me, he's not going to mess around with any buddy of Langford's."

Regan pushed his soupbowl aside and poured coffee for both of us. "So. Mr. Fanning is exculpated. Excellent."

"But let's not get carried away," I cautioned, blowing steam off my coffee.

Regan took a sip of his own coffee, staring at me over the rim.

"I mean, like I said this afternoon, if Jerry won't let us use the alibi, we're no better off, right?"

Regan just smirked. He can be exasperating.

"Look." I clanked the cup back into its saucer. "The killer's a psycho,

74

okay? Meaning he's killing at random. So who is he? Before, we knew it had to be one of fourteen million people in the greater metropolitan area. Now that Jerry's eliminated, we're down to thirteen million, nine hundred and ninety-nine thou—"

The Bishop cut me off. "Not necessarily." Something in his tone told me he had something. Something good.

"Yes?" I prompted.

He pivoted abruptly and wheeled for the door, throwing a command over his shoulder: "Bring my coffee, David."

"Hey!" I yelled at his back, but he was already out the door. He executed a precise right turn and disappeared down the hall.

What would he do, I fumed, if I didn't tag along? But the glint in his eye and the tone in his voice . . .

I just had to trail along like a true gofer, trying not to spill coffee on myself.

In the office, the boss was exercising, wheeling back and forth, from the south wall to his desk and back again. *Not* aimlessly. I set his coffee on his desk, mine on the little table next to my chair, and had a seat. He spoke on the move.

"I have an idea, David, which could reduce the list of probable suspects to a manageable level." Regan stopped moving and swung to face me. He had my absolute attention.

"What is the outstanding anomaly in this series of murders, David?"

I stared at him. He stared back. I finally shrugged.

"All right," he went on, "a hint: of the four victims, three were prostitutes, one not. Any significance in that?" The boss wheeled to the window as I pondered.

"Sure," I said to his back. "The killer made a mistake. He thought Penniston *was* a prostitute. Understandable. Beautiful young woman wearing plenty of makeup and possibly a slinky outfit, walking alone near Times Square at night. Very natural mistake—unfortunately for her."

Regan was wheeling back to his desk by the time I finished. He settled there, seemingly through exercising, at least for the time being. Thank God. He took a sip of coffee without taking his eyes off me.

"So, David: a killer's mistake. Thus the wisdom of the *Dispatch*. And, apparently, Inspector Kessler as well. As a superficial explanation, before examining all the evidence: perhaps. But it fails to explain a certain crucial fact."

I looked away and thought about it. I got an idea, though I didn't see where it fit.

"Something to do with the earrings? The killer didn't rip them off her the way he did the prostitutes."

Regan frowned. "An excellent point, David, one that bears investigation. But that doesn't happen to be the anomaly I'm focusing on at the moment. Frankly, I'm at a loss as to the meaning of the different treatment the murderer gave Miss Penniston's body as regards the earrings. It's probably significant, but I'll need more data before I'll be able to make anything of that. But it's a different anomaly that presently concerns me. Any other ideas?"

I just shrugged. Again. Regan's tone sharpened.

"The newspapers, David, have reported that *none* of the victims put up the slightest semblance of a struggle. True?"

I nodded. He raised a triumphant finger.

"And what stands out about that fact?" I shook my head. He scowled. "Come, come, David. It all but leaps out at one!"

I looked at him for a minute, then threw up my hands. He had me. I guess when your I.Q.'s 220 things leap out at you that don't leap— or even creep—out at other mortals.

"I give," I replied wearily. "Tell me, in your infinite wisdom. What is it that leaps so merrily out at you but not at me?"

"Wisdom has nothing to do with it, David, infinite or otherwise. It's a matter of analyzing the pertinent data and finding a theory that fits. And the most pertinent datum at the moment is that the killer was able to strike down all four victims without the slightest struggle. *In every case.*"

My boss seemed to be settling in for a seminar, but I didn't mind. This one I wanted to hear.

"Approach it from the killer's perspective, David. If one assumes (as apparently everyone, including the police, has) that he was a stranger to these women, how do you explain his ability to get close enough to each one to slip a garroting wire around her throat—without a struggle?"

He'd given up waiting for my wisdom. "For the three prostitutes," he continued, "the question answers itself. The very essence of the intercourse—make that the relationship—between a prostitute and her client is physical proximity. She'd have no reason to be alarmed at his closeness, physical proximity being part and parcel of the service she offers. Prostitution is said to be the oldest profession. That's unlikely.

But it is certainly the most dangerous. Constant physical proximity to strangers in the midst of extralegal activity makes it so."

I frowned at him as the ever-patient teacher waited for my comment. "I don't see where you're heading," I said finally.

"But surely it's plain—" He took a deep breath. "Now here, David. The killer's ability to achieve physical proximity to three of the victims requires no explanation. It follows from the very nature of their work."

"Yeah, I got that."

"What are we then to make of Miss Penniston? A beautiful, wealthy, successful woman. And certainly no prostitute. Apparently no one knows what she was doing at or near Ninth and Forty-ninth that evening, but—for now—that need not concern us. Whatever her reason for being there, she permitted the murderer to approach her, accompany her, throw a wire around her neck and strangle her. All without a struggle."

"Yeah. Just like the other three. So what?"

"*Precisely*, David: *just* like the other three! The question no one is bothering to ask—not you, not the police, not the newspapers—is this: *if* he was a stranger to her, how did the murderer manage to gain the proximity needed to murder her without a struggle?"

I stared at him. "Uh, some pretext, I suppose. I guess he just—I don't know, asked her for directions or something."

The Bishop shook his head. "No. It simply isn't possible that a woman of Laura Penniston's intelligence and standing would have permitted a stranger to gain that degree of proximity. Not at night and not in a strange neighborhood. Even under normal circumstances, I'd need some convincing to believe it. Given the well-publicized menace of a strangler on the loose, it's untenable. I refuse to accept it."

"So?" I was puzzled. "What are you saying? She wasn't killed the way they think?"

"I'm saying, David, that she *was* killed the way the three others were. But how can that be? For the others, their profession is sufficient explanation. Not for her. For Laura Penniston, only one explanation suffices. She *knew* her attacker, knew him well. She was killed by a close acquaintance, probably a friend." Regan watched me, waiting for my reaction. I thought before I spoke.

"Okay, maybe. But where does that leave us?"

The Bishop nodded briskly. "I believe it leaves us with only two alternatives. Either Miss Penniston's murderer was a so-called copycat, taking advantage of the serial killer's reign of terror to rid himself of her; or he was one who deliberately created a reign of terror as mere camouflage for his murder of Laura Penniston. If the latter, the other three victims were no more than pawns in his overall strategy. Which alternative do you prefer?"

I remembered something I'd read in the *Dispatch*. "Well, you can forget the copycat angle. The police considered that, according to Rozanski, and threw it out. The M.O. was the same in all four cases and, from the marks on the victims, so was the wire he did it with."

"Precisely. So, David, we are looking for a monster. Someone who sacrificed three innocent victims to disguise his murder of a fourth."

I thought about it and shook my head. "The police are never going to buy it."

Regan exuded satisfaction and confidence. "Of course not, David. Especially not when they have a man in custody. Leaving the field open to us. Where do we start?"

That was the first question he'd asked to which I had a useful response.

"Well," I allowed. "I had a long talk with a buddy at headquarters yesterday." And proceeded to give him what Joe Parker had given me. When I got to the part about the picture of the dead Laura Penniston's hand, I excused myself and dashed into my office. Twenty seconds later I was back with the photostat. I didn't know how, but I had a feeling my boss might be able to make something of it.

Panting slightly, I slid the photostat of Laura Penniston's hand across the shiny wooden desktop. The Bishop glanced at it and gave me a quizzical look.

"Yeah, I *do* get ideas," I told him. "About one a year. When Joe Parker showed me that yesterday, I made a copy. What you're looking at is the left hand of Laura Penniston's corpse."

Regan stared at me, then looked down at the sheet of paper. He picked it up, frowned, glanced at me, and started studying it. After a few seconds he leaned forward, flipped on his high-intensity desk lamp and bent over the paper, eyes about two inches from it.

"Don't tell Kessler," I instructed the top of Regan's head. "He'd be a tad unhappy to know I've got it."

The Bishop studied it for a minute or two, then said, without looking up, "What do these letters signify?"

"Ah! That's the sixty-four-thousand-dollar question! Kessler and Blake would love to know, the task force would love to know. Hell, I'd love to know *myself*. So never mind the questions. I'm looking for answers."

Regan didn't answer or look up. He continued studying the photostat for another thirty seconds.

"It looks like G O S T," he muttered, then looked up at me, his face in shadows behind the brightness of the lamp. "No one has any idea what this means?"

"Right. And, to answer your next question, they don't know who wrote it. But it's a fair assumption it was either Laura or the murderer. Either way, it could be an important clue. I could tell you what Blake thinks, but won't bore you with that bit of nonsense."

The boss nodded and returned to his close study of the writing. After a moment, he said, "I'm not so sure that's really a *T*."

I walked around behind his desk and took a gander. Looking at it more carefully, I could see what he meant. Between the downstroke of the *T* and the crossbar was a fair-sized gap.

G O S T̄

"It is a strange looking *T*", I agreed. "But whoever wrote it—and the cops figure it had to be either Laura or the killer—could have been in a hurry, plus it's not easy writing on skin. I've tried it and the letters can get all distorted."

"Perhaps," Regan mumbled and continued to study the paper under the light another few seconds. He finally slid it back to me across the desk. "It was Halloween night: *ghost* misspelled?" He shook his head gloomily. "I doubt it. I just don't know," he sighed.

"Well, join the club," I said, shoving the paper to one side. "We're all trapped in a slough of nescience."

Regan looked at me and slowly shook his head. He can't stand to hear other people use three-dollar words.

"Well. Let's attack our nescience, then." He smiled evilly. "By the way, are you sure you don't mean *miasma* of nescience?"

He was being sarcastic, but the joke was on him. By tomorrow, with the help of that big dictionary, *miasma* would be a working part of my vocabulary. It's only a matter of time before I'll be up with him. We'll see what good that 220 I.Q. does him then.

Regan switched off the lamp and pushed himself away from the desk. "Let me think about those letters overnight. Maybe something will come to me. Or you. In the meantime, we—that is, you—must compile a list of Miss Penniston's known associates and begin winnowing it down to those few, we may hope, who seem to have the requisite combination of motive, ability and opportunity.

"What we now know is this: she was a talented businesswoman, utilizing natural beauty and grace, no doubt, to build a highly successful business. So we may take it as a given that she was an astute woman, a woman of substance. And at some point—if my hypothesis is correct— she incurred the enmity of someone physically powerful and extremely devious.

"That person plotted her death—again, *ex hypothesi*—in a long-headed and calculated manner. Are any of her associates capable of that? If so, which ones? Who had an animus toward her? Or a pecuniary motive?"

I thought about it. "Well, if you're right, we're certainly a jump ahead of Kessler."

Regan sat buried in thought for a long minute. "What's on your calendar for tomorrow?" he finally asked.

I shook my head. "Up to you. I have no plans."

"Good. My recommendation is that you proceed to the offices of Penniston Associates. Learn all you can about her colleagues. And any personal friends you can uncover.

"Until we know more about the people who knew her, we will be unable to test my hypothesis. And keep an eye out for any sign of GOST." He closed his eyes a moment. When he opened them again he changed the subject.

"For now, David, please phone Mrs. Fanning. Tell her we are persuaded of her husband's innocence, that we will be working to free him and appreciate her help. Tell her I will be joining my prayers to hers for his speedy release. Ask her to tell her husband that. He will know we have verified his story. You might also tell Mrs. Fanning that she has a very engaging child. *Very* engaging. A delightful boy."

He spun and rolled away, trying not to let me see him blush. Too late.

—18—

NEXT MORNING, MONDAY, a little before nine, while looking up Penniston Associates in the phone book I got a better idea. Tapping out another of the numbers I know by heart, I considered just how frank I should be with my golfing buddy, Chet Rozanski.

If I handled him right, I'd be able to weasel out of him not only the phone number I needed but also some background on the whole situation. I got lucky and caught him still at home. Of course, the way he answered the phone was atrocious, but that's just Chet.

"Yeah, Rozanski."

"Yeah, Rozanski? What the hell kind of way is *that* to answer a phone? This is Yeah, Goldman."

A pause. Then a change of gears. "Well, well, well. My old friend, Goldman, a no-show at the big Halloween bash. Are we still speaking to our fellow golfers, or have we gone *way* uptown?"

"Give me a break, Chet. Wasn't my idea. Want some free advice? If a genius ever offers you a job, run like a rabbit. They're an S.O.B. to work for."

"So quit already, Davey! But you'll never do that, you like those Catholics too much. Scheduled your baptism yet?"

Rozanski has yet to get over me—Jewish atheist that I am, and loud-mouthed about it yet—working for a Catholic bishop. But I was in a hurry.

"Enough with the ethnic humor, Chet. I'm calling, believe it or not, for a reason. Tell me everything you know about Penniston Associates, Inc. And the real story on all those business associates, friends and acquaintances in those superb stories you wrote about the Strangler's third hit."

Another pause. Then, in a guarded tone, "So. Isn't that interesting? I don't suppose you'd have a client, would you, Davey? Perchance one with initials G.F.?"

I grinned. "You got it, friend. So let me hear all about the late Miss Penniston's nearest and dearest."

"Yeah, in a minute. First of all, you're smart enough to know when to say background only. And I didn't hear that. So am I to assume your representing Fanning is public knowledge? Like in my story in this afternoon's *Dispatch*?"

"Absolutely. And, for what it's worth, you've got an exclusive. Now. Give about the lady's friends and associates."

That started a wrangle I should have anticipated. Naturally he wanted details on my involvement with Fanning, seeing a fresh aspect on a still hot story. And since he was a reporter, my request could wait. I finally cut him off.

"Hey, man, whose dime do you think we're talking on? In the famous words of a former president, I paid for this mike! So that hot story— your gratitude for which I will not hold my breath waiting for—is going to have to wait till I have *my* information. Otherwise I'm hanging up."

He grumbled a bit, muttered an insincere thank you, and gave me what I called for. Not that his heart was in it. He was obviously thinking about his new lead for that afternoon's *Dispatch*. So I didn't get much. But since it was tons more than the dribbles and drabbles I had, I took it all down.

The number-one man in Penniston's life had received a lot of play in the papers, and Rozanski gave me some dirt to go with it. Bob Theodore, partner in the successful accounting firm his dad had established back in the seventies, was tall, blond, handsome . . .

". . . and dumb as a post," chuckled Rozanski. "We didn't put that part in our stories. Paul Malone of the *Times* told me Theodore asked him what *obsequies* meant. Can you believe it? A *partner* in a substantial accounting firm, and doesn't know the meaning of a common word like that! Ah, the advantages of having a rich daddy!"

"Yeah, ridiculous," I muttered, trying to remember what *obsequies* meant. I made a mental note to look it up.

Irrespective of his lack of intelligence—or who knows? Maybe because of it—Laura had liked Bob Theodore plenty. They'd been a hot item for a couple of years, cutting a wide swath in society circles, unquestionably the most photogenic couple in town since Ivana Trump dumped the Donald—or was it the other way around?

Following Laura's death, the *Post* had run several photos of the couple in happier times: cutting a rug at the Muscular Dystrophy Ball at the Waldorf, Laura's blond hair and full-length gown swirling as the tuxedoed Bob Theodore spun her, his own blond coif stylishly long.

And again, the two blondies, identical smiles splitting their gorgeous faces, toasting George Burns at the Christians and Jews United benefit.

Betty Donovan was the other side of the coin. As ugly as Theodore was handsome, she was Penniston's business partner and, by all accounts, a very astute lady. While Rozanski described her, I was studying Donovan's photo in a two-week-old *Dispatch*.

The woman's round face didn't really have a double chin—the skin was too tight for that. Her age was difficult to guess, as it so often is with people that fat. But I didn't have to guess. Rozanski told me Betty Donovan was fifty-five. The only lines on her face, in fact, were her most attractive feature: laugh lines alongside both eyes. They gave her face a warmth that made up for the overall plainness.

"She'd been Penniston's financial adviser," said Rozanski, "almost from the time Penniston came here from Kansas eight years ago. Three years ago they decided to go into business together—combine Laura's charisma with Donovan's business acumen—and it's been a huge success. People say Powers, DT& L, and the other biggies are starting to look over their shoulders. I have it on good authority that Penniston did nearly three million in billings last year, and that they're *very* profitable.

"Laura was point man for the outfit, Donovan the brains. You never saw anything about Betty Donovan in their press releases, but she made the whole thing work. Some speculate that Donovan was miffed about playing second fiddle. Not so. Donovan's a private person, hates the limelight."

Next on Rozanski's list was George McClendon, the new kid on the block, a would-be new partner in the enterprise. He hadn't got much play in the newspaper coverage, even in the *Dispatch*, but Rozanski had some facts and figures.

"I didn't even put McClendon in my articles, and neither did anyone else. He didn't really fit in, and we had too many other points of interest to cover. He was strictly a Johnny-come-lately in the Penniston *ménage*.

He'd been introduced to Donovan and Penniston by their banker, Lee
Stubbs. Stubbs, by the way, is an exec at Mid-City National, where
Laura and Betty banked. He was another one who got little or no press
coverage following the lady's death.

"Stubbs was their main financial support when the two gals got
started, three years ago. He provided the loan they desperately needed
at the time. I haven't met Stubbs, don't even know what he looks like.
I did meet McClendon, though. Now *there's* a memorable dude. Must
be about fifty, looks like a lumberjack—big and burly, with a bushy
beard.

"Anyway, word is, Penniston and Donovan went to Stubbs last summer to ask for an increase in their line of credit. Victims of their own
success, I guess. Their business was growing so fast they were running
out of cash. Stubbs apparently didn't want to go any further with them,
told them they ought to put in more equity. But where the hell are a
couple of gals going to come up with equity? I mean, they're making
some significant bucks, but they've got taxes to pay and plenty of expenses. They had no excess cash to stick into the business.

"So Stubbs put them in touch with his buddy McClendon. He'd been
running a successful advertising agency, had lots of bucks and a yen to
be in a sexier business, and was attracted by Penniston's beauty and
her company's success. So he was interested. Word on the street is he
was all but in the door when Penniston was killed. Now I hear he's
dickering with Donovan to buy the whole shebang."

I thought of something. "Who inherited Laura's share of the business?
What do you know about that?"

Rozanski's voice changed. "Hey, you're getting into motivation. Wasting your time, buddy. You're never going to catch a psycho by studying
motivation. And if you're thinking copycat, you'd better see my column
of last week."

"Don't need to, Chet. Read it and respected it. But my guy, Fanning,
is playing a very tough hand. Just answer my question, okay?"

"Okay, whatever you want. Yeah, I can tell you who inherited. Her
parents back in Wichita, Kansas. That's where they took the body for
burial, by the way.

"See, one hundred percent of the shares of Penniston Associates were
in trust, with Laura and Betty the sole beneficiaries—Laura two-thirds,
Donovan one-third. The trust agreement provided the trust would stay
in existence till the deaths of both. If just one died, her heirs would

take over as joint beneficiaries at the same percentage. So Laura's parents are now in effect co-owners at sixty-seven percent, along with Betty Donovan, still at thirty-three."

I considered. My first attempt at finding out who benefited was looking like a dead end. What were the odds against her parents having hired someone to knock off their daughter and three bimbos besides? Astronomical. Forget it.

"How sure are you about all this inheritance jazz?" I asked.

"It's gospel, Davey. Or Torah, if you prefer. For one brief shining moment I was a close and dear friend to one Sandra Norville, quondam office manager of Penniston Associates. She's one of those gals who make me wish I was young, single and unscrupulous like you." He sighed.

"Anyway, physical attributes aside, she's the one who gave me all this stuff. Showed me everything they had, including the partnership agreement between Penniston and Donovan. Unfortunately, she got fired last week, so there went my in."

I shook my head. Chet is one of the smoothest operators around when it comes to finagling information, especially from young ladies. Even if he does throw around fancy Greek words like *quondam*. The funny thing is he's bald and pot-bellied. But he can always get people talking.

"Was it her talking to you that got her fired?"

"Afraid so. But that's her lookout. Right now, *my* lookout is getting to work before *I* get fired. Gotta run."

He didn't get away quite that fast. I managed to hold him long enough to get the layout of the place.

"Substantial outfit," he told me, talking fast. "Plush offices, lots of space. I didn't make it past the reception area, but checked with the building super. They've got nearly four thousand feet, a ton for a modeling agency. And *very* posh. Your kind of place, Davey. You'll love it."

—19—

OVERALL APPEARANCE AND GROOMING were crucial. I was heading for a place where I was unknown, unannounced and, most likely, unwanted. The choices were clear: my one button-down broadcloth dress shirt—white, of course; my one all-American red, white and blue club tie; and my one midnight-blue three-piece suit.

To complete the gorgeous ensemble, I dusted off the ultimate prop of the prosperous businessman: an elegant, alligator-skin attaché case I'd bought four years before for the unheard-of price of $298.95 plus $23.92 sales tax. A lot to pay for a prop, but if you're trying to project a first-class image you can't pay second-class prices. I've been told that even at that price, it's an incredible bargain, but you can't convince me of that.

I tried the overall appearance on the hall mirror. A lugubrious-looking undertaker looked back at me. I shrugged. What the hell, undertakers are professionals, right?

So I was feeling very professional as I hit the sidewalk. And the omens were favorable. No sooner had I raised a hand than a taxi screeched to a halt in front of me. The cabbie obviously knew a success when he saw one.

Eleven Thirty-one Madison Avenue turned out to be one of those 1970–ish nouveau arte moderne buildings that were supposed to be the trend for about five years, then turned out to have little staying power.

The lobby was some sort of dark fake marble. I rode up to the forty-second floor alone, enjoying the Muzak. Sounded like "Jailhouse Rock" as performed by the Mantovani strings.

Forty-five-oh-two was easy to find, right across the hall from the

elevator. Inside, at a messy reception desk sat an even messier receptionist, a pretty blond, hair every which way. She was obviously having
a hard time with whoever she was arguing with over the phone. The
plaque in front of her said she was Nancy Richey.

I took the opportunity to study her as she gave me a quick if anxious
smile and a nod. She held up one finger and turned away to concentrate
on the call. Nancy's long eyelashes didn't look to be her own but impressed me anyway. They went well with the limpid blue eyes and full
red lips.

Studying Miss Richey's features made it easy to be patient, which
was fortunate, because she was getting nowhere with whoever it was.
I listened with half a mind, while trying with the other half to identify
a certain acrid odor in the air. It damn sure wasn't perfume. Closer to
tobacco smoke but not that either.

". . . Well, yes sir, I know, but Miss Donovan just isn't taking any
calls right now. She's tied up in a meeting. . . No, I'm sorry, I don't
have any idea when the meeting will be over . . . Well, you can come
over, but I don't know what that will accomplish. I can't promise you
that she'll have any time whatsoever to—Oh! Excuse me a moment,
please. I have another call."

That was when things *really* got out of hand. She had just pushed
the hold button on the phone when, eyes rolling, she looked past me at
yet another visitor coming through the door. She tried to give both the
new guy and me a little smile, making a genteel shoving motion at us
with one hand. She then put her mouth—and, possibly, brain—to the
phone. Judy Holliday playing Wonderwoman.

I turned and nodded at the newcomer, getting an abrupt nod in return.
He had cold blue eyes, a beard that covered the bottom half of his face,
bulky physique and tweedy suit. I'd never seen him or his picture, but
from Chet's description I was fairly sure I'd been joined by George
McClendon, the would-be owner of Penniston Associates, Inc.

I immediately switched mental gears, putting Nancy on the back
burner. How to parlay McClendon's arrival into an invitation inside?

I squared my shoulders and turned enough to make the attaché case
more visible. The beard gave me a sideward glance and seemed to
straighten his own shoulders. Meanwhile, Nancy was talking.

"Oh, Miss Norville! How are y—? What? . . . Well, I'm sorry, but I
did give her your message . . ." The blond now had all four of our ears.

McClendon made no bones about it, getting her eye and giving her a raised eyebrow. I tried to be a little more discreet. Nancy was too flustered to notice either of us, anyway.

"Yes, I told her you wanted your back pay and your vacation pay and—What?... Yes, I told her that. I told her you were threatening to sue... No, she didn't say anything, but I thought she'd get back to you... Yes, I gave it to her yesterday... Well, all right..."

Nancy was making it clear she was being very long-suffering and patient with the party on the other end who was, I guessed, Sandra Norville, the recently fired office manager. Nancy scrabbled for a pencil, found one and dropped it on the floor. She gasped, leaned over for it, got it, then looked for a pad. Finally, ready to write, she put the receiver to her ear again.

"All right, Miss Norville, give it to me again and I'll give it to Miss Donovan again. How long will you be at this number? Till noon? Okay, I'll put that on the note."

Fortunately, Nancy's penmanship was miles ahead of any other skill she had demonstrated so far. I was able to read and memorize, even from five feet away and upside down, the phone number as she wrote it.

Finally rid of the phone for the moment, she sighed, put the phone down, one of its lights still blinking wildly, and turned to the newcomer.

"Hello, Mr. McClendon," she said, a purr in her voice I was hearing for the first time. "You can go right on in. She's waiting for you."

In no hurry, McClendon leaned over her desk and eyed her, she staring back at him with beautiful blue eyes.

"So she's waiting for me," he said in a surprisingly thin, reedy voice. "That's sort of disappointing. I was hoping you and I could kill a little time together, Nancy."

She tossed her head, winked and pointed at the phone receiver in her hand to signify she had other duties that prevented her from participating, much though she'd like to, in whatever he had in mind. It was too bad Nancy's receptionist skills didn't equal her talent for flirting.

Feeling left out of all the fun, I gave matters a push.

"Ah, Mr. McClendon!" I said in the confident tones of a successful businessman. "I'm D.J. Goldman—call me Dave." McClendon turned to me, smiling politely, a puzzled look in his eyes. Nancy gazed up at me blankly. Then her eyes widened and her hand flew to her mouth.

"Oh, Mr. Goldman, I'm *so* sorry! I didn't realize who you were." She turned to McClendon.

"This is the lawyer we've been waiting for, Mr. McClendon. He just got here." I now had a second reason to want to kiss Nancy. No bribe I could have given her would have earned me this good an entree.

I shook McClendon's hand and he allowed me the correct amount of smile and hand pressure. Showing Nancy my most lawyerly face, I said, "Thank you, ma'am," turned back to McClendon, gave him a companionable slap on the shoulder, and said, "Shall we?"

As we went through the door I gave Nancy a wave of the attaché case. She smiled brightly, her eyes fixed on it. Never had $298.95 (plus tax) been better spent.

"How long have you been working on this?" asked my new friend as we made our way down the hall. The prints on the wall were not ones I was familiar with, but they were clearly twentieth-century and very expensive. The whole place—decor, carpeting, paneling—reeked of class.

And of something else. The odor I'd detected in the anteroom was just enough stronger here for a positive I.D. I never worked Vice, but I know pot when I smell it.

Putting that bit of knowledge aside for the moment, I considered McClendon's question. How long had I been working on *what*? The most likely answer, assuming Rozanski's tip was on the money, was the proposed purchase of Penniston Associates by McClendon.

Gave me kind of a warm feeling to be taken for Donovan's attorney. Though the circumstances suggested my tenure would be short-lived— say, about five minutes. Well, gather ye rosebuds while ye may.

I pursed my lips professionally. "How long have I been involved? Well, not as long as you, of course."

Before he could comment he led me into a room dominated by a long, shiny, deep-grained mahogany table surrounded by ten or twelve matching chairs. A steaming coffee urn stood on a credenza to one side, with china cups and saucers, linen napkins and little silver coffee spoons. Class.

"Coffee, Mr. Goldman?" McClendon asked.

"Yes, thank you, black's fine. And please—call me Dave." He filled two cups with coffee, dosing his with plenty of sugar and cream while I considered the implications of all I now knew about McClendon.

For one thing, though a guest here, he was plenty at ease, offering coffee to all and sundry. When someone marches into someone else's place of business, flirts with the receptionist like he's known her all his life, finds his way to the right room and takes right over as host, certain tentative conclusions follow. I decided to test them.

"Of course," I said, still using my lawyer voice, "as prospective owner, you would naturally know a great deal more about the transaction than I, George. Actually, I only came into it very recently."

He eyed me as he relaxed into one of the chairs and blew on his coffee. I followed suit, taking the next chair, placing my invaluable attaché case (the total contents of which consisted of today's New York *Times*) carefully on the table in front of me. McClendon shot me a startled glance, and I knew why. He was surprised that, in a room filled with chairs, I'd chosen to sit practically in his lap.

Of course, grabbing the next chair had been a calculated move. If my happy life as a lawyer was to outlive the next event—Betty Donovan's arrival—I had to set the scene. I needed to give her the strongest possible impression that McClendon and I were colleagues. At the same time, of course, I needed to keep McClendon thinking I represented Donovan. This wasn't going to be easy.

The previous summer, vacationing in the Adirondacks, I'd tried to get across a stream by jumping from stone to stone. If you've ever tried it, you know the trick is making the right decision every time you lift your foot; and you can't stop in mid-air to reconsider. That time in the Adirondacks, I made five right decisions in a row, before making the wrong one. No biggie. Just wet clothes and a couple of strawberries on the behind.

What I was now embarking on gave me the same kind of feeling.

I justified the presumptiousness of sitting so close to McClendon by scraping the chair away from him a little, and tilting on the back legs, coffee cup in hand. (See? Just trying to be friendly.) His expression cleared and he answered pleasantly.

"Well, I'm glad to meet you. Though, frankly, I was a little surprised that Betty was bringing in a lawyer at all. At this stage of the negotiations, I mean." His smile widened through the brush. "Nothing against you, Dave, or your profession, but I don't like lawyers involved till all the business decisions are made."

I took a deep breath. While he was talking I'd come up with an idea. I gave him a knowing wink.

"Well, I'm also into some things that Betty may not have told you of." I smiled and raised my eyebrows at him.

"I don't understand. You mean—?"

I leaned forward, beckoning him to do likewise. "It's not a regular business, you understand," I told him in conspiratorial tones, "but I can help friends in need get their hands on certain... party favors?"

His eyes widened in understanding. I shrugged and he grinned, sitting back in the chair, slowly shaking his head. "Well, isn't *she* something! I should have known she'd use someone no one would suspect."

He cocked his head. "You have enough to spread it around?"

I nodded soberly. "Just give me a couple days' notice."

So. Another hunch hits the mark. I had begun trying to figure a way to use the information when a large woman in a wine-colored business suit swept grandly into the room.

The photos hadn't done Betty Donovan justice. They'd portrayed her as plain, but *plain* didn't do it. Nearly the height of McClendon and me, she probably outweighed me by fifty pounds and McClendon by twenty. High, sloping forehead topped by the wispy, frizzy, salt-and-pepper hair of a woman who's never seen the sense of trying to turn a sow's ear into anything else.

Her double-breasted suit was stylish—at least it would have been stylish worn by nearly anyone else. Her dishwater gray eyes narrowed as they focused on me, accentuating the laugh lines on either side.

With an effort I tried to meet those dishwater eyes as I got up to shake her hand.

Given Betty Donovan's physique, I expected her grip to be overly firm. But she gave me only her dry fingertips to grab, and those for only a second. She seemed edgy and irritable.

"Miss Donovan!" I said, taking the initiative. "How nice to see you! I believe you know George McClendon?"

It was a tense moment. I was in the middle of the stream, stepping onto the slipperiest boulder so far. The idea was to present an image ambiguous enough for Donovan to take me as McClendon's overly aggressive attorney, and McClendon to go on assuming I was Donovan's lawyer fresh from consorting with the other side. Unsmiling, Betty Donovan took me in, turned and looked at McClendon.

"Well, of *course* I know Mr. McClendon, for God's sake. *You're* the one who's coming in new. What *I* want to know is—"

Knowing her next words were going to be something on the order of
"Who the hell are you?" I headed her off. Which took a bit of volume,
she not being a woman to suffer butt-ins gladly. I tried to smooth it
over with a smile and a shrug.

"I know, I know. Excuse me, ma'am, sorry to interrupt, but you need
to know something. In fact, both of you do."

I glanced quickly from one to the other. Both showed some curiosity
about what I was going to say. Which made three of us. I took a deep
breath.

"Since Dave Goldman is the new guy, as you put it, Betty"—I smiled
self-deprecatingly to apologize for the familiarity— "and new on the
details . . . Well, uh, just see what you think of this, Miss Donovan . . .
Uh, since I'm so new to it and you . . ." I glanced quickly at both of
them to increase the ambiguity about who I was addressing. ". . . And
you are not at all sure an attorney is needed at this stage of the negotiations—why don't you just bring me up to speed on where the negotiations stand? You talk, and I'll just listen."

I beamed at the two of them. "And I'll undertake that for purposes
of this meeting, Dave Goldman is no attorney." I tried a hearty laugh.
No response. "Umm, well, after that, you" (another quick glance from
side to side) "can decide whether you even need Dave Goldman sitting
in. And, at that stage, you can decide whether *your* attorney should be
involved, or whether I should just drop out of the picture."

I silently exhaled and gave them both my patented wide-eyed stare,
wondering if either one noticed the sheen of perspiration on my face.

Donovan raised an eyebrow at McClendon, who just looked puzzled.
My whole plan was dangling by a thread. The odds were at least three-
to-one that whichever spoke would spill the beans that I wasn't his/her
attorney. Then the game would be up, and I'd be bounced right out the
door. That's if I was lucky, and it wasn't the window with a forty-two-
story drop. But my luck continued to run.

"All right, George?" asked Betty.

"Sure," answered George in a puzzled tone.

"Well, let's sit down," she said, and promptly obeyed her own instructions.

I smiled at them both as I sat back down and put the attaché case
on the floor, proof positive that I was only there to listen.

* * *

"The first thing you need to understand, Mr. Goldman," Betty Donovan began briskly, fidgeting with the buttons on her tailored jacket, "is that I've been trying to look out for the interests of Laura's parents in these negotiations. I've become good friends with Roger and Maureen over the years. Of course, you know they inherited Laura's interest in the company."

I tried to nod without moving my head, which you ought to try sometime. I had to show Betty I was attentive without giving George the notion that I was hearing all this for the first time.

"It was the day after we buried Laura," Betty continued, "that I decided to sell out. I was in Wichita for the funeral anyway, and I was able to discuss it with Roger and Maureen, though it was a hard time for us all."

I glanced at George. He looked smug. He should have been. He was sitting here (he thought) listening to the other side explain everything to her own lawyer. He had to be gloating over how well he was going to make out.

I turned back to Betty. "I'm sure it must have been hard on all of you." I gave her a sad smile.

Ignoring me, she crossed her legs, tugged her skirt down and went on crisply.

"They're flying in this afternoon, Roger and Maureen. I was hoping we could come to an understanding on the terms of sale this morning, so that we'd have something to discuss with them this afternoon and tomorrow. Of course, as Laura's heirs, they have the right to turn down any deal we strike." She gave me a cold smile. "But they've told me they'll go along with whatever I recommend. Within reason, of course."

Betty was making preparations to smoke while she talked. She'd pulled the heavy crystal ashtray toward her, got a pack of cigarettes and a silver lighter from her purse, removed a cigarette and flipped the package onto the table next to the ashtray. She now lighted up and inhaled deeply.

"Now if we're to get together on terms," she continued in a more relaxed tone, smoke drifting from her nostrils, "we're going to have to look at the overall value of the company, not just at last year's earnings. What George is buying is not earnings, it's earning *potential*. Frankly, Mr. Goldman, your client has been acting as though—"

"Excuse me, Miss Donovan," I cut in quickly, as smoothly as I could but loud enough to shut her up. Both my clients frowned at my interrupting, each no doubt thinking the other had hired a real horse's petunia for his/her attorney.

I opened my mouth, hoping whatever came out would have the right effect. On both. I smiled brightly at Betty as I launched into . . . whatever I was about to launch into.

"I'm sure you both have your own opinions about how much the company is worth. But I really don't see *that* as the main problem. For me, the main problem is bringing me up to speed." I swung around to McClendon. "My client has given me some of the background, but I'd like to hear it from your perspective. Can you just fill me in, as you see it? Especially what's changed since the unfortunate and tragic death of Miss Penniston."

"I'd say that it—" said McClendon, simultaneously with Donovan's "You mean you—?"

They glared at each other and at me. I'd done my job perfectly. Betty was eyeing me through a cloud of smoke with an exasperated look that told me she'd had about enough. I used a coughing fit—not totally faked: her smoke was starting to get to me—to buy a little time, and smiled apologetically.

"I'll tell you what, Miss Donovan. Why don't you go ahead, and I'll try very hard *not* to interrupt. But I'd like to hear it from your side, if you would. From the very beginning of the negotiations."

Betty's lips tightened and, for just a moment I thought I was about to get the heave-ho. Then she seemed to decide she'd give me one more chance. I'd just damn well better listen and not interrupt any more.

She reached for another cigarette and lit it from the first, which she stubbed out. Inhaling deeply, she readjusted herself in the chair and rolled her dishwater eyes in resignation.

"All right, Mr., uh, Goldman. I'll indulge you. For now." She glared at McClendon. Whether he reacted to that, or even saw it, I don't know. I was keeping my eyes on her respectfully, the way an attorney of my stature should. She flicked ashes nervously and went on.

"I'm sure George must have told you. Laura—Miss Penniston—and I first contacted him in the early part of this year. It must have been—when was it, George?"

McClendon stroked his beard, eyes closed tight. He opened them. "Umm, the third of March, I believe. Um, yes, that was a Monday. Laura called me. Said Lee Stubbs wanted us to meet."

"Okay." Betty sent a plume of white smoke ceilingward. "That sounds right. In any case, Mr. Goldman, we got hot and heavy into negotiations shortly after that. As you know better than I, George wanted to be a partner in Penniston Associates. We'd finally come to agreement on all the major issues but one: price."

I smiled at her and, surprisingly, she smiled back. It was the first time she'd smiled and it helped a lot. Not that it brought her within a thousand miles of beautiful, but the deepening of the crinkles around her eyes established some facial definition. Plus, her eyes almost disappeared, which had to be an improvement.

"And what did you and Miss Penniston consider the substantive issues to be, Miss Donovan?"

She squinted at me through the smoke. "Oh. Just all the things that went with giving George thirty-three percent of our business. Really, the only thing we still had to thrash out was the right price. And we'd even come to an agreement in principle on a formula, when that horrible thing happened to Laura—"

As she tried to get out the name of her late partner, Betty's voice caught. She quickly turned away, and flicked ashes into the ashtray. I caught sight of a tear glistening on her plump cheek. If the smile had helped, the tear helped even more.

McClendon's reedy voice came from behind me. "Uh, I don't know if I agree, Betty," he said. "All we'd agreed on was to get three evaluators. Who'd *do* the evaluating was still way up in the air."

"Well, all right, George, I'll concede that," she answered, dry-eyed again. "But we were making progress. You'd picked Art Baker, and Laura and I'd agreed to him. We already had an audit from Bob Theodore, but you didn't like him. So—"

"It's not a question of like or not like," McClendon snapped. "Bob's an okay accountant, at least I thought so at the time, but face it, you tried to pull a fast one. You don't hire someone practically *engaged* to one of the parties in a deal to do the valuing. *Laura* may have been that naive, but my God, Betty, *you* had to know better than that."

Betty's face was pink as she stubbed out her cigarette. "There was no attempt to cover up, George," she said calmly.

"Anyway, the death of Miss Penniston intervened," I said, looking at McClendon. He immediately dropped his eyes. Rubbing his mouth nervously, he answered in a muffled voice.

"What a tragedy! We were all simply bowled over. God! She was so alive, so . . ." He looked at Donovan. "Well, I can tell you, Betty here was just devastated."

I turned back to her. She was looking at the two stubs in the ashtray, eyes distant, hands shaking a little as they tried to find something to do. I could barely hear her.

"Yes, I was. Laura and I had been business associates for three years. And friends eight. She was the finest—" She turned away. To my dismay, she absently reached for the pack and took out another cigarette.

"It was the night," McClendon ruminated, "of the masquerade ball at the agency." He chuckled sadly. "Well, that's what Laura insisted on calling it. It was actually a small Halloween open house. For maybe fifty people. They had it every year. People were encouraged to wear costumes and lots did, so they called it their masquerade ball."

"A masquerade ball?" This sounded interesting; it was about the first thing they'd said that seemed to have anything to do with why I was *really* there.

My question was aimed at McClendon, but Betty answered. "We had it every year. Invited all the girls to attend, with their boyfriends—or husbands, those few that had them. And the whole office staff. This year Laura brought Bob—that's Bob Theodore—and I came alone as usual. I don't date much."

"I can imagine," almost slipped out, but for once I kept my big mouth shut.

"I guess I was the only outsider there," McClendon put in. "I was going to bring a friend, but she had a headache." He chuckled through the beard. "Women's favorite excuse—the ever-popular headache. Fact is, she didn't want to compete with Laura; no woman did. No woman could. I'll tell you, there's a lot of women in this town who didn't shed too many tears when Laura got it."

I looked at him, surprised. He just stared back blandly, his expression unreadable through the beard. I didn't expect Betty'd let him get away with it, and she didn't. "George, you're a miserable son of a bitch, do you know that?" She viciously ground out her just-lit cigarette.

McClendon shrugged casually. "Well, if that's what telling the truth means, okay, I'm a miserable son of a bitch." He sighed and went on.

"Laura was elegant as always. No Halloween costume. Just an absolutely ravishing cocktail dress. And jewelry to match. She wore her red cross earrings, and they were something to behold. You'd never have thought they were paste."

"You were obsessed with those earrings, George," Betty sniffed. "They were just gaudy, not beautiful. I told her that many a time. But she wore them every chance she got. Said it was because they were a gift from her parents."

McClendon smiled. "Even you, Betty? God, even *you* were jealous of Laura, weren't you?" Betty sputtered something, but George had already turned to me.

"Trust me, Mr. Goldman. Laura did plenty for those earrings and they did plenty for her. They were perfect for her. And they *weren't* gaudy. Elegant, tiny diamonds and rubies. And if she hadn't sworn to me they were fake, I'd have bet they were worth a king's ransom.

"I've seen a lot of speculation in the papers about the fact that Laura was the only victim whose earlobes weren't torn by the killer. Well, I'm convinced he must have recognized their value and didn't want to risk damaging them. She *was* wearing them that night; no doubt about it. That's probably the main thing the police questioned me about. I told them the murderer's got them. The paper hasn't said, but I'll bet that's how they nailed Fanning."

Betty glared at him. "No way, George. If they've got earrings that need identifying, I'm the one they'd be talking to, and the cops haven't said boo. This Fanning guy is a psycho. I don't think he cares anything about jewelry."

"Then how do you explain why none of the victims were found with any jewelry on them?" George objected. "And why did he rip the earrings off those other three?"

"The police have explained that, George," Betty said in an exaggeratedly patient tone. "It was his way of further humiliating and punishing them for their sins."

"Anyway, that party was the last time either of you ever saw her alive," I said, bringing them back to the subject.

Betty nodded yes, then shook her head. "Things weren't right that evening. I told her that when she came back from that phone call, but she wouldn't listen."

McClendon nodded and jumped in. "It happened all of a sudden. Laura'd been having a great time, up till about ten o'clock. Then someone told her she had a phone call. She, Betty and I were standing there talking. She was away about five minutes. When she came back, her mood had changed." McClendon stopped, lost in thought. "She was in a different frame of mind," he said at last. "Still in a good mood, but more serious somehow. And kind of excited. Said she had to go.

"We asked her what was up, and she said something like, 'Good news. For all of us. I'll tell you all about it in the morning. But I've got to go now.' We tried to get her to tell us, but she wouldn't."

Betty took over. "I've talked to George about it, Mr. Goldman, and we just can't figure out who that call was from. I had a sinking feeling about it at the time in a way I just can't explain. I even told her to be careful." Betty was weeping openly now.

I tried to sound sympathetic. "Did you tell the police about how you'd felt?"

Betty dabbed at her eyes with a Kleenex. "Oh sure," she said shakily. "Tell him what they told you, George."

I turned to McClendon. I was sorry I'd promised I wouldn't take notes. My head was starting to ache, trying to remember all this.

"They said not to worry about it," McClendon muttered. "They told me lots of people get feelings like that. They say most of it's hindsight. That the person remembers feelings they didn't really have . . ." His voice trailed off.

"That's not true," Betty said, her voice back to normal. "I *did* have those feelings that night, George. I even told you about them then."

McClendon nodded but without much conviction.

"So she took right off?" I resumed, looking at George. "After that phone call?"

He shook his head. "No, she wanted to tell Sandy something." He glanced at Donovan meaningfully. "That's the girl who *used* to manage this beehive. And did a damn good job of it, if you ask me. But no one asked me. Just fired her." He was glaring at Betty. She avoided his eyes.

"Anyway," George went on, having made his point, "Laura was in Sandy's office for several minutes before she left. I walked to the elevator with her. The police tell me . . ." He smiled complacently and smoothed his beard. ". . . I was the last one to ever see her alive." Dramatic pause. "Except for the murderer, of course."

"That's what the cops said." Betty's voice was choked. She'd gotten weepy again. "It's just not right that she left without my even getting to tell her goodbye. I don't know how she got by me. I saw her go into Sandy's office. I thought she'd be right back out, but when five minutes went by and she didn't come out, I ran into my office to get something. And when I came back, you told me she'd gone. I had such a feeling! I almost went after her, didn't I, George?"

McClendon's voice was gentle. "You're right, Betty. You *did* have a feeling."

Betty's spunk seemed to be coming back. Her voice was bitter. "I just hope they fry that son of a bitch, Fanning. If only Laura'd been more careful. It's just so—"

"Forget it," McClendon said soothingly. "Laura was a brave gal. She had no more fear of Strangler John than she had of anything else. And you know as well as I, no one was going to change her."

"She was pretty reckless?" I asked. "I mean, Laura?"

Donovan narrowed her eyes at me as if seeing me for the first time. "George!" she said sharply.

McClendon jumped, startled at her change of tone and looked at her.

"Where'd you get this guy, George?"

The executive frowned and looked around him. "Get who?"

"*This* guy. Goldman."

"What do you mean, *get* him, Betty? He's *your* lawyer."

"The hell he is!" She was on her feet, her face red. "You idiot, my lawyer's Gold*stein*, and he's meeting us for lunch! I walk in here and see the two of you. What am I supposed to think?"

She advanced on me, gesturing at me with the pack of cigarettes she'd picked up. "Just who the hell are you, mister? And how'd you get in here?"

McClendon wasn't too swift on the uptake. "But . . . I don't see . . . What's he doing—?"

"Don't you get it, George? Guy's a—a reporter, probably, a snoop. Comes waltzing in here like he belongs, and what do *we* do? We just *let* him! Who the hell *are* you?"

I glanced over my shoulder at McClendon, whose own eyes were widening in dawning comprehension. His hands tightened into fists.

I turned back to Betty. "Oh," I said wide-eyed, "so *that's* why you let me sit in! I was wondering why you were being so hospitable. No, I'm no reporter, just a guy who wants to talk about Miss Norville's back pay. But if you want to tell me about your private business, I don't guess you can blame me if I'm too courteous to interrupt."

"Norville's back pay?" Donovan's eyes narrowed. "What about it?"

"She wants it," I said smoothly. "And she'd like it now."

"Just a damn minute, Betty!" McClendon had finally decided to get into the act. "Don't say another word."

I grinned at him. "That's pretty good advice, George. Too bad you didn't take it yourself." I turned back to Donovan.

"You see, Betty, George and I were having a little talk before you came in . . . about drugs."

The woman's eyes narrowed and fixed on McClendon. "What's he talking about, George?" she demanded.

McClendon was furious. "This son of a bitch told me he was your supplier! I told him we—"

Betty slammed her pack onto the table and cigarettes went every which way. "What did you tell him, George? You stupid son of a—!"

"Now, Betty . . ." George interrupted, hands in the air. I took him off the hook.

"Excuse me, Miss Donovan. I see no need to get into accusations and counteraccusations." I seemed to have developed lawyer's mouth. "I'm not really concerned with how you spend your leisure time. All we have here is a simple little problem: the money that Miss Norville is owed. You know this perfectly well."

I hoped that was the truth. For all I knew, Sandra Norville had stolen the company blind and maybe killed Laura Penniston to boot.

"All we're asking for is Miss Norville's back pay. Are you prepared to—? *Please*, Miss Donovan! Don't, I beg you, don't light that cigarette. I'll be out of your life in a matter of seconds. Please have the decency to wait till I'm gone before you get back to killing yourself."

She looked at her hand, frozen in its grab for the pack of Pall Malls. She pulled it back.

"And if I do?" she asked sullenly. "Then what?"

I shrugged. "Then nothing. I have no desire to make trouble. So. How about the money?"

"Just who the hell *are* you?" she demanded in a final show of bravado. "And where did Sandy dig you up?"

"I already told you my name, Miss Donovan. David Goldman. And for your information, Sandy didn't dig me up. I found her. Now, what about her money?"

"All right," Betty said through her teeth.

I looked at my Timex, thinking fast. Now that I had Donovan playing ball, I wanted to orchestrate the next move for maximum benefit.

"Tell you what," I said. "It's now precisely ten forty-seven. At exactly eleven-fifteen I'd like you to phone Miss Norville at home. I happen to know she's there waiting for your call. You don't need to mention my name, but I think it would be nice if you apologized to her for the delay. And even nicer if you could tell her that the check is on its way—by messenger, perhaps?"

Betty's face was a study in controlled rage. "Anything else I can do for you?"

Sensing that particular offer was insincere, I didn't answer. Betty looked at her own watch and winced.

"The Pennistons will be landing at LaGuardia at two-thirty, and I'm supposed to pick them up." She looked at me bitterly. "Boy, I really needed this."

I grinned. "Sorry to be so much trouble. Oh, and don't bother to see me to the door. I know the way."

But Betty wasn't about to take that chance, not with a treacherous type like me on the premises. She walked ahead of me in stony silence down the dark hall and through the door into the brightly lit reception area.

Nancy was as pretty and disorganized as ever. On the phone again, she tried to split her attention between it and us. It didn't work any better than before. Donovan caught the drift of the conversation and stopped.

"But Mr. Goldstein, you were here just an hour ago, and I sent you back to see her! Haven't you seen her yet? . . . You haven't? What? You haven't even *been* here? But—" She looked up at us in dismay as she continued talking into the phone. "But, I don't understand, I *saw* you not more than—"

She took a second glance at me and her eyes widened. She said into the receiver, "Excuse me just a minute, Mr. Goldstein." She pushed the hold button on her console and looked at me accusingly. "You told me *you* were Mr. Goldstein. Who *are* you?" She turned to her boss. "Who *is* he, Miss Donovan?"

Donovan had had her fill of dumb questions. "Hang up that phone, you idiot!" she hissed.

The girl mumbled something into the receiver and hung up. Betty Donovan marched me through the outer doors into the darkness of the nonmodeling world and headed back inside. I had a feeling Nancy was about to feel the sharp edge of Betty Donovan's tongue.

"Don't forget," I called to Donovan's back, "to call Miss Norville at eleven-fifteen."

She made an obscene gesture at me behind her back without breaking stride.

—20—

OUT ON THE STREET I looked around. My next step was to find someplace to sip some coffee, get what I'd learned into my notebook before I forgot it, and strategize. And hopefully clear my sinuses of all the nicotine they'd just been subjected to.

Halfway down the next block I popped into one of those long, narrow closets we call diners in New York. You know, a foot wide and a mile long, with a counter in front that barely leaves room to get by, and a long line of narrow tables in the rear. *The California Diner*. Good name. The steam, humidity and grease smoke gave it enough of a smog to put any Californian right at home.

It was the dead time between coffee break and lunch. No one there but the beefy counterman who gave me a glum look, straightened up respectfully and drew me a mug of coffee without being asked. Amazing the effect an expensive suit of clothes has on people. I sipped coffee for a minute as I considered what I'd just learned in the Penniston Associates conference room.

It had been a good morning. I'd found out that both Donovan and McClendon were users of illegal substances and nervous about it. I wondered if Penniston had been. Then I wondered if the killer had been. And if there was any connection between the substance abuse and the killings.

I'd also learned about a phone call Laura Penniston had gotten just hours before she died. And that no one knew where she'd spent the next few hours. I made a mental note to recheck the time of death; the papers had it at around one A.M. Could that be wrong? That phone call, I felt sure, had been the lead-in to the murder. The more I thought about it the more I realized how urgently I needed to get my morning's activities in shape to report to Regan.

But even more urgently, I needed to get on the horn to one Sandra Norville. Assuming Betty Donovan didn't blow it—and I didn't think she would—Miss Norville was going to get a phone call at 11:15, now ten minutes away, giving her the good news about her back pay. To benefit from this event, I needed to talk to Sandra before it happened. It took me half a cup of coffee and about four minutes to think of an approach.

I went to the pay phone next to the front door (trusting that no one would need to get in or out of the diner while I was using it), inserted a quarter and punched out the number I'd memorized. In two rings I had a hello as warm, musical and feminine as any I've ever heard. My kind of office manager.

"Miss Norville?"

"Yes, what is it?" she snapped. The warmth had only lasted two syllables. She'd obviously been expecting someone else.

"My name is David Goldman, I'm an investigator, and I've got a proposition for you I think you'll like." I paused for a response. Got none. But at least she stayed on the line.

"It's a sporting proposition, Miss Norville. I'll bet you that within . . ." I looked at my Timex ". . . five minutes, you'll get a call from Betty Donovan telling you your paycheck is on its way to you by messenger. That's my bet."

Silence. Finally, "Who the hell are you? How do you know anything about me?"

"Let's just say I'm a person who doesn't like to see people cheated out of what they've earned."

She said a bad word. "Tell me who you are, or I'm—"

"Hey," I cut her off, "I don't mind telling you who I am or how I got involved. In fact, I think you'll get a kick out of it. But do you want the bet?"

I suppose the desirability of getting her dough had some effect. She was beginning to sound a little less hostile. Even a little interested.

"What are the stakes?"

"Oh, you're going to like them—Uh, excuse me a minute." Two

pretty young things were trying to wiggle past me into the diner. I took the receiver from my ear and flattened myself against the wall. Nice perfume. Even nicer friction. I resumed the phone conversation, brushing plaster dust off my expensive suitcoat.

"Sorry to keep you waiting, Miss Norville. They're doing some work around my office. You were asking about the bet. Okay, the deal is if Betty calls and says what I said she'd say, I win. In which case you'll have lunch with me today at a restaurant of your choice."

"Who pays? Me, I suppose."

"Oh no. I pay. Either way, I pay."

"And if you lose?"

"I owe you a lunch at place *and* time of your choosing. It wouldn't have to be today—of course, it could be, but that'd be your choice."

Silence. Then a click. For a scary moment I thought I'd been hung up on. Then realized it was her call-waiting.

"Just a minute," she said. "May I put you on hold?" I opened my mouth to say it was okay, but she was gone. It was 11:12. Could Donovan be calling early? In just about a minute Norville was back.

"You still there? What did you say your name was?" Her tone had changed. She sounded slightly awed.

"David Goldman," I answered. "And I'll bet that was Betty Donovan."

"It was," she breathed. "She's sending the money over to me by messenger. What did you do, seduce her? I haven't even been able to get *through* to her!"

"See?" I pressed my advantage. "Maybe now you'll be a little more trusting. You've lost your bet, so where do you want to have lunch?"

"I *am* very grateful." Her tone was seductive.

"Good. That's the way I want you. Now. Where shall we meet?"

A pause. When her voice came again, it had acquired another level of sexiness. "You *do* sound interesting. Are you as hard to resist in person as you are on the phone?"

"Hard? Try impossible! Look. You decide where and when, and I'll be there."

An even longer pause, but it was worth the wait. "Well, I suppose I could do lunch. Marty's on Twelfth Street? One o'clock?"

"Right. Now where is . . . ?" But she was gone. Along with a very sexy voice, this girl had a bad habit of asking a question and not waiting for the answer.

I scratched my head as I hung up. Would Norville be there? More important, where the hell was Marty's? Did it even exist? I pulled out the Yellow Pages and found Marty's Continentale, 129 W. 12th St.

Heading back for my coffee mug, I checked the time: eleven-nineteen. From Forty-eighth and Madison to Sixth Avenue at Twelfth this time of day should be about a fifteen-minute cab ride. So I had plenty of time. I decided the California Diner would be an adequate spot for some note-taking. Provided they didn't kick me out when the lunch crowd started coming in.

To head that off, I slipped the counterman a sawbuck, rent for the stool I was using, in lieu of ordering. He agreed to the arrangement, though he wasn't exactly jumping for joy over it.

I didn't get full value for the tenner. Using my unique brand of shorthand, I managed to get the morning's activities in the notebook by noon, by which time hungry people were on either side of me, rustling newspapers, asking me to pass salt and pepper, raising the noise level, and generally making my life miserable. I walked out at 12:04. The counterman ducked my eye as I left, probably to forestall discussion of a partial refund of the security deposit.

Outside, the weather had turned fine, warmer and sunnier than November has any right to be. Having an hour to kill, I decided to hoof it down to the Village.

A good idea, as it turned out. The sky was blue with scattered white clouds, the temperature crisp and autumnal. The lunchtime crowds were festive and most stores carried Thanksgiving decorations. Tur-keys—feathered live ones and stuffed dead ones—were getting plenty of play. I was even approached by a pilgrim in black suit and buckled shoes. Wanted to sell me a pocket calculator or some damn thing.

I managed to resist that and all other appeals for money, and reached Marty's just in time for my appointment with Sandra Norville—two minutes to one.

—21—

MARTY'S CONTINENTALE MAINTAINED a low profile. The small brass plate beside the front door of the unobtrusive brownstone—*Marty's Continentale: Second Floor*—was the only clue to its existence. Didn't faze me: the brass plate outside the Bishop's house is even smaller.

I proceeded through the unlocked front door into the foyer, climbed a curving flight of stairs and entered a dark, richly paneled room reminiscent of the Bishop's chapel except for a lower ceiling and no stained glass windows.

The noise level was sedate and the twenty or twenty-five tables were about half-filled. I soon spotted a brunette sitting alone at a banquette for two and implored the gods that she be Sandra Norville.

Snapping dark eyes. Eyelashes longer than Nancy's. Shiny black hair that danced with highlights every time her head moved. Elegant cheekbones and full, red lips.

She sighted me about half a second after I spotted her, and smiled. The smile finished me off. I didn't care who she was, this was the girl I was spending the rest of my life with. Or at least lunch.

I'll admit it up front. I'm the world's worst interviewer of beautiful young women. My mind won't concentrate on what it's supposed to and I end up asking the wrong questions. And when I happen to ask the right ones I forget to listen to the answers.

My chances of getting any useful information out of Sandra Norville seemed to have gone up in smoke the instant I saw her.

I took the opportunity to check her out as I waved off the hostess and headed for the booth. Her tailored dark suit made an accurate appraisal of her figure a matter for later study, but what I could see of it told me that the surveillance wouldn't be tedious. I smiled as I reached the table.

"I guess Betty must have sent the dough."

She grinned impishly, beautiful eyes atwinkle. "Oh yes, indeed. Are you a miracle worker?"

I slid next to her in the banquette, feeling her warmth as our hips collided slightly, and got just a hint of perfume. I couldn't tell if it was My Sin, but I hoped so. Settled, I found myself dazzled by her closeness.

"Congratulations. You've proved you're a detective," she said demurely. "No one but a detective could have found this place without directions."

I waved grandly. "What's to find? Any experienced CIA agent would have this place bracketed within a week, easy. Piece of cake. I'm just surprised they don't have an unlisted phone number and a sliding panel in the front door."

She leaned closer. "You've got to tell me how you got Betty Donovan to send that check," she whispered. "And then you can tell me what reward you'd like."

I glanced up at the young waiter hovering, trying to pretend he wasn't paying attention.

"Not just now," I grinned. "X-rated. Not meant for the ears of children." Whether this lunch produced any information or not, it was sure starting out promising. We looked at each other after the waiter took off with our drink orders—Pouilly Fuissé for her, beer for me.

"Before we get into the matter of rewards, Miss Norville, maybe I'd better warn you—I'm after a murderer. And I'll resort to anything to get him."

"Umm," she murmured. "Then you'd better call me Sandy. How vicious are you, Dave? Would you resort to torture?"

I sneered. "You kidding? Women I hold down and tickle till they tell me everything I want to know. Not a pretty sight, Sandy. Not a pretty sight at all."

We were both smiling when the drinks arrived. Having had too many beers ruined by waiters who lack the foggiest notion of how to dribble it down the side of the glass to stop the head from forming, I insisted on pouring my own. To his credit, the lad didn't pout. I told him to check back with us in five minutes. Sandy and I saluted each other and sipped. She eyed me speculatively.

"So. Who *are* you? You've proved you can find a carefully concealed restaurant and extort blood money out of Betty Donovan. And you claim you're a sadist. Who the hell *are* you?"

I grinned at her. "It gets worse. I'm so unscrupulous, I'll tell beautiful women I'm after their gorgeous bodies when all I really want is information."

Sipping her wine, she gave me a sidelong glance that upped my pulse rate.

"Hmm. Pretty unscrupulous, if you ask me. Unprofessional, in fact. But go ahead if you must. Though I have to warn you, I'm ticklish in only one spot, and it might take you forever to find it."

I shrugged. "Temptation won't work, Sandy. It's been tried by experts."

I got serious. The fun and games—I hoped—would come later. We got rid of the still-hovering waiter by ordering lunch. Then I gave her my background in a sentence or two and explained about Dave Baker.

"He's the attorney for this Jerry Fanning, the supposed strangler." Sandy nodded, now as sober as I. "I've gotten into it enough to be convinced that Fanning's innocent. But for a certain reason, I can't take it to the cops. So I'm investigating to see if I can't find something—anything—to get the guy out of jail."

Sandy looked at me speculatively. "I'll tell you all I can, Dave. But before we get into that, you've *got* to tell me how you got in to see Betty. And how you got her to cough up what she owed me. She's not an easy mark; I've learned that the hard way."

I told her how I'd inveigled my way in.

"So Nancy got you in there," Sandy giggled, shaking her head. "If Nancy had the intelligence God gave a low-grade chimpanzee, she'd be the finest model in this town, I'll swear. She's gorgeous and slinky, with a perfect model's body. I'd kill for that body! But when it comes to brains, well, I've got blouses that are smarter than her."

I chuckled with her and surreptitiously admired the contents of one of those high-I.Q. blouses while the waiter put plates before us—chef's salad for her, Reuben for me. I quit scoping the scenery and reached for the Grey Poupon.

"Anyway," I said, slathering the mustard on liberally, "now you know why I went there. And why I want to talk to you. My theory is, the killer knew Laura Penniston. More importantly, *she* knew *him*. Which means I've got to talk to anyone that knew her. I suppose you've been all over this with the police?"

Sandy's lips curved slightly as she toyed with her salad.

"Well, I've been over it with them. I wouldn't call it all over. Some officer named, uh, Blake, I think it is . . ."

I nodded. "He's in charge of the investigation."

"He questioned me for, oh, maybe six or eight minutes, you know?" Sandy took a small bite of salad, then seemed to take forever to chew and swallow. She studied her fork, twirling a small leaf of lettuce in the salad bowl. Finally she resumed.

"He asked about Laura, the party, where she might have gone when she left the party, and especially where she might have been from the time she left the party till the time she was killed."

"Yeah? And what did you tell him?"

Sandy shrugged and took a sip of wine. She finally met my eyes. "The same as everyone else, you know? That I have no idea."

I nodded.

"But he really didn't ask me very much. He didn't seem very interested in anything I knew."

I pushed back my empty plate and looked down at the linen tablecloth with its intricate floral pattern. Without looking up, I asked, "Who do you think might have wanted her dead?"

Her answer was almost inaudible. "You don't mess around, do you, Dave?" I looked up and our eyes locked. "So you don't think it was a psycho that got her?"

I didn't answer. She shook her head and looked away.

"I honestly don't know anyone who'd have wanted her dead. But if someone I know did kill her, they're no friend of mine. I'll do anything I can to help you."

"Okay. First of all, when did *you* start with Penniston?"

She sipped wine. "I arrived in New York six years ago. Laura'd come from Wichita two years before that, so she knew what I was going through, me fresh out of Omaha. I wanted to become a superstar model like her. But that was not to be." She put down her glass, picked up her fork and resumed with her salad.

"Frankly, I'm surprised," I said. "Call me a flatterer, but I've seen lots of photos of Laura. Nothing against her, Sandy, but you're a better looker. I know you hate to hear that, but it's true."

"Flattery like that may get you somewhere," she murmured with a brief Mae West shrug. She took a bite of salad. "No, seriously, Dave, it's not a question of beauty. Or only partly. Laura had this quality of— the camera loved her face. She just came through a lot better than me, you know?

"Plus, our figures. I'm short and dumpy, you know?" I rolled my eyes. "Well, all right, Dave, short and plump. It doesn't matter. I suppose men like to look at my body, but trust me, fashion designers *hate* a body like mine.

"Laura's was perfect: five-ten, a hundred and ten, no hips, no bust, tiny waist. And a very nice girl to boot. I really miss her." Her voice trailed off. I picked up the slack.

"So you and Laura were already buddies. Then she brought you into Penniston Associates?"

"Right. It seemed like a big favor at the time. I'd been getting less and less work. I'd lost a couple of good lingerie contracts." Sandy grimaced. "I was getting old, Dave. As long as my face still looked like a teenager's, they'd put up with my shortness for the sake of my youth— and my bust, I suppose. But when a wrinkle or two started to show— well, even the undie folks like them younger and taller.

"I was really scratching. Talk about desperation! I was even thinking of going back to Omaha. Then I get this call from Laura asking would I like to go to work for her and Betty. They were just starting up this new modeling agency. Said they needed an office manager. They'd go twenty-five hundred a month, which was as much as I'd netted on average my best year modeling. God, I could have kissed both of them!"

Sandy looked down and her voice hardened. "What she didn't tell me was what they really needed was a glorified gofer. Someone to run her legs off twelve to sixteen hours a day. And they had me by the short hairs, because we both knew they could get some bright young thing with stronger legs than me who'd do it for half my pay. So they didn't have to worry about me quitting. I couldn't. This back-pay thing is just the last in a long line of screw jobs that I've got from dear Laura's fat friend, Betty Doodly-Donovan."

I was surprised by the bitterness in her tone. I thought of pulling out my notebook. Canceled the thought. I didn't want to inhibit Sandy just when she'd decided to tell all.

The waiter brought coffee. While he was pouring, Sandy showed signs of realizing she'd been a tad too frank.

"Not that Laura and I weren't friends to the end, you know?" she said, gently touching my arm. "She never realized how Betty took advantage of me. It wasn't her fault."

She picked up her coffee, looked at me over the rim as she sipped, and waited.

"So," I said, reaching for my own cup. "Tell me about Laura Penniston and Bob Theodore."

Coffee sloshed over the rim of Sandy's cup into the saucer.

Muttering an unladylike word, she set cup and saucer back on the table. Checked her suit for a stain. Not seeing one, she cleared her throat.

"Sorry," she muttered, eyes looking everywhere but at me. "What about Bob and Laura?"

I didn't want to blow this opportunity. Sandy had slipped badly, and despite her looks, I'd caught it. (Maybe, Lord deliver me, I'm getting old.) I took a few seconds to blow on my own coffee while I thought.

"Nothing, really," I said innocently, staring into my cup. "Had they set the wedding date or anything?"

"Oh!" Sandy seemed to relax. "Well, uh, I doubt if they were really going to get married, you know? They were just good friends. Oh, sure, Laura enjoyed seeing all the write-ups in the papers about what a romantic couple they were and everything, but that was just hoopla. I don't think either one of them was ever really that serious about the other, you know?" She looked directly at me for the first time since she'd spilled her coffee, smiling brightly.

"Well, I can understand that," I said offhandedly. "Tell me about the other people at Penniston."

Relieved at the change of subject, she relaxed and talked about several of the models, a couple of the secretaries. She didn't mention Donovan. So I did.

"Would you say," I asked, trying to phrase my question delicately, "that Betty is sort of a—free spirit?"

Our attentive waiter showed up to pour a fresh cup of coffee for Sandy. She waited for him to leave, watching my face, a small smile playing on her lips.

"Free spirit? Very deftly put, Dave." She allowed herself a throaty chuckle, and took a sip of the fresh coffee. "Is she on drugs, you mean?" I shrugged.

Sandy got serious. "I think I caught Betty once, in the washroom at work—doing coke, you know? She jerked away fast, tried to pretend she was just having a nosebleed. That was the only time I know of. But there was talk around the office. Nancy told me just last month some guy named Harv would come in every couple of weeks and exchange packages. Nancy said Betty'd leave a small package with her, first thing in the morning, tell her that a messenger would come in to pick it up, and just bring her the replacement package. Then Harv would arrive and make the exchange. Nancy said the guy made a couple of passes at her, but she cold-shouldered him. Said he was a real scuzzball."

So by the time our lunch was over, I had a couple of new facts to play with: Sandy's strange reaction to the Bob Theodore-Laura Penniston relationship; and the mysterious Harv, Betty Donovan's messenger boy. I decided to table the second and pursue the first. As our waiter put the check discreetly on the table, I asked Sandy a question I already knew the answer to.

"By the way, did Bob Theodore come to the masquerade ball?" Sandy's eyes got very round and very innocent.

"Why do you ask?"

"What do you mean, why do I ask? What makes that such a tough question?"

"Oh, I just wondered, you know?" She blushed and dropped her eyes. "I mean, whether you thought there was any connection between that party and Laura's death."

"Since you bring it up, let me ask you. Was there?"

"I have no idea," she said hastily. "But you must think so. Otherwise why ask the question?"

"Good thinking." I looked into her beautiful eyes and smiled. "Also, you're very good at ducking the issue. I still want to know about that masquerade ball. Was Bob Theodore there?" I laid two twenties on top of the bill. About an eighteen-percent tip. More than enough, considering that the kid had managed to arrive at all the wrong times.

Sandy's face was flushed. She probably wasn't used to men seeing through her evasive tactics. "All right, Dave, let's talk about the party. Yes, as you probably already know, Bob Theodore did come. *With* the lovely Laura. The center of attention. But they didn't leave together. I don't know why." She was avoiding my eye again.

"Which one left first?"

"I don't know," she said sullenly. "I just know they left separately."

Everything in the room suddenly seemed to be a lot more fascinating than me.

I grinned at her. "How do you know they left separately if you don't know who left first?"

She looked at me, eyes brighter than ever, her pretty face a nice shade of pink. She made a show of remembering.

"Oh yeah, I guess Laura left first. Yes, that's right, she came into my office and told me she was leaving, you know? It was early—maybe ten or a little before. And Bob was—Bob was still there."

By the time Sandy'd got all that out, the flush in her cheeks had spread to her forehead. I was beginning to get an idea why she didn't want to talk about Bob Theodore or the party.

I sipped some coffee and considered how to test my theory. A way to do it began to take shape. Maybe a certain someone could be persuaded to help out. The Timex read 2:49.

Seeing me look at my watch, Sandy said, "Mind if I powder my nose before we go?"

I immediately pushed the table away to let her up. "Fine," I said. "I need to make a phone call anyway."

Hurry the call as I would, she still beat me back to the table.

"Sorry to keep you waiting," I said, somewhat breathless, trying not to let my face show my jubilation. I escorted her downstairs. "Well, it's been real," I told her as we paused in the foyer. "When can we get together to discuss my reward?"

Sandy was still tense and not doing a good job keeping up her seductress pose. "Any time, dear one," she said, reaching up to pat my cheek.

"Oh!" she said suddenly, as a new thought struck her. "Let me have your number. I might need to call you sometime." She smiled invitingly.

I gave her the office number, and she frowned. "I'd better write that down. Got a pen?"

As I handed it to her I noticed her hands were empty. "Forget your purse?" I asked. "Want something to write on?"

"No, and no," she smiled, and carefully wrote my number on the palm of her left hand. She looked up at me and handed me back my pen. "No, I don't need paper and no, I didn't leave my purse. I seldom carry one."

I must have looked surprised. "It's a habit I got into," she explained, "back when I was modeling. You have to change clothes so many different places, one of the first things you learn is never carry a purse. Oh, if you're doing studio work, you *could* bring it, but even some of the studios get robbed. And if you're in a show, you *damn* sure can't carry it around with you. So you get used to getting along without it."

I was too on edge to enjoy my education in the tricks of the modeling trade. I had a problem. I'd just set up an important appointment and time was short.

As we came out the weather was turning ugly. A bitter west wind had picked up, and the gray, scudding clouds threatened rain. November in New York: never a dull moment.

Shaking her head at my offer of a lift to wherever she was going, Sandy gave me a final, uneasy smile and a wave. She walked west, heading for Seventh Avenue, leaning into the chill wind. I watched her go, skirt whipping around her thighs. I wondered if those were the legs of a murderer. They were certainly, I'd concluded, the legs of a liar.

I flagged a cab and told him to get me to 778 Park Avenue on the double. I was ten minutes late for a very important date. And on this one, timing was everything.

—22—

Now, about that phone call. Sandy's need to powder her nose had fit right in with my plans.

(Why "powder my nose," by the way? Why not "put on mascara," or "brush my hair"? I've never met a woman yet who *needed* to powder her nose. I made the mistake of asking Sally Castle that question once, and got treated to twenty minutes of Freud. Don't ask.—Sally's a psychiatrist, an occupation that has proven to be a burden about as often as it's been a blessing.)

So while Sandy powdered her nose I located the public phone in the restaurant foyer and looked up Theodore, Blaise and Theodore. I got an operator who put me through to a receptionist who put me through to a secretary. Which, in their system, was where the buck stopped.

That secretary was tough. She tried the old "Mr.-Theodore-is-extremely-busy-may-I-tell-him-what-this-is-regarding" routine—her tone implying a snowball had a far better chance of lasting a year in hell than I had of ever getting through to Mr. Theodore, Junior—but I didn't get where I am in life by letting female staff sergeants push me around. Restraining my tendency for smart-aleck replies, I went with the old *savoir faire*.

"You certainly may," I said in a $298.95-attaché-case voice. "Tell him it's an extremely important and highly confidential matter regarding Miss Norville. It has to do with a certain . . . masquerade ball."

A moment of silence. Then, in an even chillier tone—this one approaching absolute zero: "One minute, please."

But less than a minute went by before a new phone got picked up and a masculine voice said abruptly, "Yes, this is Bob Theodore."

"Mr. Theodore, this is David Goldman. I'm just moments away from your office." Catching sight of Sandy returning to the table from the ladies' room, I smiled and waved. She smiled back. I wondered whether she'd smile if she knew who I was talking to. "In view of the things I've been learning about you and Miss Norville, I think it would be in your best interest for us to have a little talk. Can you meet me in the coffee shop downstairs in your building in five minutes?" I closed my eyes and crossed my fingers.

The twenty seconds of silence that followed were music to my ears. My guess had paid off. When he broke the silence, his "Absolutely not!" had a delightfully hollow ring to it. He followed with, "I have a meeting going on right at this very moment. Make an appointment with my secretary. I think next week—"

I stopped that nonsense. He was doing his best with a losing hand, but the twenty-second pause had blown his cover. I'm a rotten poker player myself, and I sympathized.

"No, no, no, Mr. Theodore," I laughed easily. "That's not the way it works. Look. You interrupted an important meeting to take this call. So let's drop the games, shall we?" I looked at my watch. "Tell you what. I'll be in the coffee shop downstairs in ten minutes. If you're not there when I arrive, I'm going straight to the police."

I hung up without waiting for a reply and immediately realized I'd given myself a serious timing problem. Theodore's office was a good twenty-minute cab ride away, and I wasn't free of Sandy yet. How long would Theodore wait?

But it couldn't be helped. I had a hunch that the second Sandy Norville waved goodbye to me she'd go to the first phone she saw and call a certain Mr. Robert W. Theodore, Jr. For my plan to succeed, I needed to get to Theodore *before* his girlfriend could talk to him. Meaning I had to quarantine him from his office and phone till I got to him.

Which was why I'd been anxious to get clear of Sandy. All the way to Theodore's building, in a cab that seemed afflicted with a terminal case of the slows, I wasted energy, brainpower and time thinking up three different and better ways I could have handled it.

We rolled up to 778 Park, in the shadow of the Waldorf-Astoria. The Timex said we'd made it in sixteen minutes. I was so relieved I tipped the cabbie a five, which isn't like me. He glanced at it and screeched away without so much as a nod. There's no pleasing some people.

I wouldn't have been surprised to find the coffee shop Theodoreless, the guy having gone back to his office to call Sandy and find out what the hell's going on with some shyster named Goldman. But he was there, solitary customer in the place, elbows on the counter, without so much as a cup of coffee to entertain him.

The middle-aged waitress on the other side of the counter—the only other person in the room—was talking to him, but he wasn't listening. I knew it was Theodore, and not only by his doleful demeanor. His stylishly long blond hair, his patrician nose, noble chin and superb physique made him hard to hide. Now that I was laying eyes on him in the flesh for the first time, I could see how he'd made the Ten Top Eligible Bachelors the last five years in a row. He looked at me balefully as I approached.

"Mr. Theodore," I intoned. "David Goldman."

Ignoring my outstretched hand, he got to his feet, made a big show of looking at his watch and moved in on me. He was big—an inch or two taller than me—and tried to use the height advantage, challenging me with his eyes.

"You're late, Goldman. What the hell do you think you're pulling? Because whatever it is, I'm not buying."

A person could get a stiff neck talking to this guy. I'm not used to looking up at people, especially from an inch and a half away. I grinned at him.

"Hey, let's sit down, okay? You can chew me out just as easy sitting as standing." Without waiting for an answer, I plopped my butt onto the stool nearest me, placing my briefcase on the surprisingly clean counter.

He stood glaring down at me for a second or two, perhaps thinking how easy it would be to coldcock me in that exposed position. Resisting that temptation, he finally took the next stool. He sat staring at the counter, probably groping for a terrific follow-up to his opening salvo. I took him off the hook.

"Look, Mr. Theodore," I said, getting his eye. "We're not going to get anywhere that way. You blustering at me and me sneering at you. See, all I want is answers to a few simple questions. Then I'll get out of your hair and you can get back to your meeting."

Junior's blue eyes looked worried. "All right. What do you want?"

I showed him a smile half the size of the one inside. I had him dead in my sights.

"Good. Let's get right into it." I took a deep breath while continuing to hold his eye. "Mr. Theodore, I've just come from a long lunch with Sandy." He winced at the name and I paused to give him a chance to try another bluff.

"Sandy who? What are you talking about?"

I shook my head mournfully and threw up my hands. "All right, Mr. Theodore," I sighed. "If that's the way you want to play it, I'll just take what I've got to the cops. I don't need this." I reached for the attaché case.

"Wait!"

He tugged the sleeve of my dark suit. I looked distastefully at his hand and he removed it.

"Sorry," he muttered, "but just hold on. Please!" I looked at him expectantly. "Okay," he admitted, looking away. "That was silly of me. Of course I know Sandy. Sandy Norville? You had lunch with her?"

I nodded. "At Marty's. Likes to play the field, doesn't she?" He reddened, but kept his mouth shut. He was learning. "Anyway, she told me a lot about the two of you. A *lot*, Mr. Theodore. Like what happened the night of the masquerade ball. Care to give me your version?"

He looked at me for a moment, shocked. His reaction confirmed my hunch. He paused, no doubt trying to think of another bluff, then spoke, his eyes wary.

"What'd she tell you?"

I just grinned at him and shook my head. His shoulders sagged.

"Care for some coffee?" he said, and, getting my nod, called to the waitress, who'd been keeping a cautious distance ever since our opening confrontation.

"Rosie! A couple of coffees—regular." No checking on how I liked it. If I held all the cards in the poker game, well, by God, at least he could control the refreshment concession.

Rosie parked two mugs in front of us and retired to her neutral corner at the far end of the counter. Theodore picked up a spoon, added some sugar and stirred.

"We never should have tried it," he mumbled, frowning into his cup. "I told her that. But she'd been fired anyway, so we—" He looked at me. "Won't you tell me what she told you?" His tone had turned to one of pleading.

I gave him another grin and took a sip of the tepid coffee. He followed suit, then gave me a wide-eyed look. It was the identical look I use when I'm trying to buy the pot with nothing. I waited for the lie.

"Okay, Mr. Goldman, here it is, and this is the truth, so help me. See, I gave Sandy a little kiss—just a friendly peck, really. Well, you know how women are. She probably thought it meant something. But it didn't. So when she—Where are you going? Wait!"

"I *told* you not to lie to me, man." I had my attaché case and was moving. "I've had it with you. I'm going to the cops. See you in court, pal."

Big as he was, Theodore could move when he had to. He was between me and the door before I took my third step. But this time it wasn't a fight he wanted.

"Please, Mr. Goldman," he said, his face anguished. "I'll tell you the straight story. Come on back, please!"

Reluctantly returning to my seat, I plopped the attaché case back onto the counter and got his eye. "Just the truth this time."

He nodded wearily and proceeded to give me the story of the masquerade ball. And this time I was pretty sure I was getting it straight.

* * *

Bob and Sandy had discovered they were attracted to each other that night. Bob had arrived with Laura a little after eight, prior to any of the guests. Sandy, of course, as office manager, was already there, getting things ready. Since Laura was hostess she had to greet everyone and Bob was soon at loose ends. He'd somehow wound up talking to Norville.

"It was nothing we planned to do," he assured me. "Sandy was feeling down. She'd worked so hard to have things just right, and then Laura didn't even thank her. Sandy sort of unloaded on me, just because I was handy, I suppose. I didn't really know her all that well, but after a couple of drinks we decided to go into her office and talk.

"One thing led to another, and next thing we knew, we were just—well, you know, kissing and whatnot. We'd only been in there fifteen minutes or so, when in came Laura."

"What time was it?" I asked.

"Just after ten."

The sight of her office manager/friend in her boyfriend's arms had not been appreciated. Laura had fired Sandy on the spot.

"That never came out, did it?" I said, surprised.

"No, it didn't. But look. We both knew Laura didn't mean it. Sandy decided she'd just wait it out till Monday and go apologize to Laura. We both figured Laura'd change her mind. Of course, by Monday poor Laura was dead. So Sandy went to work as usual and soon discovered that Laura apparently hadn't told anyone else. End of episode." Theodore took a sip of coffee, watching me out of the corner of his eye to see if I was buying it.

I was beginning to suffer from information overload. Laura had caught Sandy and Bob kissing—and God knew what else—that night. I recalled McClendon saying that Laura had gone into Sandy's office right after the mysterious phone call. That must have been when the blow-up happened. About ten o'clock, just before Penniston left the party, never to be seen alive again.

"Did Laura tell either of you about the phone call she'd received?" I asked. Junior looked away and thought a moment. Then further postponed answering by picking up his coffee and taking a long sip. Finally he tried to meet my eyes.

"Uh, yeah, I think she did." He was having trouble keeping a steady gaze and looked away as he continued. "Said something about a phone call. Said she had to go somewhere. I don't recall exactly. It was a tense time, you know. Laura was mad as hell, Sandy was upset, I was embarrassed . . ."

His voice trailed off. He was lying again. About what, I didn't know. I had an idle thought. If this guy was as rich as everyone said, it'd be nice to get him into a game of liar's poker.

Trouble was, at the moment I had no good way of breaking his story down. I tried a different tack.

"So Laura fired Sandy. And then Sandy went to work the next Monday as though nothing had ever happened. Got it. Now. What did Laura say to *you*?"

Mr. Handsome reddened noticeably for the first time. He looked away, and I saw his Adam's apple bob up and down. He took a deep breath and turned to face me.

"She fired *me*, too," he muttered, with an attempt at a smile. "She said it was all over between us."

Junior shook his head and tried to up the wattage of the smile. "Of course, she'd never have gone through with it. We were too—well, she just wouldn't have."

I was thinking of something while he talked. Putting myself in his shoes (having been there once or twice), I asked a question I was pretty sure I already knew the answer to.

"Did you take Sandy home?" Theodore blushed and looked away. I waited.

"Uh, yeah, I did. Or, rather, uh, I took both of us. To her place." He looked at me, his blush growing. I finally finished his thought for him.

"And stayed there?" He nodded, and the blush began to subside.

"Yes. I stayed there all night. She fixed me breakfast next morning, late. We were sitting there, just talking, the radio on, when the announcement came about Laura being killed." He picked up his coffee, hand trembling. "Then I went home. We agreed we'd never tell anyone. But you might as well know the truth."

I nodded. "Did you tell the police?"

"They never asked!" Theodore looked irritated at the negligence of the police, which I found curious. Of course, since they were looking for a psycho, they wouldn't have been interested in alibis. Still . . .

"So they let you off the hook. Well, what *did* they want to know? Did you tell them about that phone call Laura got that evening?"

"I would've if they'd have asked," Bob said. "They never asked. I was questioned by someone named, uh . . ."

"Blake," I supplied.

"Right! A jerk if I ever saw one."

I looked at Junior with new respect. He continued.

"Blake wasn't very interested in what I had to say. He really only wanted to know if I had any idea where Laura went. I said I didn't. If he'd asked a couple more questions, I'd have been glad to tell him about that phone call. But he didn't ask. Sounded like he was in a hurry."

Theodore looked down and thought for a minute. Suddenly he was angry. "Satisfied now?" he said, his voice rising. "Got everything you want?"

I doubted it. Not that I didn't have plenty. Too much, in fact. I'd collected more information in one day—from Donovan, McClendon, Norville and Theodore—than any one brain could process in a week. Well, any brain but the Bishop's.

But of everything I'd learned, that phone call to Laura looked like the cream of the crop. And it looked like Bob Theodore knew more about it than he was saying. But I had no leverage—at least none that I could think of—to get it out of him.

Suddenly I got a new idea. Or rather, a variation of an old one. After all, why tamper with success?

"Well," I shrugged nonchalantly. "You've certainly given me lots to think about. But I'll have to collate it with all the other information I've picked up before I'll know whether I'll need any more."

We got to our feet. I snapped my fingers as though I'd just remembered something.

"Hang on just another sec, will you, Bob? Uh, where's the nearest phone?" He tilted his head wordlessly to indicate the door to the lobby. "Just hang in there, will you? I'll be right back."

I didn't want him to get away while I made this call. He wasn't happy about it, but I didn't give him the chance to argue. Finally he nodded abruptly and collapsed back onto his stool.

My luck held: Sandy Norville answered on the second ring. I was very upbeat.

"Sandy! Dave here. I've got a couple more questions. I can't come back down your way, but could you meet me up on Thirty-seventh Street in half an hour?"

"I'm afraid not, Dave." The tone was cool. "I've really answered all the questions I'm going to. For today, anyway."

"Oh? You've answered all the questions you're going to? Then I'm afraid I have a problem," I said with a sigh. "Bob Theodore and I have been talking..." I waited for the gasp. She didn't disappoint me. "...and Bob has just been telling me a number of things about that night at the party, and about what Laura said to the two of you when she caught you playing footsie. Sounds like you haven't been totally honest with me, Sandy."

She started to answer, but I wasn't done.

"So here's my problem: do I take what I've got to the police, or do you and I sit down and discuss it? Of course, if you don't have time—"

"I've been trying to *reach* Bob! Where *are* you? I want to—"

I cut her off. Time to get a little tougher. "Look, Sandy. We're through with the fun and games. It's time to talk turkey. You dressed? Good. Get a cab and go to Eight-ninety West Thirty-seventh Street. It'll say Catholic Archdiocese, Bishop's Residence on the door, but don't let that stop you. Just tell them who you are and they'll let you in.

"Now, don't fool around. I'll be there inside of twenty minutes, and if you're not there when I arrive I'm just going straight to the police. I've had it with you."

I hung up without waiting for her response. I'd bounced from Sandy to Bob, and now—I hoped—back to Sandy. I was beginning to feel like a pinball. Still, each time I seemed to be getting a little more of the truth.

Back in the coffee shop, I didn't bother to sit down. "No more questions, Bob," I said abruptly, grabbing my attaché case. "Got to run. It's been real." Theodore got up and offered his hand, perhaps to show there were no hard feelings. I grabbed and shook it, amused at the relieved but puzzled look on his handsome face.

I was even more amused by the certainty that the first thing he'd do when he got back upstairs was call Sandy. I'd probably caused more phone calls today, with fewer results, than anyone since Hitler tried to find out if Paris was burning.

"Then I'll be hearing from you?" he called after me in a worried voice.

I gave him a brisk thumbs-up with my free hand and kept right on walking.

—23—

SANDY WAS SITTING, beautiful and lonely, in the tiny foyer of the mansion when I let myself in. Before grabbing a cab, I'd called Ernie with explicit instructions. Sandy was to be admitted but not given access to any phone and discouraged from leaving for any reason. I wasn't ready to lift the quarantine yet.

She was beginning to look a little worn around the edges. But the tailored suit still flattered her. The figure she'd called dumpy, then plump, struck me as well-rounded or even voluptuous. Too bad she was such a liar.

Her greeting, as I invited her into my office, was strained. For which I couldn't really blame her.

"Let's get right down to it, Sandy," I said as she got herself arranged. Her perfume began to fill the room. "I need to know about a certain phone call."

"What phone call?" She examined her fingernails.

"The one Laura got at the party. You remember. The one that made her come look for you. The one that got you fired by Laura two weeks before you got fired by Betty."

Sandy turned red. She opened her mouth, then closed it and eyed me.

"Bob's an idiot!" she said coldly. "If he—" She stopped. "What did he tell you?"

"Never mind what Bob told me. Look, Sandy. You and Bob are in a potload of trouble. I can't even begin to tell you how tired I'm getting of him saying, 'What did Sandy tell you?' and you, 'What did Bob tell you?' Why don't you just tell the simple truth?"

"Truth! You're a fine one to talk about truth! You didn't even tell me

123

you *knew* Bob! You just let me talk on and on." She glanced at the door. She was about an inch away from walking out.

"Look," I sighed. "Sandy. I told you, I'm representing Jerry Fanning. I also told you, he's innocent. That's not a guess, that's a fact. He couldn't have done it. To Laura or *any* of those women." The big dark eyes were attentive.

"So I need to find out who *did*. All I'm asking you to do is tell the truth. Now, I'm not going to tell you I can protect you from police harassment, but I can damn sure help—*if* you get me on your side. What you need to understand is there's just one way you can do that: answer my questions.

"No, make that two things: answer my questions, and answer them truthfully. Do that and I swear to you, I'll do my damnedest to keep you and Bob out of trouble."

She studied me, then looked at her watch. I did the same: 5:06. Guessing her thoughts, I said, "The sun's over the yardarm, as they say. Care for a drink?"

Turned out she did, and I decided to join her. Ernie was breaking some eggs and separating the yolks from the whites as I came in the kitchen and pulled a jug of Chablis and a Heineken's out of the fridge. I waited for the usual interrogation.

"So, David, a beautiful girl."

I nodded and grabbed a wine glass and a beer mug.

"So is she Jewish?"

I had to suppress a smile before giving her my considered response: "None of your business, Ernie."

"Umm-hmm," she simpered in that smug, self-satisfied, knowing way of hers. Returning to my office with the drinks, I saw that Sandy's chair was a little closer to the desk. I instinctively glanced around the room to see if anything was out of place. Nothing that I could see. My trust in the lovely brunette obviously went about as far as I could see her.

Sandy took a sip and met my gaze squarely for the first time. "So what do you want to know, Dave?"

"Like I said. Anything and everything you can tell me about what happened with Laura the night she died, especially that phone call she got."

"Okay." She nodded and took a nervous sip. "It was Bob's idea not to tell anyone about it." She was having difficulty meeting my eyes again. "I almost feel I'm betraying a confidence, you know? He was so embarrassed. Does the name Steven Sarnoff ring a bell, Dave?"

I frowned at her. "Sarnoff? No. Should it?"

Sandy gave a slight shrug. "That's who called that night."

That didn't remove my frown. "Who's Sarnoff?"

"I don't know. Well, I do, actually, but I've never met him. He was a friend of Laura's. He runs the outfit we get most of our models from." She smiled bitterly. "I should say, *they* get most of *their* models from. Models for Hire, it's called. He's the one who called Laura."

"What makes you think that? Did Laura say so?"

"Something like that. And that's why Bob didn't want to talk about it, you know? Because Sarnoff's been cheating Laura for at least a year. And Bob missed it in the audit."

I stared at her as I pulled out my notebook. "Okay. Tell me everything you know about him. And about that phone call he made to Laura the night she died." I was beginning to get somewhere.

She took a sip of wine. "I can't really tell you much about Sarnoff. And as far as that call goes—well, Laura said . . ." She frowned into her glass, then up at me.

"I'd better just tell you everything that happened. It's complicated. See, when Laura walked in on us she was furious! I'd never seen her so mad. She was out of control. For no reason. I mean, Bob and I hadn't been all that—well, passionate. We were just—well, *you* know." Sandy tried a smile, took one look at my face and got serious again.

"Well, Laura went after *me* first. You can imagine what she said. I'd stabbed her in the back after she'd tried to help me, and so forth and so on. I just sat there, stunned, you know? Bob was up, walking around. But any time he'd get close to her, she'd yell at him, 'Stay away from me! Don't you touch me!' Things like that.

"And she climbed all over me, told me I was fired. Even tried to get me to clear my things out of the office right then and there. I just sat there, not knowing what to do. I didn't say a word. I felt so *awful*! You know?" She looked at me and I nodded.

"Well, I was just about to start clearing my things out when Laura forgot about me and started back in on Bob. By this time she was starting to get *really* vicious. And that's when she first mentioned the phone call. Said something like, 'I've got to go meet my *dear* friend, Steven Sarnoff.' Sounded really contemptuous, you know?

"Then Laura *really* started screaming at him. At Bob, I mean. 'If you'd done what I paid you to do, instead of the half-assed job you did,

I wouldn't even be *having* this problem with Sarnoff. But it doesn't really matter, because we're through, you and me!'"

Sandy took another sip. "Then she got even nastier. Her voice got real low and mean. Said, 'I'm going to tell your dad about this, you scumbag! I tried to help you, tried to keep your stupidity our little secret! Well, it's not a secret any longer!' Bob was just white as a sheet. He tried to talk to her, but she just slammed out." Sandy looked down. "And that was the last time either of us ever saw her alive."

Now I was getting somewhere. So someone named Steven Sarnoff...

"Just what did she say about the call, Sandy?"

She squinted into space, took another small sip of the Chablis and turned the squint on me.

"Uh, let me see." She put her glass down. "Laura said . . . she was going to see him." Sandy's eyes widened. "Yes! She said—she was talking to Bob—she said, 'Your buddy Sarnoff just called, and I'm going to have it out with him.' Those exact words. That was when she started in on Bob about what a lousy accountant he was and all."

I had a feeling this was straight, and I wanted more. "Okay. I want to hear about this audit. What do you know about it?"

"Plenty." Sandy smiled grimly. "After Laura slammed out, Bob told me all about it. See, Betty and Laura went to Bob last spring. Asked him to do a complete certified audit of Penniston Associates. Point was to set the price George McClendon was going to have to pay to buy in, you know?

"Well, Laura'd been real happy with the audit—at first. Because it showed the firm was worth something like nine million bucks. So George would have had to pony up three just for a one-third partnership. Laura was bubbling over the day she got the results. I know it was a lot more than either one of them had expected to get. Of course some of it would have gone into the company, but lots would have gone to the two of them. But then, oh, maybe early September, everything changed."

Sandy closed her eyes, remembering.

"Let's see, McClendon came in to the office . . . When was it?" Her brow wrinkled. "Well, it was right after Labor Day, I remember that. I remember everyone was working on the winter schedule, which always starts Labor Day week. Anyway, George and Laura had a long meeting in her office. And she was in a foul mood after he left. Slamming around and being impossible, you know? After lunch, she and Betty went into the board room and spent the rest of the afternoon there, just the two of them. They were still there when I went home about six. And Bob—"

"Excuse me," I interrupted. I was taking notes rapidly. "You say this was in September? Two months ago?" Sandy nodded, taking another sip.

"Right. Like I say, it was the week of Labor Day. It was Tuesday or Wednesday of that week. Anyway, I ran into Bob getting off the elevator. And he looked worried. I remember, he was loaded down with two huge briefcases—suitcases, really. He asked me where Laura and Betty were meeting. And what kind of mood they were in. I teased him about how worried he looked, but he wasn't in a joking mood, so I just sent him to the board room. I remember wondering what was going on.

"And I never found out—till Laura blew up the night she died. After she stomped out, I asked Bob, 'What was *that* all about?' And he told me.

"Seems this guy Sarnoff had been overcharging Laura for his models. For a year or so he'd been providing most of our models, only he was overcharging by thirty or forty percent. Bob said he should have caught it when he did the audit but didn't. And Laura'd been understanding about it—up until that night."

"How'd they happen to start using Sarnoff in the first place?"

Sandy frowned at me. "I know. That's the strange thing. I always thought he and Laura were friends. Laura started doing business with him, oh, a year or so ago. Laura'd send him a check every month to cover all the jobs his models had done the previous month. Funny thing is, these were all *our* models. I always figured there was some sort of tax reason we were doing it that way.

"Well, as Bob explained it to me, it didn't have anything to do with taxes. Sarnoff just charged us one-and-a-half times the going rate and pocketed the difference. So when Bob missed it in the audit, he'd have been in deep doo-doo if Laura and Betty had wanted to sue. But they didn't. Much to Bob's relief."

I frowned. "So Laura—and Betty—did Bob a real favor."

"Right. I guess it was *Betty* who'd taken most of the heat. I mean, Betty was supposed to be the financial whiz, so it was really her fault. At least that's the way Laura felt. Or so Bob said. But he said Laura'd never got mad at *him*, even though he'd blown the audit."

I sensed a breakthrough. "How do I get hold of this Sarnoff?"

Sandy shrugged. "I've never met the guy. But I'm pretty sure you

could locate him. Maybe through your friend . . ." Sandy grinned at me.
". . . Betty Donovan. She must know him. Or talk to Lee Stubbs. Know
who he is? Lee's our banker at Mid-City National. And Sarnoff's, too.
I was the one who made the deposit to Sarnoff's company every month,
you know? Models For Hire. In fact, I'm the one who opened their
account."

"*You* opened the account?" I was puzzled. "You opened the account
and you didn't even know him?"

Sandy nodded. "I know, I know, this whole thing's kind of strange.
Here's how it went.

"A year ago last spring, I got an office memo from Laura giving me
instructions to open an account for Models for Hire. I was to handle it
through Lee—Mr. Stubbs. Along with the memo was a check Laura'd
signed—two thousand bucks, as I recall.

"So I got the stuff I needed from Lee—Mr. Stubbs . . ." Sandy blushed
and flicked me a glance. "I got Mr. Sarnoff's signature on everything—"

"Hold it, Sandy. You never *met* Sarnoff. How'd you get his signatures
on all those documents?"

"I just sent all the stuff to him through the mail—that's what Laura
told me to do." Sandy frowned. "Come to think of it, I *did* think it was
funny at the time. It was a box number. I remember wondering where
the heck the guy was located."

"You don't remember the number, do you?"

"Nope, sorry. Anyway, Lee opened the account, and after that, every
month I'd get a check from Laura like clockwork for all the models we'd
used from Models for Hire for the previous month. And I'd make out
the deposit slip—I had a supply of them for Models for Hire—and I'd
go to the bank and make the deposit, and send the receipt to the
company—to Models for Hire—at that post office box."

I was writing fast. "How much were the checks?"

Sandy shrugged. "All over the place. Biggest one might have been
thirty thousand. Usually they were around fifteen or twenty. I thought
it was a funny way of doing business, but what did I know? You know?"

"Did you ever talk to Laura about it?"

"I don't think so. I don't think anything ever came up—till that night.
It was just a real smooth deal."

"Who else knew about Sarnoff? Did Betty?"

Sandy gave that some thought, then shook her head again. "Nope. I don't think I ever heard her mention the name. My impression was this was Laura's private deal and we weren't supposed to talk about it. That was just my impression."

That was all Sandy could—or would—tell me about the mysterious Steven Sarnoff. (You know?) So I changed directions. I asked her the same question I'd asked Theodore earlier, wondering if I'd get the same answer.

"Did Bob give you a ride home? On the night of the party, I mean."

Sandy studied me for several seconds, a slight smile playing on her full lips. She took a deliberate sip of wine and put her glass down.

"Oh, yes," she finally said, meeting my eyes, her voice at its most musical. "He took me home, all right. And came in. And had his own wanton way with me." She smiled lazily.

I looked at her. "He stayed all night? And left when?"

Sandy abruptly got to her feet, walked around her chair, put her hands on the back of it and faced me challengingly. "What difference does it make?"

"No difference, probably. Any reason not to tell me?"

"I suppose not." She shrugged. "He left early. I offered to give him some breakfast, but he had to get going."

I nodded slowly and thought fast. "Then did he call you when he heard what had happened to Laura? Or did you call him? Or did you even talk about it?"

"Why talk about it?" She'd turned sullen again. "Nothing we could say would bring her back to life. Or change what happened the night before."

"Well, when *did* you hear about Laura? About her death, I mean?"

"I don't remember." Sandy was getting restive. My office is too small for pacing and she was beginning to look like a caged tiger. She took a breath.

"Look. I want to go. I'm really grateful for you getting me that money, Dave. I won't forget it. And as far as Laura's concerned, I want the guy who did her caught, you know? And I'll do anything to help. You say Fanning's not the guy. Okay. Maybe he isn't. But I'm tired and just a little upset, you know? Nothing against you, Dave, but I really do want to go."

"Fine," I said casually. "Just sit down for a second while I tell you about a dilemma I've got." She sat, looking worried. With reason.

"Thanks," I said. "Now, here's my dilemma. I've got your story, and

I've got Theodore's, and they don't agree. Oh, you both agree that he came home with you and that you went to bed together. But that's all. The details are all wrong. So my dilemma is, do I call the cops and tell them about it?"

I grinned at her. "See, it's a murder case, and it's just possible you two decided to cook up an alibi. But go ahead and run along, Sandy. I'm sure I'll come to a decision soon. Probably about the time you call Bob to warn him that your stories don't jibe. My advice is to get together right away—before the cops get to you—and work out your story better. And for God's sake, get your details straight. Because, after what I tell them—*if* I tell them—they're likely to be pretty tough on you."

Sandy had reddened when I started talking. But when I got to the part about how tough the cops were going to be, the color left her face.

"That's not true, Dave." She was on her feet again. "Bob *did* spend the night!" She leaned over the desk, eyes flashing, perfume wafting. But the effect was diminished by her skin tone, which had turned blotchy under the makeup.

I shrugged. "Fine. I'll get the police over here and we'll work it out right now." I reached for the phone. Her hand came down on mine, hard.

I looked at her, eyebrows raised. Sandy, shoulders sagging, took her hand off of mine and fell back in the chair.

"Don't call them, Dave." Her voice sounded defeated. "I'll tell you the truth."

I sighed. "Yeah, it's about time. You're just lucky the cops weren't interested. You'd have been booked before you got halfway through that ridiculous story."

Sandy bit her lip and looked down. "I guess so," she mumbled, and proceeded to give me the latest version. Bob had taken her home that night, kissed her and left. But when the news broke about Laura's death the next morning, they'd decided to cook up a mutual alibi.

"But why?" I wondered aloud. "This was obviously another Strangler John killing. Why'd either of you even think you *might* be suspects?"

She was ready for that one. "But the first news reports weren't all that clear, Davey. They said it *resembled* a Strangler John murder. So we panicked. I mean, after that big blow-up the night before, we both had motives."

They certainly did (I thought). In fact, what if they'd cooked up the plot to kill Laura after she left? And carried it out together? I began to reconsider whether Laura's murder might have been a copycat.

"So you cooked up a story. Over the phone?" Sandy nodded. "Who called who? I mean, that morning, the morning you found out Laura was dead."

Sandy hesitated before answering. "It was me. I heard the news on my radio almost as soon as I woke up. I called him right away."

I nodded. "And who suggested this alibi story?"

Another pause.

"It was both of us." She looked for my reaction and saw my skepticism. "All right, it was me," she muttered sullenly. "You don't think old Robert Redford could have thought that one up on his own, do you?" I grinned. She stayed glum.

"Yeah, it was my idea. I had the notion we ought to cover ourselves. Can't you understand that?"

I shrugged. "Well, don't worry, I'm not saying anything to the cops. Just yet. But one more question." She nodded, watching me warily.

"How much of this stuff did Blake ask you about? I mean, the phone call. Bob taking you home. The audit."

She laughed bitterly. "None of it. All that trouble Bob and I went to, and I never got to use it—till *you* came along. And neither did Bob. I tried to tell Blake about that phone call Laura got, but he cut me off. Said he already knew about it.

"Well, it was no skin off my nose. I knew he'd interviewed Betty, and Betty knew about the call. But *she* didn't know it was Sarnoff. Bob and I are the only ones who knew that. And Blake didn't ask either one of us. What was the other thing? Oh, the audit. That never came up either.

"Really, the only thing Blake seemed interested in was finding out whether I knew where Laura spent those two or three hours between the time she left the party and the time she was killed. When he decided I didn't, that was it. I probably wasn't with him more than ten or fifteen minutes."

I was out of questions—I thought—and phoned for a cab. But while we were waiting, I thought of one.

"Oh, yeah—what about those earrings, Sandy? The ones Laura was wearing that night. They're missing. Was she wearing them when she was in your office?"

Sandy finished the last of her wine. "I didn't notice. She had them on earlier." Sandy smiled sourly. "Her famous red cross earrings. She let me wear them once on a job. I found them terribly uncomfortable; too heavy. My lobes were sore for a week.

"Laura wouldn't admit it—after all, they were gifts from her parents—but she found them uncomfortable, too. If she had to wear them for very long, she'd take them off when she went to the loo, give her ears a rest. But I can't recall if she had them on there in my office."

It was 5:53 when I returned to my office from seeing her to the cab. Seven minutes till the Bishop finished his daily stint with the word processor and would be available to hear everything I'd learned. I had an idea. Maybe I could pull off one more coup on this day of brilliant coups. The way my luck was running, anything was possible.

I keep my phone directories—several of them, fat ones—in the deep bottom drawer of my desk. Among them they cover the entire metropolitan area. I pulled them all out and looked up *Sarnoff* in every one. But my luck had run out. Not a *Steven* or even an *S. Sarnoff* in the lot.

At 6:01 I tapped on the connecting door and entered. The boss glanced up at me, back at the screen, frowned and checked his watch. He sighed and turned off the computer.

"Yes, David, time to quit. Thank God. I'm drowning in my own turgid prose."

I grinned. "Maybe I can resuscitate you. After you hear everything I learned today about the friends and business associates of one Laura Penniston, you'll feel much better. I've got some stuff you're going to love."

"I'll be the judge of that," the Bishop growled. "All right. I'm listening."

—24—

Enjoyable as it sometimes is, briefing the boss is probably the hardest of all my many jobs. Even with the help of the notebook, it usually takes all my memory power to give him everything every time. He has an amazing ability to juggle hundreds of seemingly disconnected facts and find the two that fit. Since I'm never sure which facts will turn out to be the ones that fit, I have to be sure he gets them all.

When Sister Ernestine called us for dinner at a quarter to seven I'd gotten as far as my meeting with McClendon. While we ate dinner— and I don't have a clue what we had—and returned to the office, I kept right on going. As we walked—in his case, rolled—back to the office, I was telling about my trip to Theodore's building. And when, at 10:08, I finished telling how I'd sent Sandy home and then had failed to locate any S. Sarnoff anywhere in any New York City area phone directory, I was satisfied the boss did everything I did. I was also as exhausted as I've ever been.

Regan was sitting, a bit slumped in his wheelchair, eyes closed, chin in his hand. He didn't say anything for a good thirty seconds after I finished.

"Well, well, well, David." He opened his eyes and shot me a glance. "Your usual thorough job of reporting. A busy day. And as productive as it was busy."

"Productive? Sounds promising. Are you onto something?"

The Bishop pursed his lips and shrugged. "Umm. A conjecture, perhaps. Nothing worth troubling you about. Not at this point, at any rate. But I do have a question."

"Yeah?"

"Yes. Haven't you an obligation to tell the police about that concocted story? I refer to Miss Norville and Mr. Theodore attempting to convince you they spent the night together."

I gave that suggestion the treatment it deserved. "You kidding? Look. *If* they'd lied to the cops *and* I knew it—maybe. But Blake never even gave them the chance. He doesn't even care whether those two *have* alibis. So why should I tell Blake that the alibis he *should* have asked about but didn't would have been lies if he *had* asked?"

The boss subsided. When it comes to police procedure, he always defers to me. Well—almost always.

Next point: my program for the following day.

"As I see it," I told him, "I should go back to Penniston Associates and talk to Nancy some more—assuming she hasn't already been fired. I have a feeling that little girl could tell me some things."

Regan sniffed. "I noted your description of the young lady, David. Forgive me for saying so, but your predilection for comely young women may be distorting your normally good judgment."

I didn't answer. That was obviously unfair, but I was too tired to start a fight over it. Regan glanced at me, saw my lip was zipped, and continued. "My own recommendation is that you go see Lee Stubbs first thing in the morning and find out everything he knows about Steven Sarnoff and related matters."

We compromised. Next morning, promptly at 9:00, I was at the desk of Priscilla Moran, receptionist, on the eighth floor of Mid-City National Bank, asking to be shown to the office of Lee Stubbs, Vice-President.

Not knowing what the day held, and in light of my previous success at power dressing, I had re-equipped myself in everything from the day before, the now soiled white shirt excepted. Since I owned no other white dress shirt, I hoped a blue button-down would serve as well. Naturally I brought the magical attaché case. I'd stuck another New York *Times* in it to give it a little more heft.

"I really do need to know what this is regarding, Mr. Goldman," said Priscilla. This lady was as cool and in control as Nancy was harried and disorganized. And about a quarter as pretty, which was fine by me. I'd had about all the prettiness I could stand—at least for a while.

At that, in her severely tailored suit, Priscilla fit the decor nicely. The Commercial Accounts department of Mid-City National Bank took up the whole eighth floor of a modernist skyscraper on Sixth, just south of the Park.

The reception room was subdued and sophisticated, with plenty of abstract art on the walls overlooking several well-padded chairs. Two of the latter were currently occupied by expensively garbed old geezers who looked like their pacemakers needed repairs. I watched them nervously out of the corner of an eye, hoping I remembered enough CPR to do the honors in case either or both collapsed.

Worried about the prospect of a life-threatening emergency, I must have made a face, because Miss Moran said icily, "I *have* to ask that, Mr. Goldman. It's my *job.*"

"Sorry. That frown wasn't for you. I just had an unpleasant thought." She responded with a tentative smile that did wonders for her appearance.

I smiled back. "Just tell Mr. Stubbs it's the gentleman that I.I. Schwartz spoke to him about."

As Priscilla picked up the phone to call Stubbs, I said a quick prayer to the gods of Wall Street that Ike hadn't forgotten to call Stubbs. Ike Schwartz, a charter member of the Irregulars, is probably my closest friend and has been, ever since both of us were toddlers down on Delancey Street.

I'd called him the night before, right after Regan and I decided I needed to talk to Stubbs. As a partner in a Big Six accounting firm, he knows lots of bankers. Turned out Ike and Stubbs were racquetball buddies, a break for me.

"Be glad to put in a good word for you, Davey. Or should I tell him the truth?" Ike's always had a cruel sense of humor. But he soon got serious and told me some things.

"Lee's an okay guy, Davey. He'd give you the shirt off his back. He does have a temper, though. I heard he had some nasty things to say about Laura Penniston when she threw him over for Bob Theodore. And I can remember when he—"

"Hold it! Did I hear you right? Stubbs used to date the woman?"

"Sure, Davey. Hot and heavy, up till a year or two ago. He'd set her up in business with the original loan. Then when she dropped him and started dating that hot accountant, Stubbs was furious. But she apparently calmed him down. I can tell you this: he was as upset at her death as anyone. Even flew out to Wichita for the funeral.

"One thing, though. For God's sake, don't try any of your so-called humor on him. Guy's got no sense of humor whatsoever. Typical banker." (This from an accountant.) "And don't use his first name, which is Marion. He hates it." Ike promised to give Stubbs a call first thing and give me a good intro.

Waiting for Priscilla Moran to reach Stubbs, I took a closer look at the art on the walls, especially the largest and most abstract one. I decided it was either a three-legged octopus or a portrait of a badly decayed Elizabeth Taylor.

I was still studying it when a man in a suit a shade darker than mine came bustling into the room. Lantern-jawed, balding and athletic-looking, he was half a foot shorter than me but compensated with vigor and sparkle.

He scoped the room quickly, located me and gave me an FDR smile: chin up, teeth shining. All he lacked was the cigarette holder.

"Mr. Goldman? Any friend of Ike Schwartz is a friend of mine!" I gave him my hand and tried not to wince as he crushed it. "I'm Lee Stubbs! Come on back!"

I followed the banker into a large, oak-paneled office with some large plants in the corners and three more examples of someone's idea of art on the walls. These three seemed to run to differently tinted squares of various sizes. The largest was a series of blue rhombuses (rhombi?) running off to the horizon, tilting westward as they did. Stepping closer, I checked the title. "Untitled." Good choice.

"Like it?" Stubbs said to my back.

"Oh, yeah!" I enthused. "I'm really into baseball!"

"Oh?" he said doubtfully, squinting at it through new eyes. "Ah, yes, I can see what you mean. It really is a baseball motif, isn't it?" He waved for me to sit in the chair in front of his desk. I obeyed but, feet planted wide, hands behind his back, Stubbs didn't take his eyes off the picture.

"Yes, I definitely see what you mean," he went on in a more assured tone, nodding at it. "I see what you mean—the diamonds and all. Yes, definitely baseball. I wonder why I never saw it before."

I raised my eyebrows. It was nice to finally find someone agreeable. But I sent myself a memo: no leading questions with this guy. I could wind up with lots of information all fed from me to him right back to me.

Stubbs got over his frenzy of baseball fever and down to business.

"Well," he said, settling in behind his desk. "Ike tells me you're a private detective. What can I do for you?"

"I'm just looking for information about a Steven Sarnoff. I gather he was a friend of Miss Penniston's and a customer of yours."

Stubbs frowned, closed his eyes, then nodded abruptly. "Yep, that's right. I believe he owns Models for Hire. Yes. May I ask why you want to know?"

"Of course. I'm working with the lawyer who's defending the Strangler John suspect, this guy, Fanning. We believe he's innocent, so I'm investigating the four deaths, concentrating for the moment on Miss Penniston. I have reason to think Mr. Sarnoff may know something about it and I'd like to talk with him."

"Fair enough, Davey. But just how does he fit in?"

"I'm not even sure he does, Lee. But it looks like he may have been stealing from Penniston Associates. Laura had just found out about it and was plenty hot. She got a phone call from someone just hours before her death. She went out, apparently to meet whoever called her; and her body was found next morning. I'm pretty sure that call was from Sarnoff."

The banker's eyebrows went up. "Wow! Is that right? Then why the hell aren't the police looking for him?"

I nodded. "Well might you wonder. They're not looking for him because they've never heard of him. And they haven't heard of him because they're so sure they've got the murderer in jail, they're not asking any questions. As I told you, I don't think Fanning did it. So I'm looking for Sarnoff. And I hope you can help me."

Stubbs nodded soberly. "Sure. I'll tell you what I can. What do you want to know?"

I leaned forward. "First of all, do you know Sarnoff? I mean, personally."

"Nope. Not personally or any other way. Never met the man." I must have winced, because Stubbs added, "Sorry about that."

"But he's a depositor in your institution, isn't he?" I mentally shook my head. Now I was starting to sound like a *banker*. It was time to retire the dark suit. Permanently.

"Well, yes he is," Stubbs was sounding even more doubtful. "Or rather, not exactly. I mean, his *company* is, Models for Hire, but I don't think *he* is. Just a minute." He pushed a button on his desk and waited. In a few seconds a tall, thin brunette with a bad overbite stuck her head in the door. Stubbs looked up, gave a brief smile. "Cindy, get me the Models for Hire file, will you? My desk file *and* the credit file, if you would."

Cindy disappeared.

"The file will show," Stubbs went on, "but I don't think we have anything personally from Mr. Sarnoff. Nope. I don't think so." His voice trailed off. He glanced at me, at the baseball picture, and back at me. Possibly he was beginning to realize he'd been had. He seemed to be examining that possibility from all angles when Cindy returned, bearing a large folder.

"Here's your desk file, Mr. Stubbs. I'll go over to Credit and get the credit file." She left. Lee leaned forward and started paging through the file.

"I keep some information on my accounts with my secretary so it's close at hand," he said, repeatedly licking a finger as he paged. "Copies of memos, things like that. Let's see. Models for Hire, Models for Hire. ... Ah, here it is. Now let's see what we've got." He squinted and turned more pages.

He gave me a quick glance. "I'm just seeing if we have any memos describing his having come in here. Or our going to him. Umm, it doesn't appear like it. Seems the only one we can be sure of who knew him was Sandy." Stubbs blushed and cleared his throat. "That's, er, Sandra Norville, the office manager for Penniston Associates. According to this, she opened the account and brought the resolution and sig cards originally."

"Uh, sig cards . . . ?"

"That's signature cards, sorry."

"May I see?"

Getting his nod, I got up and came around the desk and read over his shoulder. The memo started with the date—April thirteenth, a year and a half earlier—and the initials MLS. I read the short memo. For all the good it did me. Here's exactly what it said:

Opened a/c for MODELS FOR HIRE this day. S. Norville of the related a/c, PENNISTON ASSOCIATES, INC., brt. in sig. cards and res. Res. signed by Steven Sarnoff, Secy. Op. dep. of $2000 per check of PAI, signed by L. Penniston, Pres. Ave. bals. will be low 5–figures. PAI will be making disbursements into the a/c moly, in pymt for modeling fees. Res. does not authorize loans.

"Is there a glossary?" I asked.

"Oh, no, we don't need—" Stubbs stopped, looked at me and laughed. "Sorry. I suppose it *is* kind of incomprehensible to a non-banker, Dave. A/c means 'account,' *res* is 'resolution.' And there's lots of other abbreviations. What it says, Dave, is that Sandy had Sarnoff fill out some signature cards and a resolution form. Then Laura gave Sandy a check for two thousand dollars to bring here and open the account. That's the minimum balance for a small commercial account." Stubbs paused to take another squint at the memo.

"Sandy told me Penniston pays its models monthly, said Models for Hire would now be a conduit for the fees. See, Models for Hire is just an affiliate. Laura just wanted to save some taxes. We've never had any reason to question it. It doesn't borrow—you'll notice, the last line of the memo says the corporate resolution didn't authorize any loans—so we didn't bother to run a credit check. And the account's never overdrawn. I get a daily overdraft list, and Models for Hire's never been on it."

Cindy returned with another folder as large as the first but with a shinier cover. "Ah, the credit file," said Stubbs. "Thank you, Cindy."

"Did you want the statistical file?" she asked.

Stubbs glanced at me, got no answer there, and shrugged.

"No, that's all, Cindy." He looked at the file, fingered the cover and started to open it. His eyes suddenly widened. "Cindy!"

She reappeared, eyebrows raised.

"This says Closed!"

"That's because the account closed," Cindy said. "Didn't you know about it, Mr. Stubbs?"

"No!" Stubbs was aggrieved. He looked down. "Closed November sixth. That's what? A week ago yesterday? Last Monday. What's going on, Cindy? Why wasn't I told?"

I looked back and forth from Stubbs to the secretary. Something was haywire. And I had a strong feeling it had something—maybe a lot—to do with Laura Penniston's murder.

"Why didn't I *tell* you?" Cindy said in hurt tones. "It was only an account closing. I didn't know that you—"

"Okay, okay," Stubbs interrupted, raising a hand. "You're right. But stick around a minute, would you, Cin?" He spun in his chair to face the computer on his credenza. "Excuse me, Dave," he muttered, playing with the keys, getting a display on the screen in front of him. "This is strange. I need to see what's . . ."

His voice trailed off as he studied the tube. He tapped keys, and words and numbers began running down the screen. He watched intently, still manipulating the keys, finally seeming to get the display he wanted.

"Here we go," he said. "Look at this, Dave. You too, Cin."

Cindy and I obligingly came around behind the desk and looked at the screen over his shoulder. He looked up at me inquiringly. I shook my head and shrugged helplessly. He smiled and nodded.

"Okay, let me explain it, Dave. This is the Models for Hire account history. See those numbers? This is a running total of what the company kept in the account." Stubbs pushed a key and produced a new display. I was beginning to catch on. That was a bank statement on the screen before us, a little like the one I get every month. Every transaction on it changed the balance in the right-hand column.

Models for Hire, I soon saw, had been a very active account. It had opened with two thousand dollars nineteen months earlier and showed a deposit every month since in amounts ranging from ten to forty thousand dollars. The withdrawals were more numerous, and in smaller amounts. The account balance had never quite reached fifty thousand. The average seemed to be more like ten. Just as I was starting to catch on, Stubbs caught the biggie.

"Cindy!" he erupted, jabbing his finger at the screen. "Can this be *right*? Look at all those ATM withdrawals!" His tone had the sound of someone who'd just discovered he'd come to work without pants on.

I shifted a little so Cindy could move in. I was finding I didn't care for her perfume any more than her teeth.

"I don't know, Mr. Stubbs," she said, helplessly staring at the screen. She sounded as worried as he did.

"What's wrong?" I asked, looking from one to the other. I got no answer. The crisis was apparently too acute to waste time on stupid questions from non-bankers.

Stubbs was shaking his head. "I can't understand this."

"Will someone *please* tell me what's going on?" I demanded. "And, while you're at it, what's ATM?"

Stubbs's eyes remained glued to the screen. "Uh, I guess you better go get me the stat file, Cindy." She left. The banker finally answered my question, his eyes still glued to the screen.

"ATMs, Dave, are those machines that people get money out of. Automated Teller Machines. We call ours Money Depots. You've surely seen them around."

His next sentence was barely audible. "But what's this account doing with all those damn transactions? Sandy told me usage would be minimal!"

I was catching on. Under the column reading *DR* (which apparently meant "withdrawals"), the entries seemed to break into two categories. About half of them had the symbol *DD* beside them, which, Stubbs explained, meant "checks." (How you get *DD* out of *checks* and *DR* out of *withdrawals* was something I decided I didn't really want to know.) The figures under *DD* were in amounts from a few hundred up to a couple of thousand dollars.

Then there were the entries with an *MD*. Those, I gathered, meant "Money Depot." Every one of those entries was for $300, as far as I could tell, and there were lots of them—six or eight a week. And I began to notice another pattern: they came in pairs. That is, any day there was an *MD*, there were always two. Never one, never three.

Stubbs spun his chair back around to his desk, a sheen of perspiration on his face.

"This isn't right," he muttered. He sat for a minute biting his lip, staring at nothing. Suddenly he grabbed the phone and jerkily punched in a number. He drummed his fingers on the desk and threw me a glance.

"I'm getting Operations." Which told me nothing, but at least he hadn't forgotten I was in the room.

"Why are they all three hundred dollars?" I asked. "And always two a day?"

Stubbs nodded, opened his mouth to answer, then abruptly raised a finger. He spoke into the receiver. "Uh, yeah. Lee Stubbs in Commercial Accounts. Joe around?"

Stubbs tilted his head to get my eye, swiveling the receiver so he could speak around it. "Simple, Dave. Our machines are programmed not to give out more than three hundred dollars at a time. And to prevent theft, we don't permit any one account to take money out of a Money Depot more than twice in one day. It looks like this guy—" He put the finger up again, and moved the receiver to his mouth.

"Joe! Look, buddy, can you get me a complete account workup and summary on this account number?" He spun to the screen. "Uh, here we are. Seven, nine, double-oh, four, seven, three. "What? Oh, 'Models for Hire'. . . Yeah, right. Anything else you need besides the account number, Joe? Good. How soon can I have it?. . . Uh, tell you what, Joe. Just call it over, will you? Thanks. Get back to me in the next five minutes and I buy you lunch, okay?. . . Hell yes, you get to pick the place. Thanks a million, Joe."

Stubbs pulled out a handkerchief and wiped his brow. "Hot in here," he informed me. "That was Joe Todd. Good guy. We'll have the account info shortly. Meanwhile, I'll fill you in on what's going on."

I grinned. "I can tell *something*'s going on."

The banker didn't smile back. "Well, I don't know. It may be okay. I *hope* it's okay. Or my ass could be in a sizable sling.

"See, when Sarnoff opened that account, he asked for an ATM card— our 'Depot Ticket,' we call it. So I—"

"Excuse me," I interrupted. "I thought you said you never met the guy."

"Yeah, right, I haven't. All our dealings have been through Sandy— that's Sandra Norville. The office manager at Penniston. Or *was*—till last week.

"Anyway, shortly after the account opened, a year and a half ago, Sandy called and said Models for Hire would be needing cash at odd times—something about the models needing taxi fare or some damn thing. I don't recall. I *do* recall that she assured me it'd be seldom and for small amounts of money. Nothing like *this*!" He waved his hand at the computer like the whole thing was its fault.

"I've never seen *anything* like this. It's got to be a glitch." He wiped his forehead again. It was a lot of forehead to wipe—most of his head, in fact.

"I guess I should have met the guy—Sarnoff. I *told* Sandy to set up a lunch or something, but she never did." His tone implied it was all Sandy's fault. I wished he'd settle on just who the guilty party was. The phone rang. Stubbs grabbed it.

"Stubbs here. Yeah, Joe. Thanks for getting back so quick. . . You got it, buddy." Stubbs pulled a pad toward him, yanked a pen from its ornate holder on his desk. "Fire away, Joe," he said, pen poised over a yellow legal pad. He listened, head bobbing in agreement, for a few seconds. Suddenly he sat up straight, grimaced, and switched the receiver to the other ear.

"Joe, you have got to be *kidding*! One hundred twenty-two thousand dollars coming out of the ATMs in a little over a year? I don't believe it!" Stubbs rolled his eyes at me and continued. "You're telling me that someone took a hundred and a quarter big ones out of the Models for Hire account in greenback dollars, and no one around here knew a bloody thing about it? You have *got* to be kidding!" With plenty of feeling he added a word I'll omit. Joe appeared to have no answer to that. Lee frowned at the floor in silence for a moment before speaking again.

"Okay, tell me which ATMs they were, Joe . . . Uh, hang on." Stubbs glanced at me, muttered, "They used several," and started jotting on the pad.

"Okay, Joe, fire away. Grand Central? Gotcha. Keep going." Stubbs spent the next several seconds taking down locations.

"Okay, Joe," the vice-president said when he'd finished the list. "Get me a memo on it. *Today*, babe. I'll try to get in to see the prez before lunch, and I need to have that when I do . . . What? Yeah, I wish. Keep your fingers crossed. If Tom's in a bad mood, heads are going to roll. Yeah, I'll let you know. Before lunch. Then we can decide where to go for lunch. If we still have jobs."

The banker hung up, shaking his head. He looked at me. "They used eight Money Depots, all in midtown, four on the east side, four on the west side. I've got to get Betty Donovan on the phone. God, I hope she can straighten this out!"

Stubbs somehow managed to get Nancy to put him through. "Betty? How are you? Lee Stubbs."

He explained the situation, using about twice as many words as I felt were needed. He was winding up with, "Anyway, Betty, I was hoping you could help me figure out what's going on. If you could just give me Mr. Sarnoff's phone number—"

The vice-president got well and truly interrupted. For the next two minutes he listened, getting in only two "But—"s and one "But, Betty—." From the redness of his face, I gathered he wasn't getting full and complete cooperation from the new, if temporary, proprietor of Penniston Associates. He finally managed to get in a full sentence.

"All right, Betty. I'm sorry for bothering you in the middle of a meeting. This may not seem very important to you, but to me—" He glanced at me, shrugged and cradled the receiver. "She hung up."

"What's eating her?" I asked.

Stubbs shook his head. "Oh, I guess she was in the middle of a meeting with George McClendon and Laura's parents over at their offices. You knew she was selling the company to McClendon? Well, I guess they're right in the middle of trying to come to terms. She was mad at being interrupted. Plus, I guess the negotiations aren't going so well, and she had a few choice words for me about *my* cutthroat friends—namely McClendon. You see, I'm the guy who introduced them—Betty and Laura—to McClendon."

"So, I take it, we're not getting any help from her in locating Sarnoff?"

"Oh yeah! Sarnoff. I almost forgot. No, she can't help us. Part of that . . ." Stubbs pointed at the phone." . . . was her telling me about him. Says she never met the guy, doesn't know anything about him. Says he was a friend of Laura's. In fact, she's pretty mad at *Laura* right now. Says Laura brought Sarnoff in and he stole them blind." The vice-president shook his head.

I was thinking fast. I was still hitless in my primary goal: locating Steven Sarnoff. But I'd hit a homer—of sorts—in learning about the missing cash. This was looking more and more like a case of embezzlement followed by murder.

We were getting close. I was now convinced that Sarnoff was the key witness, if not the murderer himself. Trouble was, how were we ever going to find him?

25

I DECIDED TO hike home.

A real tribute to my intrepidity because the gods of meteorology had decided that one day of sunshine was enough and were now favoring us with a bit of serious winter right in the middle of November. The wind whistling across the Hudson had been picking up speed ever since leaving Ohio and was finding the steel forests of Manhattan a terrific playground to cavort in. The snow and sub-freezing temperature didn't help matters any.

On second thought, make that *stupidity*, not intrepidity.

I managed to keep my hat for a while by anchoring it to my head with a free hand while the other hand clung to the attaché case. But halfway between Fifty-fifth and Fifty-fourth, on Seventh, I had to do something about the icicle that was forming on the end of my nose. I tugged the hat firmly down to my eyebrows and reached into my pocket for a handkerchief. Seeing its opportunity, a huge gust hit me from behind and got leverage on the hat brim. Before I could jerk my hand back out of my pocket, there went the hat. Several harried fellow-pedestrians helped me watch it bounce and roll across Seventh until a city bus put a sudden end to its short escape to freedom, crushing it flatter than my wallet two weeks before payday.

Those of you that are wondering why I didn't just grab a cab are obviously not from New York. As any New Yorker could tell you, every taxicab in the city disappears the instant the weather takes a turn for the worse.

My reason for walking had been the hope that the exercise would stimulate my brainstem into solving the puzzle of the missing Sarnoff.

145

Forget it. The only workout the brainstem got was monitoring me for signs of incipient hypothermia.

By the time I staggered into the mansion and slammed the door behind me I was convinced I'd never get warm again. Pitching the useless topcoat in the general direction of the hatrack, I headed down the hall to the Bishop's office, trying to stop shivering.

Regan, at his desk, threw me a casual glance over the reading glasses, then a more serious look. He pulled off the specs and stared.

"David, your face is bright red. And your ears! Shouldn't you—?"

I waved it away. "Naw. It's good for me." The words came out a little mushy. "I've decided to try out for the Winter Olympics in kayak-racing. Time trials on the North Slope in three weeks. I think I'm ready."

I was trying to get a comb through my hair as I talked. "One thing about it, for the first time ever, my hair's even messier than yours."

Regan automatically started a hand toward his silvery mop. His lips tightened. "You must be all right. Your persiflage is as puerile as ever. Sit down, if you have anything to report."

I sat down, rubbing my hands together.

"As a matter of fact, I do. We're onto some kind of scam here. What I can't figure out is how to solve it. My brain's coming up empty, mainly because of that damn monsoon out there. I think it's—"

"That is *not* a monsoon, David. Not even metaphorically. A monsoon is . . ."

I'll skip all that. When we eventually got tired of arguing meteorological inconsequentialities, Regan was all business.

"So this Sarnoff, whoever he is, has been withdrawing substantial funds from his bank account every week?"

"Well, *someone* was. In three-hundred-dollar—no, *six*-hundred-dollar—chunks. Every time he did one, he did two." I flipped the three sheets of computerese Stubbs had given me onto the Bishop's desk.

The boss leaned over them, tracing a fingertip quickly over the figures. He looked up, frowning. "This MD notation refers to the cash withdrawals you mentioned?"

"Yeah. From the ATMs the bank has, all over town. I'm surprised you had to ask. I thought a guy of your intelligence—"

I shut up. No point taunting someone who's obviously not listening. Two minutes later Regan looked up again and shoved the papers dismissively across the desk.

"So, David. Cash withdrawn: $122,300; checks paid: $163,140. I presume that amount represents legitimate business expenses. And one other debit, negligible: thirty dollars. This, from an initial $2,000 deposit, and seventeen subsequent deposits—one a month—totaling $281,470. Leaving zero. If the $122,300 cash withdrawn all went to him, Mr. Sarnoff skimmed forty-three percent off the top. Rather substantial profit margin, that."

I stared at him. Stubbs had come up with the same results. Only it had taken him half an hour and he'd needed a desk calculator. The boss was showing off.

"Naw," I said contemptuously, glancing into my notebook. "You're way off. The real figure's 42.967 percent. That's the kind of sloppy thinking that's going to get you in trouble one fine day if you don't start shaping up."

A hint of a smile played over the Bishop's lips. "Thank you for the correction, David. From now on I shall strive to be precise." The smile vanished. "However. Important as precision is, even more important is finding Mr. Sarnoff. Whether he's the murderer or not, we certainly need to talk to him. Any progress in that effort?"

"Not really," I admitted, and proceeded to fill him in on the rest of the morning's happenings. The boss wheeled around the office aimlessly during the final ten minutes of my report, but never stopped paying attention. When I finished, Regan stopped rolling. He sat for a few seconds, eyes closed in concentration.

"How very intriguing. Elusive gentleman, this Sarnoff. One begins to wonder if he even exists."

"Oh, he exists, all right," I assured him. "In fact, I can tell you several important things about him." The Bishop swung to face me, gave me a nod and his full attention.

"First of all, he's smooth. Laura Penniston was no chump, I've learned enough about her to know that, and he tricked her good. That's why she was in such a rage that night with Sandy Norville and Theodore. She said as much.

"Second, Bo knows banking." Regan cocked his head and frowned. "Oh yeah, I always forget how little TV you watch. Never heard of Bo Jackson?" The boss just stared at me.

"Put it this way: Sarnoff knew how Mid-City operates. How would a person go about finagling over a hundred grand in untraceable funds out of a bank? I've been around the horn a time or two, and I couldn't have told you that. Till now. Turns out it's a piece of cake: you get an ATM card and pull the money out a little at a time. Of course you end up with a huge pile of double-sawbucks, but there are worse problems.

"Mid-City's in a real snit over it. Stubbs is meeting with their in-house attorney right now: do they have enough evidence that a crime's been committed to notify the FBI? They think they do, but they want to discuss it with Betty Donovan and her lawyers first.

"Way it looks, Sarnoff knew Mid-City didn't permit over three hundred dollars per single withdrawal, nor more than two withdrawals a day. So six hundred bucks is the max you can take out of the machines in any one day. And every day the account had enough in it, that's what he took.

"But—" I raised a finger "—he never let the account get below two thousand dollars. Close, but never below. Seems he knew that Mid-City had a policy of contacting its commercial customers any time they let their accounts get below that. So he made sure he stayed above it. At least, till he was ready to make his getaway. Last week, for the first time, he ran the account down and finally zeroed it out with a final withdrawal of two hundred twenty dollars. Causing the account to automatically close."

Regan was back behind his desk, eyes closed. He tugged abstractedly at the silver chain around his neck. Hanging from that was the crucifix the Pope sent him after the shooting. (Regan's proud of that gift. He once showed me the note that came with it, handwritten in English by JP II himself: "We now have *much* in common, you and I.")

"You've obviously given this some thought, David," Regan murmured. "Please go on. What else have you deduced about Mr. Sarnoff?"

I gave him a suspicious look. He was either making fun of my puny ideas or handing out some rare praise. Hard to tell. I decided to give him the benefit of the doubt.

"Thank you. Point three. Despite his being so close to Laura Penniston, I haven't been able to find a single friend or associate of hers who ever met the guy. So he knows how to cover his tracks.

"One final point. He needed money, fast and bad. He put plenty of time and effort into planning this scam. And once he had it in place, he jerked the money out as fast as he could—but never too fast. So he's extremely patient. He had a great scam going, but played it very cool. Not a single slip-up with the account in the entire year-and-a-half it was open. This guy makes ice water look lukewarm."

I flicked a hand in a gesture of modesty. "And that's what I deduce about Steven Sarnoff."

The Bishop, now over by the windows, had spun around and moved toward me.

"I applaud you, David. Very good. I don't suppose you'd object to my adding a point of my own? Along with a refinement?"

"Be my guest. All I ask is for you to remember where credit is due, if any of that leads to Sarnoff."

Regan smiled. "But of course. I simply want to add a peripheral point or two to the very descriptive—and, I think, accurate—picture you've drawn. I would suggest the following for an appendix: Mr. Sarnoff has at least one other name. Which he uses as and when needed."

I stared. "I don't see where you come up with that. There's been no indication of any alias."

"Not explicitly, no. But there are sufficient hints to suggest it. Consider, David. As you pointed out, not a single one of Miss Penniston's associates—at least none you've been able to reach—has ever met Mr. Sarnoff. Query: how could Miss Penniston have been close enough to the man to trust him as fully as you correctly say she must have, without any of her friends meeting or seeing him? Probable answer: they have indeed met him. But not under the name Sarnoff.

"I would offer considerable odds, were I a betting man, that at least one of the people you've interviewed has met, or at least spoken with, Mr. Sarnoff. Perhaps unawares.

"Put yourself in his position. He had cash to dispose of. You spoke of his plethora of twenty-dollar bills, saying that there are worse problems. No doubt. Nonetheless, I find it hard to believe that the man simply hid one hundred twenty thousand dollars in cash under his mattress. No. He must have had means of depositing it quickly, conveniently and undetectably. Without a pseudonym, that would have been impracticable to the point of impossibility.

"So I think we may safely conjecture that the man is operating under two names. In fact—" The door chime interrupted. I looked at Regan. "Go ahead and see who it is," he muttered, reaching for a book on his desk. "We'll resume this later."

It was Ida Mae with a friend. As I came down the hall Ida gave me a small wave through the glass, but no smile. Her companion was a young black man about her age and height in a black leather jacket.

Hands buried in the pockets of his jeans, he shifted weight from side to side in his unlaced Michael Jordan high-tops.

I opened the door. The guy flicked me a quick glance and looked away.

"Mr. Goldman!" Ida Mae exclaimed. "You got to help us! Jerry's in trouble!"

—26—

WONDERING HOW THINGS could have gotten any worse for Jerry than they already were, I hustled the two visitors in and closed the weather out.

"This here's Henry Justice," Ida said as I took her coat and hung it up.

I turned to her friend, extending my hand. His jacket was already off and he awkwardly shifted it to his left hand as he gave me his right. He looked away while we shook; his grip was reluctant. Several things about him suggested he'd spent some time in jail; the odor of disinfectant he gave off told me the time had been recent.

"Welcome, Mr. Justice," I said, taking his coat and hanging it from the hatrack next to Ida's. "I guess you're a friend of Mr. and Mrs. Fanning?"

Henry looked at Ida Mae. I briefly wondered if the kid was mute. The girl nodded encouragement and he turned back to me.

"Yessir. Mist' Fanning, he brung me to the Lord. And he ast me to come see his missus when I got out this morning. I had to tell her what's gone on with Mist' Fanning in there. And it ain't good."

Ida Mae started to add something, but I cut her off. "Come with me," I said to both of them. "I think the Bishop will want to hear this." Regan looked up over his glasses as we came into the office.

"Mrs. Fanning," he said, his tone friendly but businesslike. "Come in. Sit down, please. What can we do for you?"

She opened her mouth again and I interrupted her again. "This is Henry Justice, Bishop, a friend of the Fannings. And I believe he's got some news about Jerry. Bad, I'm afraid. Right, sir?"

While talking, I was pulling up chairs for the visitors. The Bishop, meanwhile, was putting his book back on his desk and maneuvering into position to listen and converse. Amazing how having a friend in trouble can improve your hospitality.

Neither of the guests seemed to want to use the chairs I offered them. They finally did, Ida with her knees together, dress primly pulled down; Henry with his feet splayed apart. Neither sat back; both looked uncomfortable and declined my offer of drinks.

Regan tried waiting for someone to begin, but had to give up on that. Henry seemed preoccupied with his Nikes; Ida fidgeted, opened her mouth, closed it, glanced appealingly at me. I opened my mouth but Regan decided to go ahead and lead the discussion himself.

"So, Mrs. Fanning. Your husband is in need of help of a new kind?" Ida met his gaze for a moment, then looked away.

"I'm sorry to be bustin' in on you like this, Bishop, but I don't rightly know where else to turn." She looked at the black youth. "Tell him, Henry."

Justice screwed up his courage and met her eye, shifting in his seat uneasily. "Tell him," she repeated. Henry, looking at the floor again, shook his head stubbornly.

"He come to see me this morning, when he got out of jail, Bishop," Ida said. "Jerry's—" Her voice caught. "He's in trouble, Bishop. Please tell him what happened, Henry. Please!" The kid glanced at her, then finally gave the Bishop more than a second's worth of eye contact.

"Mist' Fanning, he in big trouble, sir," he said, and stopped to clear his throat. "He in trouble with a couple them bad-asses in the joint. They beat him up yest'dy. Hurt him pretty bad, too, I think."

"There was a fight?" I asked. Henry didn't look at me. He smiled a sad little smile at the floor.

"No sir, it wasn't no fight. Michael and Calvin, they just stomped him."

"Who are Michael and Calvin?" the Bishop asked softly. "And what, if any, was their complaint against Mr. Fanning?"

"Like I say, they two bad-asses in the joint. Michael Habbaz and

Calvin X. They Muslims, you know? And they don't like Mist' Fanning talkin' so much 'bout Jesus, know what I mean? Mist' Fanning, he turn my life around. My momma, she always try to get me to accept Jesus, but I never did. I quit school four years ago, started shootin' up and gangbangin', you know?" Henry's voice was muffled.

"I knew Michael before; we hung out together, you know? He's the one give me my name: Pee Wee. And Calvin got to be friends with Michael in the joint." Justice took a breath and looked Regan straight in the eye for the first time. "Guess it's my fault Mist' Fanning got hurt. Soon as he started telling me 'bout Jesus, it was like I was a new man, just like he said I would be. And he told me I just had to spread the word, you know?

"So I went to Michael. I wanted the Lord to touch him, way He touched me, you know? Only He didn't touch Michael a-tall. Michael, he big, you know? Michael grab me and slap me up side the head, say, 'You dumb nigger, you don't know no better'n to listen to some jive honky tellin' you all about Whitey's God?' He got with Calvin and they was both plenty mad. I laid low after that, but they both knew I'd gone over.

"Michael and me, we're blood, you know? So Michael, he ain't gone hurt me none. But he and Calvin, they went after Jerry—Mist' Fanning." Henry swallowed. "They waited for dinnertime yest'dy, then they got him right outside the mess hall. Calvin, he started messin' with him, gettin' in his face, you know? And Mist' Fanning, he finally swung at Calvin. And then the two just whupped Mist' Fanning good, knock him down and stomp on him."

Henry looked at Regan as though he expected some questions, but Regan just waited. "Guards, they was right there, so didn't last long. And Calvin just got his blade con-fiscated, so Mist' Fanning, he didn't get cut none. But they hurt him good anyway, you know? Mist' Fanning had to go to the infirmary. And he's not walkin' so good today. All humped over like it hurt him, you know?"

Justice took a breath and looked at Ida Mae but she was focused on Regan.

"That's why we come to you, Bishop," she said. "I hate to ask it, but can you do anything? Anything at all?" She looked at me and asked me the same question with her eyes.

Regan's eyes were closed and he was rubbing his face wearily. Everyone waited for him to respond. He finally did.

"You say you saw Mr. Fanning this morning, Mr. Justice?"

"Yes sir," Henry said softly. "Saw him at breakfast. He come in, walkin' real slow and humped over, you know? But soon's he gets there, he starts talkin' to one of the brothers, tellin' him about Jesus, same as he first talked to me, you know? And Michael and Calvin were there, too, just starin' at him real mean-like. But he just stared back." Justice shook his head admiringly. "That man ain't 'fraid of nothin' or nobody." He frowned.

"Onliest thing is, Calvin say he gone to find him another blade and off the dude, you know? That's why I come to Miz Fanning. Mist' Fanning, he need some help, and he aint gone to help hisself none, no way."

Justice shut up, looked at Regan for a moment, then resumed the study of his Nikes. Regan gave him a long look, then turned to Ida Mae. She met his gaze squarely.

"I'm sorry, Mrs. Fanning," he said. "I'm not sure there is much that Mr. Goldman or I can do. But we'll try." He frowned in concentration for a moment. "I should tell you something. Your husband is innocent. Mr. Goldman, through certain investigations he has done, has established that." Ida looked at me and started to speak, but the Bishop cut her off. "Unfortunately, our information is privileged, and we can share it neither with the police nor with you. Consequently, our ability to use it is limited. For the moment." He ran his fingers through his hair, for him a sign of desperation.

"Mr. Goldman and I need to discuss matters. Since it now seems that your husband's life is in jeopardy, it may be that we should take bolder steps to get him released. So—if you have nothing further . . . ?"

I saw Ida Mae and Henry out. She turned to me while putting on her coat and started to say something but changed her mind and looked away. I promised her I'd call, and wished Henry good luck.

Back in Regan's office, I followed up on his closing remark to Ida.

"So what about it? You sending me down to the jail to talk Fanning into releasing us from that vow of silence?"

"Vow of silence," he muttered, shaking his head. "It's really too bad you're not Catholic, David. Your multifaceted misunderstanding of theological terminology would qualify you to enter the seminary of your choice. But—yes, I would like you to go to the jail and speak to Mr. Fanning." He looked at his watch.

"You'll have to skip lunch. Or rush it. Regrettable, but can't be helped. Under the circumstances. Why should we waste time and energy proving him innocent, if he is going to use equivalent time and energy getting himself killed?" He sighed. "We must get him out of there. Talk to him, David. Tell him if he releases me from the seal—which is *not* a vow, by the way—I'll do my best to set things right with his wife. Tell him—"

Regan grimaced, put his head back and looked at the ceiling. His eyes closed tighter and tighter. I began to wonder if he was having a heart attack and was halfway to my feet, when his eyes suddenly popped open and he gave as deep a sigh as I've ever heard from him. "I must go," he groaned.

I was amazed. "Are you sure you want to, Bishop? I—"

"No!" he snapped. "I'm quite certain I *don't*." He groaned again. "Make arrangements, David. We'll go immediately after lunch."

—27—

SURE. "MAKE ARRANGEMENTS." Easy for him to say. He ought to try making them sometime.

Getting Fred at the garage to bring the car around was duck soup, due purely to the dumb luck of him having a slow day. But arrangements at the jail were a different matter. Fran Wilson being unavailable, it took Davis L. Baker, famous attorney-at-law, to get it done.

Not that Regan cared. He just expects things to happen, and they usually do. One of these days I'm going to quit for longer than a day, and he'll find out what it's *really* like to fend with the cruel world on his own.

The Bishop was too glum to enjoy Sister's elaborately prepared lunch. He'd just come down from changing clothes, replacing the purple robe and beanie with his clerical black suit. That's got to be part of his aversion to going anywhere: for a paraplegic, changing clothes is not the simple affair it is for you and me. And, naturally, he won't let me help.

The weather he had to go out into wasn't calculated to make him feel any better. I checked it from the south window while he changed. The sleety snow had switched to sleety rain and the wind had, if anything, gained in intensity. While I was looking out, a sizable garbage can came rattling down the courtway from the west, bouncing off fences and dribbling contents as it made its way for Tenth Avenue.

I had my own problem with Ernie's lunch, for a totally different reason.

My mother made the mistake, years ago, of sharing a few of her Jewish recipes with her friend, Sister Ernestine. Ernie—who with her gentile dishes is not a bad cook at all—uses my mom's recipes all the time and not one tastes the way it should. Maybe you have to be Jewish, I don't know.

To the "Shabbat stew" Ernie served that day, I added about a quarter pound of salt and pepper, thus rendering it close to edible. Ketchup would have helped even more, but that would have hurt Ernie's feelings. Sister beamed at seeing me eat and I tried to smile back.

Fred brought the car around at 12:50, and I got the Bishop down the steps, him keeping his hat in place with both hands. Going crosstown, I began to see the wisdom of having walked home that morning. Horrible as the weather was, at least walking you could make *some* headway. Half the population of Manhattan had obviously decided to drive around town and watch all the unattached flotsam and jetsam blow around. We did well just to be twelve minutes late for our 1:00 P.M. appointment.

Jerry didn't look as bad as I'd feared. I've seen a few victims of battery in my day, and Jerry looked no different than most. Below his eye was a black-and-blue lump, and his puffed-up lower lip made him even harder to understand than usual. But his eyes were defiant and unafraid. Saturday, he'd been a man with a mission. Today he was a man who's seen his mission start to succeed.

Regan opened the conversation, operating the button on the phone like he'd done it all his life.

"I'm sorry about your condition, Mr. Fanning. What can we do?"

Fanning tried to smile, winced, and straightened his lips. But the smile stayed in his eyes. "Thankth for coming, Bithop," he lisped around the puffy lip. "You shouldn't ha' bothered."

"Nonsense!" Regan answered briskly. "My pleasure." Pleasure. I didn't dare look at him. Fanning flipped me a wink. He didn't believe him either. Regan got down to business.

"Mr. Fanning. We have just spoken with Mr. Henry Justice, whom I believe you know. Your wife brought him to us." Jerry nodded. Regan took a breath.

"He told us of your altercation yesterday with those two inmates. He also told us that he regards it as probable that you will be attacked again—more severely attacked. It is important that you leave here. Today." Jerry scowled and looked away. The Bishop waited. Jerry finally faced Regan again. Holding his eye, the Bishop pleaded.

"Jerry. We have now established independent verification of your presence at that theater on those four evenings. If the police knew that, you would be exculpated and released from here immediately. So I am now asking you, I am begging you, to tell them about that—"

"Nossir," Fanning said into the instrument. His voice sounded thin and distorted. He smiled with the uninjured half of his mouth and shook his head at the Bishop. "That's no good. Let me tell you what's going on."

Regan nodded abruptly, pressing the receiver tightly against his ear.

"See, I got some of these ol' boys listenin' to the message, don't y'see, Bishop?" The fundie's face was animated, his voice lively in spite of the lisp. "It's the first time since I got to this here misbegotten city that anyone's taken me serious. They're *really* listenin', Bishop. And they want to know what the Lord's saying to them. Course, Satan don't want none of that, and he provoked those two to do what they did.

"But the Lord turned the tables on Satan. I could see the expressions on some of the other guys' faces. Bishop, they were looking at me like I was *somebody*."

Fanning looked at the far wall and blinked a couple of times. He glanced at me, immediately looked away and went on, avoiding both our eyes.

"I just *can't* tell the police—or anybody else—about my sinnin', Bishop." He snuck another glance at me, presumably for signs of any reaction on my part. "It'd just tear up everything I'm starting to accomplish in here. Don't you see?" He gave Regan a look of appeal.

I tapped on the glass. Jerry turned his face to me, and I noticed how bloodshot his left eye was—the one with the lump under it. I tried a grin and my most persuasive voice.

"Come on, Jerry, give yourself a break, man. Sleaze is a part of life and no one's going to blame you for spending a couple of hours in a sleaze parlor. It's no big deal."

Fanning obviously didn't agree. He blushed, shook his head and turned away. I shrugged and gave the boss a glance. He ignored me and kept after Jerry hard. For fifteen minutes he launched every attack he could think of on Jerry's position, but got no further with that than he had two weeks before when he'd tried to stick holes in fundamentalism.

Regan finally threw up a hand.

"All right, Mr. Fanning," he growled. "I understand your position, but you're making a big mistake. I have to tell you, when I came down here, I had resolved, if you refused to let us go to the police with the truth, that I was going to leave you to your fate. You're not being fair to yourself, your wife, your child—and certainly not to God."

Regan shot me a sidelong glance. "But we will continue. For now." He glared at Jerry.

Jerry started to answer, but Regan cut him off. "Just remember, if you change your mind, tell Mr. Baker to get in touch with Mr. Goldman immediately. We will get you out."

"Thanks," Jerry answered calmly. "I'm sorry you don't agree, but at least you see what I'm trying to do here. If you could just see the looks on these fellows' faces when they hear about what the Lord wants to do for them! I tell you, Bishop, it's—"

"Please, Mr. Fanning," Regan said wearily. "Don't, I beg you, waste your time and mine trying to justify your recalcitrance. Let us know when you've had enough of this place." Without a look at Jerry or me he spun his chair around and pushed for the door. I gave Jerry a quick glance over my shoulder as I hustled to open the door for the Bishop before he tried to ram it. Jerry gave me a goodbye wink.

—28—

BACK HOME, Regan went up to his room to change into his robes. And I found a note on my desk, Ernie telling me to call Cheryl. Turned out Cheryl'd had a visitor while the Bishop and I were visiting the jail.

"A Betty Donovan came busting in here an hour ago, Davey. Thinks she's the Queen of Sheba or something. Demanded to know where you were, how she could get hold of you. I don't think she likes you too well."

"Hey, women have all kinds of different ways of showing affection, Cheryl. Take you. If I didn't know how much you cared, I'd sometimes think you—"

"Will you get *serious*, Davey? I'm telling you, this gal is steaming! She's ready to go to the police. Says you pulled a scam on her and some other people. And Davey, she *knows* you represent Fanning; she says you tried to hide that from her. I mean she's mad, Davey, and I really think she might go to the cops."

I took a minute to calm Cheryl down a little.

"So I did right in *not* giving her your home address?" she asked anxiously.

"Oh, yeah," I grinned. "You got that right. I want her popping up on my doorstep about like I want a second head. But if she calls again—or comes by—try to reach me. I'd like to talk to her."

"Yeah, well, she sure wants to talk to you, pal, I can tell you that. I've got a feeling she'll be back."

Which didn't bother me as much as Cheryl thought it should. Because I had a few questions of my own for Miss Donovan. In fact, I had a lot more questions than Betty could answer.

I decided to go to the Answer Man. Rozanski was available, but not to talk. At least not for more than thirty seconds.

"Yeah, yeah, Davey, I'd love to talk to you, but we're going nuts down here. Got anything that's absolutely got to go in this afternoon's paper?" Chet paused, but not long enough for me to say anything.

"Obviously not," he rushed on, after about a second. "If you can't think of it any faster than that, it can wait for tomorrow. See ya."

"Hold it!" I roared. He grunted impatiently but didn't hang up—yet. I talked fast.

"I've got something hot for you on the Strangler John case. But it'll wait . . ." Chet started to interrupt, but I rode over him. "Hold it, Chet! It's no good for today. For now, I need to ask you one question. How much have you got on those five people we discussed yesterday—Donovan, Theodore, McClendon, Stubbs and the lovely Miss Norville— that you haven't already given me?"

Chet sighed loudly. "You never quit, do you, Davey?" He took a deep breath. "I've really got to go, man. But yeah, I might have a couple of facts and figures beyond what I told you about, yesterday."

"Good. I thought so. Stop by after work tonight and I'll give *you* a few facts and figures *you* haven't got. Some of it off the record for now, but all of it good. And you'd better bring something of your own, or you get nothing."

Rozanski sounded bored. "What's up? You trying to build a case that one of *them's* Strangler John?"

"Nope. Not Strangler John. But one of them knows him. I just don't know which one. And you can take that to the bank."

Chet suddenly decided he had more time than he thought. He started pumping. But when he saw he'd get nothing till I had what he had, he subsided. Not without an insult or two.

"All right, you sandbagging piece of horse manure. You've got me interested, I'll give you that. I'll be by at eight o'clock with everything I've got. But you better *have* something."

Ten minutes later, I joined Regan in his office to see if we could brainstorm up any more ideas for finding Sarnoff. This gave us half an hour, it being 2:30, since his schedule—in this case, writing from 3:00 P.M. to 6:00 P.M., daily—takes precedence over everything.

The Bishop's face was lined from fatigue. The case was getting to him. He sipped coffee Ernie'd brought, presumably trying to wake up his brain cells.

"So, David," he began, frowning at his cup. "Any ideas?"

"Ideas? Yeah, two. One, our client won't help himself. Two, there's a murderer out there we don't have a clue how to find."

"Ah! Not so fast. Your portrait of Sarnoff this morning was very illuminating. Nicely done. Let's consider some possibilities."

Regan took another sip, put the coffee on his desk and headed for the windows. He looked out, probably checking to see if there was anything left in the courtway that hadn't blown away. He couldn't have done a complete inventory, because he spun to face me after only a couple of seconds.

"When Mrs. Fanning interrupted us this morning," the boss said, "I was putting a few finishing touches on that portrait of Mr. Sarnoff you drew. Since then I have come up with a further idea to explore, after which we can discuss optimal deployment of the little information we have. I agree with your assessment that Sarnoff is the key.

"I suggest a modification of your first point—namely, that Sarnoff is very astute, as evidenced by his ability to trick Miss Penniston. I suggest that he is not only astute, he had an accomplice in his depradations. It strikes me as unlikely that he could have carried out the scheme he did without inside assistance."

I thought about it. "Yeah," I said, nodding. "Yeah, that could be. That could explain how he was able to pull it off so smoothly for so long."

Regan nodded. "Then, when Miss Penniston suspected something, he killed her. And in such an elaborate and contrived way that no one would suspect she was other than one of the victims of a psychopathic serial killer."

"Yep," I said. "Now all we've got to do is find him."

Regan grimaced. "Which has proved devilishly difficult. But if my theory of an inside accomplice is correct, pinpointing the accomplice may be equally productive and a great deal more easily done.

"We need to formulate a plan, David, though at the moment I'm stumped. Too many missing pieces in the puzzle."

So we worked and plotted and devised and, frankly, got nowhere. Regan went from snappish to friendly and back to snappish again. At five minutes to three, no closer to a program than ever, he was at his snappishest.

"David, if you don't like my program, I assume it's because you have a superior one. All right. Let's hear it."

"I didn't say I had a better one. I'm just saying going back over old ground isn't getting us anywhere. Why don't—"

"We're *not* going over old ground. I have in mind—"

The doorbell interrupted. I took three steps down the hall, saw who it was, and came back into the office on the gallop.

"Looks like company. And very interesting company, at that. George McClendon, for openers. And Betty Donovan. And a couple who, I strongly suspect, are Mr. and Mrs. Penniston. Laura's parents."

Regan looked at me and glanced at the clock on the wall. One minute to three, the start of his sacrosanct three hours at the word processor.

"Oh, don't worry," I assured him. "I'm sure it's me they're after. I can squeeze them into my office. Or take them into the dining room."

The Bishop glanced back at the clock to see if it had changed its mind any. He shook his head and tightened his lips.

"No," he sighed. "Bring them in here. It's a day for breaking precedent. We'll need both our brains if we're to solve our conundrum. And this has all the earmarks of an unprecedented opportunity."

I was delighted—and amazed—but didn't let it show. "What if they don't want to see you? As I said, they're probably here to see me."

"Don't offer them the choice, David," he said testily. "Just bring them in."

I shrugged and headed for the door as it chimed again. And again. And again. Good. They were revved up and ready to talk. Well, we were ready to listen. To anything.

—29—

"WELCOME! DON'T STAND THERE shivering! Come in!"

My cheery greeting was not what they were expecting. Donovan, in stylishly matched royal blue topcoat-and-hat combination, was in the lead. It was obvious they'd picked her for their spokesperson.

She flounced past me through the door, if someone that size can be said to flounce. Without waiting for me to help, she whipped off hat and coat and hung them on the rack. Her dishwater eyes gave the foyer a thorough going-over.

Following her was the woman I was guessing was Laura's mother. I introduced myself (Betty being in no mood to do the honors), and had the guess confirmed. Nearly my height, even in medium heels, she was a pleasant-enough-looking woman, but it was obvious that, whatever her daughter had inherited from her, it hadn't been her taste in clothes.

Not only was the cloth coat she wore too light for the weather, it was hopelessly out of style for anywhere. And when *I* can recognize something's out of style, well, it's been out for a while. The dress under it, I noticed as I hung her coat up, was no improvement. Though the figure it covered could have been a model's figure. Sandy's description, "no bust, no hips, tiny waist" came to mind. The woman also carried herself well. Most women that tall tend to stoop. This one kept her neck extended and her chin up, looking down regally on all she surveyed.

I also had to introduce myself to the husband, who was a good six inches shorter than his wife. He was the kind of bouncy, chubby little guy that no one ever takes seriously. His horn-rimmed specs made his eyes look big, round and inquiring. His wife had coolly introduced herself as Mrs. Penniston, but he was at pains to get us on a first-name basis.

"I'm Roger Penniston, uh, is it David? Pleasure to meet you, David.

162

And this is Maureen." Roger was the type who beamed a lot. And seemed to mean it.

McClendon was willing to shake my hand. I thought I even detected a twinkle in his eye behind the beard, though he said nothing.

When all the coats and hats had been deposited on the rack, I allowed the small silence to grow. Before I said anything, I wanted to hear what they'd come for. Betty broke the ice—no surprise there.

"I suppose you didn't think we'd find you," she said in a gloating tone, smoothing down the front of her jacket. "That hen over there on Broadway tried to give me a hard time. Said you'd call me. Sure you will." Mr. and Mrs. Penniston had the grace to look embarrassed. McClendon, behind the beard, was unreadable.

"Yeah," I answered. "I guess I'm a little surprised. Maybe someday you'll tell me how you did it. I'm always looking for new detective tricks. But in the meantime, what can I do for you? Any of you?"

Roger opened his mouth to answer but Betty cut him off. She was the spokesperson and wasn't giving it up to any Johnny-come-lately.

"Lieutenant Blake—your former boss—gave us your address. He told us what you're *really* up to. Which has nothing to do with Sandra Norville's back pay, by the way." She sneered at me and gave me a chance to defend myself, but I just waited. Seeing I wasn't going to respond, she glanced at her companions and continued. "We're here to find out why you're trying to free the man who killed Laura. Mr. and Mrs. Penniston have a special right to ask, but George and I deserve to hear your answer, too. So—"

"Please," I interrupted her. It was time to bring Regan into the discussion. Or, rather, vice versa. "I think my partner in crime should hear this. Through that door, please." I extended my arm down the hallway.

I wasn't sure whether Regan was simply pondering what he was going to say, or just being dramatic. As the four entered the office, they were treated to the sight of a brooding presence at the window. Hunched over in his wheelchair, looking down on the alley, in purple robe and skullcap, he looked like something out of a medieval morality play. I heard a gasp from someone, I think Maureen.

"Bishop Regan," I called to him across the room. He spun the wheelchair to face us, face unreadable in the glare of the window behind him. "May I present our visitors?"

He nodded, and pushed off in our direction, circling his desk and pressing the flesh with all four as I pronounced names. Even the redoubtable Betty seemed in awe. Momentarily.

Regan was gracious. "Please, sit down and be comfortable. Not a pleasant day to be out and about. Anything to drink? Ah, Sister Ernestine!"

I'd heard him ring for Ernie while I was in the foyer, and here she was in the doorway. As the visitors mumbled polite negatives to Regan's offer, Ernie spoke up.

"I have some milk on, ladies and gentlemen. May I bring everyone some hot chocolate?" After a brief hesitation the vote was unanimous, in favor. Including Regan and me. Sister beamed.

The Bishop, now behind his desk, studied the visitors fanned out before him on chairs I'd hastily assembled from around the room. I'd had to get one from the dining room for me. I put it over close to my office door where I could keep the whole room in view. Having their undivided attention, the Bishop spoke.

"Before you tell me why you came, let me offer you my condolences on the loss of your daughter, friend, business associate. Especially you, Mr. and Mrs. Penniston. It's not an easy thing to bury one's offspring." Both parents' heads bobbed as one, and the wife spoke up.

"Thank you, Your Excellency. We appreciate it." Regan winced slightly at the "Your Excellency." He can't abide that title, even if it is technically correct. He was opening his mouth to respond when ever-ready Betty butted in.

"Thanks for the sympathy, but we're all here to register a complaint and make a demand. Lieutenant Blake has told us all about you—and your man. So maybe you ought to hold your pieties till you hear what we've come to say."

If Betty wanted to get under the Bishop's skin, she'd succeeded. He tightened his lips and flicked her a sideward glance. "Of course, Madame. I didn't realize I was mouthing pieties. By all means, register your complaints. Make your demands. If we are able, Mr. Goldman and I will remedy the situations complained of and comply with your demands."

Donovan's own lips tightened. "I'll bet," she snapped. "I'll just bet you'll comply. But okay, here's the complaint. This individual—" She flicked her thumb in my direction "—came charging into our office yesterday—"

"And hoodwinked two of you. I know what he did, Madame. I've heard it from his own lips. Is that your complaint?" The Bishop has a knack of cutting people off without offending them. I wish I knew how he did it. But Betty wasn't ready to give up the floor.

"That's one of my complaints. Not the only one." She suddenly leaned over, picked up her suede purse off the floor and placed it in her lap. Her eyes found the Bishop's. "I see there's no ashtrays. Does that mean I can't smoke?"

"It does, indeed, Madame. I'm sorry not to be able to accommodate you. The more expeditiously we proceed, the more speedily can you leave this tobacco-free zone."

Betty put her purse back on the floor with an angry flourish. "You people . . ." she muttered, then got loud again. "All right. We'll hurry." She turned to her right. "Roger? Want to tell him what Lieutenant Blake said this morning?"

Mr. Penniston blushed. He looked, blinking, from the Bishop to me and back to the Bishop.

"Er, yes," he said. "We saw—"

"Excuse me," came Ernie's soft voice from the doorway. She'd arrived with six big mugs of hot chocolate and a plate of homemade chocolate chip cookies. Each mug had a sizable dollop of whipped cream on top, which struck me as a bit excessive. I jumped up and helped Ernestine distribute the goodies. As she left, all eyes returned to Roger and he looked more uncomfortable than ever. He turned to his wife, sitting to his immediate right.

"Uh, why don't you tell it, dear?" Maureen glanced at her husband and took in Regan. She put down her mug and took a deep breath.

"Yes, all right. My husband, Your Excellency, doesn't—"

"Please, Madame." The Bishop can't take two of those in one sitting. "I dislike that honorific. I pray you, call me Father, call me Mister, call me anything. But please don't call me Your Excellency."

She shrugged. "What then? I'm certainly not going to call you Mister!" Regan shrugged back. "'Bishop' is most acceptable."

"Fine." Maureen was happy to have the whole thing settled. "In any case, Bishop, we went to see Inspector Kessler this morning to find out how the police are progressing on the murder of our daughter. You can imagine how we feel, living a thousand miles away, not knowing what's going on. We saw in the Wichita Eagle that the killer—the alleged killer—had been jailed, and was being held.

"Of course, nothing's going to bring our daughter back, but knowing that the man who did it is in custody has helped us a little. I'm sure the mothers of those three other girls must feel the same way. Anyway, we met briefly with the Inspector, and he referred us to Lieutenant Blake. Mr. Kessler told us the lieutenant is responsible for the case and that, furthermore, it was his brilliant questioning of one of the witnesses that destroyed this Fanning's alibi once and for all and made it definite that he's the murderer."

Maureen reached out her hand and Roger took it. I wouldn't have thought she needed any support, the way she sounded—firm and steady. She continued and, sure enough, her voice did begin to crack a little.

"Well, Bishop, just imagine how we feel. Laura came to this big city. For eight years Roger and I worried about her—and she was just fine! Then this monster has to come all the way here from Oklahoma and murder our little girl. I just—" Maureen stopped. Tears began. But she didn't avert her gaze from the Bishop's face, nor look for a hanky, nor let go of Roger's hand. Just sat there, proudly, weeping, looking at the Bishop.

"Some tissues, Madame?" Regan said. "No? As you wish." He waited for her to get herself together. "Madame. You—and the police—are under a misapprehension. The misapprehension that Mr. Fanning murdered your daughter and those other three women. He did not. I can—" I don't suppose Regan was surprised at the interruption. So he remained placid when McClendon jumped in, beard atremble, reedy voice even more high-pitched than normally.

"You have got to be a maniac, sir! Roger and Maureen told us all the evidence the police have. We even know about some that hasn't even been released to the general public." He glanced to his left. "Okay, to tell him, Roger?"

Penniston nodded solemnly, still holding his wife's hand.

"I don't see why not," Roger said. "After all, the man's a Bishop." He blinked at Regan good-naturedly. The Bishop just glanced at him and answered McClendon.

"You're wasting your breath, sir. You were, I presume, going to reveal that Mr. Fanning is known to have left his residence at around midnight on the night of all four murders and returned home after the murders were committed. And that he lied to the police about those sojourns, claiming he was home in bed when, in fact, he was not. Yes?"

McClendon was thunderstruck. "But if you knew that—"

Mrs. Penniston interrupted imperiously. "Please, Mr. McClendon, allow me." She released her husband's hand and lifted her jaw higher than before. Her eyes burned into the Bishop's. He didn't flinch.

"Yes, Bishop," she said. "If you knew that—if you *know* that—why do you go on working for that—monster? Lieutenant Blake told us that you and Mr. Goldman and some lawyer named Baker are doing everything in your power to interfere with the police investigation and get this Fanning back out on the streets so he can murder again." Her voice rose for the first time.

"That's the man who killed our daughter, Bishop, and we want him put away. *Why* are you doing this? *Why* are you protecting him? *Why?*"

Maureen reached into the purse on her lap, pulled out some tissues and blew her nose. Everyone in the room was looking at her and she knew it, but she wasn't meeting anyone's eye. Just sitting there, straight and proud.

The Bishop's response was soft. "Madame. The police have been unusually forthright with you. As parents of one of the victims, I think you were entitled to that. I'll try to be equally so, though I'm at the disadvantage of having to safeguard a professional confidence.

"I said before, Mr. Fanning murdered no one. I'm not at liberty to divulge the full story, but you can trust us, Mr. Goldman and I know his whereabouts during the time of every single murder. Our knowledge is based on Mr. Goldman's interview with an unimpeachable witness. Mr. Fanning could *not* have murderered your daughter.

"I have no animus toward the police. It is not their fault that Mr. Goldman and I happen to be privy to this information and they are not. They have every reason to believe they have the right man. But they don't. And in the fullness of time they will realize it. Only then will they start looking for the real killer. Which is what Mr. Goldman is attempting to do now. With some help from me." Regan leaned forward and turned up the palms of both hands.

"Mr. and Mrs. Penniston. You have no quarrel with me. Or with Mr. Fanning. He didn't travel here a thousand miles with his wife and baby to commit murder. He came attempting—perhaps not always wisely or too well, but sincerely—to convert people to Jesus Christ.

"That he is behind bars is his misfortune and the murderer's good fortune. In a real, if limited, sense he has something in common with your daughter. He is also the murderer's victim. Mr. Goldman and I have a twofold mission: to free an innocent man and to put the guilty one away. Your interests and ours are, for all practical purposes, identical."

From where I was sitting I could observe all four of our guests. All paid close attention, but the one who seemed most affected was, to my surprise, Betty Donovan. When Regan began his speech she was her usual fidgety self, probably dying for a cigarette. By the time he finished, she was hanging on every word. I suspected she'd be the first to respond, never mind that the Bishop was talking to the parents. She didn't disappoint me.

"That's amazing, Bishop," she said. "You're really certain of the man's innocence?"

Regan didn't take his eyes off Mr. and Mrs. Penniston, holding hands again, but he nodded and answered.

"Yes, Madame. We are certain." He swung his eyes to her, then back to the parents. "Which is my excuse for asking your cooperation. Mr. Goldman and I have a few questions of you. If you'd be kind enough to indulge us?"

Slight shrugs around the semicircle. As usual, Betty had the last word. "I guess so, sure. Fire away, Bish."

—30—

So, for once, the Bishop's routine self-destructed. A red-letter day, that Tuesday, November 15. Because that's the day he laid not so much as a fingertip on the old word processor. Instead, he spent the time gathering information on a murder. It may never happen again.

Anyway, the four acceded to his request. They answered his questions—most of them. And I got it all down in my little black book. For all the difference the little black book made. The fact that led to the solution didn't even get written down. But it entered the boss's cranium, the only receptacle that really mattered.

At least writing gave me something to do. With Regan doing all the questioning and no one accepting my occasional offers to bring them more hot chocolate, more cookies or a wide variety of drinks, I had a choice: play stenographer or sit there with my finger up my nose.

The Bishop started with Mr. and Mrs. Penniston. He seemed to be trying to find out everything he could about their daughter's upbringing, which irritated me till I saw where he was heading. Sarnoff *might* have been someone from Laura's past. Maybe someone from her Wichita past.

And the name Sarnoff was certainly an attention-grabber. As soon as it came out of the Bishop's mouth, everyone's ears perked up. McClendon's most of all.

"What do *you* know about him, Bishop?" he demanded, almost spilling his cocoa in his excitement. "He's the joker who's really screwed up this whole negotiation."

"How so?" the Bishop asked, cocking an eye his way.

"Two reasons." McClendon put down his mug. He was more assured than I'd seen him. Though he toyed nervously with his beard, his reedy voice was quick and definite. "First, what it showed about the company's financial controls—or, rather, lack of them. The fact that this guy was able to siphon so much money out of the company over so long a time with no one catching it shows that no one was minding the store. So—"

"George, that's an insult!" said Betty Donovan, red-faced. She was sitting with her weight forward, feet splayed in front of her, her posture ever since she sat down. I'd obviously wasted the most comfortable chair in the house on her. "Dammit, I did a *good* job of controls. My only mistake was trusting Laura. *She* told me Models for Hire was legit."

Another uproar. Roger and Maureen both spoke up at once, stopped, looked at each other. Roger shut up and the family spokesperson took the floor.

"Miss Donovan," Maureen said imperiously, looking down her nose at Betty. "Mr. Penniston and I resent what you're implying about our daughter. For you to say she was party to some illegitimate—"

Betty raised a hand. "I'm sorry, Maureen. That didn't come out the way I meant it. I apologize. As you know, no one loved Laur—" She stopped abruptly and bowed her head. Maureen just waited, as Betty cleared her throat. "Excuse me. But you know I'd never say anything against Laura. I just meant that Sarnoff was *her* friend, and Laura was *my* friend, so I didn't question how she dealt with him. It was a sweetheart arrangement, but it was her business, and I wasn't involved. That's all I meant."

Apparently that satisfied Roger and Maureen. McClendon retook the floor.

"And I apologize to *you*, Betty," he said. "I didn't mean that as criticism. I just meant that as an outside investor, I needed to know what was going on, and I didn't. Not from you, because you were leaving that part up to Laura; not from Laura, who had her own reasons—perfectly good ones, I'm sure—and not from that idiot Bob Theodore, who didn't have the sense to look behind the Models for Hire numbers in that so-called audit he supposedly did."

No one stuck up for Junior. They'd finally found someone they could insult without fear of contradiction.

The Bishop had suffered all the interruptions patiently. I knew he was doing the same thing I was: listening for clues in the midst of commotion. I couldn't tell if he'd gleaned any. I'd picked up the obvious one but didn't consider its implications, with unfortunate results later on for me personally. But I'm getting ahead of myself. For now, Regan had the floor.

"In any case, I take it, neither you, Miss Donovan, nor you, Mr. McClendon, ever met Sarnoff." Nods from both. "What about the two of you, Mr. and Mrs. Penniston? Ever hear your daughter mention the name Sarnoff? Or, have you yourselves ever known anyone named Sarnoff? In any connection whatsoever?"

Maureen shook her head immediately and decisively. Roger wasn't so sure. He squinted at Regan through his thick glasses and scratched his bald head.

"Umm, I might have had a student by that name, back in the mid-eighties," he muttered. "Kid from the West Coast, I think. Bob...? No, Bill Sarnoff. Jewish kid. Bright. Came from the L.A. area."

"Did your daughter know him?" The Bishop sounded interested. "And do you know where he is today?"

Roger shook his head. "Nope. No idea. Anyway Laura never met him."

Regan glanced around at his audience.

"So. Except for that boy years ago, none of you knows—or knows of—any Sarnoff. Is that right?" Shrugs from the men, shakes of the head from the women. "All right. Tell us about the circumstances of your daughter's leaving Wichita, if you would, Mr. Penniston."

Roger reached for his wife's hand as he spoke. "It was hard on us, Bishop. I guess anyone with just one child is bound to think she's special, but Laura really was. We had such high hopes for her when she graduated high school. She had acceptances at CalTech, Stanford and M.I.T. She was a math whiz, which made me proud because that's my field. I teach mathematics. I was—"

Maureen wasn't going to let *that* go by without comment. "My husband is too modest, Bishop Regan." She threw Roger an affectionate glance and said, teasingly, "Teach mathematics! My husband, Bishop, is a full professor at Wichita State. He's written three textbooks on differential equations and a host of scholarly articles. Last month, his piece on surds was the featured article in the *Journal of Mathematics*." Her husband blushed clear up into his bald scalp and smiled apologetically at Regan.

"Yes, well. That, and sixty cents will still buy you a cup of coffee— at least in Wichita." He glanced at his wife. "But thanks for the plug, dear." They smiled and touched fingertips. The Bishop had perked up, no surprise to me, when he heard the man was a professor.

"So," Regan said. "You're a mathematician. Differential equations?" Roger nodded. "*I* was interested in mathematics, in my youth. In fact, it's a regret of mine that time constraints have made it impossible to keep up with the field. I'm sorry that our time today doesn't permit us to—" He shrugged. "But it doesn't. Please continue, sir."

"I'd enjoy talking mathematics with a bishop. Maybe some other time." Roger smiled, then continued, "In fact, the year Laura graduated from high school, I was department head, not that that's all that big a deal. But it did make it that much nicer to see my daughter following in my footsteps. I'd started her on math problems before she was in kindergarten, Bishop, and she was a natural. By the time she could read, she could add, subtract, multiply and divide. Numbers were easy for her."

"You spoiled her penmanship with those early studies," his wife reminded him.

"Oh, God!" Roger laughed. "Did I ever! That was the worst part of her high-school work, Bishop. She'd put the right answers down, then her teachers couldn't read them! Her mind was quicker than her hand.

She was always in too much of a hurry." Roger flashed a knowing smile at his wife, who smiled back and chipped in.

"Yes. Her numbers were usually just squiggles." She demonstrated, her hand cutting a quick zigzag through the air.

Roger nodded. "I could never get her to change. But even if it was hard to read, her teachers all loved her work. By the end of her junior year she was already through calculus, which was as far as her high school went.

"So I helped arrange with the university for her to take an introductory course in differential equations—from another prof, not me—her senior year in high school. She wound up with the highest scores in the class," he concluded proudly, "even with all those bright college kids in there with her. And some of *them* grad students, at that.

"But by then she was already into modeling. Started when she was just a sixteen-year-old sophomore. By her senior year, she was in real demand around town. What can I tell you? She was always a photogenic little girl. And that never changed right up to the day she—" The proud father looked down, swallowed, and finally continued. "So when she graduated, she told us it was what she wanted to do with her life. *Not* math." For a minute, it was touch and go whether Roger would be able to continue. His eyes filled, and he rubbed the scalp on top of his head. But he quickly regained control.

"It *was* a disappointment," he muttered, wiping his brow with his handkerchief. "She was so darn good at it. But she was a darn good model, too, and that was her love. She *was* good, wasn't she?"

He looked around the room. McClendon looked uncomfortable. Donovan spoke up.

"She was terrific, Roger. I can tell you she was the best damn model in this town. You can both be proud of your daughter. Very proud."

"So you were not fond of your daughter's choice of profession," the Bishop prompted, "but you accepted it. How long after high-school graduation did she come to New York?"

"Three or four years," the mother said, taking over. "Let's see. She was eighteen when she graduated and now she's—*was*—thirty. And she's been in New York just . . . I think, eight and a half years. So she must have stayed in Wichita just over three years."

The Bishop stayed with the Pennistons for another half hour, which struck me as a bit excessive. In fact, he was probably just being kind, giving them a chance to talk about their loved one. And they took advantage of the opportunity.

Their faces glowed. Take Maureen's description of the red cross earrings. Roger and Maureen had given them to Laura to celebrate her opening her own agency.

"We had B. C. Bigelow—the finest jeweler in Wichita—design and make them. They were the most expensive we could afford. B. C. designed them in the shape of little crosses. Small diamonds in the center, rubies on the edges. She loved them, wore them every chance she could. So we . . ." Maureen bowed her head for a moment. When she lifted it again her eyes were moist, but her voice was firm and vibrant. "Excuse me, Bishop. I was thinking how horrible it is. Those earrings mean so much to Roger and me, I just *hate* it that he—that monster—should have them."

The Bishop, finally satisfied he'd got everything he was going to get out of the Pennistons, turned the spotlight on Betty. About time, I thought. Now, maybe, we could learn something useful. Maybe even something that might lead us to Steven Sarnoff.

"I met Laura six years ago, about two years after she'd come to town. I had my personal financial advisory service, and I'd done some work for a couple of other successful models. One of them had Laura call me. She was already a sensation and making plenty of bucks, so I was happy to hear from her. Not only was it good to get a successful client, but I figured she'd direct some more clients to me."

"Just what services do you render your clients, Madame?" Regan asked.

"None, any more." Betty smiled. "Once we started the agency, I had to drop my private practice. I tried keeping it for the first few months, but Laura complained, and I couldn't blame her. The business was more than a full-time job for both of us." Betty frowned, and added, "I guess I'll be going back to consulting, now that I'm selling the business to George.

"But, to answer your question, I'd look at a client's financial status and income and make recommendations, depending on their wants and needs. What kinds of investments to make, what kinds of returns to look for, what levels of risk to assume. Those kinds of things. Are you interested, Bishop? Like I say, I'm getting back in the business."

Regan cut that off fast. "Not at the moment," he murmured, and steered the conversation back to Laura. "When did you and Miss Penniston decide to go into business?"

"Oh, God," Betty said. "We *talked* about it almost right away. She was saying how poorly managed most of the agencies were, how they'd send girls to the wrong places for shots, mishandle the payments, that kind of thing."

Regan was frowning. "Mishandle—?"

"Oh, they're mostly awful. Few of them would carry group insurance—that was the first thing Laura put in at Penniston Associates. They'd screw up the FICA, take too much out or not enough. And they wouldn't give girls enough lead time for a session. Things like that.

"So Laura began to think about how many friends she had who might come to her if she opened an agency and ran it right. She was the idea woman all the way." Betty glanced over at the parents. "She really *was* bright, Roger. And not just in mathematics. Everyone used to say she was the beauty and *I* was the brains of the outfit. Not so. She was both." She smiled, her eyes crinkling.

"Just to give you an example of what I mean. I noticed one thing about her right away, back when she was modeling. She was so much sharper than any of the other models. She kept a little black book with every phone number that she might conceivably ever have a use for. So she was always ahead of all the other girls in getting new jobs. She used the phone like a master, calling clients to thank them, calling to see if they needed anyone for this or that job. She was always miles ahead, and that little black book was part of it.

"It came in handy after we were partners, too. Any time I needed a phone number, Laura'd probably have it in her little black book. I've seen her take time to take down numbers that I thought couldn't possibly have any use at all. I even accused her of having a number fetish! But she always said, you never know when you might need it. And, sure enough, I'd constantly find myself asking her for some phone number I really needed, a number I couldn't get any other way—and she'd always have it. Amazing!"

Maureen nodded with a sad little smile. "She was that way since she was little. Part of her fascination with numbers, I suppose." Betty and Maureen exchanged smiles.

"Anyway," Betty went on, "Laura had this idea about starting her own agency. Right away she started trying to talk me into helping with the financial end of things. I gave her a little help—strictly as an adviser, at first." Betty grinned, deepening the laugh lines even more. Her eyes practically disappeared.

"My main advice, frankly, was to stay the hell out of it. I hated to see her put all her eggs into one basket. 'You're a successful model,' I told her. 'Why throw that all away to do something you don't know anything about?'

"We went round and round. She kept saying she *knew* she could do it. I kept pointing out problems, and she kept solving them. Gradually, I got interested. After spending all that time telling her what a dumb idea it was, I wound up asking to join her. She was delighted that I'd changed my mind, and I became her one-third partner. She kept two-thirds for herself, which was fine.

"I introduced her to Lee Stubbs at Mid-City—Lee's been a client of mine for years—and he did the loan. And the business just took straight off."

It was the most enthusiasm I'd seen the woman show. I couldn't tell if the Bishop was impressed or not, but he was interested.

"But there came a time," he said, "when you needed another partner. And that's where *you* come in, Mr. McClendon. Please tell us how you came to know Miss Donovan and Miss Penniston."

"My turn, hmm? All right, why not?" The burly businessman glanced around at the others, settled back comfortably in the straightback chair and smiled complacently through his beard.

"I've been reasonably successful in everything I've tried, Bishop. I've run my own advertising agency for twelve years, managed to make a little money at it—started as a commercial artist, eventually got my own set-up. Lee Stubbs—" McClendon glanced at Betty—"Betty mentioned she's done business with him for years. Well, so have I. Lee phoned me early this year, told me the two gals were in need of equity money." McClendon looked back at the Bishop. "I was friends with Betty and Laura. I'd used their models. In fact, I'd about decided to use them exclusively, they were so good. Of course, Lee and I go way back—he helped *me* get started. So when the gals went to him for an increase in their line of credit, he asked them if they'd talk to me. Right, Betty?"

Donovan looked startled, then nodded. Out of the limelight now, it looked like her craving for nicotine had returned. Her hands were looking for something to do, tapping the chair arms, smoothing her skirt over her thick thighs, patting her hopeless hair.

"Yes, that's right," Betty spoke in quick, staccato syllables. "Lee thought we were getting stretched a little thin, that we needed an infusion of equity, not more debt. Laura didn't want to hear that, but I told her Lee was right. And he knew you were trying to get into the business. We liked you, liked the way you worked with us, the way you'd moved more of your business to us. So we said we'd give it a shot."

McClendon sounded downright lazy after that burst of machine-gun fire. "Right. Well, Stubbs set up a lunch for the four of us—Laura, Betty, him and me. And everything went great after that—till Bob Theodore's audit." He glared at Betty and she glared back. The sore point was still sore.

"Bob was already suspect, far as I was concerned, since it was common knowledge that he and Laura were engaged. He wasn't—"

"They were never engaged!" The outraged mother. "Laura told me everything. And she was never engaged to anyone. Least of all to that— puffed-up playboy!" Mrs. Penniston glanced at hubby, apparently to make sure he was on the team, and redirected her glare at McClendon. Teeth gleamed through the beard. He raised a hand of peace.

"Maureen, Maureen." He said soothingly. "Don't take me so seriously. Okay, they were—friends. And everyone knew it. Their pictures had been in every paper in town for a couple of years. They were what we call here an item. Surely she sent you some of those pictures." Maureen turned away, but Roger acknowledged George's point with a nod.

"That's all I meant," George continued. "Anyway, I took a close look at those numbers and had my company accountant do the same. And we both noticed that the models' fees paid to Models for Hire were about half again as high as what they were paying their other models. But they were capitalizing the difference as Goodwill, so they were overstating earnings by nearly one hundred thousand dollars a year. In a company that was only making two-and-a-half times that! In other words, earnings were overstated by nearly forty percent, while an absolutely meaningless asset was growing by the same amount. And Bob Theodore passed it right by without so much as a nod.

"I was being asked to buy in at nearly double the realistic value, if you think twenty times earnings is realistic, which . . ." He grinned at Betty. ". . . I guess it is, in view of their growth." He'd lost me with all the financial mumbo-jumbo, but Regan was hanging on.

"So," the Bishop said, "they were valuing the company at five million, giving you a one-point-seven-million-dollar cost to buy in. But a true valuation would have put the value at three million, meaning you should have been able to purchase your one-third for only one million."

"You people listening?" McClendon chortled, looking around at his three cohorts. Maureen sniffed, Roger nodded agreeably and Betty's face reddened.

Aiming his big smile at the Bishop, McClendon said, "I should have brought you in as an expert witness, Bishop. But, yes, that was the problem." The businessman settled back, as comfortable in that hard chair as Betty was uncomfortable in her soft one.

"Of course, my first reaction was that the girls were out to screw me. I shot right over to Laura's office to have it out with her."

"Exactly when was that?" Regan demanded sharply. Everyone looked at him.

McClendon took a minute to consider. He pulled a small notebook from his pocket. "No need to guess," he muttered. "It was, umm, September fifth, two months ago. Yes, the day after Labor Day. I'd been in my own office plenty over that weekend.

"Anyway, Laura's first reaction confirmed my worst suspicions. She turned red, stuttered and stammered. It was obvious to me she was covering up. Finally, she said she had to talk to Betty. Alone. That it was all a mistake, she was sure they could straighten it out. I first insisted on joining them, but she got her back up, so I gave in.

"At that point, I was pretty sure the deal was dead. I certainly wasn't about to get in bed with anyone—even someone as pretty—" George remembered Laura's parents and backed away from whatever he'd been about to say. "Anyway, they came back to the office, the two of them, and they got me to believe them. Right, Betty?"

Donovan managed to stop fidgeting for a moment.

"Right, George. Laura came into my office, all flustered. She almost broke down. She explained that Steve Sarnoff was an old friend of hers, she'd had to do this deal with him, she'd explain the whole thing to me later. She said—"

"Just a moment, Madame." Regan. "Weren't you already aware of this arrangement through your financial responsibilities with the company?"

Betty met his gaze and shrugged. "I agree I *should* have been. If that's criticism, your point is well taken. That's one thing I warned George about this morning. Right, George?" McClendon nodded.

"I told him to make sure the new financial VP, or whatever he's going to call them, take responsibility for the whole operation from day one. Laura and I operated a lot looser than that. I kept my hands off the people part of it—the models. That was Laura's bailiwick, she was good at it. She decided what they should be paid, who we should use, who worked best with which photographer, the whole thing. I left it up to her, and she did a great job of it. Till this.

"Well, she felt so awful. Like she'd let me down." Betty looked at the parents. "She was *not* out to cheat me, Maureen. I never had the slightest suspicion of that. She just hadn't been able to tell me, for her own good reasons. She was going to, I'm as sure of that as I am about anything. She just never got the chance. She—" Betty's voice caught, and she dropped her head.

"And did Miss Penniston ever tell you what that explanation was?" Regan asked. Betty raised her head immediately and looked Regan in the eye.

"Never."

Regan nodded and looked back at George, who resumed gently, with a sympathetic glance at the woman.

"Right. And Laura never had it in mind to cheat *me* either. When she and Betty came back in, they both assured me it had been a mistake. Laura took the whole blame, said she just forgot to warn Bob about it. She didn't lay it on him, either, though it had to be embarrassing for her, his being her boyfriend and all." George looked Maureen's way but she didn't seem to object to *boyfriend*. Just *fiancé*.

"Well, Laura was just so sincere about it," McClendon went on, "and Betty certainly hadn't known anything, though she was embarrassed about it slipping by her, her being the financial factotum." Betty nodded, blushing. "And I'm not one to hold a grudge. I just told them in no uncertain terms that I didn't want Theodore coming near the company any more. And that was the end of it. We were going to go ahead and get the whole thing revalued. But then Laura—" McClendon stopped abruptly.

The Bishop filled the silence. "Couldn't you merely have eliminated Goodwill and used the resultant value?"

"You kidding?" McClendon was contemptuous. "Theodore's blow-up on that threw his whole audit into the ashcan. I'm willing to forgive and forget, but I'm not stupid."

"So the negotiations were still very much alive the night Miss Penniston died?"

"Oh, yes," Betty said. McClendon nodded.

The Bishop's questioning went on for another hour, but you don't need to hear it. None of it came to anything. Regan wound it up just at six without so much as asking me if I had any questions.

"Thank you for indulging me," he murmured. "I don't know if you've gotten me any closer to my goal—freeing Mr. Fanning and locating Mr. Sarnoff—but if not, it hasn't been for lack of effort."

Roger was on his feet. "You mean you won't tell us how you know that man is innocent?"

"I can't, Mr. Penniston." Regan shook his head decisively. "Not without breaking a sacred confidence."

Response to that wasn't enthusiastic. Maureen sniffed, Roger scowled, the other two glanced at each other.

I followed the four down the hall, helped them into their coats and saw them out onto the stoop. Having exhausted every known method of precipitation, the sky had dried up, but the wind was just as fierce and it was even colder than before. I was happy I didn't have to go out.

"I'm exhausted, David," said the Bishop when I returned to the office. He looked it.

"We've got Rozanski coming over at eight o'clock," I reminded him. "Do you want to bug out on that? I could take plenty of notes. *You* know," I added sarcastically. "Like I did this afternoon."

The sarcasm went right over his head. "No, I'll join you. But I want to rest first. Please tell Sister I'm foregoing dinner.

"In the meantime, I need to ponder—and you might, also—the rather interesting similarity between certain letters of the alphabet and certain numerical symbols when written by a person in a hurry."

—31—

Rozanski arrived ten minutes late for our eight o'clock appointment.

"Sorry, Davey, sorry," he said, bustling down the hall. "The damn paper's going to hell in a handbasket, I swear. I was on my way over here a half hour ago, when . . ." And so forth. I believed him. Chet's the promptest person I know, outside of myself. But you don't need to hear all the things that can go wrong with an evening daily just when the presses are ready to run on a Tuesday night.

As he sank gratefully into the chair, I saw lines and wrinkles in Chet's tanned face I'd never seen before. He was tired.

If Rozanski's had a few more lines in it, the Bishop's face had a few less. It was puffy from his evening nap. Just as well Rozanski'd been late: the Bishop hadn't come down till a minute after eight himself.

The Bishop likes Rozanski. Evidence: Chet's one of the few people he grants permission to smoke in the mansion. This time, he even invited it. "Please, Mr. Rozanski. Feel free to enjoy a cigar. I've been looking forward to the aroma ever since I found out you were coming." Rozanski grinned and pulled out a cigar.

"Well, I wouldn't want to disappoint a man of the cloth." He carefully clipped off the tip and lighted up. Puffing a white cloud in Regan's direction, he peered at the prelate through the smoke.

"Smell good?"

"Marvelous." But that was as far as the levity went. The Bishop got right to work.

"Now, Mr. Rozanski. Let us explain—to the extent we are able—why we are convinced Mr. Fanning is innocent of the charges against

180

him. Then perhaps you can tell us about some of the people you have researched in your own investigations."

Regan filled Chet in without getting into the porno flicks. Of course, being deprived of our privileged info didn't make Chet happy.

"Come on, Bishop!" he complained. "You can do better than that! You haven't given me a thing I can even use." Chet looked in my direction. "Davey, give me a break. Tell him what good all this is going to do me. Like none."

But with the Bishop's vow of silence—or whatever he called it—we couldn't help him.

"See here, Mr. Rozanski. I understand your point and sympathize. All I can tell you is I am not at liberty to give you my reason for knowing the gentleman to be innocent, beyond telling you that it is cogent." Regan paused and leaned forward. "But I do offer my assurance—and David's—that you will be the first—except for the police, of course—to know anything we know about the true killer, once we learn his identity."

"Okay, Bishop. Since it comes from you. If it were Davey talking, I'd tell him to stick it where the—well, I just wouldn't accept it."

Unsmiling, the Bishop nodded. "Very prudent of you, Mr. Rozanski. Now. What can you tell us about Miss Penniston's friends and associates?"

Rozanski slumped comfortably into the chair and exhaled smoke. "Quite a bit, actually. I've dug up a few things I didn't know when I talked to Davey yesterday morning. Let's start with the partner."

Chet kept the floor for the next hour and a half with very few interruptions. About halfway through he got a little dry and accepted the beer he'd declined the first time I offered.

I joined Chet with a beer for myself. I didn't bother asking the Bishop if he'd have anything. He quit drinking before I knew him, right after the shooting. I don't know why. A few subtle hints from Ernie suggest he had been in the habit of having a drink or two—maybe even more—before then, but those are just hints.

As Chet talked, I jotted down the items we hadn't heard before. There were several. In fact, he gave us at least one thing we didn't already know about each of the five players.

The reporter opened with Betty Donovan. Five years before, Betty had gone on a tough weight-loss program. She'd tried everything from diet pills to Chung-Mu-Quan to bicycling around Central Park a half hour every morning. And every diet from Scarsdale to liquid to fasting—you name it, she'd tried it. This had gone on for six months. Results: twelve pounds gained.

"My sources say it didn't bother her that much," Chet concluded. "But one thing. There are rumors that she got into drugs during the weight-loss kick. Marijuana and possibly worse. Which brings up the next person on the list of associates: George McClendon."

Rozanski had more—and dirtier—dirt on McClendon than he had on Donovan. He was a known drug user, first of all, but it got worse. He'd been charged twice with battery in sexual situations. Both times the prostitutes involved had dropped charges—most likely following a payoff by George.

"I've met McClendon," Rozanski said, "and I'd never have guessed it, but he's a real fetishist. Gets off on bondage and torture. Both those cases with the prostitutes apparently started with comparatively innocent sexual role-playing, involving spanking and maybe some light whipping—leather and chains, you know?" Rozanski glanced at Regan. "Sorry, Bishop."

The Bishop shrugged. " 'There but for the grace of God . . . ' How badly were the two women hurt?"

"Badly enough, I guess. I've got their names and addresses; I'll leave that with Davey. Neither of them had any lasting injuries, but one had to be hospitalized. Happened in hotel rooms. They made a racket, other guests reported it, and the police got called in.

"Which makes you wonder how many *other* times the guy's done it but never got caught. Also makes you wonder how far the guy'd have gone if he hadn't been stopped. An informant of mine who happens to be on Vice told me George was just getting started when the cops arrived—one of the times."

The Bishop didn't look as shocked as I thought he should have. Or as I was. McClendon—a seemingly decent human being. And successful businessman. You never know.

"And as I said," Chet went on, "the guy's also a known druggie."

"What about Laura Penniston?" Regan asked. "Did she use drugs?"

Rozanski shook his head. "No, why would you think that? Oh—birds of a feather, you mean. Nope. Not that I've heard, anyway."

Next, Chet talked about Sandra Norville. "Beautiful gal. I met her, as I told Davey. Both a friend and an employee of Laura's. But I got it from someone reliable that maybe they *weren't* such good friends. Maybe Sandy resented Laura's success.

"And—get this!—*Laura* was jealous of *Sandy*. Yeah! Hard to believe, but Sandy had stolen two of Laura's boyfriends in the past. People were wondering when she'd get around to stealing this guy Theodore." I didn't say anything, just glanced at the Bishop. He didn't meet my eyes.

"Which brings us," Chet went on, oblivious to my reaction, "to the man in Laura Penniston's life: the last of many. He'd hung on with her longer than most. Laura was always in the news, you know. She seems to have had a nose for publicity that told her just which men would help her the most. A real self-promoter, this gal, no disrespect to the dead intended.

"Bob Theodore was well wired-in, a scion of wealth, as we journalists put it, plus good-looking, debonair, knows which fork to use. For Penniston's purposes, perfect.

"But there's some other stuff on him, too. Word is, when he got out of school the old man put him in charge of the company pension fund. Junior promptly invested far too much of it in oil stocks in the late seventies and early eighties—exquisitely bad timing. When oil prices crashed in 'eighty-two, he got clobbered.

"After that, daddy kept a tighter rein on him, but he kept fumbling balls. Word is, daddy's about had it with Junior.

"For some time now, Junior's had to live on straight salary. Partnership distributions at Theodore and Theodore have been nil for three years, due largely to Junior's stock market screw-ups. But that hasn't stopped him from cutting a wide swath on the party circuit, or from heading over to Antibes, Capri or the Seychelles whenever the urge strikes him."

"How about this banker, Stubbs?" I threw in as Chet picked up his beer. "I understand he used to date Laura."

Rozanski looked at me, took a small sip of beer and put his glass down. "Just coming to him, Davey. Met him?" I nodded. "Well, you're right. He was Penniston's steady guy till Theodore came along. If you know Stubbs and Theodore, or even what they look like, you know there's no comparison between the two, looks-wise. Am I right?"

I grinned. "The prince and the frog."

"Yeah. Well, early last year—it was at the mayor's big Valentine's Day gala—Stubbs brought Penniston to the party, but she left on Bob Theodore's arm."

"That would have been February, twenty-one months ago," the Bishop murmured. I looked at him. It was the first time he'd opened his mouth in the last ten minutes.

"Umm, right," said Chet. "Stubbs apparently just shrugged it off. Of course, Penniston Associates is one of Mid-City's biggest accounts, so I don't suppose he'd want to jeopardize that. Plus, he must have realized a mere bank vice-president can't compete with the son of the founder of a big accounting firm. Especially when said son is taller, blonder, younger and better-looking. So I guess Stubbs lumped it. He and Penniston stayed on speaking terms, and her company continued to bank at Mid-City."

Rozanski said plenty of other things by the time he walked out at 9:40, but nothing you need to hear. When I returned from seeing him out, the Bishop had selected his book for that evening's reading in bed—something highly philosophical by a couple of Frenchmen, Garigou and LaGrange—and was wheeling for the elevator.

"I'm exhausted, David," he told me without slowing down, "and disgruntled. I have to get my mind off this case. Goodnight."

I watched him gun down the hallway and into the kitchen. I was tired, too. A good, solid night's sleep would do us both a world of good.

Right.

—32—

MY SOLID NIGHT'S SLEEP never stood a chance.

I'd been drifting in and out of a nightmare—in which Sarnoff, a six-foot-six giant of a man with gleaming eyes and a jet-black bushy beard, tightened a garroting wire around my throat—when I sat bolt upright, dripping wet, wide awake.

What *was* that noise? And where was it coming from? It wasn't my alarm clock. Ugly sound, halfway between a buzz and a wail.
Suddenly I knew. My face went cold. When I'd last heard it, six years previously, I'd hoped never to hear it again. Regan's emergency alarm signal.

Trowbridge, the Bishop's neurologist, had recommended it, insisted on it, actually. A month after I first moved in, he'd gotten worried about the remote but real possibility of the Bishop's paralysis suddenly spreading without warning.

"Your respiration could be impaired," he'd told Regan, "and if it happens, it will be sudden. You'll need immediate help or you could die."

So Regan had me get a summoning device. I'd installed it myself, running the wire under the carpet between the two rooms. The sender was by Regan's bed, the receiver by mine.

He'd loathed the sound of it. "I promise you, David, I shan't use it for anything less than the ultimate emergency. That caterwauling would awaken the dead."

That had been the last time I'd heard it. Until now.

* * *

Fumbling frantically, I finally got my bedside lamp on. (How long had he been buzzing before I woke up?) Swung my legs over the side of the bed. Tried—and failed—to find the unit to push the respond button. (Encouraging thought: if he could still buzz, he must still be alive.) To hell with responding, this was an emergency.

I burst across the hallway into Regan's room.

And there he was, placidly sitting up in bed, bedside lamp on, signaling unit in hand, his disheveled hair the only out of place thing in the room.

A jumble of thoughts: he's having a heart attack; he's gone nuts; he's playing a practical joke; this is chapter two of my Sarnoff nightmare. But Regan's eyes were calm.

"Sorry to trouble you, David. Please sit down."

I just stared.

The boss's face showed irritation. "Sit down, David! Please! I want you to do something for me."

I looked around, grabbed the one chair in the room, pulled it to the side of the bed and sat. Thinking, "This had better be good."

It was.

His eyes were now higher than mine. He uses a hospital bed and now had it angled at nearly ninety degrees.

Beside the bed is his jungle gym, a set of pulleys and bars that he uses to get in and out of bed, and in and out of his wheelchair. It's also what he uses for a half hour every morning at five, to do his exercises. His upper body is—well, you ought to see it. A hint: don't ever try arm-wrestling him.

"Again, my apologies, David. But the answer to our puzzle—one of our puzzles—came to me in my sleep, and I was anxious to share it." To brag, he meant.

Not that I wasn't interested. And getting back to sleep was certainly out. Maybe forever. My pulse rate was probably still over one-twenty.

The Bishop explained. "That message on Miss Penniston's palm. I now think I know what it means. Would you get the photostat?"

The photostat? I looked at him, shook my head and hustled back across the hall. I quickly put on slippers and robe, grabbed the sheet and hurried back.

We examined it together. I studied the G O S T, wondering what he'd come up with. The boss didn't keep me waiting.

"Yesterday, Mr. and Mrs. Penniston gave us the two bits of information we needed, David.

"The first—that Miss Penniston wrote her numbers sloppily—was one. As I thought about it, I realized that the symbols we were taking to be letters might very well be numbers. Take a look."

I scanned the writing again, through new eyes.

"Okay," I said, nodding slowly. "I see what you mean. The G could be a six. O is zero. S is five." I frowned, thought about it, and shook my head decisively. "But you can't get a number out of T."

Regan immediately raised a finger. He'd expected that. How lucky for him to have such a good straight man.

"That was what was troubling me, David, when I went to sleep last night. You'll recall that we noticed that the upper cross bar of the T seemed to be separated from the vertical lower portion? That gap was very much on my mind when I went to sleep." He paused, frowning. "Your description of Miss Norville writing a telephone number on her palm made me wonder if the four characters—be they letters or numbers—could represent a phone number. But how do you get a seven-digit telephone number out of only four characters? This was troubling me as I went to sleep. One possible answer came to me in my sleep, just five minutes ago."

"So what is it?" I demanded. "Have you got it?"

"Very possibly. The moment Mr. Penniston told us his daughter was a mathematics aficionado, I *knew* that was a key—to something. But I didn't know what. Well, perhaps in my subconscious. There is a certain convention in mathematics which—how far did you progress in mathematics, David?"

I was pained. "You would have to bring that up. I struggled for a hard-won C-minus in high school algebra. If I never see another equation, it'll be too soon."

Regan was neither contemptuous nor amused. He'd already pulled a pad and pencil from his night stand. "Very well. Then try to attend."

Regan wrote "3.333 . . ." He looked at me. "Do you understand that, David?"

"Of course I do," I said contemptuously. "Newton's Grand Unified Theory of Relativity. Everyone knows that."

He was patient. When he's excited or proud of himself, he's hard to irritate. When he's both, forget it.

"Close, David," he smiled. "But not quite a direct hit."

"No, it's shorthand for an infinitely repeating decimal. The three dots imply that the digit immediately preceding is to be repeated to infinity." I shrugged, but he didn't even see me. He was too busy educating me.

"Alternatively, one could write it like this:"

Regan added symbols till the pad read:

$$3.333\ldots = 3.\overline{3}$$

He looked at my face for a reaction, got none and continued. "As the equal sign implies, the expression on the right means the same thing. Thus, the final three is to be repeated."

I sat back down in the chair and thought about the implications. I got an idea and grabbed the picture of Laura's palm. "So you think the T is a one with a bar over it to indicate repetition?"

"Precisely!" Regan exclaimed. "I suspect it was her personal shorthand for any symbol to be repeated indefinitely. It's the kind of shorthand a mathematician would use. I've used it myself." He stared at me, waiting. I stared back. "I *think*," he added significantly, "it leaves us with a certain *telephone number* we ought to look into."

"Six-oh-five, one-one-one-one?"

"*Yes*, David!" He was triumphant—briefly. Then he frowned. "At least I think so. You should look it up in the Reverse Directory."

For once, I was ahead of him. I was going through the door before the words *Reverse Directory* were out of his mouth, heading for my office.

As you probably know, the Reverse Directory is a phone directory—with a gimmick. Using a normal directory, you start out knowing the name of who you want to call and look up the number. The Reverse Directory is for when you know the number but not the name.

In my office I pulled it from the shelf and found the 605s. As I looked, I was giving odds on the name I'd find. *Unlisted* was the favorite at five-to-two (my normal pessimism); right behind that were the five suspects: McClendon, Donovan, Norville, Theodore and Stubbs. Not wanting to play favorites, I had them all at six-to-one.

I lost all bets. The entry opposite 605–1111 was "Jos. B. Ingram, Exp./Imp., 601 W.49."

A definite downer. I double-checked by putting the tip of my finger under the number and tracing the little dots across the page. Old Joe

Ingram it was, the export/import king of West Forty-ninth Street. No doubt about it.

But as I trudged dejectedly back up the stairs at about a tenth the speed I'd raced down, something began to niggle me about Ingram's address. I'd seen 601 W. 49th, or something similar, not long before. But where?

Then it hit me, and my blood started racing again.

The bodies of Joy Foxworth and Laura Penniston had been found below the stoop of 603 W. 49th. Six-oh-one had to be the building right next door.

Maybe Mr. Ingram had something to contribute to this case after all.

—33—

IT WAS NINE O'CLOCK Wednesday morning before I got anyone to answer 605–1111. Not for lack of trying.

When I'd got back upstairs at 3:22 A.M. and talked it over with the Bishop, we'd agreed there was nothing more to be done for the moment, and went back to bed. But not before he told me, "Look into it in the morning. If you get a lead, come up to the chapel and discuss it. I don't want you going anywhere before you talk with me."

I lay down in bed and tried to figure how and why Jos. B. Ingram, Exp./Imp. figured into the whole affair. And if. Next thing I knew, some newscaster was informing me about Gorby's latest adventures in *perestroika*, wherever that is. Seven-forty-five in the A.M. My first reaction was to turn the damn radio-alarm off and go back to sleep. Then I remembered our breakthrough and was immediately wide-eyed, if something less than bushy-tailed. Breakfast helped. A little.

I tried the number at 8:30 and an answering machine provided another riddle. (Why can't detective work *ever* be simple?) Getting answered by a machine wasn't the puzzling part (these days, it's puzzling when you're *not*); the puzzling part was what the machine said. I took it down verbatim. A youngish male voice gave me the following message: "Rice Realty here. Your call is important to us. At the beep, please leave your name, time of call and phone number, and we'll get back to you as soon as we can. Please wait for the beep and have a nice day." I didn't wait for the beep. As to having a nice day, we'd see.

That had to be a wrong number, so I tried again, more carefully. Same result.

I looked up both "Ingram, Jos. B.," and "Rice Realty" in the directory—the regular one, this time. Both were listed. Ingram at 601 W. 49, just like in the Reverse Directory; and Rice at 222 W. 58. Unquestionably, I hadn't got the Rice number by mistake—even stone drunk, I couldn't get 286–3000 out of 605–1111. Certainly not twice. The phone company seemed to have some crossed lines.

Before calling New York Telephone, I decided to wait till nine and try again. This time I got a human being. Feminine-type. Youngish. Lilting tones. "Rice Realty."

"Seems I have the wrong number," I said. "I'm trying to reach Joseph B. Ingram."

"Mr. Ingram is on sabbatical . . ." (sabbatical?) ". . . We're handling his calls. May I help you?"

Well, at least I hadn't misdialed. But what the hell was going on?

"Are you at the corner of Forty-ninth and Ninth?"

"Uh, no. We're at—wait a minute, yes we are—*they* are. That is, Mr. Ingram's office is." She gave a little giggle. "Let me explain. In Mr. Ingram's absence, he is offering the office for sublet and we're the agent. So we're having Mr. Ingram's calls forwarded to our office—that is, during periods like now when there's no subtenant in there. I'll be happy to take a message for Mr. Ingram. He calls in once a week."

"Oh, it's not important." I cradled the receiver. Before I said another word I wanted to think about it.

Ingram gone, office available for sublet. I had lots of questions to ask, but getting answers out of Rice Realty could be a problem. I needed a plan.

I reviewed the situation. About Joseph B. Ingram and his office I now had three hard facts and one strong maybe.

The three facts:

One. The office was in the building next door to the spot where Laura's body and that of one other victim had been found.

Two. The office was under sublet, had been for some time, and was presently empty.

Three. It had a working phone, with a number (605–1111) listed under Joseph Ingram's name.

The strong maybe: for some as yet unexplained reason, the office's phone number had been on Laura's palm when she was murdered. That conjecture rested on four assumptions: (a) Laura had had a habit of writing on her palm; (b) the Bishop's interpretation of that *T* on the palm was accurate; (c) the number—assuming it *was* a number—was a phone number, not a social security number or safe deposit box number or God knew what; and (d) if it *was* a phone number, it was in the 212 area code. I.e.: New York. Not Hoboken or Wichita or Sydney, Australia.

A lot of assumptions. Still, its being a phone number for an office next door to where Laura Penniston's body had been found supported the theory. Besides, I didn't have any other line of reasoning to pursue.

I scratched my head. Since I was trying to reason like the Bishop, what would *he* think about next? For one thing, how about the questions left to be answered? I wrote down some questions. The more I wrote the stronger my feeling grew that the answers were inside the office of one Joseph Ingram, Exp./Imp.

First of all, what was the office like? Big? Little? A suite? Furnished? Was the phone in service the night Laura died?

Second of all, was it under sublet during the murders, especially during Laura Penniston's murder?

Third, was Steven Sarnoff involved with it in any way?

Fourth, did *anyone* who knew Laura—Sarnoff or anyone else—have any connection with the office?

I came up with an approach that seemed to have a chance of getting me some answers. It was going to take some guesswork along the way, but I didn't see that I had a lot to lose.

I called 605–1111.

"Rice Realty."

I went with my deep basso, Richard Burton voice. No point tipping her to the fact that I was the same guy that'd called before.

"May I speak with the manager?"

"That would be Dan Rice," said the voice, suddenly brisk and businesslike. "May I tell him who's calling?" (Why can't anyone just put you through?)

"David Goldman. I'm interested in the Ingram space."

Within three seconds I was speaking with none other than Dan Rice. The same voice I'd heard earlier on the answering machine. A man desperate to know what he could do for me.

Decision time. I had a couple of options, neither of them, naturally, involving anything as simple as the truth. After all, I needed information. And nothing truthful I could tell Dan Rice was likely to be persuasive. Especially when I couldn't tell him *why* I wanted to know. I made a snap decision. My favorite kind.

I dropped Richard Burton and became a prissy businessman.

"Ah, my good man. David Goldman here. I believe you know Mr. Sarnoff?" I held my breath. Three seconds of silence. "Well, do you or don't you?" I was an *impatient* prissy businessman. "Mr. Sarnoff was telling me about that office. That *is* the one at Forty-ninth and Ninth, is it not? . . . Hello! Is anyone there?"

"Oh, sorry," Rice said hastily. "Uh, yes, that's our space. I only paused because, uh, I never actually *met* Mr. Sarnoff."

Bingo.

I chortled aloud to buy time while my mind raced. Another footprint of the elusive Mr. Sarnoff. Was *anyone* ever going to admit to actually having seen the guy?

"Never met him, hmm?" I improvised, thinking furiously. "Well, Steven *does* have his little ways. He *is* a dear boy!" I chuckled again. "I suppose he insisted on the usual: payment with hundred-dollar bills."

Rice seemed to relax. "Well, almost," he chuckled back. "Twenties, actually, sent through the mail." He clucked disapprovingly. "Rather poor business practice, that. I mean, where's your proof you sent it, should a question arise?"

"Of course, he *did* phone me to be sure I'd received the money. By the way, does Mr. Sarnoff have laryngitis?"

I filled the phone with words, while considering Sarnoff's laryngitis. I didn't want any uncomfortable pauses to roil the still waters of Rice's current level of trust in me.

"Well, that kind of thing sort of runs in his family, don't you know. His father used to be troubled . . ."

While I blathered on I was mentally fitting the pieces of a puzzle together. Sarnoff's laryngitis was one piece; the strange voice of the Whisperer who'd called the *Dispatch* was another. Did they fit?

"Steven, the poor boy," I concluded, "tends to sound as though he's, er, *whispering*—wouldn't you say?"

"That's it!" Rice exclaimed. "At first I couldn't understand him. Finally I figured out who it was, that he wanted to be sure that the money he'd sent me was safe, and to arrange to get the key. Asked me to mail it to him. Of course, we don't like to handle things that way, we like to see the people we're doing business with, but he said he wasn't feeling well, so he couldn't come in. Asked me to mail him the key along with the lease.

"Anyway, since he'd paid in advance, I accommodated him. Does he handle all his business dealings that way?" I chuckled again and was about to ask another question when Rice added something.

"But I'm glad you called, Mr., er . . ."

"Goldman."

"Ah, yes. Mr. Goldman. I'm glad you called, because we haven't been able to get hold of Mr. Sarnoff. He was all paid up on his rent. But he had asked us to replace Mr. Ingram's name on the door with the name of his company. I can't think of it at the moment. Er . . ."

"Models for Hire?"

"Right! Models for Hire! Well, he told us to bill him for it. By the time we got around to billing him, he'd canceled the office. So we mailed the bill to him at that box number, but it came back, Moved, Left No Forwarding Address. Can you give me his correct address? We've offset what he owes us for it against his security deposit, but we'd like to settle up for our records."

I nodded to myself. This guy Sarnoff was something else when it came to covering his tracks. But we were gaining on him.

"Quite," I assured the realtor. "I may be able to help you with that. In point of fact, as I mentioned, I'm interested in the space myself. Could you be a good fellow and meet me there, say, in half an hour? Meanwhile, I'll rustle up Steve's current address and just bring it with me."

I had another thought. "Oh, and say! Would you be so kind as to bring a copy of that sublease with you? I asked Steven to give me a peek at it, and he couldn't find his copy." I chuckled as prissily as I knew how. "I'll take him another copy, and we'll get this entire matter straightened out. Could you be so kind?"

Rice not only could, he would. I headed upstairs. Time to confer with my guru.

As I opened the door into the chapel's little anteroom, I heard a rhythmic sound. I cocked my head, listening. A power saw, three blocks away? Some new kind of smoke alarm going off next door? A bus on Eleventh Avenue, periodically revving its engine? It took me about two seconds to figure out the answer: none of the above. What we had here was snoring, right in the sacred confines.

Regan's chin was on his chest, prayerbook in his lap, one hand dangling at his side. It was a race between the beanie and the prayerbook which would hit the floor first.

I considered just letting him sleep, but he'd never forgive me if I went off to see Rice without telling him what was up. I approached and cleared my throat explosively.

His chin jerked up, eyes flew open, one hand automatically grabbed and reset the beanie. The prayerbook slid off his lap onto the floor. He glared at it, then at me.

I picked up his book and grinned. "So *this* is what you're doing up here every morning when Sister Ernestine thinks you're deep in prayer! Not to worry, though. Slip me a salary hike—say, fifty a week—and my lips are sealed!"

"You'll clown at your own funeral, David," the boss muttered disgustedly. He blinked and gave his head a doglike shake. "I suppose I should thank you for waking me. I didn't come up here to sleep." He shook his head again, even more vigorously. He eyed me.

"So, David. What news?"

"Paydirt!" I gloated.

—34—

THAT REALLY WOKE REGAN UP. His eyes gleamed as I filled him in on the conversation with Rice. And when he heard the office had been sublet to none other than Steven Sarnoff, he got positively ecstatic. He insisted I give him every word of both phone conversations, both the one with the secretary and the one with Rice.

When I finished, the Bishop sat a minute, eyes closed, thinking. He came out of his trance, opened his eyes and rubbed his face. He looked awful. His eyes were bloodshot and he'd gouged his chin with the razor. Plus his hair was even more of a disaster than usual.

"All right, David. You're meeting the realtor at that office building?" I nodded. "Fine. Inspect the office thoroughly. Meanwhile, I'll try to pray. This looks promising. I think we're getting close."

I went to my office. Yesterday the Bishop had left four personnel files to be updated. They were still on my desk. I took one look at them and decided they weren't going to get worked on. Not today. At least not by me. I took off. I still had fifteen minutes left in the half hour I'd given Rice, so decided to walk.

The sun was low to the southeast. If its job was to produce heat, it was malingering. The air was nippy. Good weather for walking fast. I strode up Tenth till I got to Forty-ninth. There I made a right turn and was on the long block that included 601.

I stopped in front of 603. The steps on either side of the stoop leading down to the fatal spot were blocked by makeshift barricades, on which was displayed a sign: ACCESS BARRED BY ORDER OF THE N.Y.P.D.

Coming down the block I'd noted that access to the below-stoop areas of all the other brownstones on the block was blocked by wrought-iron fences with locked gates. On both sides of the street. Not that the fences were high enough to stop an athlete from vaulting over; but it would've been awkward to lure a live lady or schlepp a dead one down any of them. The murderer had taken advantage of the one site on the block where he could do his work in seclusion.

I leaned over the barricade and peered below. No signs of violence—or anything else. I headed next door.

The lobby of 601 was old and gloomy. About half the bulbs in the four ancient chandeliers were burnt out. To the right was a shuttered newsstand, dust thick on the black Formica counter and gray metal shutters.

Three birdcage elevators with old-fashioned grille doors took up most of the rear wall. Above each one was the clocklike dial you never see any more, floor numbers going around in a semicircle, and a pointer to tell you where the elevator is. Only one seemed to be working, the arrow moving slowly from 10 to 9. Behind the cloudy glass under it a loop of cable jerked fitfully.

The left or west wall consisted mainly of a glass-enclosed alphabetical directory. The way it looked, the names on it hadn't changed since the building was new, which had certainly been well before I was born. Or my father. Or *his* father.

Appearances notwithstanding, it had what I was looking for: IN-GRAM, JOSEPH B.: EXPORTS & IMPORTS . . . 320. I quickly scoped the names of the other twenty or thirty tenants. Nothing I recognized. I was considering risking a ride up to Three on one of the ancient elevators when a thin guy about my age and height with thinnish blond hair and horn-rimmed glasses burst through the revolving door from the sidewalk. He approached me.

"Mr. Goldman?"

I nodded. "And you must be Rice." He nodded back. We shook on it.

"So! Delighted to meet you, Mr. Goldman!" His eyes met mine with the exact degree of confidence they teach you in salesman school. His smile radiated sincerity.

"I assume Mr. Sarnoff told you all about the office, Mr. Goldman. It's priced right in your range, and if you move fast I'm sure I can tie it up for you. Of course, as Mr. Sarnoff may have told you, you'd have to give it up in June. But we can have something else just as nice ready for you, then. In the meantime, we can dress this one up any way you say if the furniture arrangement isn't everything you need. Shall we go up?" He didn't explain how he knew what my price range was, and I was afraid to ask.

"Actually," I said, speaking to his back as he pushed the elevator button, "I'm interested in knowing a little bit about the history of the office. Who is Mr. Ingram and how long has he been gone?"

Rice turned to me, puzzled but affable. After all, the customer is always right.

"Mr. Ingram? Well, he's been gone since August. His wife had an opportunity for a sabbatical in Italy—she's a professor at NYU—so he closed up the office and went along with her." Rice grinned. A good grinner, this guy.

As we rode up, Rice talking a mile a minute, the elevator made some noises that made me question its longevity. But it got us to Three, which was really all I had any right to ask.

Three-twenty was a small, square office. Plaster walls, off-white, in need of a new paint job. Two desks, forming an L in the corner next to the single aluminum-sash window. Only one of the desks had a phone, a plain-Jane black one. Leather couch. Three fluorescent lights in the ceiling. Your basic drab. Some signs of poor maintenance—cracks in the walls and dust on the floor—but nothing to send you screaming out into the street.

Where did this little gray office fit into Sarnoff's plans? And how had its phone number got onto Laura Penniston's palm? I sat down at the desk with the phone. Had Laura sat in this chair the night she died?

The instrument had a label that read 212/605–1111. I took out a handkerchief, draped it over the receiver and picked it up. Rice gawked. I put the receiver to my ear and heard a dial tone. Rice started to open his mouth but I frowned and raised a hand as I replaced the receiver. Why had Laura come here the night she was killed? And why had she written that number on her palm? My mind was doing a great job of coming up with questions; too bad it was so empty of answers.

I got up and walked around aimlessly. I wanted to explore. Privately. Rice was being courteously silent after his rapid-fire commentary all the way up on the elevator and down the hall. I turned to him. His eyebrows went up and his head thrust forward. He was so eager for me to rent, he looked like a dog ready to fetch.

"Yes," I said nodding at him sagely and giving the room another slow scan. "I can see why Steven recommended it so highly. Oh! Did you bring that lease along?"

At that, Rice's mood changed. He was suddenly nervous. Possibly my lack of sleep was making me a lousier liar than usual. Eyeing me suspiciously, he laid his briefcase on one of the desks and pulled out a document. He frowned at it for a moment and came to a decision.

"This really is a confidential document. Could you show me some identification, Mr. Goldman?"

"No problem." I showed him everything in my billfold. He took a second look at the private investigator's license, looked at me and started to ask a question. Then decided against it.

Semi-satisfied that I was who I claimed to be, he handed me the agreement. I made a show of checking it over. But I really just wanted a look at that signature. I'm no expert, but, to my eyes, it looked exactly like the *Steven Sarnoff* I'd seen scribbled on the Models for Hire signature cards at Mid-City National.

"It's a fairly standard agreement," Rice assured me. "It was only written for one month, as you can see. But I told Mr. Sarnoff originally I'd be glad to offer him a month-to-month option to continue. I was never able to get in touch with him after that. I guess he left town?"

I ignored the question. "This lease looks fine," I muttered, folding the document and slipping it into my inside coat pocket. I glanced around. "One other thing. Mr. Sarnoff has been missing a couple of important papers, and he asked me to check around for them while I'm here. Would you mind?" Seeing the uncomfortable look return to his eyes, I added, "Oh, you can stay." Rice looked relieved. "In fact, you can help me look."

I'd have preferred to do it alone. If he hadn't been with me, I could have given the place a thorough shakedown. Of course, that could still be done, if the boss wanted it. I'd paid attention to the lock. A Tinker. I can pick one of those in fifteen seconds on a slow day.

But my gut told me there was probably nothing there that would help. So much for my gut.

"Let's look!" the realtor said. I got him started happily on the desks. I was going through the desultory motions of checking behind the cushions of the leather couch when dammed if I didn't feel something.

I pulled out a small object wrapped in Kleenex and unwrapped it carefully. Even after I saw what I had, it took me a couple of seconds to realize it.

Like two eggs in a nest, in the tissue paper lay a pair of matching earrings. The settings looked intricate. Each was a cluster of tiny gems that looked like rubies and diamonds. The rubies (if that's what the red ones were) formed a sparkling cross in each earring.

I could see how someone might call them red cross earrings.

Sometimes I'm almost as quick on the uptake as I think I should be. This was one of those times. I knew right away those earrings were Laura's and, almost as fast, that they were important evidence in a murder case. And right behind that, the thought that I had to avoid compromising my find. I must have gasped or something because Rice was looking. And I was glad he was.

"Mr. Rice!" I said, surprising both of us with the loudness. Rice's eyes widened.

"Did you see me find these in the couch?" Rice nodded, staring at the earrings in my palm.

"Yes, I did."

"Good," I said, thinking fast. Rice having seen me find them was good. Now I was coming up with an idea: how about Dan Rice as temporary custodian for the prize? I looked up from the jewelry into his frowning face. "These look valuable. Let's think for a minute about what we ought to do."

We looked at each other, then simultaneously back to the loot in my hand. Rice started babbling. "What do you think we—?"

I raised my hand. All kinds of thoughts were rumbling through my head but I now knew how I wanted this to go. The idea of Dan Rice taking custody was looking better and better every minute.

I wasn't ready to go to Kessler—yet—but the inspector was almost certainly going to be in on it at some point. Meaning I needed to handle it so Kessler couldn't charge me with tampering with evidence—that is, charge me *and* make it stick. Furthermore, and more importantly, I didn't want to screw up the chance—the excellent chance, it seemed to me—that these trinkets could get Fanning sprung from his current address.

"Do you know any reputable gemologists, Mr. Rice?" I asked the realtor. He stared. I snapped my fingers at him. Rude, but it worked.

He blinked and shook his head. "Gemologists!" I repeated. "Experts on jewelry. Do you know any?"

"Gemologists?" The realtor was trying to get on track. I just smiled. Patience is one of my strong points, never mind what Regan tells you. Rice finally woke up.

"Gemologists. Gemologists. Yes, as a matter of fact, I do. There's one next door to my office. Harold Brady. He's a jewelry wholesaler. Why?"

"Well, these look valuable." I examined the jewelry with a cop's eye. I could see no surface remotely large enough for even a partial fingerprint. The diamonds and rubies looked even more impressive from close up. They did strange things to light, even in this dingy office.

I eyeballed Rice. I hoped he was as innocent as he looked.

"Here's what I think, Mr. Rice. I'm not going to touch them. And I don't want you to, either. Would you take them, please?" Rice held out his hand and I placed the earrings, still in the Kleenex, into his palm. I wrapped the Kleenex around them again. "Just take them as they are to Mr. Brady, would you do that?" I was improvising, but I liked it.

"I've got a feeling," I went on, "that these belong to a friend of Sarnoff's. And don't worry, I'm fairly sure they're not genuine. Thing is, we need to be *sure*." Rice looked willing. So I continued. "I take it you trust this Brady?" Rice nodded. "Good. Let's leave the earrings with him—*after* he appraises them. Is he likely to charge for that?"

The realtor shrugged. He seemed back on track. "Just nominal, I'm sure. If anything."

"Good." I put my arm around his shoulders and started him for the door. "Tell Mr. Brady to guard them with his life. Uh, because Sarnoff'll have a fit if anything happens to them. Oh, and tell Brady it's a rush job." Rice, closing the door behind us, looked at me, surprised. (Yeah, why *was* it a rush job?) "Umm," I said, arm back around his shoulders, heading for the elevators, "because I'd like to be able to tell Mr. Sarnoff for sure whether they're his, uh, friend's."

"But I thought—" Rice was all the way back. Thinking logically— too logically for comfort. I needed to end the conversation.

"I really don't have time to talk about it, Dan," I interrupted as we got on the elevator, "I've got an appointment. Just be a good guy and do it, will you, Dan? And rush it, please? Oh!" I said, as we got off the elevator. "And have Brady call me—at this number." We were going through the revolving door. I handed him my card. "It's very important."

I left him on the sidewalk staring at the card as I hailed a cab. I had to get to the Bishop before asking my brain to do any more improvising. It was starting to go into overload.

—35—

"BUT WHY IN THE NAME of Heaven did you leave the earrings with that realtor?"

Regan had been as excited as I'd been when he heard about the discovery of those earrings. But he about blew a gasket when I told him I'd given them away. He wanted to look at them. For which I couldn't blame him. But, brilliant as he is, rules of evidence are not his strong suit. I had to set him straight.

"You're not listening, Bishop. Let me repeat." Regan rolled his eyes but I ignored it.

"Look. Bishop. Custody of those earrings is crucial. They're absolutely vital evidence—certainly in the death of Laura Penniston and at least indirectly in the others as well. One way or another, those earrings, if they do nothing else, are going to get Jerry Fanning out of the slammer. But if they're going to do that, I can't let them get contaminated."

"Meaning what?"

"Meaning I can't permit the slightest suspicion to exist that they could have been switched or tampered with. The way the cops feel about me, the last thing I need is to have those things in my possession even for a second without a corroborating witness.

"Now, what I did wasn't ideal. Ideally I should have put the earrings into an envelope, had Dan sign his name over the seal; me likewise. Then, both of us go straight to the gemologist and have him sign a receipt testifying to the manner of delivery. But I didn't want to do it that way for a couple of reasons, one being that I wanted *you* to know about it as soon as possible." I snuck a glance to see if he appreciated my concern. He didn't look very thankful, the ingrate. I went on.

"But what I did will hold up in court—if it has to. No one's going to doubt this guy Rice. He's not involved and doesn't suspect a thing. The only risk is that he'd pocket the jewelry and take off, but he's not going to do that. Not the type. An eagle scout.

"The important thing is, I never laid a finger on those earrings without a witness present, and Rice will testify to that. *He* was there when I found them, and he'll back me up that he's the only person—besides me and Brady—who ever touched them. That might be important if we need to convince Kessler—or, even more so, a jury—that we're not pulling a fast one."

I took a breath.

"And that's why I did it that way." Regan glared at me for a few seconds, but I stared him down. For once, he didn't criticize.

"All right," he grumped, looking away. "What's the next step?"

I stared at him. "The next step? Hey, don't be that way. How would *I* know what the next step is? You're the stepper. *You* tell *me*."

"It seems you have taken care of everything. I'm at a loss. I have nothing to suggest."

Talk about a big baby. "Okay," I cajoled. "I apologize for making a decision on my own. But you can't go into hibernation. We've got a buddy down at the old jailhouse, remember? Let's get Fanning out of stir, *then* we can fight."

He spun his chair around, pointed it at the windows, changed his mind and spun back to me. "You're right," he said in a more encouraging tone. "In fact, you're probably right about the earrings. It's just that I'm afraid to move forward without being certain they're Miss Penniston's. But you are? Certain, I mean." I nodded.

He shook his head in disgust. I started to object, thinking he was scorning my opinion, but he overrode me. "No, no, David, my chagrin is not directed your way. At least not at this time. I was simply wishing for a scenario of action comparable to our coup in the McClain matter. What an evening *that* was!"

"Yeah," I muttered. "And your chariot still has the scar to prove it." Regan glanced smugly down at the dent on the left side of the wheelchair. I continued. "And so does my heart. I don't *ever* want to go through anything like that again. Please."

THE FUNDAMENTALS OF MURDER

"Ah," he said contentedly, "there was never any real danger." There's a word for statements like that, but him being a man of the cloth, I didn't say it.

"In any case," he went on, after a few more moments of pleasant reverie, "I should be adroit enough to dream up a new way to put our knowledge to use. Do you think—?" He stopped and frowned. He cocked his head at me. "David, what are the chances that those earrings were deliberately left there by the murderer?"

I gave it some thought, and slowly shook my head. "No, I can't see it. At least I can't see any reason for it."

Regan nodded. "Nor I. Which means that—" He broke off, put his head in his hands and began rubbing his eyes. His voice muffled, he went on, "I'm pondering a theory, David, even as we speak. Think along with me, please. We know that Miss Penniston received a phone call from Mr. Sarnoff at her office the night she died. When she left that party it was undoubtedly to meet him. It now seems that they met in the office Sarnoff had sublet. What happened there?"

Regan raised his head and looked at me but I outwaited him. He didn't get that irritated look he gets when he wants an answer I can't or won't give, so I guess he was just thinking. He finally resumed, holding me with his eyes.

"We may assume that Miss Penniston did two things while there. She removed her earrings and she wrote the phone number of the place on her left palm. As I say, these are only assumptions as yet, but they give rise to an interesting working hypothesis." ·

I frowned. "Well, we know she was in the habit of keeping any and all phone numbers. But why did she take off her earrings? That's what I—"

Regan shook his head at me. "No, David. You're asking the wrong question. The important question is not *why* she took them off, but where was Sarnoff *when* she was taking them off? *And* when she wrote that number on her palm. I find it inconceivable that Sarnoff—and for now let us assume he is the murderer we are after—would have left those earrings there for you to find more than two weeks later, had he known she put them there. Or that he wouldn't have scrubbed that number off her palm, had he known she wrote it. I conclude that Sarnoff was out of the office when she did both.

"Yet Sarnoff must have been there to admit her—nothing suggests that Miss Penniston had a key, and much suggests she didn't. And, assuming he was the murderer, he was there when she died. Then what prompted him to leave? Having gone to such lengths to get her there, why leave her alone—for several hours, apparently? And why did she remain there?" Regan shook his head.

"And there is a final puzzle. Given the murderer's penchant for removing his victim's earrings, why didn't he return to that office and retrieve the earrings?"

We stared at each other. The expression on the boss's face suggested he was looking for me to come up with an answer. I hated to disappoint, but I didn't have a clue.

The phone rang in my office. Saved by the bell. I made tracks. "Goldman."

"Mr. Goldman, this is Harold Brady. Mr. Rice asked me to call you."

The Bishop was in the doorway, eyebrows raised. He was really getting into it. I covered the mouthpiece and mouthed the words *the gemologist*. Regan got even more excited. Pushing himself all the way into my office, he stage-whispered, "Tell him you'll call back. Get his number and hang up." I frowned at him but finally obeyed, leaving Brady puzzled.

The Bishop was third-degreeing me before the receiver hit the cradle. "Did he say anything about the earrings?"

"How could he? You cut me off before I could even—"

"I want to talk to that man," the boss interrupted, spinning and heading back through the door. "Call him back on my line, David. And tell him I'm joining the conversation."

I would have liked to know how he wanted to be introduced but he was in no mood for delay. I shrugged and punched out Brady's number.

"Mr. Brady. Dave Goldman again. My associate, F. X. Regan, would have a word with you." The even more befuddled jewelry expert mumbled something along the lines of "Okay." I stayed on the line.

"Mr. Brady," said Regan from his office. "Mr. Goldman is still on the line, but he has asked me to ask you some questions. What can you tell us about those earrings, sir?"

"Er, yes, er, Mr. Regan. Well, each earring has twenty-one imitation diamonds and twenty imitation rubies, all tiny ones, an eighth carat each. Whoever did the setting is a superb craftsman. The design is very unusual. Were the stones genuine, it would be a very costly set. At a distance of several inches, one could be fooled—even I. Looked at carefully, up close, the material in the stones is obviously cubic zirconia."

"Cubic zirconia, Mr. Brady?"

"That's right . . . um, crystallized zirconium dioxide."

"Ah! Could you give me an approximate dollar value for the set, sir?"

"Well, I hesitate to give an estimate."

"I assure you, sir," said Regan, "I shan't quote you. I'm simply looking for an order of magnitude. As much as a thousand dollars, say?"

"Oh, perhaps. But probably not. Wholesale, as they are right now, perhaps four hundred. Retail, with luck, eight- or nine-fifty. Very difficult to say. The setting is lovely, but with imitation stones . . . On the other hand, they've been well cared for; only one tiny scratch on the setting, almost invisible to the naked eye." Brady sighed. "Perhaps a thousand. It's hard to say."

"Indulge me, sir," the Bishop said, applying plenty of lubrication. "Again, not for publication, could you give me an estimate of the set's worth, were the stones *genuine* diamonds and rubies."

Brady chuckled. "That I don't mind doing, since it's pure fantasy. With high-quality gems—no, say, *highest* quality gems, twelve-point diamonds and rubies, well cut—that set of earrings, with the kind of crafting that's gone into the setting, could be worth easily fifteen— maybe even twenty-thousand dollars. Easily."

"Thank you, Mr. Brady," said Regan. "I'll leave the conversation, now. I think Mr. Goldman may have a question or two for you." The Bishop rang off.

I thought for a moment. "Just one question, Mr. Brady, what were Mr. Rice's instructions to you, as you understood them? As regards those earrings?"

"He said to keep them in a safe place. And that I was to give them to no one except to you *and* him. Jointly."

"An honest man," I commented. "I couldn't have thought of a better arrangement. I hope it doesn't come to it, but they could be important pieces of evidence in a criminal case. Guard them with your life." I hung up on a no doubt thoroughly confused jeweler.

The Bishop looked up when I reentered, and his look started my spine tingling. He was onto something. I grinned.

"You look like a lion that smells fresh meat. What's up?"

"This: the questions I was raising when Mr. Brady called are probably unanswerable till we have more facts. But is that important? Perhaps we can come up with a working hypothesis based on some educated guesses and design a plan around it to trap Mr. Sarnoff.

"First of all, let's take the questions: why did Miss Penniston remove her earrings? And why did she go to that office in the first place?

"Using facts that we know, I think it's a fair assumption that Sarnoff invited her there. He let her in and left. How did he get her there? And why did he leave? Those are doubtless important questions, but since I see no way of exploring them, let them go for the nonce. She came, he left. Miss Penniston was left for several hours to her own devices. Query: how did she occupy her time for those two or three hours? Any ideas, David?"

"I know what I'd do," I grinned. "That leather couch in there wasn't in the greatest of shape. But it was good-sized. And it looked comfortable."

"Exactly." Regan nodded with satisfaction. "You might have taken a nap. If Miss Penniston took a similar course, what do you think she would have done with a pair of heavy, valuable—?"

"—earrings?" I interrupted excitedly. "She'd take them off!"

"No doubt," said the Bishop. "And wrap them in a tissue."

I was thinking fast. "So when the killer arrived . . ."

"She wasn't wearing them," Regan finished. "And either forgot she had taken them off, or decided, for whatever reason, not to put them back on. And the killer paid no attention."

"Then why didn't Sarnoff return for the missing earrings? Certainly he knew she'd been in that office; and he knew the earrings were not on her ear lobes."

Regan raised his left thumb. "Either he didn't know she'd been wearing earrings, or . . ." right thumb up. ". . . he knew but didn't consider the jewelry of sufficient value to bother looking for."

"Okay," I conceded. "I can buy it. So where does that leave us?"

"Advantageously situated," the boss said. "Consider. We have now accumulated two or three pieces of vital information known neither by the police nor, more to the point, the murderer.

"We don't know what drew her there, but we do know with a fair degree of certainty that Miss Penniston spent her last hours in that office. We know that she—or someone—left those earrings there. And we know the office was rented under the name Sarnoff. Of course, two of those facts are also known by Sarnoff. What he *doesn't* know is that anyone else knows."

Regan set his brake and leaned forward, elbows on the desk, holding me with his eyes. "Nor does he know that Miss Penniston wrote the office phone number on her palm. Therefore, he has no reason to think that anyone knows he was using the office. Yet. How can we use what *we* know—but Sarnoff doesn't—to our advantage?" Regan tilted his head back and squinted at the ceiling.

"Sarnoff's mysterious identity," he mused, head back, "continues to intrigue me. No one has seen him; he hides behind post office box numbers and false addresses. The only person who knew him—Laura Penniston—is dead."

The boss released the brake on the wheelchair, and began to pace. On his third pass from the east wall to the west, I said, "Call me when you need me," and headed for my office. He didn't seem to hear me. When he's pacing, he often doesn't hear or see anything.

But I didn't make it. I was two strides from the door when he exploded.

"David!" I turned to him, miffed.

"Hey! I was only going to wait in my office. If you—"

Regan waved it away. "Sit down, please. I have an idea, but it's problematic. I need your advice."

—36—

I SOON UNDERSTOOD why the Bishop wanted my input. Rolling around in his wheelchair, he'd come up with a doozy of an idea. Trouble was, it conflicted with his inconvenient code of morality and he needed me to assuage his tender conscience. Myself, I loved it as soon as I heard it.

"But," he said mournfully, "it entails a direct contravention of the truth."

"Yeah, but look at the reason why. To nail a murderer and get Jerry Fan—"

"—Fanning out of jail," Regan finished for me. "A man we know to be innocent. But David, one can't violate a commandment simply to obtain a good result. 'The end justifies the means' flouts the very essence of Christian morality or any other morality." I didn't ask the boss if that was a knock against me. I was afraid I knew the answer.

"Well," I said instead, "figure out some way around it. I've seen you do it before." *That* got him. He turned various shades of pink and gave me a glare that would have melted steel.

"I have *never*," he huffed, "subordinated morality to my own needs or desires, and you know it! That is the rankest kind of—"

I threw up my hands. "Hey, I take it back. But haven't I heard you talk about something called broad mental reservation?"

"Well, yes, there's that," the Bishop allowed, partly assuaged by my semi-apology. "That can sometimes apply. But clearly the type of statement I am envisioning would not fall under that rubric. Regrettably."

So we had a lengthy discussion of the whole situation. What Regan could and couldn't do, morally. And—more to the point—what he could and couldn't let *me* do. It was all very interesting if somewhat academic.

For myself, it wasn't an issue. As I said, I thought he'd come up with a dandy, and was ready to go with it, morality be damned.

"All right," he finally said, quasi-capitulating, "go ahead and explain our dilemma to the Pennistons. It's not my wont to let others make my ethical decisions for me. But a little discussion with them might clarify matters."

I guess I should have thanked him for including me on his high moral plane by calling it *our* dilemma. I made the call—and got lucky. Caught the Pennistons just as they were going out the door.

"Oh, Mr. Goldman," Maureen said. "Nice of you to call. Mr. Lancer, our attorney, is just now taking us to lunch. Roger and I came upstairs to freshen up. After lunch, we're going over to Mid-City National with him to open Laura's safe deposit box. Then he's taking us to LaGuardia in time to catch the five o'clock flight back to Wichita." I glanced at my watch: 11:53 A.M. Things were moving too fast.

"Do you have a second phone in your room, Mrs. Penniston?" I asked. "I have something I need to discuss with both of you, and since you're on your way to lunch I'd like to do it over the phone—if you don't mind taking a minute."

Roger got on. I wished the Bishop would too. It was tricky and I was afraid I'd screw it up. But his morality wouldn't let him participate— beyond watching me do it. I outlined Regan's immoral idea.

"What we—I mean, what *I*—have in mind is a trick to pull Sarnoff out of hiding. I think there's a good chance that one or more of your daughter's friends knows Mr. Sarnoff and either doesn't know it—because he was using a false name—or doesn't want to admit it. This trick involves your daughter's earrings. How much did they cost? Does either of you remember?"

A pause. Then Maureen's voice, quietly, "Roger?"

"Yes, I do." Roger was positive. "They were twelve hundred and fifty dollars. And well worth it. They were beautiful. And Laura loved them. She said she'd always—" The doting father had to stop and clear his throat. No one said anything for a few seconds.

I decided Roger had said all he was going to, and broke the silence.

"Thank you. Now let me tell you what I have in mind. I'd like to ask you to get the word around that those missing earrings were really terribly expensive. I'd like you to tell everyone that the diamonds and the rubies in them were *real*. That those were *twenty-thousand-dollar earrings*. Could you do that for us—I mean, me?"

More silence. Finally, from Maureen, "I'm afraid I—what are you saying? You want us to *lie* about them? Lie about how valuable they were?"

"Well, I'd prefer to call it a broad mental reservation, not lying," I said, glancing at the Bishop. He blushed and looked irritated. "But, yeah, basically that's it. I think if you're willing to do that, we can find the man that murdered your daughter."

"Whom should we tell?" Roger asked.

"I'd like you to call George McClendon, Betty Donovan, Lee Stubbs, Sandra Norville and Bob Theodore, and tell them all. All of them saw her that evening, so it would be natural for you to ask them: are they absolutely sure they *were* the red cross earrings? Because you know just how valuable they are. You just can't believe they're now in the hands of some murderer."

"I don't understand." Roger put in. "How could that possibly help?"

I held a two-second debate with myself regarding how much I should tell them. I decided to give them a piece of the puzzle.

"Okay," I said. "Because I think Sarnoff needs money bad. He cheated your daughter and Betty out of one hundred twenty thousand dollars. And I think if he sees a way to get twenty thousand more, he'll go for it. And I think I know where he thinks he knows the earrings are. And I plan to be there to nab him when he goes after them."

A short silence. Then Maureen said in a shocked voice, "You think this Sarnoff's the one who murdered Laura, don't you, Dave?"

"Frankly, I do, Maureen. I don't have time to go into all the reasons, but—yes."

Roger had another objection. "But doesn't Sarnoff—or whoever killed her—already have the earrings? If she was wearing them, and they were missing when the police found Laura, he's probably got them."

"Nope," I assured him. "The earrings are in a very safe place. When this is all over, I'll return them to you."

"We'll do it," Roger said grimly. "If you really think it might do some good, Dave, I'm willing. Count us in." A murmur of conversation between the two of them. Then Roger gave me the kicker. "We'll postpone our flight back to Wichita, Dave."

"Thank you," I said, relieved. "I appreciate it. Suppose I come over to your hotel so we can discuss it."

The couple agreed to meet me in the Hilton lobby at 2:30.

"I don't like this, David," Regan fretted as I hung up the phone. "I am aiding and abetting direct and blatant disregard of the truth. I can't permit it. Call them back."

That did it. I blew up. "Look, dammit! I don't know where you dig up that so-called morality of yours! But if you're more concerned about telling a little white lie to a bunch of suspects in a murder case than you are about a guy who set up and knocked off four broads, all I can say is—"

Regan blew right back at me. "I'll not tolerate that kind of sexist vulgarity in my presence! *Broads*, indeed!"

We glared at each other. Regan broke eye contact first.

"Very well. Vulgarity aside, your point about the overarching need to identify and apprehend this criminal is well taken. All right." He headed slowly for the window. "Let's talk about strategy, David. We can discuss situation ethics at a later, more convenient time." Regan spun his chair and faced me.

"Mr. and Mrs. Penniston can make the calls this afternoon. And you will be in place in that office. With just a *soupçon* of good fortune on our side, we may soon know exactly who and what Mr. Steven Sarnoff is."

—37—

MAYBE YOU SEE now why I liked the scam. It had an excellent chance of working, for all the Bishop's ethical qualms. Frankly, I found it easier to appreciate the scam than to understand his qualms. To me, catching a guy like Sarnoff is a helluva lot more important than to have the truth come charging out of your mouth every time you open it. Well, to each his own.

But the idea! True, Laura had told people the earrings were paste, but that could be written off as nothing more than a strategy to discourage thieves. Don't people often try to protect their jewelry by getting the word around that it's worthless?

So the Pennistons telling the world that those red cross earrings were worth $20,000 struck me as a dandy way to lure Sarnoff out of whatever hole he'd jumped into.

"How would you assess the probability," I asked the Bishop over lunch, "that Sarnoff will head for that office?"

"Impossible to say, David. Too many variables. All we can do is hope we're right—that one of those five will inform Sarnoff of what the Pennistons are alleging. He will know that she was wearing them that night. And it shouldn't take him long to calculate that the most logical place she could have left them was where she in fact did leave them— in that office—an office about which he has no reason to believe anyone else knows."

After lunch, I went to my office, loaded my .38 and donned my armpit holster. This Sarnoff was giving every indication of being a very scary individual, even if he wasn't the towering monster from my nightmare. I wanted to be ready for him.

I went over the script with Regan once again. We agreed that I should—assuming they let me—stay with the Pennistons when they made the five calls, to lend immoral support. We also agreed that the simpler the script, the better.

No need for it to be anything but simple. They were going over the estate, and just wanted to be sure those earrings were really missing. Extremely valuable, real rubies and diamonds, you know. What? Laura told you they were *paste*? Hardly! Twenty thousand dollars is a lot of money to pay for paste. So she was definitely wearing them the night of the murder? Then there was nothing more to be done, was there?

Before leaving the house, I made two key phone calls. First to Rice, telling him I wanted to rent the office for a month. He was delighted, promising to meet me there with the key and a rental contract at five that afternoon.

Then I called Dennis Kelley. Dennis is a fellow Irregular and a damn good private detective. I was going to need some back-up if this turned out to be a several day stake-out. Or maybe even if it didn't.

Kelley was happy to hear from me and was available. He promised to meet me in the lobby of 601 West Forty-ninth at ten to five. I told him I'd explain everything then.

The plan was as follows: I'd stay with the Pennistons while they made the first call or two from their room at the Hilton, but leave them no later than four-forty—whether or not they'd reached everyone yet—and go meet Kelley and Rice at the stake-out. I wouldn't let the Pennistons make the first call till four-thirty so as to avoid the slightest chance that Sarnoff might come, look for the earrings, and leave before Kelley and I got there to wait for him.

I didn't really expect to see the Pennistons much before three. Lunch with their lawyer, inspecting their daughter's safe deposit box—these things take time. So I was surprised when we bumped into each other at two-twenty as I walked into the Hilton.

"Well, Dave," Roger said jovially, his face ruddier than normal, "this is fortuitous timing." He had a little trouble getting out the *fortuitous*. His lunch had obviously been at least part liquid. A quick glance at the frau told me she was also a little happier than she'd been the day before.

I decided our first order of business, once we got up to their room, had better be a rush order of coffee from room service. I wanted Roger and Maureen stone sober before they started making those phone calls.

You'd have thought I was a long-lost friend. Flanking me on either side, they chattered all the way through the big lobby to the elevator. I didn't pay much attention to the small talk, having other things on my mind. At least, until we got on the elevator. As the doors closed and Roger pushed 26, I heard Maureen say something about Stubbs, Donovan and McClendon joining them at the bank.

"Oh?" I said, turning to her. "How'd that happen?"

"Well," she said, lurching as the elevator jerked upward, "Betty and George just wanted to be with us when we looked. Just being friendly, you know."

Roger grinned at her and joined in. "Yes, and Lee wanted to be sure everyone in the bank was treating us okay, you know?"

"You'll be proud of us, Dave," Maureen said. Something in the way she said it made my stomach tighten.

She moved closer to me, taking my elbow. Roger moved in with her. The other four passengers listened carefully while pretending not to. In a stage whisper, she said, "We've already done it, Dave!"

I looked from her beaming face to Roger's. The air was redolent of fine scotch.

"Wonderful!" I beamed back, my gut not feeling the joy my face was trying to show. "Done what?"

We were slowing for the twenty-sixth floor. The doors opened and Maureen put a cautionary finger to her lips. In the hall, on edge now, I turned to face them.

"What did you do?" They suddenly looked sheepish. Maureen gave Roger a look that was an appeal for help. Roger stepped in, his smile losing a little of its wattage.

"We really pulled the wool over their eyes, Dave." I stared. Roger got serious. "We told them how expensive the earrings really were, Dave. We told them just what you told us to."

I grabbed Roger's arm. "Told who?"

"George and Betty. And Lee Stubbs. We told them they were twenty-thousand-dollar earrings."

Maureen, looking at my face, looked worried, though not nearly as worried as I felt. "Is something wrong, Dave?" she asked.

"Yeah," said Roger. "What's wrong? Isn't that what you wanted us to do?"

I had lots of choices. Curse, swear, stomp on the floor. Shake the two idiots till their teeth rattled, either separately or as a team. But business before pleasure. At the moment, I had to be somewhere else. Namely, at 601 West Forty-ninth Street. Before Sarnoff got there. Or, at least, before he got away.

"When was this?" I snapped, pushing the elevator button. For a tenth of a second I considered taking the stairs, then remembered I was twenty-six floors up. I gave the button several more sharp jabs.

"About two hours ago," Roger said, nervously looking at his watch, then back at my face. "Before we went to lunch. Why? What's wrong, Dave? Did we do the wrong thing?"

I glued my thumb to the damn elevator button (I know, I know, that doesn't help, it's stupid. All I can say is, *you* try standing there doing nothing while Steven Sarnoff is probably on his way to West Forty-ninth Street).

"Don't worry about it," I said automatically, trying to think. And actually came up with an idea.

"Here!" With my free hand, I pulled out Dan Rice's business card. "Call this guy. Right *now*! Tell him to *meet* me in that office he's subletting. Tell him five o'clock's too late. I need it *now*. *Right* now!" The doors chimed. "Tell him there's a *bonus* if he gets there in ten minutes."

The doors opened. I groaned audibly. Packed with kids in school uniforms. How much was *this* going to slow me down? I squeezed on anyway, still talking to the flustered Pennistons.

"Tell him to hurry! *And* call Bishop Regan." The doors closed in my face and I raised my voice. "Tell him everything that's happened!" The kids stared. I looked at my watch and tried to ignore them.

Anything else I should have told the Pennistons? Too late to worry. I had to get to Forty-ninth and Ninth and hope to hell Sarnoff hadn't already come and gone.

—38—

I LOOSENED MY TIE and ran all the way. Not far to run, you say? Sixth to Ninth is only three blocks, you say? You'd better bone up on your geography.

First of all, it's not three blocks, it's four, because Broadway's in there. Second, those are the four longest blocks in the world. Third, you wouldn't *believe* the idiots that inhabit the sidewalks of New York— half of them gawk like fools at anybody in a hurry, and the other half go out of their way to slow them down.

In spite of everything—schoolkids on tour, gawkers and obstructionists—only eleven minutes had elapsed from the moment I squeezed into that elevator to the moment I pushed through the revolving door at 601 West Forty-ninth.

I was covered with sweat, especially my left armpit under that nylon holster. And naturally the lobby was being prepared for a sauna party, with the temperature at a balmy ninety degrees or so. In seconds, sweat was starting to come through the suit in patches.

But how I looked was the least of my worries. I loosened my tie a little more, wishing I wasn't packing that damn weapon so I could take off my suit coat. I tried to think logically. Were there any other exits from this place? If so, did Sarnoff know about them? Would Rice show up?

The last question got answered when Rice came bustling into the lobby just three minutes after me. Barely enough time for me to have resumed normal breathing. The Playmate of the Year in a sheer negligee couldn't have looked any better than Dan Rice coming through that revolving door.

"Mr. Goldman! What's the rush?"

"I'm just anxious to get started," I answered in as cool a voice as I could muster, giving the elevator button a couple of hard jolts. I immediately gave him the program I'd thought up while I waited.

"Do me a favor and go up first, would you, Dan? Mr. Sarnoff was going to meet me here about now, and he didn't say whether it would be here in the lobby or up in the office. I'd hate to pass him going up on one elevator while he's going down on the other. So I'll wait here a minute while you go up."

Rice started to say something but I rode over him.

"Don't go in, though. Umm, I think he may have kept his key, and you'd only embarrass him. If he—if *anyone*—comes out of that office, don't bother introducing yourself, just stay with them, all right?"

Rice was puzzled and wanted to argue. The elevator arrived and the doors opened.

"Just humor me," I cajoled, easing him onto the elevator by the elbow. "I'll be up in two minutes. Anyone comes out of that office . . ." The doors closed and I raised my voice. ". . . you come back down with them!"

I was starting to get sick and tired of elevator doors closing in my face while I was still talking.

I hadn't found the greatest partner in the world. Replacing Rice with Dennis Kelley would've made me feel a lot better. But, weak reed or not, Rice was what I had. Kelley would join me in a couple of hours. Then we could enjoy a chuckle over my senseless mad rush.

Because I was beginning to think a little more rationally. After all, even if the three who'd heard the Pennistons' earring story *had* included Sarnoff's informant, it wasn't likely they'd reached him already. And even if they had, he had no reason to think there was any rush. If he showed at all, it probably wouldn't be before tomorrow. Or even the next day. My heart rate was beginning to subside. I wished my suit would dry as fast.

I gave myself two minutes. The lobby wasn't getting a bit cooler or any less deserted. I went up.

Rice was waiting, as instructed, in the hallway by 320. Something seemed to tell him it was no time for idle chatter. He inserted the key and opened the door. I muscled past him and went in fast, hand on the .38 inside my coat.

The office was a wreck. Furniture askew, bits of foam rubber scattered around. The cushions on the couch had been slashed and ripped apart. The rug, partly rolled up, was pulled over into one corner.

I was on the verge of cursing when, over Rice's breathing and my own, I heard a sound from behind one of the desks. Old habits took over. Out came the .38. I was down on one knee, arms extended, both hands on the automatic.

"Come out from behind there!" I yelled, weapon trained on the desk, hoping to hell whoever came out wouldn't come out blasting. A long and silent second passed. Then, like the moon rising over the eastern horizon, the round face of Betty Donovan appeared over the desktop, dishwater eyes wide with apprehension.

—39—

THE THREE OF US froze. Till I saw that Betty wasn't showing any signs of resistance. Then I put my .38 back in its holster. Thinking a comment of some kind was called for, I came up with "Where's Sarnoff?" Not a top contender for Wittiest Remark of the Year.

Rice looked too stunned to say anything. Betty struggled to her feet and cleared her throat. Something about her was out of kilter, I couldn't tell what. She ran her hands over her skirt, trying to smooth it down.

"I've already told you, Mr. Goldman," she said, in a valiant attempt to recover some dignity. "I don't *know* any Sarnoff. What are *you* doing here?"

So she was going to brazen it out. She went on. "Just look at this room! Someone has vandalized it." She seemed to focus on Rice for the first time. "Oh, hello," she said, approaching him with extended hand. "I'm Betty Donovan. Please excuse the mess." Grace under pressure.

Rice uncomfortably took her hand, and, as they shook, I realized what was cockeyed about her. Her eyes. They were unfocused and wandering. She had to be high on something—speed would have been my first guess, coke right behind.

But what she might or might not be on was near the bottom of my list of concerns. Nearer the top was the discovery I'd just made: I'd found Sarnoff's accomplice. Which translated into Strangler John's accomplice.

But at the peak of the list was a question: what the hell was I going to do now? Looking at Donovan's jittery eyes, I guessed she was asking herself the same thing.

"It's okay, Dan," I said. "Miss Donovan and I know each other. Tell you what we're going to do." I strode to the desk. Betty just watched me, her moon face twitching.

I picked up the phone, facing Donovan. This was one lady I definitely did not want to turn my back on. She stood watching me, fingers writhing on the purse she held.

The phone was dead. I tried jiggling the button. No good. I looked at Betty.

"I know," Betty said in a strange-sounding voice. "I tried it myself a few minutes ago. Here. Look." She pointed at something on the floor, hidden from me by the desk. She took an abrupt step back, still facing me, leaving room for me to maneuver around it. I didn't move. So she bent with a grunt and picked up the phone line. Held it up, pointed at the tear. "I guess whoever ripped up this office must have done it," she said, accentuating her words with jerky nods.

"Yeah, probably," I said skeptically. "Let me see your purse, Betty."

She stared at me blankly for a moment, then gave me a quick, unpleasant smile and handed it over. I riffled through it quickly, not finding anything lethal, unless you counted the ciggies. I handed it back.

Rice moved to my side. "What the hell is going on here?" he demanded, looking angrily from Betty to me. "Why'd you tear this room up? I want to know what's going on!"

"Tell you what, Dan." I kept my voice matter of fact. "Someone's got to call the police. And it looks like you're nominated."

I removed my billfold without taking my eyes off Betty and handed it to him. "My private investigator's license is in there. Find the nearest phone and call the police." I gave him the number for Homicide. "Tell them I'm here and making a citizen's arrest." No reaction from Betty.

Rice started to move, but I stopped him. "Wait a minute, Dan. You need to remember this woman's name. Betty Donovan, got it?"

"D-Donovan," he said in a scared voice. "B-Betty Donovan."

"Right. Don't forget it." Betty just stood there, blinking and licking her lips, clutching her purse in both hands, her fingers clenching and unclenching. I repeated the phone number.

"Call that number, Dan. Can you do that?"

"Right. I'll find a phone and be right back." He left.

Betty sank into the swivel chair behind the desk and put her purse in her lap. She swung abruptly around, giving me her back, and looked out the window. "You can't really believe what you're saying, Mr. Goldman."

I held a brief caucus with myself over whether or not to debate with her. I won *that* debate—What the hell, I'm a born talker.

"You couldn't be more wrong, Betty. I not only believe it, I know it. I knew it as soon as I saw you in the midst of all this rubble. Did you do all this alone, or did Sarnoff help you?"

Betty swung the swivel chair to face me, and the look on her round face shook me. How could she be that calm and have been accessory to the death of her best friend?

She shook her head sadly and began swiveling back and forth, purse teetering in her lap. The chair squeaked in protest with every movement.

"David, David, David," she crooned. "You're *so* naive. Sarnoff's my *guy*. Don't you understand anything?" She was as high as a kite.

"What are you on, Betty? Uppers?"

She giggled, and pivoted away from me. "Oh, David. If you only knew." This was getting spooky.

"Why'd you help him do it, Betty?" Silly as she was acting, she might actually tell me something. And, no longer being a cop, I didn't have to inform her of her rights. When she didn't answer, I just waited. The chair got still. All I could see of her was the back of her head.

"That damn Harv," Betty finally said, in a near whisper. "He hooked me. Then he upped the ante. Higher. And *higher!*"

The last word was almost screamed. This was getting out of hand. In addition to wondering whether Harv was Sarnoff's real name, I was starting to wish for a back-up. For once in my life, even Charlie Blake would have been a welcome sight. I tried to calm her down.

"Harv was your pusher?"

"Damn straight. The son of a bitch. I should've—awww, poor Laura. That poor damn Laura." Betty swung her chair to me and I saw she was crying. Real tears. This lady was wired like Consolidated Edison.

"So who's Sarnoff?"

She looked up at me with eyes that refused to focus. A vertical streak of mascara streaked her fat left cheek almost all the way to the corner of her mouth. She smiled slyly. "Does it matter, Davey? I needed him and he needed me, know what I mean?" She steadied the purse on her lap. "And nobody knew! Didn't tell a soul! Fooled 'em all, Davey. Sandy was point man and she didn't even know it." Betty giggled like a ten-year-old girl.

"So who's Sarnoff?" I persisted.

Her eyes got sly again. "Want to meet him, Dave? Want to meet Steve Sarnoff?"

"Sure." She didn't seem to hear me, so I raised my voice. "Where is he, Betty? Where is Steven Sarnoff?"

But I couldn't reach her. She was back in her private world. Her voice softened. "Kept giving Sandy memos about the account, using Laura's signature. Made everyone think Laura was the one. I just needed the money, can you understand that?" Her voice suddenly turned vicious and she ground the next words through her teeth. "It was that damn Harv!"

"Was that Sarnoff's other name, Betty?"

She stared at me thoughtfully, looked away and shook her head. "Then that damn McClendon had to go blow the whistle. And Laura *knew*! So she had to go." Her eyes filled with tears. "I didn't want anything to happen to Laura. I *didn't*! But Harv had me in a box! What was I going to do? God! I couldn't live without that damn crack! I couldn't!"

Donovan got up and lurched to the desk. Suddenly she dumped the contents of her purse onto it. Billfold, lipstick, toilet articles skittered across the wooden desktop. And five or six joints. She picked one up and offered it to me, smile slack, eyes wandering crazily.

"Want some, Dave? It's good stuff—mostly tobacco, with a little something extra. Here!"

I took it from her and sniffed it. There was crack in it all right. It had that unforgettable, acrid, vinegary odor. I flipped it disgustedly back onto the desk.

"Don't like crack much, do you, Dave? Well, neither do I, buddy, neither do I. You get hooked on it, and it's damn expensive, boy. *Damn* expensive!"

I felt sorry for her. Big mistake. Dumb mistake.

—40—

I DECIDED THE BEST THING would be to let Betty sleep it off on the ruins of the couch. By the time the police arrived, she'd feel better.

"Why don't you lie down, Betty?" I suggested. Donovan nodded blearily, her eyes still unable to focus. "Maybe you're righ', Dave," she allowed. "Gimme an arm, willya, buddy?"

The woman seemed ready to collapse. Feeling half disgusted, half sympathetic, I put an arm around her and tried to help her to the couch. She put all her weight against me. She was even heavier than I'd thought. I staggered a moment, righted myself and managed to get her moving, her feet trying to keep up.

I had one warning. Her right arm was around my shoulders. Out of the corner of my eye, I saw wrapped around her right thumb a loop of wire, the end of it running up her arm into her jacket sleeve. That didn't register fast enough. Had I acted immediately when I saw that . . . But I didn't.

Drugs fool everyone. They fool the user and then they help the user fool you. They make the users high; they can also make them unnaturally quick and strong. As I was about to find out.

We were almost to the couch, her right hand around my neck, left hand hanging onto her right hand across my chest. I was watching her face. (I'd have been better off watching her feet.) Suddenly her eyes rolled upward, her knees gave way and I had her full weight.

I should have realized that if she'd lost consciousness, her hands would have let go of each other. Instead, they clung tight.

The extra weight made me stagger. I took a step forward to keep my balance. Or tried to. But one of her feet was suddenly in the way and

I started down. The fall was abruptly accelerated by a sudden knee in the back from the no longer comatose woman. I was in big trouble.

I hit the floor hard, face first, the wind knocked out of me. I tried to roll, but Donovan's whole weight was on me. And like a flash, a wire was around my throat, jerked hard and tight. I must have instinctively tightened my neck muscles. Which probably saved my life. Without that, the wire would have crushed my windpipe in that first second.

Everything went momentarily black. The neck didn't hurt that bad— that came later—but I saw purple circles of light expanding out to the edge of my vision, new circles replacing the ones that disappeared. My sight partly returned and I was able to see the carpet a half-inch from my face, swimming and shimmering in the expanding circles.

Just one thought kept running through my mind: you idiot, Betty Donovan is Steven Sarnoff, Donovan *is* Sarnoff. Good timing there, Dave.

Meanwhile, Betty's knee sought better purchase in the small of my back. I could hear her grunt with effort as she tugged the wire tighter, trying to snuff me out.

My neck muscles were straining, and the skin of my neck was starting to tear with the sawing action of the noose. Attempting to roll to either side was out of the question. I had to try something else. The noose tightened. I needed to get over on my back to bring my arms into play, but I couldn't move.

A hoarse, rhythmic, animal sound filled the room. I vaguely realized it was Betty grunting. I could visualize her, teeth bared, eyes popping, in the effort to strangle the life out of me.

My oxygen was going. I fought to free my right arm, trapped under my body. Donovan responded by rolling her weight to put more pressure on my back.

That's where she blew it. In shifting her weight she gave the noose a little slack. I sensed a slight lessening of the pressure around my neck and reacted to it. Violently. Abruptly arching my back, I lifted my head as high as I could, relieving the pressure still more. She realized she was losing leverage on my throat and immediately rocked backward to recover tautness. As I felt her rock back, I snapped my head forward. The wire dug deeper into my neck, but I ignored that and rolled right.

That roll cost Betty the noose. But not the fight. I was now on my back and she went straight for my face. Her fingernails sliced into my cheek and jarred against the ridges above both eyes.

One of my arms was still trapped under me, the other was shielded by her shoulder. My only immediate defense was closing my eyes and rolling my head away from her probing fingers. Fingernails ripped across a tightly closed eyelid.

Betty's knee crashed into my groin. I reacted with an instinctive hip roll. I had to stop playing defense and start fighting back, but she wasn't letting me. She was a fury. And I was exhausted. I was running out of oxygen fast.

Summoning strength from somewhere, I finally got one arm free, then the other. I went for her hands, still gouging at my face. I blindly managed to get hold of one wrist. God, she was strong! It took both hands just to hang on.

Once I did, I thought I had her. I didn't. She could now use my own leverage against me. Feeling her other hand leave my face, I opened one eye to a slit to see what was happening. The answer came sooner than I wanted: her free fist was coming straight at my face from over her head.

I jerked my eyes shut again. Her fist slammed my head into the floor so hard I damn near lost it once and for all. A lot of pain, more expanding circles, more flashes of light.

Another smash wouldn't be far behind. Not caring to leave my brains on the dusty floor of this godforsaken office, I released her wrist and spun to my right. I felt her lose purchase. Her fingernails futilely slashed the back of my neck, and I kept right on rolling. I opened my eyes as I rolled. Nice to be able to do that without immediate risk of losing them.

Two-and-a-half rolls later, my back to Betty, I dizzily got partway to my feet and started my hand for the .38. A whisper of air and that damn wire was around my throat again. How could anyone that fat be that quick!

But this time I surprised her. Instead of trying to break free, I went the other way. I was up as the noose hit, and backpedaled fast. The noose loosened slightly, then I felt and heard a gasp as I slammed into her. I dug my heels in and backpedaled harder. Your basic move to box your man off the boards in unrefereed schoolyard basketball. Presumably not having played schoolyard basketball, Betty didn't know the countermove.

She must have let go of the wire at that point, but I was too busy to notice. She lost her footing and went down hard. Blindly, I followed her down, ramming my elbow deep into her abdomen as I did, bringing another gasp.

Betty's body went still. The fight was over. Except . . .

I'd rather skip what I did then. The woman was clearly out. One glance at her ashen, contorted face left no doubt. She was doubled up, struggling for air. But I was . . . I don't know. I went into her chest with my elbow again, the weight of my whole body behind it. As I later learned, that blow broke three ribs and collapsed one lung. And came within a hair of acing her.

I could argue, "All's fair" or "Hey, she played possum before." Or "She had it coming." But those are rationalizations. Police training is clear: No excessive force, meaning you don't hurt someone more than the minimum required. That final slam to Betty Donovan's midsection was excessive force. I was sorry for it the second I did it. And I'm sorry for it today.

I'd just got to my feet, panting, and begun to feel around my face and neck to see how much damage the maniac had done when I heard a key turn in the lock. A second later, Dan Rice was in the room. The realtor took one look at the gasping woman on the floor and another at me, and his eyes grew huge.

"My God, Goldman, what—?"

That was as far as I let him get. "No time, man! Get the hell back to where you came from and get an ambulance. Tell them on the double! She may be dying."

He ran, leaving the door ajar. As I bent to see what I could do for the woman, I could hear through the window the faint but growing sound of a siren.

—41—

JUST LIKE OLD TIMES. The place lousy with cops and medics. Kessler insisting I had to check into the hospital for observation, me telling him he was full of it. Like riding a bike, some things you never forget.

Of course, all that was after the two paramedics had hustled Betty out on a stretcher. The looks on their faces said what they wouldn't: Betty Donovan wasn't going to make it. And the way she was breathing— or rather struggling to breathe—they had logic on their side. They failed to reckon with the woman's stubbornness. She was her normal self a year later when she stood to face the jury and heard them proclaim her guilty on all four counts of Murder One.

Rice—my "weak reed"—had done splendidly. He'd sent the police up straightaway and waited downstairs for the ambulance, which came in less than ten minutes. The two patrolmen had been with me in the office for nearly eight minutes by then, none of us able to do anything about Betty other than watch her try to breathe. They were green but handled themselves pretty well.

The paramedics looked just as green at first, but they took one look at Betty and went to work like pros. One of them had an oxygen mask on her, the other monitored vital signs. They got her stabilized, on the stretcher and out of there in about a hundred and fifty seconds.

The patrolmen stuck around but resisted the impulse to ask me any questions. I guess they knew Homicide was on the way. Homicide doesn't take kindly to being infringed upon.

Kessler and his usual sidekick, Sergeant Mike Burke, popped in a minute or two after the stretcher went out. They were their typical cool selves. The more bizarre the circumstances, the cooler they get.

225

After asking me if I was okay, Kessler wanted a rundown on what the hell was going on. I told him. I was hoarse and feeling lousy, mentally as well as physically. I kept the jokes to a minimum.

"I didn't buy in," I explained, "to Fanning being the Strangler, so I kept on looking. Which resulted in my bumping into Miss Donovan here in this office just twenty minutes ago. We had a slight altercation."

That didn't strike his funny bone. "Yeah, an altercation. Are you telling me you think *she* murdered those women?"

"Hey, I don't *think* anything, Inspector. I *know* she did. She told me as much.

"Furthermore, Officer Holmes there," I gestured at the tall young patrolman with the mop of tousled brown hair who was standing uncomfortably to the side, "has taken a certain piano wire into custody— where'd you put it, Officer?" Holmes pointed to the wire on top of the desk.

"That's an interesting little item, Inspector." I kept talking to Kessler's back as he walked immediately to the desk to study the wire. "You'll obviously want to check whether it's the one. But I'll give you dollars to doughnuts it is. But, whether it is or not, the M.O.'s definitely the same. I can testify to that. So can my neck. And if you want to compare the marks it makes on the victims' throats, you don't have to look any farther than right here." I lifted my chin and pointed at the wounds and bruises all around my neck.

"Judas Priest!" Kessler took a step closer. "That Donovan woman did *that*? I saw what she did to your face and eyes, but—! What the hell happened?" He spun around and yelled. "Mike!"

The beefy sergeant, whom I had greeted when they arrived, was in the midst of taking Rice's statement. He looked up.

"Take custody of this weapon," Kessler snapped. "It may be the Strangler's." As fussy as Kessler is, he didn't say a word to Burke about being careful with it, which said a lot about his opinion of Burke. Burke's a damn good cop. I know that myself. He was my direct supervisor the first two years I was in Homicide.

The inspector came back to me. I gave him the full story—everything but my sneaking that Xerox of Laura's palm. Kessler had a hard time understanding how I got a phone number out of G O S T."

"Yes, I can see that the G could be a six. And the S a five. I'd thought of that myself. But where'd you get the four ones?"

I tried to give the inspector a lesson in repeating decimals but got hopelessly tangled up in the math. He finally cut me off.

"All right, Davey," he sighed. "You've got a genius penned up over there on Thirty-seventh, with no workable legs, nothing to do but pray, and no one to talk to but a putz like you. So what's he got to think about but your cases? I'm not surprised he doped it out. Next time, though, you'd better have him explain it to you a couple more times until you get it straight." He gave me a friendly wink.

"You know," Kessler went on, a grin now showing through the beard, "I actually considered showing him that photostat myself, just to see what he'd say. Dammit, I *thought* maybe he was the one guy who could figure it out. But . . . I never did." He shrugged. "What I'll never understand is how you two doped that Fanning was innocent. For my money, he had guilty written all over him. Bishop Regan's clairvoyance acting up on him again?"

I shrugged. With the vow of secrecy my boss had laid on me, that was about all I could do. Which didn't make my *former* boss very happy.

For that matter it didn't make *me* very happy either. The shrug had rubbed my collar up against my neck.

"All right," Kessler went on. "What the hell did Donovan use *this* office for, then? *Assuming* that she's it."

I nodded—and winced again. "Yeah, I've been asking myself that same question ever since I heard about it this morning. I first thought it might be where she went to shoot up, or where she had her drugs delivered. But that's not it. For one thing, her pusher, Harv, came to her office. For another, she only rented this office a month or so ago."

I swung around—with my whole body this time—and looked over the room. "What I think is, Laura came here that Friday night. Betty'd told her Sarnoff was here. Or at least that he'd be coming here. Then Betty came instead. And killed her."

Kessler nodded then yelled, "Burke!" The sergeant looked over again. "Are you planning to dust this place?"

"What for?"

"Do it, Mike. I've got a feeling we could find some of Laura Penniston's prints around here."

Burke nodded. With absolutely no curiosity. That's why he's Kessler's favorite gofer. And why he'll never get any higher than sergeant. If Laura had left a trace of a print in this room, Burke'd find it. But he'd never think to ask why the hell he was looking for it in the first place.

"Only thing I want to know, Dave." Kessler was back to me again.

"How'd you let that woman get the drop on you? Didn't you have her tagged the moment you walked in?"

I looked at the inspector. I didn't want to tell him I'd thought she was only an accomplice till the wire was around my neck. I didn't want him to know the Bishop and I had been chasing our own tail the past three days, looking for a guy named Sarnoff who didn't even exist.

Most of all I had no desire to talk about the fight. This one I wasn't proud of. I'd been suckered like a ninny, come through it more marked up than the other guy, and ended it with a very cheap shot after the buzzer. And the other guy was a woman. So I tried the light touch.

"My mistake, Inspector. I asked her to demonstrate—on me—how she did those women. She got a little carried away with it, and I had to subdue her. That's about it." I gave him a big, false grin. Kessler scowled. "Well, I've got some people to see." I turned and went.

"You go straight to the hospital, Davey!" Kessler yelled after me. "And when you finish there, I want you down at Headquarters for a statement."

"Yeah, yeah," I muttered. I wasn't heading for any hospital, but I also wasn't going to argue about it. I just wanted out of that damn building. Forever.

—42—

I TREATED MYSELF to a cab ride. Figured I'd earned it. The cabbie did a double-take at my appearance, both my face and my suit. (The more expensive of the two, I sadly realized, was going to have to be pitched.) He started a comment, took another look at my face and shut his mouth.

I spent the ride mentally working up a report for Regan. Damn good one, if I say so myself. Insightful, modest. Listing all the clues that led me straight to Betty. How I deduced that she was Sarnoff. Good piece of fiction. Shame I never got to deliver it.

I was barely in the mansion before they were all over me like fleas on a dog. At the sound of the door opening, Ernie came charging out of the kitchen, almost getting blindsided by Regan blasting out of his office, hands a blur on the wheels. Normally a near-miss like that would have got him a good chewing-out. Not this time. They ignored each other and headed straight for me. Both started talking at once.

"Oooh, David! Your face! Shouldn't you . . . ?"

"In Heaven's name, why didn't you call? I wanted to . . ."

". . . be in the hospital? Come into the kitchen and let me . . ."

". . . give you some advice. I'd finally deduced that the Donovan woman and Steven Sarnoff were one and the same. If you hadn't . . ."

". . . put some ointment on your face—oooh! And your *neck*! David, you must have . . . !"

". . . acted so precipitately, I could have warned you about her."

Amidst the torrent of words, "the Donovan woman and Sarnoff were one and the same" hit me right between the eyes. When I can help it I avoid showing awe at Regan's mental gymnastics. This time I couldn't. I stared at him as Ernie fussed over the wounds on my neck.

"What did you say?" I demanded, wincing as Ernie's not-so-soft fingertips probed around my Adam's apple.

"I said you should have called! I had—"

"Not that. About Sarnoff and Donovan. Being one and the same."

"Oh, that." Regan waved it away. "After you left, I realized that Miss Donovan *was* Steven Sarnoff. And that she must therefore be the murderer. Had you only gone to the Pennistons' hotel room before rushing off, you would have found my urgent phone message. I assume the damage to your face and neck were inflicted by her?"

There was something wrong with his tone (it lacked the gloat it normally has when he's pulled off a feat), but I didn't stop to ponder that. I was too flabbergasted. How had he figured it out? I grabbed Ernie's hand to stop her fussing. I got her eye. "Ernie. Did someone call within the last half hour? Or show up?"

Normally that kind of suspicious question would have drawn a smirk from Regan. Instead, he turned away. What was going on?

"No," Sister Ernestine answered, with a quick glance at the boss. "Mr. Penniston called an hour ago. Right after that, Bishop Regan called me in, told me my prayers were needed right away. He said something about Mr. Penniston's call told him you might be in grave danger. I went straight up to the chapel. I said five decades of the rosary for you, and some other prayers." I was surprised—and touched—to see tears in her eyes. She gulped and continued.

"I turned on the phone up there, so I'd have heard it if it had rung. I only came back down ten minutes ago. I asked the Bishop if anything had changed. He said nothing. Since then, I've been praying in the kitchen. David"—Ernie looked stricken—"I'm so relieved to see you here safe!"

"My surmise," Regan said gruffly, giving Ernie a chance to regain her composure, "was that Miss Donovan would go straight from the bank to that office to look for the earrings. And that when you walked in on her, you would think she was only an accomplice, rather than the murderer. And, from the looks of you, my surmise was accurate."

I looked at him. His voice sounded dejected. Was he sinking into one of his depressions? I hoped not. Life around the mansion is a bitch when he's depressed. What was wrong? Hadn't I shown enough enthusiasm over his accomplishment? Well, I could certainly remedy that.

"How did you figure it out?" I asked admiringly. "I don't see how—"

Regan interrupted, even more dejected-sounding. "It's not important. I was too late to be of any use, anyway. In the meantime, your injuries look serious. Shouldn't you be in the hospital?"

"Probably," I muttered. "If you mean the psychiatric ward. I need treatment for stupidity, not for these scratches." I wished people would start shutting up about hospitals.

Ernie finally managed to get me into the kitchen for her nursely ministrations. Regan, though invited, declined to join the bandaging party and headed for his office. Ernie was anxious as she applied antibiotic ointment. And not about me.

"Is he starting another one?" she asked fearfully. She didn't have to explain. I knew all too well what she meant. These fits of his come along every few months, and neither of us has yet devised a way of getting through them without winding up depressed ourselves. I shrugged.

"But you have to *do* something, David!"

"Yeah, you always say that, Ernie. But you never tell me—do *what*?"

She applied salve to my right eyebrow. "This should have stitches," she fussed, saw my scowl and gave it up.

"How do I know?" she asked, returning to the original subject. "Just *do* something!"

Women.

But I did try, at least. I badly needed to get out of my damp, filthy, ruined clothes and into something clean and comfortable. But the Bishop's situation couldn't wait. I headed straight for his office.

He'd closed the door. I tapped once and entered. Regan was over by the window, reading. It was a depression all right. Reading during working hours is a dead giveaway.

"Want to know what happened?" I asked brightly. He looked up from the book and nodded, not enthusiastically. He wheeled—slowly—in my direction. The book, I saw, was McMurtry's *Lonesome Dove*. A birthday gift from me. He'd read it through (along with dozens of other books, of course), each of his last two depressions. This was looking grim.

"I take it that's a yes," I said. "Then may I suggest something? We owe Rozanski plenty, mainly for the help he gave us the other night. Let me call him and you listen in. When I'm done, you can tell me how you doped it all out."

He gave an almost imperceptible nod. I got Chet and reported. I did it the way Chet's taught me: first the basics—who, what, when, how and where—and then the details.

Regan watched as intently as Chet listened. He also asked fewer dumb questions. Though, to give Rozanski credit, he asked only one really dumb one—at the end: "How are you feeling, Davey?" I'd have made an appropriate comment, but I was getting hoarser and my throat was starting to burn. Just as well I didn't, because Chet followed the dumb question with a surprisingly sincere thank-you.

"Your timing on this is impeccable, Davey. Our guy at Headquarters picked up a rumor fifteen minutes ago that something big had gone down on the Strangler John thing, but he couldn't find out what. We've both been trying to get hold of Kessler or Blake, but they're incommunicado. I was just giving up on today's edition right now, when you called. So I really appreciate this, buddy. Next time you call me for some info, maybe I won't bitch and moan so much."

"Yeah, sure you won't," I croaked and hung up.

"You should be in the hospital," Regan growled, and headed for the window again. The spark of interest that had been in his eye was gone.

"Hey, weren't you going to tell me how you figured it out?"

He didn't stop moving. I could barely make out his mumbled response.

"At some later time, perhaps. You should see a doctor." He reopened the book. I couldn't think of a thing to say or do, so I left.

Back in my office, I called Kelley to tell him the job was off, but my mind stayed on Regan. He'd never started one of these so soon after a case. I was especially worried about his unwillingness to crow. Crowing is the sugar and cream in his coffee.

I was sitting there, feet on the desk, fruitlessly trying to dream up a plan to jolly Regan out of his funk, when the phone rang. Dave Baker. With the solution to my problem, though I didn't know it at the time.

"Hey, man, I hear you went three fast rounds with Strangler Joan, the Minutemaid! Tell me about it!"

"What do you want, Dave," I rasped. "I'm pretty busy right now." I didn't feel like talking, not even to a fellow Irregular.

"Well! Are we a mite testy today? And what's with the voice?" I was thinking of a suitable response when Dave got serious. "Pretty rough, huh? I just talked to Kessler. He says you looked like something the cat drug in."

"Piece of cake," I croaked. "Put a woman in the ring with me and I'll whip her butt damn near every time."

Silence for a few seconds. "Well," Dave finally said, "I'm at the jail right now. They're processing our boy out of here. Harrington's dropped all charges. Jerry's extremely grateful—to you and the Bish, not to me. Which is only fair. I didn't really do anything."

I thought fast. An idea was building.

"Is he grateful enough to call me, Dave?" I asked.

"Fanning? Oh, I'm sure he would be. You want me to tell him? They're almost done here."

We left it that Fanning would call within the hour. I sat back, feeling a lot better now that I had something to work on. I'd caught a murderer; now I could rescue a man from his sulks. Not a bad day's work. Of course, I hadn't pulled the second one off yet. And it was probably going to be a lot tougher than the first.

The phone rang again in less than five minutes. Not Fanning as I expected, but Kessler. Discovering I hadn't been to the hospital, he bawled me out—gently, for him—and then got down to business.

"Mr. and Mrs. Penniston are with me, Davey, and I've been telling them of the . . . new development in the case. They would like to see you. You and the Bishop."

It took me less than a second to see that that might fit nicely into the plot I was devising.

"Could they come over here?"

A short jumble of voices on the other end. Then: "They'd be happy to, Davey. They'd planned to catch the late flight back to Wichita, but now they're planning to stay over. In view of what's happened. You don't sound so good, though. Is today okay?"

"Feeling better every minute, Inspector." A light flashed under one of the buttons on the phone. "I've got another call coming in. Could you hang on?" I put him on hold and depressed the button. "Bishop's office."

"Davey, it's me." Fanning's jubilant voice. "I got to thank you for all you've done. You and that Bishop."

"Nice of you to call, Jerry. Uh, Jerry . . . ?"

"Yessir?"

"Would you like to stop by with Ida Mae and Joe Bob?"

"Shoot, yes!"

"How about today?"

"Why, heck yes."

"Then hang on." Two more bounces from line to line, and I'd done it. Two Pennistons and three Fannings were stopping by at six to see the Bishop and me.

Naturally, Kessler horned in. And, naturally, I let him. After all, he'd just been nice enough to give me till tomorrow to come in and give my statement. Besides, you never know when it'll come in handy to have a friendly police inspector in your corner.

Then came the hard part—getting Regan to see them. This was one meeting where getting the guests to come was going to be a whole lot easier than getting the host to play host.

—43—

"ABSOLUTELY NOT!"

Exactly the response I'd expected. I'd have appreciated his looking up from the book to give me the turndown, but you can't have everything: rudeness *and* eye contact too.

"Hey," I wheezed, "why beat around the bush? If you don't want to see those people, just say so." I plopped onto a chair and yawned. Audibly.

Regan closed the book and hefted it, probably calculating *Lonesome Dove*'s throw weight, the optimum arc of trajectory and the probable damage to my head. He decided against it, dropped the book in his lap, and rolled my way.

"David. You know I have nothing to say to those people. *You* apprehended the killer. *You* exhibited intrepidity, quickness and strength. Also percipience, in spite of my failure to warn you. I have nothing to offer."

So that was it. He was miffed that I'd solved the case without him. That I'd have never got to first base without him, much less second or third, didn't count. He'd wanted to be at home plate for the finish, like in the McClain thing, and he'd missed out. He was pouting.

We wrangled for fifteen minutes and I was getting nowhere, beyond making my throat worse. And perilously close to telling him exactly what was eating him. Which, of course, would have sunk the whole project.

Ida Mae—or rather Joe Bob—saved the day. The boss and I were still haranguing when Ernie appeared in the doorway, looking very nervous. Regan didn't see her till she found a gap in the uproar and interrupted us in a small voice. "Excuse me, Bishop, but—" His glare would have wilted a tougher maiden than Ernie. She was turning to flee when I stopped her.

"Hold it, Ern." I turned to Regan. "Look. She's not involved. Don't take it out on her."

Ernie gave me a look that reminded me of a line of poetry way back in high school English, something about "wee poor timorous beastie, what a (something)'s in thy breastie." Burns, right? And Regan says I have no soul.

"What is it, Sister?" Regan said in a kindlier voice than I'd heard out of him in several minutes.

"Excuse me, Bishop, I didn't know if you were taking calls. It's Mrs. Fanning. She says it's important."

Regan's lips tightened. Without glancing at me, he spun to his desk and picked up the phone. Ernie departed, giving me a grateful look. I winked at her with my good eye.

"Yes, Mrs. Fanning." Courteous, but barely. The Bishop listened for a few seconds. "But Mrs. Fanning, I'll not be able to join you. A previous engagement makes it impossible. I trust you—" He listened some more and either I was imagining things or his face actually began to soften. "Well, I don't know . . . Well certainly, Mrs. Fanning, if you feel Joseph would be helped by seeing me, I suppose I—all right. I'll see you at six. And your husband. And, of course, Joseph."

Regan cradled the phone gently and wheeled away toward the windows without a glance at me. He *did* throw back over his shoulder the last word of what *had* been an argument.

"Mrs. Fanning seems to think my presence would be therapeutic for Joseph. He's not feeling well. Perhaps she's right. So I'll join your meeting. But I'll stand mute. I was not involved."

He'd stand mute? That was a laugh. For openers, he can't stand. And he'll probably stand a long time before he'll ever be mute. On any subject whatsoever. But I was in no mood to quibble. Ida Mae had done what I couldn't—got the Bishop to join our party. As for his standing mute, well, we'd see.

I barely had time to shower—very gingerly—and change into comfortable slacks, sweater and loafers before our guests arrived. I was actually feeling pretty chipper. Till I discovered Kessler had brought his mutt.

I refer to Blake. The four of them—the Pennistons, Kessler and Blake—arrived at five to six, five minutes early. Fortunately, I saw Charlie through the glass before opening the door.

I made a quick decision. Checking to be sure I had my house key, I stepped outside, closing the door behind me. This made the stoop a bit crowded, what with five of us. Kessler was decent enough to back down onto the top step.

"Roger! Maureen!" I croaked, shaking hands. "So nice of you to stop by." Maureen took a look at my face and gasped; Roger mumbled something. I wasted no time getting to Kessler, grabbed his elbow and turned the two of us to face the street.

"What's the ape doing here?"

"He insisted," Kessler mumbled, unable to meet my eye. "As the officer in charge of the case, he wanted to be here. And I—"

"And you caved in. Well, I'm not, brother. Caving in, that is. He's not getting in. Bishop's orders. You know better than this, Inspector. You're going to have to get rid of him. When you do, you'll get in. If not, you're not."

Kessler's face started to redden but I didn't wait. Turning, I ignored Blake, gave Roger and Maureen a bright smile and croaked, "Come on in! Uh, Charlie, the inspector wants a word."

Blake glanced rapidly back and forth from me to Kessler. The look in his eye told me he was thinking of forcing his way in with Roger and Maureen. I sort of hoped he'd try. No way he could be as hard to handle as Betty.

But something in the inspector's face, possibly combined with consideration of the weak job market, persuaded Charlie to go slow. He glared daggers at me but stayed behind.

I gave Kessler about four minutes to get rid of him. I was wrong. The doorbell didn't chime again till ten after six and when I went, it was Baker and the three Fannings. Plus Kessler. As I held the door for them, Blake peeled away from the curb in his Chevy like some dope-crazed teenager. Pretty childish if you ask me.

—44—

So by 6:15 everyone was in place. Over at the south window, the Bishop had his buddy, Joe Bob, on his lap. Ida Mae kept glancing over, but the baby was giving less than two hoots to anything but Regan.

Jerry, Roger and Maureen were pelting the guy in charge, namely me, with questions. Kessler, over in a corner, looked amused. I don't know if it was at me, running things from behind Regan's desk, or at Regan, playing baby sitter while I held court. And Baker, in the other corner, kept looking at his watch like he had to be somewhere else. Typical.

Roger, speaking for all, demanded an explanation. "But I still don't understand how you deduced it wasn't a religious psychopath. And *Betty*! My God, Maureen and I *knew* Betty, or thought we did, and it never occurred to us that she might be capable of—this!"

"The guy with the answers is my ecclesiastical ally over there," I told him, aiming a thumb over my shoulder. All eyes moved to the Bishop. The only sound was a gurgle by Joe Bob, who was testing out Regan's pectoral cross as a teething device.

"Joe Bob!" Ida shrilled at the desecration. She jumped up and headed for the baby. The Bishop stopped her with an upraised hand.

"Please, Mrs. Fanning. 'Suffer the little children . . . ' Yes?"

He smiled at her. She smiled back. And promptly made the appeal I'd asked her to. Her twangy Oklahoma accent helped. But knowing the boss, I think it was her youthful sweetness that carried the day.

"*Please* join us, Bishop. Joe Bob won't be no trouble. And we'd all be proud to hear how you figured it out."

237

Regan's smile faded. He surveyed the group, ending at me. He had me. I shrugged and tried to look innocent.

The boss sighed, murmured "Hang on, Joseph," and, to the baby's delight, rolled quickly to the desk. I yielded the place of honor. With pleasure.

Ensconced at his proper spot, Regan patted the baby absently and took in the group, looking longest at Kessler in the corner.

"First of all," the boss finally said, "I have a confession to make." He paused, frowning at the cooing infant in concentration. Suddenly he lifted him, causing a scream of glee, high over his head.

The smile on Regan's face, as he craned to look up at the baby, vanished abruptly. Joe Bob's mouth, wide open with laughter, was developing a sizable leak, and a dollop of drool was heading Bishopward. The prelate quickly jerked his face out of harm's way and settled the baby back into his lap. Plenty of laughter, especially by Joe Bob.

Ida Mae hopped over to wipe the boy's mouth, and gasped. "Bishop! Your robe! It's all wet. Joe Bob, you—!"

The Bishop stopped her. "Madame. Joseph simply did what babies do. This soutane is not stained. If it is, I'll wear it anyway, in honor of my small friend. Eh, Joseph?" He smiled, first at Joe Bob, then up at Ida.

"Nonetheless, perhaps you'd better take him, Mrs. Fanning. For now."

Rid of his tiny burden, Regan got to the point. "I said I had a confession. The confession needs to be linked to an apology—to Mr. Goldman." Regan glanced at me. "You have all seen the angry scars on his neck and face. Miss Donovan did that today in her earnest and nearly successful attempt to kill him. The damage she inflicted is directly attributable to my nonfeasance. I failed abjectly to warn him about her till it was too late to be of any use.

"Too late to warn Mr. Goldman of the extreme danger he'd be in if he were alone with her. All credit for her apprehension belongs to him. But—" He looked at Ida Mae "—since you ask, let me see if I can explain my thought processes."

Regan turned to Kessler. "Inspector. You asked Mr. Goldman today how we could be so certain that Mr. Fanning was not the murderer." The Bishop glanced at the fundie. "Mr. Fanning and I are Christians. We have prayed together. I went to see him in jail and asked him point-blank if he was guilty. He responded that he is guilty of a great many things—but not of murder. I believed him. As a fellow Christian, I could do no other. Mr. Goldman, though no Christian, was willing to share my conviction."

Kessler looked skeptical, with good reason. In the silence that followed, he started to speak, glanced at Fanning and subsided. I could have told Kessler how justified his skepticism was. But I left it at rolled eyes and kept my mouth shut.

Fanning spoke up, his expression two parts sheepishness, one part defiance. "I have to confess, Bishop. I told Ida Mae this morning, and I want to tell all of you."

"Surely, this isn't necessary, Mr. Fanning," Regan said.

"Yes it is, Bishop,"Jerry answered immediately and confidently. Ida Mae nodded. Joe Bob was now sleeping noisily, his face scrunched into her shoulder.

So we all got treated to Jerry's confession. He probably got more sympathy for his porno-movie peccadillo than he would have if everyone hadn't wanted him to shut up. We wanted to hear the Bishop's explanation.

Though Jerry's sincerity was moving. He ended with, "I still love my wife and baby, and I just hope the Lord'll be as good to me as they are." He looked at Kessler. "Now you know where I was, Inspector. See why I didn't want to talk about it none?"

Kessler nodded and gave a slight smile through the beard. He turned to Regan. "And *you* couldn't tell me, because of the seal of the confessional." The Bishop nodded. Kessler's a Presbyterian but I guess he knows Catholic lingo.

"Okay," Kessler said. "Now: how'd you figure out it was Donovan?"

Regan closed his eyes. "I must first explain how I reasoned that Miss Penniston must have known her attacker."

Kessler stared. Regan proceeded to lay it out: how Laura's failure to resist had tipped him. Kessler nodded as he listened.

"Not bad," he said when Regan finished. "So based on that, you had Davey sniff around the Penniston agency?"

"Indeed. The first thing we were looking for was a motive. And a likely one came to our attention almost immediately, with the discovery of the Models for Hire fraud. As you know, Mr. Kessler, a Steven Sarnoff had been looting Penniston Associates for a year and a half.

Uncovering the swindle was child's play for David. As was the identity of its perpetrator—or so it seemed. Except that Steven Sarnoff was nowhere to be found.

"So we began looking for him. And as he studied the man's *modus operandi*, Mr. Goldman came to certain conclusions about Sarnoff's personality and character. He deduced that he must be patient, devious, intelligent and, above all, familiar with banking practices and policies.

"My own contribution at that stage was nugatory: that 'Sarnoff' must be an alias. Well . . ." Regan reddened slightly and looked around. The room seemed to hush a little.

"Well," Regan said in a quieter voice, "I did consider the possibility that Sarnoff might actually be one of the five friends of Miss Penniston David had talked to. As I compared each to the template that David and I had projected, Betty Donovan alone possessed all the requisite characteristics. But . . . she was a woman." Regan smiled grimly.

"Now I'm not so foolish as to think a woman incapable of using a man's name for a pseudonym. Or of murder, for that matter. But I *was* foolish enough to believe—albeit unconsciously—that a woman wouldn't commit crimes this heinous. And that was criminally foolish."

Kessler was interested. "So what finally disabused you of that, er, misapprehension?"

Regan sighed. "It wasn't easy. Let me begin at the beginning. Operating on the theory that 'Sarnoff' was a pseudonym for one of Miss Penniston's associates, I was certain that her discovery of his identity precipitated her death. So, who was 'Sarnoff'? In my foolishness, I was sure he was a man."

"So you were down to the three men in the picture," muttered Kessler. "Theodore, Stubbs and McClendon." Regan nodded.

"At first, yes. Yet none fit the mold. First of all, Stubbs. He had motive, of a sort. Miss Penniston had thrown him over for Mr. Theodore eighteen months before—coincidentally, at the very time 'Sarnoff' was beginning his raids on the Penniston treasury. But Mr. Stubbs was exculpated by height considerations. At five-seven, he is three inches too short to have been the killer. Correct, Inspector?"

Kessler nodded. "The marks on the throat showed that the killer had to be at least as tall as any of the victims. If Stubbs is five-seven, he's a good three inches shorter than either Morgan or Pen—" The Inspector reddened. "Or your daughter," he ended lamely, nodding at the parents.

Regan jumped back in. "So Stubbs was excluded. Which brings us

THE FUNDAMENTALS OF MURDER

to Robert Theodore. Mr. Theodore had a motive—he was short of funds, despite his wealthy father. And he was certainly of sufficient height and strength.

"But his temperament and, frankly, his intelligence did not seem up to the demands of the job. Furthermore, the fact that he was caught in a dalliance with Miss Norville by Miss Penniston just hours before her death argued against his guilt. It was inconceivable to me that a killer as patient, intelligent and cold-blooded as this one could have been so distracted by lust in the midst of his crime as to fall prey to temptation. Unless the dalliance were a deliberate act designed for some ulterior motive, and I could imagine no such motive.

"So I refused to accept it, thus ruling him out of consideration, at least provisionally. And Miss Norville as well, incidentally, had she not already been excluded by several other considerations—most notably, her slightness of stature. And, of course, her gender." Regan made a face.

"But they cooked up that alibi together," I objected. "Couldn't they have also—?"

"No," the boss snapped. "Whoever this killer was, his plot didn't begin the night of Miss Penniston's murder. That foolish attempt at an alibi was as exculpatory as anything those two could have devised. I refused to believe this cold-blooded, cautious, farsighted monster could be capable of that kind of jackassery."

"Leaving McClendon," commented Kessler. "A very unsavory individual. Were you aware he has a police record?"

"Oh yes," Regan murmured. "But reflective of a different kind of violence. His were crimes of passion, however twisted the passion. Nothing about those sadomasochistic episodes with prostitutes suggested the foresight this criminal exhibited.

"Furthermore, he was in no position to set up the scheme which defrauded Laura Penniston's—and Betty Donovan's—company of well over a hundred thousand dollars. Getting memos to Miss Norville with Miss Penniston's forged signature on them, arranging payments so that the models got their expected fees with plenty left over for the thief— McClendon was in no position to do any of that.

"No. Examined coldly and objectively, Miss Donovan was the only possible candidate." Regan began to tick off points on his fingers. "First: she was in a prime position to loot the company. She alone held fiscal responsibility. Second: motivation. Miss Donovan's chain-smoking hinted at an addictive personality. Also her use of marijuana. And several informants suggested use of stronger drugs. If true, and if that use had passed on to addiction, there was the possibility of a need for funds to support her habit. Visits of the mysterious Harv with his mysterious packages transformed possibility into likelihood. Third: ability. That was answered when we learned that she had studied Chung-Mu-Quan."

Maureen Penniston interrupted. "I thought that was a form of karate. Isn't that a peaceful philosophy?"

"On the contrary, Madame. Practitioners of Chung-Mu-Quan boast of their ability to use many and various instruments to inflict death. Miss Donovan's leaning seems to have been in the direction of piano wire."

"But where'd she get the wire?" Roger asked.

Kessler intervened. "We're working on that, Mr. Penniston. Thanks to Davey, we have the wire itself. I doubt that we'll ever find out where she got it, but that doesn't matter. We've got plenty to indict and convict. Miss Donovan's in custody at City Hospital and her condition has stabilized. We'll be able to ask her a few questions in a day or two. Not that I'm counting on getting many answers."

All eyes went back to Regan as he continued. "But my fixation on Miss Donovan's femininity had me convinced that she could be at most an accomplice in the crimes." He shook his head and looked down. "This prejudice—which is what it is—is, I now realize, a part of me, and has been since my childhood. That it is, for the most part, unconscious is no excuse. Discovering its presence within me has been as humiliating as any experience I've ever had." Regan took a breath and resumed.

"Thus I stayed on the trail of the elusive Steven Sarnoff long after it was—or, at least, should have been—painfully obvious he didn't exist. This perverse blindness persisted until today, after David left.

"At that point a chance vulgarity of David's brought to mind the same vulgarity, used by the final victim. The manager of the motel where she died told one of your men, Inspector, that the woman—an Afro-American named Billie Morgan—had said, 'Not bad for an old *broad.*' This, while displaying a one-hundred-dollar bill she had just received from her customer. Do you recall the remark, Inspector?"

Kessler frowned. "Yes."

"To whom did you imagine Miss Morgan was referring when she used that expression?"

"Herself, of course. Who else?"

"Who else, indeed? That was the question I finally got around to asking myself this afternoon. I am not an expert on Afro-American culture, but I have kept my ears open. It suddenly struck me that use of that particular epithet is uncharacteristic of Afro-Americans. To confirm it, I telephoned Sheriff Langston of Catskill County, an acquaintance of Mr. Goldman's and mine. I believe you also know him, Mr. Kessler."

Kessler scowled. Langston's a sore subject between us because of the Bishop's unorthodox tactics in the McClain case.

"Mr. Langston," Regan went on, unperturbed, "is Afro-American. He confirmed my suspicion. In black street argot, the term *broad* is seldom used. And when it is, it almost always refers to *white* women. Almost never to Afro-Americans. Making it highly unlikely that Miss Morgan was referring to herself. If not herself, then whom? Was it possible her 'john' was a *woman?*

"A woman. Suddenly, scales dropped from my eyes. I realized that sexism had been coloring my perceptions, and quickly reevaluated the other pertinent data. As I began to consider—seriously, at last—all the other evidence pointing to Miss Donovan, everything fell into place.

"Take the whispered warning to the *Dispatch*. Why did the murderer whisper? The call wasn't being taped. *But*: if the caller wished to disguise her gender, what better way?

"But by now I was helpless. Failing to reach Mr. Goldman at the Hilton, then learning from Mr. Penniston that our earring ploy had been prematurely activated, I knew instantly where Mr. Goldman had gone and his possible peril. But there was nothing to do but pray. Which Sister Ernestine and I proceeded to do. With fortunate results."

Kessler snorted. "Yes, very fortunate, Bishop. Considering you were in possession of several key facts in a murder investigation you didn't see fit to entrust to me. Now, I'm as much for prayer as the next guy. But we Protestants have a saying: The Lord helps those who help themselves. You could have helped me—*and* Davey—if you'd seen fit to give *me* a call this afternoon. I'd have at least *tried* not to mess up your little scheme."

Regan faced the angry stare and shrugged. "And done what, Inspector? I dearly longed to call you. But what could I have said? That, for my own good and sufficient reasons, I'd deduced that Betty Donovan was the Strangler, and that she might be lying in wait for David in that office? Can you honestly say you'd have paid the slightest attention to such a call, given your belief, bordering on conviction, that you had the true murderer in custody?"

A brief staring contest. Kessler blinked first. He shrugged. "Maybe not, Bishop, maybe not. But it'd sure be nice if you were ever to get me involved in one of your cases before the murderer has tried to kill you or Davey."

Regan smiled. "Next time, Inspector. You have my word."

The interchange seemed to wake Dave Baker up. Tearing his eyes away from his watch, he had a question. "What happened the evening Laura Penniston died, Bishop? I don't understand how Betty Donovan could have made that call to Laura when she was at the party the whole time."

Regan shook his head. "We only *assumed* a phone call was made, Mr. Baker. At no time did Miss Penniston say she had talked to anyone on the phone. She said Mr. Sarnoff had called, and that she was going to meet and unmask him.

"What must have happened is this: Miss Donovan left a message for Miss Penniston on her desk and arranged for someone to summon Miss Penniston to her office. The note was probably on the order of 'Sarnoff called. Go to Room 320 of 601 West Forty-ninth and wait for him.' It was undoubtedly signed by Miss Donovan, whom Miss Penniston trusted. And with it would have been the key to the office to which she was being dispatched.

"Miss Penniston went as instructed. While there she did something without which the crime might never have been solved. Following her highly useful practice—now second nature to her—she jotted the number of the phone in that office on her palm. She did so in her own unique shorthand which remained impenetrable to all decoding efforts—until last night.

"I think she also took a nap. Divesting herself of her earrings, she probably leaned back on the couch and fell into a deep sleep. No doubt the phone call from Miss Donovan, when it came, was alive with urgency. Miss Donovan was downstairs, Sarnoff would appear at any moment, they must hurry. In her haste Miss Penniston forgot her earrings. And never returned for them, because her friend, on the pretext that Steven Sarnoff awaited them, lured her to the passageway under the stoop next door and there garroted her."

"But what had made Laura think that this Sarnoff even existed?" grumbled Kessler.

"From Miss Donovan," Regan answered. "Miss Penniston had left affairs so much in her friend's control that in all likelihood she would never have discovered her malfeasance had Mr. McClendon not come along.

"The day she learned of it from him must have been horrible for Miss Penniston. To discover that her friend had been taking advantage of her! Miss Donovan no doubt admitted all and pleaded for mercy—in private. That's why Miss Penniston was so distraught and her excuses so lame. She wasn't covering for herself; she was covering for her friend." Regan's angry voice filled the room. "And while Miss Penniston was protecting her, her friend was plotting her death in as elaborately cold-blooded a manner as can be imagined." The Bishop looked around and, seeing nothing but respectful faces, glowed. The end of a funk.

I grinned. Not only had I got Regan to tell how he solved the case, I'd rousted him out of his depression. That last got confirmed right after I let everyone out.

I'd left his office door open. As I went to close it I peeked in and caught him red-handed, putting *Lonesome Dove* back in its proper place on the shelf.

—Epilogue—

So—ALL'S WELL that ends well. And I guess it all ended as well as it could.

The Pennistons headed back to Wichita. A day later than planned, but knowing that their daughter's murderer—the real one—was behind bars and that they'd played a part in putting her there. Even if they did sort of screw it up.

Jerry and Ida Mae were heading back for Oklahoma, the object being for Jerry to go into prison ministry there.

"It's the perfect place for me, Davey," he told me when he called to say goodbye. "And Ida Mae's all for it. I just never had people so happy to get to know the Lord as I did there in that jail here in New York. I think that's why Jesus come to me in jail in the first place—to let me know where I belong. Oh, I'd be proud to stay and work on the Bishop to get him straight on the Bible . . ." He chuckled. ". . . but that'd be a big job and I think the Lord's got other work for me."

And Regan, the depression—his shortest on record—having ended, was back at his computer, putting the finishing touches on his latest, totally indecipherable masterpiece of obfuscation.

Leaving only me in the dumps. And I couldn't seem to shake it, even after a good night's rest. I moped around the house all day Thursday, ignoring and being ignored by Regan and Ernie. My face and neck were healing but not me. What the hell was wrong? I *never* get depressed.

I'm not much for psychiatry, but when your girlfriend *is* one, what have you got to lose? I called her Thursday night right after dinner.

Sally was testy at first. "Well, as I live and breathe! The magical disappearing detective! What hole did *you* just crawl out of?" I remembered that I'd promised to call her the day after the Knicks' game.

"Point well taken," I answered humbly, surprising her.

"Hey! Have I got a bad connection here? Whatever happened to David Goldman, the renowned sleuth? The man who says macho means never having to say you're sorry?"

It was good to hear her voice, but she wasn't doing much for my mood. "Go ahead, Sally, have your fun. But I need to talk. Like soon."

A pregnant pause. When Sally broke it, she was all seriousness. "Sounds like you mean talk to a shrink, not to a girlfriend." I didn't answer.

"Okay," she said briskly. "Of course. When?"

"How about now?"

"Fine. You know where I live."

Thirty minutes later, I was at her door. Sally opened up and gave me a big smile. Getting no smile in return, she changed expressions, gave me a peck and invited me in.

She put me on her couch in both senses of that expression. Only, instead of lying down, I sat, she beside me.

I talked, she listened. She gave me her eye at first but gradually sank back till her head was resting on the back of the couch, her eyes closed.

When I finished, she sat forward and took my hand. Her beautiful blue eyes held mine.

"Davey, sweetheart, listen to me. You have nothing to be ashamed of. Nothing. Shh. Hold it, Davey. Just listen for a minute, will you? Let's say the force you used *was* excessive—and you haven't convinced me that it was; this babe sounds like a very dangerous person—but say it was. You were in a life-or-death struggle. Your adrenalin was pumping for all it was worth—more than in a normal fight, because your oxygen supply had been curtailed. When that happens, the adrenal glands have to work that much harder to compensate. And then, suddenly, it was over."

She grinned briefly. "Now I'm not going to sit here and tell you no thoughts of revenge were in your mind. But—and this is key, Davey—*that* wasn't what caused you to sock the lady that extra sock. That was fear, my dearest; fear, pure and simple. Except that fear is never pure and seldom simple. You were, in a word, terrified. Scared out of your wits. You'd thought you were about to die. Fear like that you don't turn off like a faucet."

Sally interrupted her speech for a little interpersonal involvement. She got up, deliberately and demurely sat on my lap, put her arms around me and gave me a very soulful kiss, as only she can. I concluded I was forgiven for my latest offense. When we came up for air she resumed her therapy, murmuring in my ear.

"I love you for what you are, sweetheart. You're all man, but you're also a vulnerable human being. You were scared and now you're feeling guilty, but it's going to be okay."

When I left—some time later—the depression was gone. I still wouldn't call myself a big fan of psychiatry, but I'm no longer quite so skeptical. My recommendation is, if you want to see a shrink, go ahead. And if you can work it, get one with honey-blond hair, a lot of affection and plenty of skill in interpersonal relations.